shattered souls

HALSTON U PART THREE

R.A. SMYTH

Finding my daughter is all that matters now.

Aurora is out there somewhere, and I'll do whatever it takes to bring her home. Thankfully, I'm not in this fight alone. I have Logan, my rock, who is always ready to catch me when I fall. Royce, who is learning to trust and opening his heart, and Grayson—still haunted but finding strength in our connection. Together, we're unstoppable.

We're racing against time, piecing together clues and facing our worst fears. But Bertram, the monster from my past, is hellbent on taking everything from me. He's relentless, and he's not playing by any rules.

Then there's my mother, the ultimate narcissist with her own twisted agenda. She's proven she'll go to any lengths to destroy me.

This final showdown will test us in ways we never imagined. Can we rescue Aurora and finally find peace? Or will Bertram's obsession shatter our fragile world once and for all?

My daughter's life is on the line, and we'll risk everything to save her —even ourselves.

HALSTON U PLAYLIST

Keep Your Head Up Princess – Anson Seabra
Naked – James Arthur
Said So – Alexander Stewart
Confidence – Steven Ryan
Hope it Haunts You – Citizen Soldier
Elastic Heart – Sia
Titanium –David Guetta, Sia
Wake Me Up – Tommee Profitt, Fleurie
Addicted To You – UNSECRET, Anna Mae
Don't Try – Extreme Music
Praying – Kesha
Breath – Breaking Benjamin
Battlefield – Jordan Powers
...And many more

TRIGGER WARNINGS

- History of sexual abuse (discussed; not on page; not by MMCs)
- Attempted sexual assault (on page; not by MMCs)
- Kidnapping of a child
- Child Trafficking
- Noncon (not by MMCs)
- Primal Play
- Degradation
- Violence

CONTENT WARNING

This book is a dark, contemporary, new adult reverse harem romance, meaning the FMC will end up with 3+ males.

This is the final book in the series and will result in an HEA.

AURORA

PROLOGUE

"Breakthrough Academy, how can I help you?"

"Good afternoon. My name is Bertram Van Doren. My stepdaughter, Riley, is a new student of yours and I wanted to know how she was settling in."

"Oh, Mr. Van Doren, what a pleasure. Riley has adjusted to life here quite well. There have been no issues so far."

"I'm glad to hear that. I want to send her a care package. Something to help her feel more at home."

"Of course. Students are not allowed personal items in their rooms—we find regiment and uniformity help to keep everyone in line. However, you are welcome to write her letters, and we do, of course, have Parents' Weekend twice a year, which you and your wife are welcome to attend. The first one of the academic year will be next weekend."

"Unfortunately we will be unable to attend," I state brusquely. Now that I have what I called for, I'm done with this conversation.

"Oh, that is such a shame. I know Riley was hoping to see Aurora."

I pause. "Aurora?"

"Her, uh, daughter? God, I hope I remembered her name correctly."

Daughter?

"Oh, Aurora, yes. Yes, of course." The cover falls seamlessly from my lips. "Apologies, I was unaware that you knew of her. Thank you so much for your help. I'll be sure to write to Riley shortly. Goodbye."

I hang up before she can respond, staring at the payphone as the receptionist's words drill into my skull.

Daughter.

"Aurora." I say the name slowly, grinning slyly.

Well, isn't this an interesting turn of events.

GRAYSON

CHAPTER ONE

With one hand wrapped around the handle to keep the front door from opening, I blink stupidly at my father. My father, who is standing on my front stoop, even though he's supposed to be in prison for another sixty-seven days.

Yeah, I've been counting. Although, perhaps I shouldn't have been avoiding visiting him, or I'd have known he was being released early instead of being blindsided first thing in the fucking morning.

"So?" He arches his brow in that arrogant way of his when I don't respond to whatever he said. *What the fuck did he just say?* Oh yeah, some bullshit about getting the entire family back together—what the hell that even means. "Are you going to invite me inside?"

Fuck no.

Hoping my shock is entirely explained by his unexpected appearance at my door and not his uncanny timeliness after last night's botched *Save Aurora* plan, I paste on a fake as fuck smile.

"You know what? I was just on my way out to get a coffee.

Why don't you join me?" I surreptitiously pat my pockets. I definitely don't have my wallet, but thankfully, I have my phone with my cards loaded onto it.

My father's gaze drops, his lips pursing in disapproval at the gray sweats and black undershirt I'm wearing. Yeah, this isn't my ideal going-out outfit either, but it's not like I'm going to change and leave my father standing here, risking him running into one of the guys—or worse, Riley.

Uncaring, I stuff my feet into a pair of trainers tossed haphazardly by the door. That'll be Logan's doing, and the shoes are a size bigger than mine, but that's the last thing I care about right now.

With a forced smile directed at my father, the door snicks shut behind me, and side by side, we walk down the street toward the corner coffee shop.

He's silent while we walk, which gives my brain time to catch up to the reality that my father is a free man—walking casually down the street like he hasn't served a sentence behind bars for the last four years.

Like he shouldn't *still* be locked behind those bars.

Like he isn't a menace to society—or, more accurately, a direct threat to the broken woman I just left passed out between my two best friends after a night of crying because we failed to bring her daughter home.

There's a tightness in my chest at our failure. We tried so hard to spare Riley from this pain. Now, not only does she have to deal with the loss of her daughter, but I'm going to have to break the news of my father's release. Just thinking about adding more to her overloaded plate has my stomach twisting. Except, I can't focus on that right now.

Dragging my hand down my face, I push aside my exhaustion. I need to be on my game for this conversation with my father. If he's on my doorstep at the ass crack of dawn, he's here with a reason in mind.

Side-eyeing him, I ask, "Were you just released this morning or…"

"This morning." My father grins at me. "My first stop was seeing my son." Lifting a hand, he squeezes my shoulder, a gesture I once would have viewed fondly—a father-son bonding moment—but now, as his fingers dig into my trapezius muscle, I see it for what it truly is: a passive-aggressive display of control.

The blinders I've been wearing when it comes to my father are damaged beyond repair, and in their place is so much anger I can barely withstand it, along with a hefty amount of self-disgust that I *allowed* myself to be blinded when it came to him. The potent mixture is toxic, poisoning my veins every waking moment. If I weren't so selfish, I'd give Riley up, knowing she deserves far better than me. But I am my father's son. I'm not a good man. Riley is mine, and there isn't a goddamn thing on this planet that will stand in the way of that—including my father.

"Since you haven't been to the prison recently."

Aaand another manipulative talon slices into me, this time in the form of guilt.

"Sorry." *Not.* "Senior year," I give by way of explanation. "It really is as brutal as everyone says."

My father chuckles, a charismatic laugh that immediately ingratiates people to him. Now, I realize it's part of his repertoire—a skillset he uses to distract people from seeing the contemptible soul beneath his polished veneer.

"Everything will be easier now. We can be a family once again."

That's the second time he's referred to family, and my brows furrow, trying to read between the lines as we enter the coffee shop. The place is empty, too early yet for the morning rush before work and classes. I'm fortunate that anywhere was even open at this hour.

We place our orders, and I pay for our drinks before we sit at a table at the back of the cafe where we won't be disturbed.

"What do you mean *we can be a family again?*" I ask, eyeing him over the rim of my espresso cup. God knows the double shot I ordered will barely hit the exhaustion and stress already riding me hard today.

Blowing on his black coffee, he gives me a sly grin as he slowly sets his cup down, prolonging the suspense.

"I *mean*, we can all finally be a family again. The four of us—you, me, Lydia, and your sister, Riley."

"Stepsister," I quip, unsure why I'm focusing on *that*. Probably because it's the only aspect of that entire sentence that doesn't make me want to throw my steaming cup in his face. "I thought you and Lydia were divorced?"

My father's brows furrow. "What gave you that impression?"

Aware I'm treading in shark-infested waters, I shrug casually. "I just assumed, you know, given the allegations..."

This time, my father's laugh is dipped in arrogance. "Lydia knows there was no substance to those accusations. We both agree Riley was going through a difficult time—struggling to adjust to her new life and no longer having all of her mother's attention and affection."

I practically choke on my next sip. I'm certain Lydia isn't capable of motherly affection, nor would Riley *want* to be the focus of her mother's attention. Even if Lydia wasn't a narcissistic bitch, Riley isn't—nor was she ever—the type of girl who demanded attention.

"We decided that while I was..." my father grimaces before spitting out in distaste, "*incarcerated*, Lydia would live her life, focusing on giving Riley everything she needed. Now that I'm released, we've agreed to give this another try. To focus on our *family*."

I tense at the emphasis he puts on the word *family*. It's clear this isn't purely about him and Lydia—it's about the four of us, and the coffee burns a hole through my stomach at the notion of Riley being anywhere near either of them.

Unaware of my rampant thoughts, my father graces me one of his winning smiles. "I've asked Lydia to move in with me, and I've arranged for the four of us to have dinner on Saturday. You'll be there."

It's not a question.

Knowing there is no other response, I give a curt nod. However, my thoughts are a million miles away—well, not that far. They're down the street inside the brownstone where the devastated woman who has become my obsession is currently sleeping and wondering if this news will be the nail in the coffin of her sanity.

How thinly can you be stretched before you snap?

How much pain can a soul endure?

How many scars can a heart carry before breaking?

Wherever that boundary lies, I can sense Riley teetering on its edge. She's already traversed the unfathomable, overcoming trials that would shatter most. She's fashioned her trauma into armor, resilient and unyielding, but recent events have left it marred and vulnerable. Each blow has chipped away at the sturdy facade she's built. I fear this latest revelation—this expectation of my father's—may deliver the fatal strike, shattering her carefully forged defenses beyond repair.

My father makes small talk while we finish our drinks. Frankly, I'm not listening to a word he's saying. I nod and smile at all the right times, but otherwise, I'm absent from the conversation.

The longer I sit there, the more unbearable the itch to get away from him becomes. Simply being in his presence sickens me, knowing the truth of everything. I can't even think about my mother's journal, or the indifferent facade I've donned will fracture. It's taking every ounce of willpower to sit here civilly and play this game with him.

However, as tempting as it would be to call him out. It wouldn't do any good to scream and shout and tell him I know exactly who he is. There is already enough to deal with, and getting on my father's bad side is not somewhere you want to be. Better to appeal to him and figure out what game he's playing because you can bet your ass I'm not buying this *happy family* bullshit he's spouting.

With a final reminder to be at the restaurant on time on Saturday night, I parted ways with my father. *Finally.* Turning toward my front door, I notice the curtain in the living room window twitch, and I shake my head, knowing Logan has been spying. Likely, the three of them are anxious to know what's happening. Not that I can blame them.

However, when I step inside, it isn't Logan standing there but a starkly pale and timid Riley. Dressed in a pair of Royce's sweats and a Huskies jersey that swamps her slim frame, her arms are wrapped around her middle as though she's literally holding herself together. As the door closes behind me, her wide, fear-ridden eyes lift to mine, and I can't help but feel a pang of concern for her.

My gaze flicks to the hallway behind her, surprised that Logan or Royce aren't hovering nearby. That they'd leave her alone in her state.

"Where are the others?" I ask in a carefully neutral tone.

Her teeth sink into her lower lip, and her voice is weak, worn out, and exhausted beyond belief when she says, "They went to shower and get dressed. We..." She glances away, inhaling a shaky breath before hesitantly sliding her gaze back to mine. Terror has her pupils dilated, eliminating any of the captivating green of her irises. "Grayson, w-was that really your dad? Logan wasn't sure..."

The same extreme tiredness pouring out of her crashes through me, and I stumble forward. My chest collides with hers, and bending, I grasp the back of her thighs and haul her into my arms. She goes without complaint, her toned thighs squeezing my hips as her arms wrap around my neck.

I carry her into the kitchen and set her on the countertop before collapsing into her. My forehead rests on her shoulder, and now that I'm no longer faced with my father, I release a shuddering exhale. I feel like I'm in shock, my limbs shaking after the unexpected confrontation. Of having to face *him* for the first time since finding out what he did to Riley. To my mother.

Since learning the truth about the truly heinous piece of shit who makes up half my DNA.

As if sensing I'm on the brink of losing it, Riley squeezes me tighter. Her legs wrap around my middle, and she buries her face in the crook of my neck as her fingernails dig into my shoulders.

The two of us united in our grief. In our desolation.

Regardless of the shit I've put her through, of the unresolved issues between us, in this, we are allied.

She's the only person on this planet who understands the hatred I feel toward my father. The only other person who knows what it's like to be pinned and helpless beneath his manipulation.

Neither of us says anything, soaking up the other's comfort

until what sounds like a herd of elephants comes trampling down the stairs.

I slide out of Riley's comforting embrace as Logan appears in the doorway, stopping as his gaze darts between us. His hair is damp from a shower, and he's dressed casually in loose-fitted shorts and a t-shirt. One look at our faces, and he knows. "Fuck," he hisses, his features twisted in a grimace. "I was really hoping I was wrong."

Royce silently steps into view, dressed in his typical all-black attire. His expression is locked down; however, his piercing blue eyes are solely on Riley. Assessing. I can't blame him, especially knowing that I'm about to destroy the last of her sanity.

I glance at her from the corner of my eye, hating the dark circles under her eyes and her ashen complexion, which makes the freckles dotting the tops of her cheeks and the bridge of her nose stand out.

"So, your dad is out," Royce states. My eyes snap to him, finding him watching me. I nod.

"Bought his way out early," I explain before anyone can ask.

Logan frowns before marching across the kitchen and scooping Riley into his arms. He then moves to sit on a bar stool at the kitchen island, holding her protectively in his lap.

As if he's now mentally prepared to have this conversation, his hard gaze meets mine over her head, which is tucked beneath his chin. "What did he want?"

Royce moves too, standing on the opposite side of the island where he can see Riley's face and read her every thought while being close enough in case she needs him.

My gaze connects with Riley's, unblinking as I rip off the Band-Aid. "Spouting some bullshit about all of us being a family again."

She physically flinches as though my words slapped her.

"What the fuck does that mean?" Logan snaps, riled up, and I haven't even gotten to the worst part.

Leaning against the counter behind me, I cross my arms over my chest, keeping my focus on the woman in Logan's lap. "Apparently, your mom and my dad are still married and are moving in together now that he's out of prison."

Riley's nose scrunches in distaste, and I notice Royce straighten at the news.

"So they wanna play house; what does that have to do with either of you?" Logan asks, confused.

It's barely perceptible, but Riley stiffens. Just when I thought she couldn't get any paler, what little color was in her cheeks drains. "He wants to get back what he had before his arrest."

Logan scoffs, however his expression is fierce as his arms tighten around Riley. "You're not teenagers anymore. It's not like he can demand you live under the same roof as him."

I shake my head, sighing. "I'm not entirely sure what he's up to, but he's up to something." Deciding to just get it over with, I blurt, "He wants the four of us to sit down for some fucked up version of family dinner at a restaurant on Saturday."

"Well, that's not fucking happening," Logan snaps before Riley can say anything. "Over my dead fucking body is that sick fuck going anywhere near my Shortcake."

Riley shakes her head, a fierceness entering her expression for the first time since Royce and Logan walked empty-handed into the house last night and ripped her heart to shreds. "I don't give a shit about some twisted family dinner. My *daughter* is missing." She chokes over the words. "Nothing else matters except finding her."

I nod in complete agreement before my gaze slides to Royce. "You're quiet."

He scrubs his hand over the dusting of scruff along his jaw.

"I think the timing makes a lot of sense," he muses aloud. "Lydia was clearly trying to get Aurora out of the picture before your dad was released—whether or not she knew he was getting out earlier than we expected."

"You think Bertram has no idea Aurora exists?" Logan questions, brows furrowed in thought. "That Lydia kept that secret from him?" His eyes widen. "Damn, that would be something."

"I think she's incredibly insecure," Royce states. "In her mind, she lost him once to Riley. She would definitely be concerned about the same thing happening again." Royce's attention shifts to me. "And if he and Lydia have been in contact this entire time, it could explain how he knew Riley was at Halston. I can't imagine Lydia being eager to give him information on Riley, but if he asked, she might have handed it over."

"The Christmas card," Riley gasps.

Royce nods.

"So what, Lydia—because I refuse to refer to that woman as my mother given what she's done—" Riley sneers, "has been waiting for Bertram to be released so she can get her old life back? If she knew Aurora would become a… problem… why fight to have custody of her at all?"

"For control. A bargaining chip. To keep you in line, and in case Bertram decided he was done with her," Royce supplies. All theories, of course, but given what we know about Lydia, it stacks up. Even if it is all incredibly fucked up.

On the plus side, instead of breaking her further like I thought this conversation might, a furious spark has ignited in Riley's eyes. They're still dim and lifeless, but her depression has been overshadowed by anger—an emotion I'm all too familiar with using as a crutch.

"So what do we do now?" Logan asks the pinnacle question. "We could go to Lydia and demand information on the buyer."

Riley recoils at his words, and he grimaces, pressing a quick kiss to her shoulder.

"I'm going to The Depot to talk to Dax and get his tech guy to look into it. See if he can find anything," Royce states. "I think we should hold off on interrogating Lydia just yet. Riley isn't supposed to know that anything is wrong with Aurora. If we go asking questions now, it will only raise her suspicions as to how we know. Let's keep it quiet while I look into it." Staring at Riley, he says, "You could call your mo—Lydia—if you're up to it. Ask to talk to Aurora."

"We usually only talk on the weekends, but yeah, I can do that," Riley agrees. Her voice comes out strong, but the anxiety in her eyes belies her true feelings.

"What do the rest of us do?" Logan asks, glancing my way.

Sighing, I scrape my hand through my hair. "With my dad out, I need to go into the office. I don't trust him not to start pulling strings behind my back, and I'd been putting off informing everyone of his release... guess I can't do that any longer."

"Guess Riley and I will have a Netflix and chill day, then," Logan says with a frown.

Riley shakes her head. "I can't sit around this house and do nothing. It's a school day. I'm going to class. Or at least to campus. I just... I can't sit here. I'll drive myself crazy wonder-ing..." She tears up before sucking in a steadying breath and turning to Logan. "I'm going to campus if you wanna come."

"Like I'd let you go alone," he murmurs, cupping her cheek before pressing an affectionate kiss to her temple.

With that decided, everyone goes their separate ways to prepare for the day ahead. Not at all looking forward to breaking the news to my shareholders and staff, I head for a shower and to get dressed.

ROYCE

CHAPTER TWO

"Blue's keeping an eye on all methods of transport out of the country. Any mention of a little girl matching our description, and it'll be flagged," Dax states with a grim expression. We're sitting in Xander's office at the back of The Depot. By the looks of things, Dax has been here all night, talking to Blue and looking into everything. I vaguely recall him saying something to that effect yesterday, but honestly, I was so fucked up after realizing I'd failed Riley that I couldn't take any of it in. "We're looking into Lydia, too. Trying to identify the buyer and figure out how they communicated. We missed something somewhere," he states in frustration, "but we'll find her."

"We have to." My voice is choked. No other outcome is acceptable. Not after I had to watch Riley irreparably shatter in front of me last night. The second we walked through the door without Aurora, *she knew*.

The sound she made, as though she were physically dying, will haunt me for the rest of my days. I don't *ever* want to hear that noise again. Never want to fail her like that ever again.

"How is she?" Dax asks, lips pursed.

Sighing, I lean back in my chair. "Putting on a brave face, but she's... wrecked." It feels wrong to share Riley's vulnerability with him. Based on the darkness that creeps into Dax's expression, he doesn't need me to say anything more.

Unable to sit in this office that stinks of failure and desperation any longer, I tap my fingers against the desk and get to my feet. "Keep me posted."

Dax nods. "You know I will."

With that, I exit the office. Passing the bar, I lift a hand in farewell to Xander and Rome, who are stocking out before I step outside. The fresh air does nothing to calm the storm raging inside me. Nothing will until I can see Aurora safely ensconced in Riley's arms.

Climbing into my truck, I pull onto the road and head to my second destination of the day. I'd said we shouldn't interrogate Lydia yet, but that doesn't mean I can't pay her a visit. After all, she does *owe* me for my time and services.

The drive to Springview passes in a blur. I'm too lost in my thoughts, barely paying attention to the junctions and turns, until I park outside her house.

A moving van is parked at the curb, partly full of boxes. *Guess Bertram was telling the truth about her moving in with him.* I make a mental note to get Bertram's home address from Grayson as I pocket my keys and walk up the drive to the front door.

A man wearing a jumpsuit with the moving company logo walks past carrying a box, lifting his chin in greeting. When I reach the door, I don't knock or announce my presence as I walk inside. Boxes are piled in the entranceway, and peering into the living room, sheets have been thrown over the furniture.

There's no sign of Lydia, so I move deeper into the house, using my knowledge of the last time I was here to direct me to the room I know belongs to Aurora—*belonged* to Aurora. When I step inside, I do a double take, wondering if I have the wrong one.

I pop my head into the hall, looking up and down, but nope, I've definitely got the correct room. Doing a slow turn, I take in the bland, cream-colored walls and the bare bed. Gone are the soft toys that cluttered it, the pile of games in the corner. The rainbow and unicorn design on the wall. If I hadn't seen it for myself, I'd never have guessed a little girl slept in this room only two nights ago.

Knowing Lydia so thoroughly eliminated Aurora from her life this easily makes my blood boil, and my hands fist at my sides as the need for violence raises its bloodthirsty head. I'm in desperate need of an outlet.

"Ruthless?"

Simply hearing her voice grates against my skin like sandpaper, and my restraint nearly snaps in two. Forcing myself to calm down, I slowly turn to face her.

"What are you doing here?" she asks, glancing nervously around before returning her attention to me. Even though she's packing to move, she's dressed to the nines in cream linen pants and a tight tank top that can barely restrain her fake tits. Her heels are silent on the carpet as she approaches, her heavily made-up face making me want to recoil.

"You double-crossed me," I seethe, unable to hide the true extent of my anger as rage flashes across my face. Stalking toward her, I snarl, "I don't take kindly to people messing me about, *Lydia.*"

Her eyes round as she takes a step backward. "I-I didn't. That's not what—I didn't mean to." Her hands come up, palms facing me as if to stop me from hitting her. Like I'd even want to fucking touch her.

My gaze narrows as I allow Ruthless's true personality to surface. Menace leaks from my pores, and violence brims in my eyes. "You knew exactly what you were doing when you agreed to my price. Then you went behind my back to another buyer—a *buyer* you never told me was involved."

"I-I'm sorry," she stutters, visibly shaking. She might be afraid, but she's sure as fuck not sorry. But she will be. Maybe not today. Maybe not tomorrow. But one day, I'm going to eviscerate this bitch. I will destroy her so thoroughly that she'll regret crossing me. Regret ever saying a negative word to Riley. Regret the day she decided to keep her daughter instead of giving her up for adoption and at least offering her a chance at finding a loving family.

"I don't work for free, Lydia," I snap in her face. I don't give two shits about her money, but it's the only justifiable reason why Ruthless would be in her house, so I have to play the part.

"O-of course." Her gaze drops over me, and despite her fear, heat flares in her eyes, and her tongue flicks out to wet her lips.

Mine curl in disgust. "If you think I'd fuck a two-bit, plastic-filled, dried-up whore after what you did, you've got another thing coming."

Any desire is immediately snuffed out, righteous indignation replacing it as her nostrils flare in anger. "You can't talk to me that way in my house!"

I step forward so I'm towering over her. "Choose your next words wisely unless you're eager to find out what shade the carpet turns when it's drenched in your blood. I may be a criminal, but I value loyalty and honesty." My gaze drops over her, lips twisted in derision. "You have neither. Frankly, I've killed men for less."

Visibly shaking, Lydia drops her eyes. "I-I'll get you your money."

"There you go, that wasn't so hard," I purr condescendingly. "I'd suggest throwing in a substantial tip to compensate for your poor decision-making."

When she turns toward the door, I do a final sweep of the room, hating that there isn't anything of Aurora's I can bring home to Riley before reluctantly following her.

"Moving?" I ask, stating the obvious as I trail her into the kitchen. "Guess you've got enough money now to start your life over."

She doesn't supply any information, probably not wanting me to know anything more about her life than I already do. Pulling open a drawer, she lifts out a checkbook and cuts me a sizable check.

"So, will you ever tell me who my competitor was?" I'm careful to make my tone blase, as though I'm merely curious about who I lost out to.

Her lips thin in smug victory as she huffs a haughty laugh. "It's just business, Ruthless." She shrugs, having no idea how close I am to grabbing her by the throat and pinning her to the wall until her pulse stops hammering beneath my palm. "You win some; you lose some." The sound of her check being ripped out is deafening in the silent room before she holds it out to me. "Seems to me like you're still coming out on top."

Her phone chooses that moment to light up with an incoming call. Flicking my gaze toward the screen, I notice Riley's name. Lydia barely spares it a glance before silencing the call and setting her phone screen side down.

"Answer it," I say dismissively. When she shakes her head, I put more steel behind my words. "Answer the phone, Lydia."

Her eyes flick to mine, fear flashing across them before she scrambles to answer the call before it ends.

Bringing the phone to her ear, she sighs in exasperation, "Riley."

I can't hear Riley's side of the conversation, but I astutely watch Lydia's reaction. Her face is pinched, and it's clear she isn't interested in talking to her daughter. It *could* be because I'm standing over her, but I know it's not.

Her eyes flick to mine, but I don't avert my gaze or pretend to give her any semblance of privacy. "Now isn't a good time." Riley must say about calling back later because Lydia makes a noise of exasperation. "No. I'm busy. We agreed to weekends. That was *your* plan."

God, this bitch!

I take a few steps away, needing to put space between us before I choke her out right here in the kitchen with moving men directly outside her fucking door.

"You can talk on Saturday," she snaps before ending the call.

My teeth grind, and I seriously debate the merits of just killing her. It's unlikely she'll even tell us who she sold Aurora to. Does she even know who she sold her to? Still, the possibility that she *might* stays my hand—but barely.

"That sounded like a spat over custody arrangements if ever I heard one," I drawl.

She doesn't latch onto my bait, instead thrusting the check into my hand. Her tone is clipped as she snipes, "I trust this will be the end of our business."

Accepting that I'm not going to get anything else from this exchange, I give her a slimy grin as I pocket the check. That will make a nice initial deposit to Aurora's college fund. "I hope you get everything you deserve in life, Lydia."

Outside, I approach the back of the moving van and stop one of the movers, asking if everything in the van is going to the same place.

"She said that pile there could go to charity." He points to a small stack of brown boxes. There's no writing on the outside to indicate their contents. Regardless, I pluck a hundred-dollar bill from my wallet. I hand it over to him, along with my address, and ask if he can deliver them there instead. With a shrug, he takes the money.

Exhaustion tugs at my bones as I slot my key into the front door of the house later that night. I've spent the last however many hours driving around, avoiding coming home.

Avoiding facing her.

I deliberately waited until I knew Logan would have dragged her up to bed. Except, as I step into the house, a flash of auburn hair draws my eye to where Riley is sitting at the bottom of the stairs... waiting.

I stop on the threshold, realizing my plan has backfired as Riley's gaze lifts to mine, and she slowly rises to her feet. She's wearing an oversized Huskies t-shirt that belongs to Logan, a black pair of boxers peeking out the bottom and accentuating her long, toned legs.

Her loose, wild hair falls past her shoulders, framing her unnaturally pale face. In the light of the hall and the nightmare of the past few days, her hazel eyes glow darker than usual, more brown than green. I hate looking into them now. I hate the lack of spark I see there, the flatness staring back at me.

I watch as she swallows, sucking her lower lip between her teeth as she gathers the courage to ask. Not that she needs to. I already know the only question on her mind.

"You should be resting." There is nothing but weariness in my tone as I delay the inevitable a moment longer.

"Not like that's actually possible..." Her fingers twist in the front of her t-shirt, those wide, anxious eyes boring into me.

The force of her words hit me like a hurricane, and I have to steel my spine to stop myself from falling back a step. It's not that I didn't already know how impossibly hard this must be on her.

It's the guilt.

Knowing that this is all my fault.

That if I hadn't fucked up, she would be cuddling beside a sleeping Aurora upstairs right now instead of a wraith of her former self, staring at me like I might have all the answers when that's the last fucking thing I have for her.

"Did you…" Her question hangs like a guillotine in the air between us.

"Dax and his guy are looking into it." The words are ash in my mouth, and my tongue is thick and swollen as I spit them out. I don't mention her mom since that turned up jack shit.

I'd given Logan a heads-up about the boxes being delivered to the house, and he messaged earlier to let me know he'd hidden them in the spare room before Riley saw them.

I'll go through them once I've convinced Riley to go back to Logan's bed. Not that I'm expecting them to reveal anything, but I have to do *something*. The thought of just lying in bed, alone with my thoughts… nope. I can't rest until I have a lead—anything to alleviate the heartache etched into the very lining of Riley's being.

Any piece of information, no matter how small or insignificant. I just need something to go off—a breadcrumb to follow. A little girl doesn't just disappear into the ether. Aurora is out there somewhere, and you can bet your fucking ass I won't rest until I find her.

I'm sure she didn't expect any other answer, yet her face is still crestfallen at my response. I can't look at it for more than a second before I have to tear my gaze away, nostrils flaring. Despair floods the hall, leaving a tang in the back of my throat that no amount of alcohol or brushing my teeth will erase.

"Go back to Logan, sweetheart." It takes all of my self-control to keep my voice even. I keep my gaze averted, unable to meet her eyes, but I hear her. Instead of climbing the stairs like she should, she descends the final couple of steps before padding toward me barefoot.

She doesn't stop until her arms wind around my waist and her face rests on my chest, ear pressed to the staccato rhythm of my heart.

I go still, fingers itching to touch, to lose myself in her. To bury my nose in her hair and inhale her fruity, floral scent that resets me in a way that I've only ever been able to achieve by running myself ragged on the field or splitting skin in the ring.

"Hold me, Royce," she murmurs into my chest. "I need you to hold me. And I think you need me to hold you, too. We'll keep each other from breaking."

I cave instantly, my arms coming to wrap her in a hug as I lower my face to the crook of her neck and inhale like I haven't breathed fresh air in decades. I lean into her comfort as she leans into mine, and together, we hold each other up.

"I don't deserve your compassion," I murmur, my lips brushing against her soft skin. "I failed you." My words are so low I'm not sure if she hears me. I didn't intend them for her, anyway, so it doesn't matter. I said them more as a reminder to myself.

Still, her arms only tighten around me as she shifts in my hold so she can tuck her face against my chest. Her forehead rests against my pec while I hide my face in her hair. When she speaks, her voice is soft, her words clear. "You could never fail me, Royce. All you do is lift me higher. You're my wings in the storm, plucking me from the chaos and carrying me to safety."

Refusing to believe her beautiful words, which are like arrows piercing directly into my heart, I shake my head. "If it hadn't been for me, Aurora would be here—" I choke up, squeezing my eyes shut against the sting of tears.

My breathing is erratic as I struggle and fail to wrangle myself under control. All the while, Riley runs her fingers through my hair and holds me. The fact that she's the one comforting me when I should be comforting *her* is the only thing that gets me to toughen up, and I force deep breaths into my lungs.

Placing her hands on either side of my face, Riley forces my face away from her shoulder until she can look me in the eye. Despite missing her usual spark of life, a fierceness in her stare has me straightening.

"I don't want to hear you talk about yourself like that ever again," she states in a stern voice that only a mother can adopt. "I will say it again, because I get the distinct impression you don't believe me... You, Royce King, have *never*, not once, failed me." Her features soften, her thumb stroking back and forth along my cheek as she holds my gaze. "If it weren't for you, we wouldn't have even known what Lydia was up to. I'd be naively sitting here assuming everything was fine, completely unaware that my daughter..." Emotion chokes her as she glances away to compose herself.

When she looks back at me, her eyes are glassy, but her voice is strong as she continues, "We would have no fucking clue what's going on. It's because of *you* that we have this insight. That we can do everything we're doing right now to find her." She releases a long exhale, her hands sliding down to cup the sides of my throat. "Grayson only gave me the gist of it, though I can only imagine what you were subjected to in order to gain Lydia's trust... The part you were forced to play." Fresh tears glitter in her eyes, this time of gratitude, of awe, of *love*. "The fact that the three of you were willing to pay for the safety of my daughter..." She shakes her head, but her eyes remain on mine as she presses a hand to her heart. "There are no words to express how I feel in here. And even though it didn't work out the way we wanted, I know you'll do everything to get Aurora back because that's the type of person you are, Royce. You don't stop. You're not built to fail, so stop beating yourself up. Especially when all you've ever done is be there for me, even when I couldn't see it."

My hand slides to the back of her neck, giving a quick squeeze. "I'd do all of it a hundred times over if it meant you had Aurora right now," I rasp. "And you're right. I won't stop until that little girl is safe in your arms. She might have slipped through my fingers once, but I learn from my mistakes, and hurting you is a mistake I never intend to repeat."

Holding me captive with her gaze, Riley slides her hand down to mine, entwining our fingers. "Come to bed, Royce. Aurora needs us to get our rest so we can find her."

Helpless to this woman's pleas, I follow as she leads me up the stairs to Logan's bedroom. At this point in our relationship, I've gotten used to sharing a bed with him, so I don't think twice about his half-naked form sprawled across three-quarters of the bed.

Pulling back the covers, Riley climbs into the middle of the bed, and Logan immediately pulls her against his hard chest without cracking an eyelid.

Stripping down to my boxers, I slide in beside her, and she immediately tangles her legs with mine. Sharing a pillow, our faces are inches apart, and when sleep drags me into the deep beyond, I go with a newfound peace.

RILEY

CHAPTER THREE

S taring at myself in the mirror, I take in the cheap black dress that stretches across my collarbones, hugs my chest before flaring out at my hips, and falls to just below my knee. It makes my already pale skin appear ghostly, and my bloodshot eyes are like something out of a vampire movie.

My hand rests over my queasy stomach. *You can do this. You can do this. You can do this.*

Spinning, I clap my hand over my mouth. *Nope, maybe I can't do this.* Sweat breaks out along my skin, and I breathe through my mouth to quell the nausea.

Since the morning after I woke up to the reality that my daughter had been sold on the black fucking market, I've been numb. Barely existing. I move, eat, shower, and sleep, but it's all done on autopilot—an automatic action, mostly in response to nudges or orders from one of the guys.

That was until Grayson so painfully reminded me that we have that fucked up dinner with Bertram and Lydia tonight. In the midst of everything I'm dealing with, it's the absolute last thing that I need, but we've all agreed we are better off playing this game—whatever game this is—for now.

Besides, after Lydia dodged my calls all day today, I'm going to use the opportunity to corner her. She can't expect me to be dismissed for much longer. What's her plan, then? Does she think I'll give up if she keeps fobbing me off? That I'd let my daughter go without a fight? Without flying flags and declaring war? Hell to the motherfucking no!

There's a soft knock at my bedroom door before Logan's head pops into sight. He came with me back to my apartment so I could find an outfit and change. Grayson will be here soon to pick me up—if he isn't already waiting in the living room.

"Just wanted to check on you." Logan's gaze doesn't leave my face, likely reading every twisted emotion eating me alive. Without another word, he strides over and envelops me in one of his perfect Logan hugs. His hand rubs up and down my spine, and I bury my face in his hoodie, wishing I could spend the entire night curled up beside him—much like I have the last four nights since everything went to hell in a handbasket.

I've spent my days on campus going about the motions while not hearing a single word my lecturers have said. I don't care that I'm falling behind. I don't care about anything anymore. How can I when the only person of importance in my life isn't here—where she should be?

Inhaling deeply, I fill my lungs with Logan's crisp winter scent. It always works wonders to clear my mind and stabilize me. Even now, it takes the edge off my frayed nerves. Although, nothing on this earth could eliminate the overwhelming nausea of having to face Bertram again. Nothing could prepare me to sit across a table from him and act like we're family. Like I don't want to claw his eyes out. Slit his throat. Stab him in the eye with my fork. Rip off his dick and shove it down his throat.

There are so many options....

I guess I'll have all dinner to contemplate in which order I should carry them out.

"I wish I could go for you," he murmurs against my ear. "If I could take on this pain for you, I would."

I squeeze him tighter, knowing this is killing him—him *and* Royce. Knowing they have to remain behind while I literally walk into the Devil's lair.

The only upside is that I'm not walking in alone.

I never thought I'd appreciate the day Grayson was by my side, but I'm grateful for this.

We break apart at the sound of a throat clearing, and I peer around Logan to find Grayson standing stiffly in my bedroom doorway. He is wearing a pale blue shirt and gray slacks; his lips pressed into a tight line as he stares at me unblinking.

"It's time."

He says it like he's announcing the moment I walk to the electric chair.

Steeling my nerves, I nod. Stepping from Logan's embrace, I move to walk around him. However, before I can get too far, he grabs my hand, whirling me back into his arms. Logan captures the back of my head with his hand, angling my face to his as his eyes search mine.

"You're so brave, Shortcake. So strong. I know you'll survive this dinner, just like you've survived everything else—with unbelievable poise and grace. And when it's over, I'll be here. Come home to me and cry in my arms. I'll be strong, so you don't have to." Tears gather in my eyes. Before they spill over, he presses his lips to mine in a chaste yet heated kiss. One that goes so much deeper than physical affection, lust, or chemistry. It's a kiss that speaks to the profound bond we have—the love we share.

"Grayson will be with you the entire time," he assures me before reluctantly letting me go.

With a small smile, I walk over to Grayson. His gaze is fixed over my head as he nods at Logan before sliding his attention to me.

"I won't leave you alone with either of them," he repeats, his words a searing promise.

Throat thick, I merely nod before we make our way out of my apartment, down the stairs, and into his slick sports car.

We're silent on the drive out of town and toward Springview, where the restaurant for tonight's shitshow is situated.

The journey to Springview simultaneously lasts a lifetime and is over too soon. When we pull up to the restaurant and a valet opens my door, I'm still not prepared to face my worst nightmare, but I'm officially out of time.

The valet holds out his hand to help me out of the car, but before I can put my hand in his, Grayson is rounding the hood, snapping at the poor guy. "Don't touch her," he snarls, glaring at the man.

He flinches away, his hand dropping as he apologizes profusely to Grayson.

Grayson, the asshole that he is, ignores him as he moves to stand in front of me, blocking out the rest of the world as he holds out his hand with obvious expectation.

Too strung out to deal with his bullshit tonight, I shake my head as I allow him to help me out. If he didn't have such low seats, I wouldn't *need* help getting out of his car—an observation I don't think he'd appreciate right now, so I politely don't point it out.

"That was rude," I say instead, piercing him with the same glare he leveled on the valet.

He arches an arrogant eyebrow as he looks down his nose at me. "So?"

"He was only doing his job."

"He was going to touch you."

"So?" I counter, in the same tone he just used on me.

His eyes spark with possession. "*So*, no one touches what's mine."

"This misplaced ownership is getting old," I drawl, turning away from him so he can't see the flush in my cheeks from his words. I might play it off as annoying, but there's no denying his jealousy does inappropriate things to me.

"Don't care," he retorts as he moves to stand beside me. Glancing down, he offers me his elbow.

I slide my arm through his.

"Ready to do this?"

Staring up into his dark chocolate eyes, I answer honestly. "Not even a little bit."

He grins, all teeth and savage. "Me neither. Let's get this shitshow of a dinner over with."

It doesn't matter that Grayson is pressed against me, a solid strength of support. It doesn't matter that the restaurant is full of patrons and staff or that I'm not the same weak teenage girl I was when I last faced *him*.

Nothing—and I mean *absolutely nothing*—could prepare me for coming face to face with the monster who stole my innocence.

My voice.

My sanity.

The restaurant is a blur as Grayson leads me through the tables, following the maître d' to where our parents are sitting.

All I can see is his face—it looks exactly how it did four years ago. There are a few more lines at the corners of his eyes and around his mouth, and salt and pepper dust his dark brown hair, but otherwise, you'd never know he'd just been released from prison.

You'd never know the evil that lurks beneath his superior facade.

The darkness that resides under his skin.

The pit of tar that lives where his heart should.

When he spots us approaching their table, his eyes lift to mine. Outwardly, his expression doesn't change, but the second our gazes connect, a sick gleam ignites in his dark eyes, and all I see is his hidden malevolence. It makes me nearly projectile vomit, and honestly, I'm not sure how I keep moving. How I don't turn and flee. I want to. Everything in me is screaming for me to run. To get away.

I must react to the urge because Grayson's arm squeezes mine, refusing to let me slip away.

"Look who I found outside," he purrs, easily falling into the role of father's son once we reach the table. My arm falls from his as he pulls out a chair at the table—deliberately choosing the one opposite Lydia instead of Bertram—and gestures for me to sit.

Forcing my gaze from Bertram's, it inadvertently slides to my mother's as I reluctantly take my seat. The shock on her face is apparent.

"I'm so glad you could make it, Riley," Bertram says smoothly. He draws out my name, and I have to bite my tongue to stop myself from barking at him to keep it out of his sick mouth. His gaze shifts to my mother, hardening imperceptibly. "Your *mother* wasn't sure if you'd be able to."

Still staring at Lydia, I force my lips upward into the best replication of a smile that I'm capable of at this moment. "My study group canceled at the last minute."

"Their loss and our gain," Bertram continues, eyes still drilling into the side of my face as I astutely ignore him, unfolding my napkin and nitpicking as I place it over my knee. *God, will he shut up already?* "And looking so beautiful. You've truly grown into a stunning woman, Riley."

It feels like bugs are crawling over my skin, and despite my dress not being revealing, I still have the urge to cover myself up.

"Shame you couldn't have worn something smarter to dinner," my mother snipes, her lip curled in distaste. "Couldn't you have made an effort? We're in a fancy restaurant."

I merely stare at her. She's really one to speak. She might be wearing a designer dress, but it would look more at home on a twenty-year-old hitting the clubs. Her tits are practically spilling out the top, and without looking, I know the hem likely barely covers her ass.

Bertram ignores his wife, too, finally shifting his attention from me to greet Grayson. "Son."

"Dad," Grayson responds in that same tone, claiming the seat beside mine. His gaze shifts to Lydia, his smile forced. "Lydia."

"Grayson," my mother simpers. "So nice to see you looking so well after all these years."

Cue internal eye roll.

Bertram smiles, a charismatic, charming grin that fools everyone. That once fooled me until I caught a glimpse of the monster that lurks underneath.

"Isn't this nice? Having the *entire* family back together again."

Lydia turns her saccharine smile on Bertram as she leans in to place her hand on his arm. "So nice, dear. We have so much to celebrate and be thankful for."

"That we do." Bertram lifts his glass of champagne in a toast. Lydia and Grayson follow suit. Me? I can't seem to make my arms move, much less lift the glass without shaking and spilling it everywhere.

"Riley." I can't stop the flinch at hearing my name on his tongue *again* and feeling the weight of his perverted gaze on me. "I understand you are at Halston with Grayson. What are the chances?" Bertram chuckles, but there's a hardness in his eyes. *Oh, he doesn't like it one bit that I'm attending the same school as his son.* "Have the two of you had the opportunity to catch up?"

Thankfully, Grayson fields that question. "It's a large enough campus, and she's a freshman while I'm a senior. We don't exactly run in the same circles, and I haven't had much desire to go out of my way to reacquaint us," he drawls. Turning to look at me, there's none of the usual possessiveness I've become accustomed to seeing in his eyes. Instead, they're hard and cold—just like his father's. It's frightening. Terrifying, honestly. Especially when he accompanies it with that forced smile. "However, I'm willing to bury the hatchet—for the sake of *family*."

"Yes, let's leave all that ugliness in the past," Bertram agrees, his voice a touch less hostile than it was a moment ago. "You're brother and sister; you should get to know each other as such."

My insides twist. *Yeah, I have never looked at Grayson as a brother. And with how he looks at me, I'd judge he's never seen me that way either.*

"Lydia, how are you settling into the new house?" Grayson redirects.

In between the waitress taking our orders, Lydia blathers about the new house. The one that isn't as nice as what she had before, but *will do for now.*

The entire time, Bertram sneaks glances my way while sipping from his glass of whiskey. I shuffle uncomfortably in my chair, and it's evident that Grayson is the only one feigning interest in Lydia's rambling.

However, when I shift in my chair for the fifth time, he spreads his legs under the table so his thigh presses against mine. It's the only source of support he can offer, and I soak it up, leaning into his warmth.

Food is delivered, and I mostly push mine around my plate so it looks like I've eaten something while Lydia and Bertram continue talking as though this truly is a family dinner. Honestly, I'm barely listening. I'm just trying to get through this, counting down the minutes until it's acceptable to make my escape.

Anytime Bertram attempts to pull me into the conversation by asking me personal questions, my mother slyly diverts the conversation back to her. I don't care. She'd probably stop if she realized she was actually doing me a favor.

However, as the meal drags on, I see her becoming more irritated. She starts openly glaring at me across the table and making passive-aggressive remarks anytime Bertram compliments me.

By the time our main course is taken away, my mother dabs at her mouth with her napkin before piercing me with a fierce stare. "I need to use the ladies' room. Riley, accompany me."

It's not a question, though I don't argue because I do need to talk to her—*alone.*

Pasting on a fake smile, I say, "Sure, mother," as I place my linen napkin on the table and slide out of my chair. My eyes connect briefly with Grayson's, a silent reassurance that I'll be okay before I turn and follow my mother away from the table.

Storming into the bathroom, she stalks the length of it, pushing open stall doors before whirling on me. "What are you doing here?" she hisses, spitting venom now that she doesn't have an audience.

Crossing my arms over my chest, I stare her down. "Why are you dodging my calls?" I ask instead, ignoring her outburst. "I want to talk to Aurora."

Just saying her name has a fresh wave of pain slicing through me, and my hands shake as I form a fist, wanting so badly to call Lydia out on her lies.

This is how we decided to play it, though: Apply pressure while Dax and his IT guy do their thing. Royce assures me that Dax has confirmed that his computer guy is the best. If Aurora has shown up on a camera, had her picture posted online, or her name mentioned anywhere, he'll find it. We only need one digital breadcrumb to trace the footprints back to whoever has her.

The problem with that is that it means we're currently sitting on our asses waiting for said breadcrumb to materialize. In the meantime, I'm slowly losing my sanity without my daughter. And being face-to-face with the woman who fucking *sold* her is messing with my head. I don't want to play dumb.

I *want* to shove her against the wall and demand to know who she fucking sold *my daughter* to.

I *want* to wrap my hands around her throat and watch the fear that is eating me from the inside out flood her eyes.

I *want* to make her as weak and helpless as I have felt every single second since Grayson told me what was happening.

"I won't let you ruin this for me *again*." My mother continues on her tirade as though I never spoke, pacing the length of the bathroom. "You stole him from me four years ago, and I've had to suffer the consequences of your selfishness since then. I *deserve* this."

The fucking gall of this bitch!

"Please," I sneer. "We both know you only went back to him because no one else would put up with your ass. You're not twenty-two anymore, *Lydia,* and plastic surgery only gets you so far. Why have a fake, dried-up version of a younger woman when you can have the real deal?"

She stops in her pacing to gape at me. "How dare you!" Marching toward me with her finger pointed at my face, she snarls, "I can keep Aurora from you. Make it so you *never see her again.*"

Except she's already done that. She's already sold her bargaining chip—the one thing she used to manipulate and control me.

Instead of cowering to her as I typically would, I stand taller, glaring down my nose at her. "I'd like to see you try. You think all I did was get those lawyers to send you a sweet little letter?" I hiss, stepping closer. "They're going to ensure I regain full custody of my daughter. They're going to drag your decrepit ass over the coals. Reveal you to the whole world for the manipulative, narcissistic bitch that you are."

Well, that *had* been the plan. Logan's plan. And one that I'd started to believe could actually be a reality one day... until that night.

Despite the circumstances, sick satisfaction floods my veins as, for the first time, genuine fear bleeds into Lydia's expression. She takes a step back, cowering to *me* for once. I'm not stupid enough to believe my threats are enough to intimidate her, but given that the last thing she'd want is lawyers snooping around looking for a child she no longer has guardianship of, she *should* be scared.

I mean, what the fuck did she think would happen once she sold my daughter? Did she believe she could hide behind Bertram and his money? What the fuck was her end game?

The flash of fear disappears as quickly as it arrives, her face hardening once more. "Just stop flirting with my *husband*. Don't think I don't notice how you flutter your eyes at him—that whole shy, innocent act you put on to get his attention," she seethes. "Make your excuses and leave, and I'll let you have five minutes with Aurora next weekend."

It's fucked up how my heart skips a beat, and hope—the fickle bitch—beats a drum in my chest. For a second, I *almost* believe she can make that happen. I *want* to believe it so fucking bad that I agree before the reality of the situation has caught up to me.

The grim reality is that she *can't* make that happen because my daughter no longer lives with her.

Instead, she's god knows where, doing god knows what, with god knows who.

My head is still spinning from the emotional whiplash as Lydia marches out of the bathroom. Moving to the sinks, I place my palms against the granite countertop and stare at myself in the mirror, giving myself a moment before I have to go back out there.

Closing my eyes, I hang my head. *It's nearly over,* I tell myself. *All I have to do is go out there and make my excuses. Then I'm done.*

With a final, deep inhale, I open my eyes. Staring at my reflection, I nod before grabbing my clutch and walking out of the bathroom.

And straight into a hard chest.

RILEY

CHAPTER FOUR

L arge hands grasp my shoulders as I rebound backward into the bathroom door, momentarily stunned. Fear renders me paralyzed for a second, thinking Bertram has taken advantage of my moment alone to corner me. However, as I lift my head, it isn't his malicious face that I'm met with. No, this face has similar features, but they don't come together to form Bertram's grotesque shape.

Instead, it's Grayson's hard stare that greets me. He looks pissed. Actually, that's an understatement. He looks *livid*. Downright murderous.

I'd be afraid, except the way that he's slowly reeling me into his arms until I'm tucked against his chest, something fragile and precious to be protected, quells any panic.

"We only have a moment, but when your mother returned to the table without you, I needed to make sure you were okay," he murmurs against my ear. "What did she say to you?"

"Nothing worth repeating," I whisper, sinking into his embrace. It still throws me when Grayson is sweet like this. It's almost like he's two people. For the most part, he's the raging, possessive asshole who loves to drive me crazy. Then, when I'm right on the verge of dick-punching him, he reveals this softer, caring side and ultimately throws me for a loop.

"Did your dad say anything?"

"Nothing useful."

While I was arguing with my mom, Grayson was trying to figure out his father's angle. What *is* this game that he's playing?

"So tonight was a bust," I sigh. "Can we get out of here now?"

"I thought you'd never ask."

Pulling back from our embrace, he drops his hand to mine, quickly squeezing it. "You go back to the table first. I'll be right behind you."

I nod before walking out of the hallway where the bathrooms are and back into the restaurant. I've barely taken my seat at the table before I see him striding across the restaurant, his stare fixed on us. However, his eyes aren't the only ones I feel on me.

"This has been... lovely," he states once he reaches the table. He remains standing, fingers curling around the back of his chair as he continues, "But I have to head out." He glances my way. "Riley, can I give you a lift somewhere?"

"That would be—"

"No need," Bertram intervenes with a tight smile and a tick in his jaw. "I'm happy to give her a ride home when we're finished."

Yeah, no fucking way.

"Nonsense," Grayson retorts, his charismatic smile still glued in place. "I'm sure you two lovebirds would rather have some time alone, and it's a perfect opportunity for Riley and me to *get to know each other*."

"That would be perfect, Grayson," my mother purrs, jumping on the opportunity as she clamps her hand possessively around Bertram's arm. "You're such a sweetheart." With her bright, plastic smile still in place, her eyes slide to mine and harden in warning.

Yeah, like I *want* to spend another second in either of their presence.

I don't bother saying a word—I couldn't force out a fake pleasantry even if I wanted to—as I get up from the table before following Grayson toward the exit.

The fresh air is a welcome relief against my heated skin as we wait for the valet to bring Grayson's car around. We stand there in silence, both of us lost in our thoughts. I can feel the tension radiating from Grayson. He can probably feel the same thing emanating from me. Even though I know they can't see us from inside the restaurant, I can still feel the lingering weight of Bertram's sick stare. It's an effort not to scratch at my skin, and I desperately need a shower, even though he never touched me.

Just being in such close proximity to him is enough for me to break out in hives.

When the valet appears with the car, we both climb in—thankfully without Grayson going apeshit on the valet this time. I've barely gotten my door closed before he slams his foot down on the accelerator, and the wheels spin on the gravel before we shoot out of the parking lot.

"Grayson!" I gasp, reaching for my seatbelt and hurriedly buckling myself in.

"Sorry," he grinds, his hands fisting the steering wheel and his focus solely on the road in front of us. "I just have to put as much fucking distance between us as I can."

Now that we're encased inside his tiny car, the tension I felt from him before escalates, multiplying tenfold until it practically chokes me.

Concerned, I peek at him from the corner of my eye. His expression is haunted, his teeth grinding as he glares out the windshield. The leather steering wheel creaks beneath the pressure as he squeezes it.

With each mile that zips past us, the tension winds tighter, the car growing hotter until it becomes stifling. The silence sits heavy in the air, like a bubble I'm too afraid to pop—not while he's driving, at least.

When we're halfway between Springview and Halston, he suddenly pulls on the steering wheel. The car squeals as it lurches ninety degrees, and I'm thrown back in my seat before he presses on the accelerator, and we speed up a single dirt track road I hadn't noticed before.

"Uhh, Grayson?" I hedge, suddenly a lot more nervous than I had been before. I'm not afraid of him. I've never, not once, been fearful of Grayson or his moods. It's his mindset that worries me. Did being faced with his father push him too far over the edge?

He doesn't answer me as the car bumps over the uneven ground, the Xenon headlights bobbing and dipping as they highlight the dirt road, tall grass, and tree trunks as we pass by. It'll be a miracle if his tires don't get a puncture.

The trees grow thicker around us until they blot out the sky overhead, and the thick canopy casts eerie shadows over the car, making the darkness feel denser somehow. Grayson cracks his window, the scent of damp earth and pine infusing the vehicle. As we crawl deeper into the forest depths, I glance nervously at Grayson, his profile sharp in the dim glow of the dashboard lights, giving nothing away.

I return my focus to the front windshield in time to see the trees part, and before us, a space opens up, bathed in the soft light of the moon. An old, crumbling church stands in the middle of the clearing, its skeletal frame silhouetted against the night sky. Ivy creeps up its walls like grasping fingers, and broken stained glass windows glint ominously in the moonlight.

I feel the hairs on the back of my neck stand on end as we pull to a stop a short distance from the ruins. There's something eerie and otherworldly about this place, but at the same time, it's hauntingly beautiful in its abandonment.

Grayson turns off the engine, leaving the headlights on and bathing us in silence. The only sounds are the rustle of leaves in the night breeze and the distant hoot of an owl.

I can feel Grayson's emotions thrumming in the air around us, thick and heavy like a storm gathering on the horizon. The tension between us is palpable as I stare steadfastly out the windshield and wait...

My gaze runs over the weathered remains of the church. Parts of the roof have collapsed, and the windows are all either missing or smashed. It's a place frozen in time, abandoned and forgotten, yet still standing.

Beyond the church, I notice the tops of headstones peeking through the tall grass, a forsaken cemetery reclaimed by nature.

I can't help but feel a sense of awe at the sight. Despite the years of neglect and the relentless onslaught of the elements, the church still stands, a testament to its resilience and strength. I've faced my own battles, my own struggles. I'm missing pieces, parts of me that were torn away by trauma and hardship. But, like the church, I'm still standing. Still fighting. And maybe, just maybe, I'll weather the storm too.

My gaze slides to Grayson as I wonder whether he, too, will be able to survive the storm or if the harsh winds of his past or the torrential rain of what's to come will pull him under.

Or perhaps it will be the storm that rages within that will take him out.

I patiently wait for him to work through his feelings, but

minutes pass, and still, he sits in silence beside me, his hands clenched tight around the steering wheel.

Then he snaps. He drives his fists into the steering wheel repeatedly, pummeling the leather as he hisses and snarls. Wide-eyed, I watch as he breaks.

Crumbles.

Decimates.

Heaving heavy breaths, he keels forward, sliding his hands into his hair, his forehead resting against the steering wheel. His voice is raspy with emotion when he finally speaks, his knuckles red. "I don't know how you fucking did that," he seethes. "How you managed to sit there. I wanted to launch myself across the table and rip his head from his shoulders. Every second was fucking torture."

I can hear the strain in his voice. He put on a good act at dinner, appearing unaffected. I don't think I realized until now just how hard that was for him. To sit opposite his father, knowing he abused his mom. That he might have killed her. Knowing *that* and having to pretend that he didn't.

"I thought of Aurora." My voice is loud in the small confines of the car despite having spoken the words softly. "Every time it became too much, I thought of her and knew I could endure another few minutes—*for her*."

Still hunched over, Grayson lifts his head from his hands and turns at my admission. His wild gaze latches onto mine like I'm a lifeline before the anger gradually seeps out of him, slow and steady, until all that remains are the vulnerable emotions underneath—the ones he never allows himself to actually feel.

"Everything is so fucked." Shaking his head, he exhales heavily. "I don't have any right to complain when I don't even understand how you're still standing. I shouldn't have made you come tonight."

"You didn't *make* me do anything, Grayson. *I* chose to go

tonight. To confront Lydia, but also because Bertram still has so much power over me. I've learned to accept what he did to me because Aurora came out of that horrific time, and she is the best thing that's ever happened to me.

"But Bertram is still a constant presence stalking me from the shadows. Peering over my shoulder and following my every move, even when he was behind bars. As terrifying as it was, I *had* to go tonight. Not because he all but demanded it. Not because I *want* to play his game."

Glancing down, I fiddle with the hem of my dress. "As a teenager, he was this omnipotent, all-powerful being. He had full control over me. I needed to prove to myself and him that he was not in control anymore. *I* am. I'm not that terrified teenager he remembers. I took the damage he caused, and I built myself a suit of armor that is in-fucking-domitable."

Pushing open the car door, I step outside. After my little speech, Grayson appeared incapable of any sort of verbal response. He merely stared at me with admiration and lust and something far more primal that heated my skin and made a pulse throb between my legs until I couldn't sit in the car a second longer.

The cold air is a balm to my frayed nerves. It's the end of February, and although the worst of winter has passed, it's still bitingly cold once the sun goes down. I'm not dressed for exploring, but I find myself drawn to the old church regardless.

"Riley," Grayson chastises as he steps halfway out of his car. "What are you doing? Get back in the car."

Because taking orders from Grayson is something I'll never do, I ignore him as I climb the uneven steps at the front of the church. The wooden door has rotted away in places, hanging open at an angle on the rusted hinges.

Glancing back over my shoulder, I flash him a grin before I slip inside. The interior is dimly lit by the moonlight filtering through the missing roof tiles and broken windows, the air cool and musty against my skin. While my eyes adjust, I turn on the flashlight on my phone before holding it out in front of me and doing a sweep of the room.

The floor is littered with debris, fallen leaves, and bits of broken stone crunching beneath my feet as I pick my way down the aisle between the empty pews. The silence is deafening, broken only by the sound of my own breathing echoing off the walls as I run my hand along the rough wood of the nearest pew, feeling the years of history beneath my fingertips.

The light of my torch catches on a rotted Bible sitting on the bench, its pages yellowed and brittle with age, before I swing my phone toward the front of the church, where an altar stands beneath a faded and molded tapestry. Its surface is cracked and weather-beaten, the once-golden trim now tarnished and dull.

Despite its dilapidated state, the church has a sense of grandeur, a feeling of reverence that hangs in the air like a tangible presence.

"Riley," Grayson hisses from the doorway, having seemingly followed me. "You're going to break your goddamn ankle walking around in the dark in those heels." His footsteps echo off the walls as he stomps down the aisle toward where I'm standing. With each *thud*, my heart races, and I turn to face him as he approaches.

The moonlight glances off his sharp features, casting half his face in shadow and making him appear like a dark god in the dim light—powerful and menacing yet undeniably beautiful.

There's a raw energy about Grayson that sends shivers down my spine, and despite the fear that gnaws at the edges of my mind, it's excitement that pulses through my veins.

I can't tear my eyes away as he stalks closer, his every movement deliberate and controlled. There's a magnetic pull between us, a tension that crackles in the air like electricity. When he stands before me, his dark eyes ablaze with emotion, I feel a thrill run through me unlike anything I've ever experienced.

"Grayson…" There's a question in my tone, one that has him cocking his head. "Remember that time you chased me through the field?"

His eyes narrow, however it does nothing to hide the spark of excitement I see hidden in his dark depths at the memory.

"Chase me."

"Riley…" Unlike before, there's a strain in his voice as he says my name. He wants to; I know he does.

"Chase me, Grayson." My voice is barely a whisper in the silent church. "You brought us here because you wanted to forget everything for a little while… I want to forget too. I want to escape this pain, if only for a few moments." I can feel the weight of my agony pressing down on me, threatening to crush me beneath its unbearable weight. But in this moment, with Grayson's hungry gaze fixed on mine, I'm desperate for a reprieve, however fleeting it may be. "Chase me, Grayson."

I'm already slipping off my heels, first my right one, then my left, until I stand barefoot in front of him, my soles pressed against the cold stone.

A range of emotions flit across Grayson's face—uncertainty, desire, hesitation—before he finally settles on one: *Want.*

Pure, unadulterated *need.*

"You want to run, Tempest?" The deep purr of his voice is both sinful and seductive. I catch a flicker of something dark and intense in his eyes as he leans in, warm breath caressing my cheek before he whispers, "Then you better *pray* that I don't catch you, 'cause when I do, I'm going to force you to your knees and make you scream my name until you're hoarse." His lips brush tantalizingly against my skin, eliciting a full-body shiver as my temperature spikes. "By the time I'm done with you, there will be no question over who you belong to."

Adrenaline courses through my veins—a heady mix of excitement and fear, anticipation and exhilaration, as if I'm about to flee from a predator, and yet I can't help but feel a thrill at the chase.

A primal urge takes hold and implores me to run, escape, and forget.

With the heat from his body wrapped around me, Grayson plants a taunting kiss on my jaw as he strokes a light finger down my opposite cheek, before he rasps in a thick command, *"Run."*

With a quick intake of breath, I turn and sprint down the aisle. My heart pounds in my chest. The slap of my bare feet against the stone echoes off the walls of the old church. Behind me, I can hear Grayson's footsteps matching mine, the sound like a drumbeat in the darkness, driving me forward, pushing me to run faster, to forget everything but the exhilaration of the chase.

I can feel the heat of his breath against the back of my neck, and before his fingers can reach out and grab me, I grab ahold of the back of a pew, using it to change trajectory as I run between the benches to the far side.

A hysterical laugh bursts from my chest as he growls, before quickly changing direction to pursue me once more. My gaze darts frantically around the ruins in search of an escape route until I spot an archway that leads outside. The door is missing, and putting on a burst of speed, I race through it and into the overgrown cemetery.

The moonlight is brighter out here, lighting my way as I weave between the forgotten headstones. I can no longer feel the bite of winter against my flushed skin as I run like my life depends on it.

My heartbeat whooshes in my ears, and I so badly want to look behind me and see where Grayson is, but I don't dare. I can feel him close by as I sprint between the crumbling graves, my heart pounding and anticipation thrashing in my veins.

Against the soft grass, Grayson's footsteps are indecipherable behind me, but I can feel his presence hot on my heels. With every step, the tension between us crackles in the air, electrifying and exhilarating. It's a game of cat and mouse, only there's nothing playful about the way his intense, predatory energy consumes the space between us.

It's primal, raw, and entirely exhilarating—fleeing from a predator yet secretly hoping to be caught.

In the final moments before his fingers reach out and grab me, time seems to slow, each heartbeat echoing in my ears like a drumroll of anticipation. My breath comes in ragged gasps, the cold night air burning in my lungs.

I feel the heat emanating from his body seconds before his fingers slide into my hair, fisting the back of my head and dragging me backward.

My back meets his hard chest, and he uses his grip on my hair to tilt my head to the side, exposing my neck. His breath dances over the shell of my ear, heavy with exertion and need.

"You might be able to run from reality, Riley," Grayson growls, his voice low and menacing. "But there is no running from *me*."

As if to cement his point, he sinks his teeth into the tender flesh of my neck, sucking on the skin until it's raw and bruised.

Releasing me, he runs his tongue over the bite before using his hold on the back of my head to force me to my knees right there in the middle of the cemetery. The ground is unforgiving against my knees, but it's a welcome pain—a pleasurable one.

No more words are needed as he shoves me forward onto my hands before flipping up the back of my dress. My panties are wrenched to the side before he drives two fingers roughly into my tight channel.

I cry out at the intrusion, my back bowing as he finger fucks me. I'm so wet already that I can hear the squelch of my excitement with every powerful thrust of his fingers.

"There is no outrunning *this,*" Grayson growls from behind me as he continues to destroy my pussy and send me careening head-first toward what I already know is going to be an intense orgasm. "There is no outrunning the fact that you. Are. Mine." He presses down on the bundle of nerves as he says those last three words until I detonate on his fingers with a scream that bounces off the headstones and drifts into the sky.

My pussy is still spasming with aftershocks when I feel his blunt head pressed against my entrance before he slams inside in one long thrust.

"*Fuuck,*" he hisses when he's fully seated inside me. His fingers dig into the skin of my hips with enough force that I know I'll have bruises tomorrow. "I won't ever get enough of this. The way you strangle my cock, Tempest. Holy fuck."

He moves then, pulling back before slamming in. He uses his hold on my hips to yank my ass back into him, sending him impossibly deeper as I whimper and moan.

My fingertips dig into the earth beneath my hands. Soil embeds beneath my nails, and my arms tremble as I struggle to remain on my knees against the crashing waves of pleasure rolling through me.

"Grayson."

"Fuck," he hisses. Leaning over me, he fists my hair and forces me to arch my spine. It limits his movement, but the new angle has his dick hitting the perfect spot as I moan louder. He sucks on the other side of my neck, leaving a matching mark before he rasps, "Say my name again."

"Grayson," I cry out, my voice a breathless plea as I teeter on the edge of oblivion.

"Fuck, I love it when you say my name like that while you cream my cock."

God. I'm a sucker for dirty talk, and his filthy words send me careening over the edge. Birds take flight from nearby trees, and I'm sure the ghosts that haunt this graveyard are peering out at us from behind their headstones as I scream out in pleasure.

Grayson grunts in my ear as my pussy squeezes the cum from his cock until we're both left sated and breathless. My limbs are jelly as I collapse onto the ground, feeling our combined release drip out of me.

I'm still half out of it when I feel Grayson push open my thighs, and I raise onto my elbows to peer at him over my shoulder. His eyes are glued on the junction between my legs, and he stares enraptured, as if incapable of looking away. I'm about to ask what he's doing when his fingers press against my entrance. A moan slips past my lips before I can swallow it back, and his gaze snaps to mine as he pushes our cum back inside me.

"Need to make sure you're still carrying my seed when we get home. I want them to smell me all over you."

Holding my stare, he makes my pussy flood with renewed heat when he slaps my inner thigh before smirking and fixing my panties back into place.

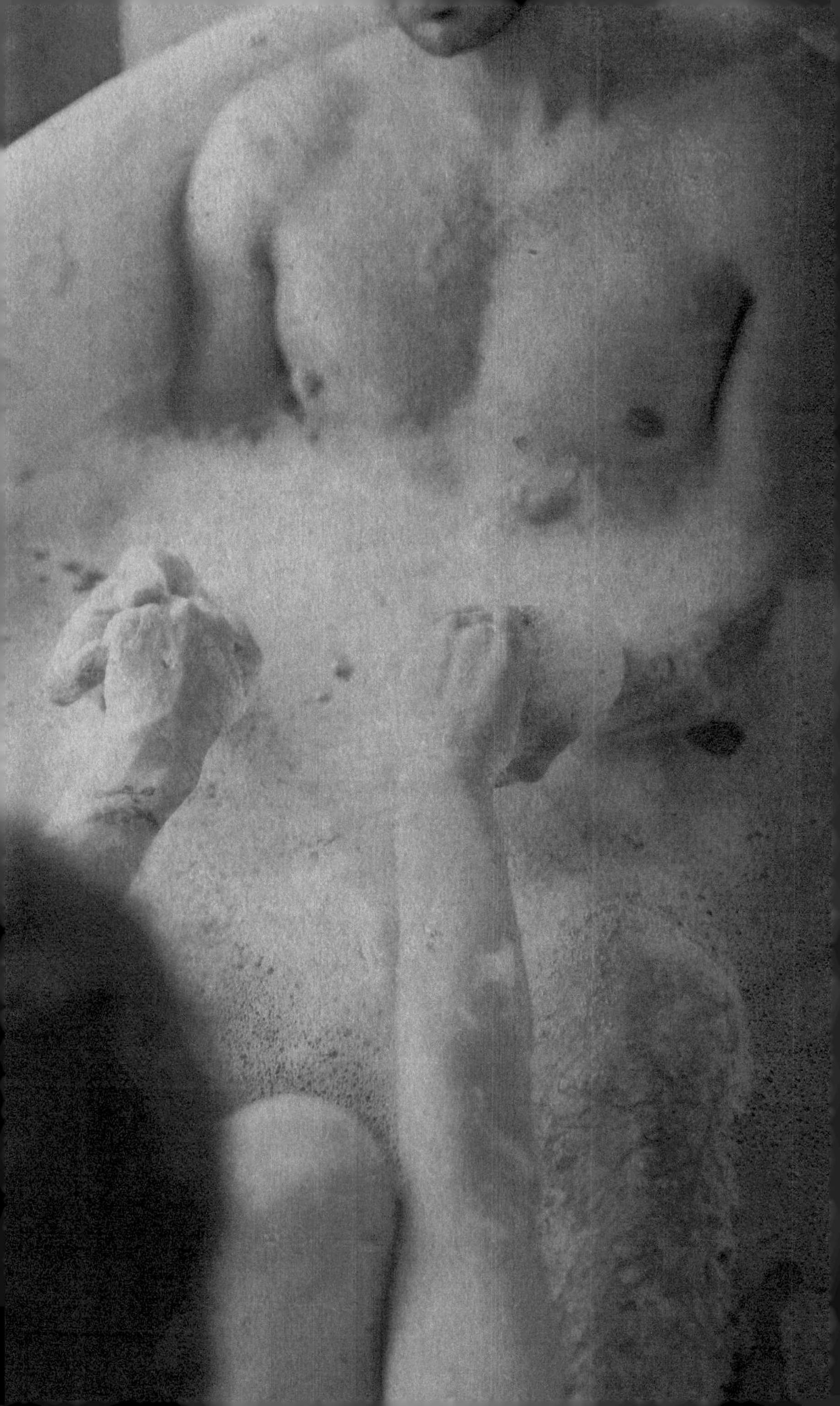

LOGAN

CHAPTER FIVE

"Ah, fuck," I curse when I stub my toe on the step before lifting my foot to cradle in my hands.

"Will you shut the fuck up," Royce hisses, glowering at me over his shoulder from halfway up the stairs.

Still holding my foot, I roll my eyes. "It's not like anyone's home."

"With the way you're banging around the place, the fucking neighbors will be able to hear you and call the police."

I let loose yet another eye roll because, *seriously?* "Their closest neighbors are a mile down the road."

"Exactly."

When he turns his back on me to continue up the stairs, I flip him the middle finger before following him to the second-floor landing.

Despite having never been in Bertram's new house, he seems to know where he's going as he turns right at the top of the stairs, making a beeline for a set of double doors that open into the primary suite.

From what little I've seen so far, you wouldn't think Bertram moved into it less than a week ago. For real, it looks as though he's lived here for years. Books line the bookshelves, and there are paintings on the walls and rugs covering the hardwood.

I wonder if he had everything put in storage when he was incarcerated or if he bought entirely new shit that some poor soul has had to find a home for.

"What are we looking for again?" I ask as we enter the main suite that he shares with Lydia.

"I don't know. Anything that might lead us to whom she sold Aurora to," Royce answers, moving straight for the nearest bedside table before yanking open the drawers. "She'd already packed up all her shit by the time I went to hers, so if there's anything to find, it'll be here."

"Surely she wouldn't be stupid enough to bring proof of her crimes here?" Despite my uncertainty, I move to the other side of the bed to investigate. We've done much speculation over the last few days as to *why* Lydia would choose now to get rid of Aurora, and the only thing that makes sense is because of Bertram. The timing is too perfect to be coincidental.

Lydia is seriously insecure and jealous. She's envious of the attention her own *daughter* received from Bertram—oblivious to how sick and inappropriate it was—so it's only to reason she'd feel the same toward Aurora.

To Lydia, Aurora is a threat—yet another female to compete with for her husband's attention.

Better to get her out of the picture before Bertram learns of her existence.

Yeah, it's a completely fucked up way of thinking!

"The last thing Lydia would want is for her husband, whom she's recently gotten back, to not only find out that Aurora exists but also the role *his darling wife* played in the child's sudden disappearance. So, I repeat, why would she be stupid enough to bring proof of her crimes into this house?"

"We've gotta at least look," is all Royce says as he rummages through the bedside table.

It's immediately apparent from the lube and combination of porn and business magazines that I have Bertram's side of the bed, so after a brief glance—and definitely no touching 'cause *eww*—I wander over to the large his-and-hers closet.

I pull open drawers, rifle through clothes, and even peek inside handbags, but whatever the fuck I'm looking for, I don't find it.

"How do you think Ry and Gray are getting on?" I ask. Every few minutes, my thoughts drift back to her, wondering how she's holding up at the family dinner from hell. It's beyond fucked up that she even had to go. I mean, we told her she didn't, but never one to back down or show weakness, my Shortcake insisted. I know the opportunity to possibly glean some info about Aurora's whereabouts was too tempting to pass up—even if the chances are slim that Lydia will spill a word about who she sold Aurora to.

At least it allows us to snoop uninterrupted, knowing both Lydia and Bertram will be out of the house for at least an hour. All it took was Dax's IT guy fiddling with the security system and Royce picking the lock, and *voila*, here we are.

"I'm sure they're having a grand old time catching up over steak and lobster," Royce drawls from the bedroom. *Sarcastic fuckwit.*

"You don't think it was a bad idea, her going? That it'll be too much for her? She's already a wreck. What if this pushes her over the edge?" Exiting the closet, I lean against the doorframe as he checks under the bed before turning to face me.

Arms folded across his chest, he stares at a fixed point on the wall, but it's clear he's not truly seeing it. "Do I hate the idea of her sitting across the table from that sick fuck? Of course I do. Will it be too much for her? Maybe. I honestly don't know. But I *do know* that our girl is resilient as fuck. I know she'll endure anything if it means getting her daughter back. And I know that no matter what the fuck happens, she has us. We've got her back. We'll pick up the pieces if she breaks. We'll wipe her tears when she cries. And when all this is fucking over, we'll make sure no one can fucking touch her or Aurora again."

Amen to that.

Out loud, I tease, "Damn, you're a sappy asshole when you're in love. Who knew?"

If looks could kill, I'd be six feet under. "Stop wasting time and go check the bathroom."

Still sporting a shit-eating grin, I push off the doorway and stride to the adjoining bathroom. Flipping on the overhead light, I scan the immaculate white porcelain and marble countertop before crouching to look through the cupboards underneath.

Royce joins me a few moments later, the two of us working silently. I crouch to go through the cupboard under the sink, pushing aside bottles of cleanser, eye creams, and god knows what other shit that Lydia uses to make herself look like less of a hag.

My nose scrunches when I realize I've grabbed a box of sanitary pads. "Bleugh." I nearly gag. As if seeing Bertram's porn magazines wasn't bad enough, now I need to live with the knowledge that Lydia still gets her fucking period. I can officially die with regrets now.

I go to let go when I realize the weight isn't quite right. The box is too heavy. Trust me, after spending far too long in the pharmacy picking out the right ones for Riley, I *know* what weight a box of sanitary pads should be.

Curious now, I lift out the box and reluctantly open it. The top is as you'd expect—filled with sanitary pads—so I tip it upside down. There's a loud clatter as an old mobile phone hits the floor. *Huh, interesting.*

"Think I might have found something."

Royce crouches beside me, reaching out to grab the phone and powering it on. He goes to the call list, but it's empty, and there is only one outgoing message in the phone's inbox.

Package delivered.

It's time-stamped the exact date and time we were due to meet with Lydia to do the exchange for Aurora, along with the digits of the number she messaged.

"Fuck," I curse. "The package is Aurora, right? I mean, it has to be," I rant. Agitated, I swipe a hand through my hair, tugging on the short, blond strands. "Should we call the number?"

Royce's eyes lift to mine while he thinks. With a one-shoulder shrug, he presses the number and puts the phone on speaker. There's a tense moment of silence before an automatic voice comes over the line. *The number you are trying to reach has been disconnected.*

"Shit," I curse as Royce sighs. "Do you think Dax's guy can trace it?"

"No idea," he answers, pocketing the phone as he stands. "I'll give it to him and see." He does a scan of the bathroom. "I don't think we'll find anything else here."

Checking the time, I'm more than happy to get the fuck out of here. Riley and Gray should be done with their farce of a dinner soon, and I wanna be at home whenever she gets there.

"This is a big ass house," I comment as we make our way

back downstairs. "How the fuck did Bertram afford something like this? Did Gray buy it for him?"

"He vetoed the *much more modest* houses Gray showed him. I don't know how the fuck he's affording to live here." Royce looks around as though only now noticing that this house should be *way* out of budget for someone who has been in prison for four years and had his accounts frozen. "Something to look into," is all he says, frowning at his surroundings.

Reaching the bottom of the stairs, I begin to cross the foyer toward the door when Royce throws out his hand, smacking me in the chest.

"Ouch, fucker," I glower. Asshole doesn't even look at me, and I follow his gaze toward a set of double doors, one of which is ajar. Through the crack, I can make out a large mahogany desk and bookcases, and I can hazard a guess that that's Bertram's office.

"Hold up. There's something I've gotta do before we leave." Before I can ask any questions, he's slipping into the office, and with a sigh, I follow.

I remain near the door as Royce stalks like a shadow around the desk, plonking his ass in Bertram's chair as he touches the mouse and brings the computer screen to life. It's password protected, but that doesn't seem to bother Royce as he pulls out his phone and calls someone.

"What are you doing?" I ask, curiosity getting the best of me as I move closer.

Royce's eyes flash to mine, but he doesn't answer. Instead, he speaks into the phone. "Yeah, I'm in front of his computer."

Whoever he's speaking to must give him orders because he pulls a flash drive from his pocket and inserts it into the computer. "Okay. Now what?"

More orders follow. Royce hits a set of keys on the keyboard before the screen goes black, and gibberish text scrolls across it.

"We're in," he says a moment later when the screen returns, no longer displaying the *insert password* display but Bertram's desktop.

Putting the phone on loudspeaker, a brusque voice I don't recognize guides Royce as he navigates to the computer's files and clicks on the flash drive.

"Download the file on the drive," the voice dictates.

We watch as the download bar steadily fills, and when it hits 100%, Royce says, "Done."

"That's it. That's all you need to do. I'll be able to monitor his activity remotely."

I'm guessing this is Blue, Dax's tech guy. I've never met the guy, couldn't pick him out in a line up, but I'm grateful for all his help in trying to rescue Aurora and now with finding her.

"And Bertram won't know it's on his computer?" Royce confirms.

"Nope. He won't have a clue, but we'll be able to see everything he does."

"Perfect. Thanks, Blue." Royce hangs up but continues moving the mouse around the screen. I watch on as he goes through Bertram's search history and scours through the files on his computer.

"Anything?" I ask impatiently after a few moments.

Royce shakes his head. "Computer's clean. Looks like it's new—there's barely anything on it, but at least we can see now what he's doing on it."

My nose scrunches. "Why do we wanna see whatever sick shit he does on his computer?"

Swiveling in the chair, Royce pierces me with a droll look. "Cause he's a sick, slimy fuck who is up to no good. I want to know what the fuck he's up to." He gives a casual shrug. "And if we happen to catch him doing something that would get him sent back to prison..." He grins savagely, but *holy fucking shit. That* is genius!

Much more invested now, I lean over the back of Royce's chair to peer at the screen. Not that I know what the fuck I'm looking at. Beyond doing assignments on my laptop and scouring the web, I have no technological interest.

"What's that?" I ask, pointing at an app on his desktop with the Bentley symbol, the same as the brand-spanking new car Grayson said he's now driving around in.

"Looks like an app for his car, probably so he can update the maps and entertainment center," Royce answers.

"So it might show us where he's been since he was released?"

With a shrug, Royce clicks on the app. Immediately, a map showing the car's latest coordinates pops up—to the restaurant where he's having dinner with Gray and Riley.

"Click *all journeys*," I tell Royce, pointing at the button. He's already spotted it and clicks, bringing up a list of the car's previous journeys. There aren't many since he's only owned the car for a few days.

Scrolling to the bottom of the short list, the first journey is from the dealership to the prison, where the car had been dropped off in time for Bertram's release. *Like, seriously? The guy couldn't have taken a cab?*

"That must be him arriving on our doorstep," I say, indicating the journey from the prison to Halston. "And look, he made a five-minute journey to somewhere else in Halston before coming here."

When you click on the journey, the map shows a street in the center of Halston, and the blue dot shows exactly where he was. Bringing up the maps on his phone, Royce street views the location. It brings up a corner shop on a street populated with individual shops, cafes, and apartment buildings. He shrugs. "He probably stopped to pick up condoms or something."

"Gross." I grimace, immediately losing interest. "If there's nothing else, can we get out of here?"

There's a ping from the computer, and a notification pops up telling us the car is on the move.

"Looks like dinner is over," Royce states. "That's our cue to leave."

Fucking finally.

After closing out of the app, Royce puts the computer to sleep, and we ensure everything is as it was when we walked in before we sneak out of the house the way we entered. When we're back in the car, Royce messages Blue, who reactivates the security system.

And it's like we were never there.

———

"Where the fuck are they?" I growl, pacing the length of the kitchen and back. Every time I pass the door into the hall, I peer through it, but there's still no fucking sign of Riley or Grayson.

Redialing Grayson's number for the gazillionth time, I put it on speaker as I continue pacing. It rings out *again*, and I immediately dial Riley. It also rings out, and snarling, I glare down the hall to the front door.

"Will you fucking chill? You're making me dizzy with all your pacing," Royce huffs from where he's hunched over the kitchen island on his phone.

"They should have been home ages ago!"

"And if something had happened, we'd know." Lifting his head to pierce me with a stern expression as I walk past, he adds, "We have to trust Gray with her."

"They're dynamite when left alone. I love Gray, but his

asshole ways aren't what she needs after whatever will have happened at that dinner."

"Maybe not, but they need to work out their differences and learn to get along. If not for each other and our sanity, then for Aurora. They have a lot of history to sift through, but if they're talking, that's a good start. Just let them do their thing."

Teeth grinding, I pace in silence until I hear the sound of a key in the front door. I wheel in time to see Riley step into the hallway, and I freeze. My eyes round as they drop to her dirt-covered feet before slowly climbing to her red, dirt-caked knees, up to the red and purple marks on her neck before landing on her flushed cheeks and messy hair.

"That does not look like fucking *talking*," I snap at Royce before raising my voice so they can hear me—or more specifically, so *Grayson* hears me. "What. The. Fuck. Happened?!" I bellow, marching toward Riley and yanking her away from him.

My hands roam over her, carefully tilting her head back so I can see her neck. Noticing the teeth marks besmirching her skin, my nostrils flare. It's not only that my Shortcake is bruised... it's that she's covered in marks that aren't *mine*.

I've never had an issue sharing Riley with Royce, but for some reason, sharing her with Gray ticks me the fuck off. I don't know if it's the way he feels the need to claim and mark her as his, like she doesn't belong to Royce or me too, or if it's something more...

A warm hand cups my face, pulling me out of my bloodlust, and my gaze snaps to her gorgeous hazel eyes.

"I'm okay." Riley's soft voice soothes some of the bubbling anger. I cast a final glance at the marks on either side of her neck before dropping to my knees to brush my fingers over her knees. Her skin isn't broken, just bruised and dirty.

"What the fuck, Grayson?" I snap, finally giving him my full attention.

The fucking idiot must be looking to get punched because he smirks at me, and the fucking spark in his eyes nearly has me lunging at him.

Sensing how close I am to snapping, Riley shifts to stand in front of me, blocking my view of the shithead.

"Logan," she says with emphasis. "It's fine. *I'm* fine."

Pushing to my feet, I keep my eyes on her as I slide my hand around the back of her neck, relishing the feel of her warm skin against mine. She places a hand on my chest, and she does seem fine, if not exhausted. Still...

"It's not fine," I grit, lifting my gaze to glare at Grayson over the top of her head. "You had an emotional night that this fucker took advantage of to get his dick wet."

The smirk drops from Grayson's face, his expression hardening to stone as he glowers murderously at me.

"What the fuck did you just say?" he snarls, stepping closer.

"Logan!" Riley snaps. When I don't look at her, too busy facing off against Grayson, she places her hands on either side of my face and yanks it down to hers. "It wasn't like that. We went somewhere to cool off after the dinner." Her eyes search mine, pleading. "*I* instigated it. Grayson didn't do anything I didn't want. He would never, and you know that." She glances over my shoulder, likely at Royce, before turning her head toward Grayson. "We've all had a rough night. Emotions are running high. We should go to bed and talk in the morning."

"Sure, Tempest," Grayson grunts, cold gaze still boring into mine before he wrenches it away to stomp up the stairs to his room.

"Fine," I concede, "but I'm taking care of you first, and I don't want to hear a word of protest, Shortcake."

Grasping her hand, I pull her up the stairs and into the bathroom. Scooping my hands beneath her thighs, I lift her onto the counter. My eyes connect with hers. "You swear you're okay?" I ask, needing to hear her say it.

Her gaze softens, her hands coming to rest on my chest before sliding over my shoulders and curling around my neck, pulling me in between her legs. "I swear it, Logan. Grayson didn't hurt me."

My hands go to her hips, squeezing. "What about Bertram or your mom?"

I don't miss the pain that darkens her expression. The sadness that seeps in. "I survived." Eyes bouncing between mine, her voice trembles as she forces herself to ask, "Did Royce find anything?"

Sighing, I shake my head, hating how her entire posture deflates. "I'm sorry, baby."

With a weak smile barely touching her lips, she murmurs defeatedly, "Not your fault."

Moving past the moment, I grab a towel and soak it in the sink before lifting her leg. Holding her calf, I clean her knee before proceeding to her foot. I move on to her other leg only when her skin is its usual creamy color.

With her hands clutching the side of the counter, I notice the dirt beneath her nails. Tutting, I take a palm in mine and carefully clean the dirt from the creases. She giggles, and the sweet sound is music to my ears. The fact that this astounding woman has the capacity to laugh while her world is being burned to ashes speaks to the strength of her resilience.

I flash her a grin and a flirty wink before fetching a nail file and removing the dirt from beneath her nails. When I'm satisfied that I've gotten it all, I move to run the bath.

While the tub fills, I lift Riley off the counter and gently set her on her feet. I reach around to her back to undo the zip of her dress, and she holds my stare as the black material peels away, falling to her hips before she pushes it down to her feet and steps out of it.

She's left standing in her bra and panties, looking like every man's wet dream. Except, I'm not doing this to get my dick wet —even if he hasn't caught on to that yet.

Divulging her of the last of her clothing, I whisper in her ear, "Get in the bath, Shortcake."

"Only if you join me."

One side of my lips quirk. "Wouldn't have it any other way."

I turn off the taps and check the temperature before she steps in and lowers herself into the warm water. She watches as I pull my t-shirt over my head before shoving my sweats and boxers down my legs and kicking them aside. Striding toward the bath, I climb in behind her before hauling her against me, her back to my chest.

I take a proper breath for the first time since Grayson drove her away from her apartment. She relaxes into me, her body melting into mine, melding until we become one.

With her in my arms, it's the closest to peace I can achieve these days.

The back of her head rests against my shoulder, and lifting it, she looks up at me, her bottom lip between her teeth. "Say the words."

The grin that gradually grows across my face is effortless and pure. She's asked this of me several times in the last few weeks, and honestly, I can't get enough of it.

Lowering my neck, I kiss the tip of her nose before looking her in the eyes and giving her what she wants, "I love you."

She sighs, like those words are all she needs to sustain herself, and I tighten my arms around her, pulling her in closer. My lips brush against her temple, and I just breathe her in.

"How was your game tonight?" she asks. "I'm sorry none of us could be there."

Sighing, I glance away as I rub the back of my neck. "I didn't go. I went with Royce instead."

"Logan," she chastises, although she's not really angry.

"My head wouldn't have been on the ice anyway," I admit to her. In all honesty, my head hasn't been on hockey all week. I've been physically present at practice, but my mind is elsewhere, and Coach said if I didn't get my head in the game not to bother showing up tonight. So I didn't.

I mean, how can I be focused on hockey—a fucking *game*—when my fucking *life* is in pieces. Aurora might not be mine, but I *feel* like I've lost a daughter or at least a friend, and I like to think Aurora and I were friends.

"I couldn't have been there when I needed to be here," I tell her. "I *wanted* to go with Royce. I'd do anything to get Aurora back. To bring her home."

Shifting so she's sitting on her knees between my legs, Riley cups the side of my neck and presses her forehead to mine. "I know. You have no idea how much that means to me. What you're doing—what you're *all* doing. But you can't lose out on your future because of this." She smiles, but it's watery at best. "What will I tell Aurora when we get her back, and you've been kicked off the team? I've been talking you up and promising to take her to a game. It won't be the same if you're sitting beside us instead of out on the ice."

I bark out a laugh even as I sniffle. "Shortcake, you can bet your ass I'll be on that ice when Aurora comes to her first game. You think I don't have the entire team practicing for their next pre-game entertainment show? I've got them learning all the moves to *Let It Go*. It's going to be epic. Aurora will love it."

Tear tracks streaking down her face, Riley chuckles. "She will," she agrees as I brush away her tears.

Gathering her into my arms, I stand before stepping out of the tub. Grabbing a towel, I wrap it around her before capturing her lips with mine. I intend for it to be a quick kiss, but just like every time I touch her, I'm incapable of pulling back.

Riley presses onto her toes, her body flush against mine as her lips part, and she deepens the kiss. One hand falls to her hips while the other slides into her hair as I give myself fully to this woman who already owns every piece of my heart.

Clinging to one another, our tongues tangle in a kiss that speaks of salvation, of the dreams we both hold dear and the futures we hope to see play out.

And I swear I'll do everything possible to ensure Aurora is front and center in that future.

RILEY

CHAPTER SIX

"I'm really not in the mood for this," I sigh, reluctantly climbing out of Royce's truck in the gravel parking lot at The Depot on Tuesday morning. It's been seven days since that awful day. Seven days where I haven't spoken to my daughter. Seven days of worrying whether she's okay. If she's even alive.

I haven't dared to voice that last thought aloud. To put it out in the atmosphere. It feels like tempting fate, and with the cards life has been dealing me recently... yeah, I'll keep those dark thoughts to myself.

Still, it's like the guys automatically know when my thoughts veer in that direction and dive in with various distractions. All three of them talk about Aurora with absolute certainty that she'll be coming home.

And not just home to me, but home to *them*.

The number of tears I've shed listening to Logan talk about Aurora attending his games and the spot he's reserved for her in Hot Shot Huskies, Royce including Aurora in hypothetical future plans like her presence in our lives is an inevitability.

Even Grayson's excitement at introducing her to the family business—or, as he phrases it, *her legacy*.

"I know." Royce's deep voice breaks through my wayward thoughts as he rounds the truck and walks beside me toward the large warehouse where The Depot is situated. I don't think I've ever been here during the day, and looking at the large metal structure, you'd never know it was a heaving dive bar and fighting ring when the sun goes down. It blends seamlessly with the countryscape around us—the open fields that stretch as far as the eye can see. "But with Bertram out of prison, learning self-defense is in your best interest. We'd all feel better about you walking around campus if you knew a few basic moves. Especially..." He sticks his tongue into his cheek, his jaw hardening.

Especially after what happened with Ben.

That's what he was going to say.

It's precisely why Tara has organized this mandatory self-defense session for all the girls who work at Lux and why she has pushed for increased security and protection for all staff members with the new club owner. I haven't been at work since everything with Aurora went down, but I've heard about the new bouncers and stricter rules from her text updates.

Under normal circumstances, I'd be all for learning to defend myself. *Especially* given what happened with Ben.

But today?

I just don't have it in me to care.

Royce pulls me to a stop before we reach the door, his hands squeezing my shoulders before sliding to grip the top of my arms as he lowers his head to mine. "I know you don't want to do this. I know this is the last place you want to be. I'm sure Tara would get you out of it if you absolutely don't want to go in there, but I think the distraction would do you good. It isn't going to fix anything, but there is a catharsis in physically expelling all that you're feeling." His piercing blue eyes search mine, soft with affection and sympathy. "You're lost right now. Everything is spiraling out of control, and you can no longer identify up from down. While I can't empathize with exactly how you're feeling, I do understand that feeling of having no control over your life.

"Stepping up to an opponent, facing your fears head-on, it's like... it's like reclaiming a piece of yourself. You can't control everything that's happening, but for those moments when you're lost in the draw of the fight, *you* control your body, your movements, your power. It's a release, a purging. You let out all that pent-up frustration, anger, and fear. And in that brief moment, you feel... liberated. Like you're not just surviving but fighting back. It won't solve everything, but it might give you a little breathing room, a break from the suffocating weight of it all."

Staring up at him, I hold his gaze before sighing. "Okay," I murmur.

He smiles, reeling me into his chest for a brief hug before we enter the warehouse. Without the usual revelry to drown out the noise, the steel doors clang shut behind us, echoing through the cavernous space. The air is thick with the scent of sweat and anticipation, mingling with the faint aroma of stale beer that lingers from the previous night.

The steel warehouse, usually filled with raucous crowds and pounding music, has been transformed into a makeshift arena for the self-defense class. The harsh fluorescent lights typically focused on the ring in the center of the room now illuminate multiple mats spread out on the worn concrete floor around the ring. Some are already occupied, and I wave as some girls I work with glance my way.

I recognize Tara's friend, Rome, standing in the middle of

the ring, wearing loose shorts and an undershirt. Her brother stands beside him, similarly dressed, as they converse quietly. The two of them, plus Royce, are our demonstrators today.

"You came!" Tara greets me with a broad yet compassionate smile as she strides toward me in a pair of skin-tight workout leggings and a bra that shows off her toned stomach. Her hair is pulled back in a sleek ponytail, emphasizing the bright pink tips that swish as she walks. She doesn't stop until she barrels into me, her arms wrapping me up in a tight embrace that forces the air from my lungs.

Despite not wanting to be here, I practically collapse into her as I seek strength from her hug. When I'd messaged her last week to tell her I wouldn't be at work for the foreseeable future, I'd dodged her texts and calls, wanting to know what was wrong. I'd thought maybe Xander would have filled her in, but it appears he was keeping everything on the downlow. Eventually, Logan took pity on her and answered her call to explain the situation.

I appreciated him doing that. I just couldn't bring myself to say the words aloud.

"You didn't have to come," Tara murmurs for only me to hear.

"It's fine." Pulling back, I give her a tight smile. Glancing Royce's way, I tack on with a sarcastic drawl, "Apparently, attempting to beat up someone else will be cathartic for me."

Tara laughs. "He's totally right. The rush is a high like nothing else. It'll give you something else to focus on for a couple of hours, if nothing else."

I arch a brow in a silent question.

"What?" she chuckles. "I grew up around a group of guys who know how to fight. You think I didn't pick up a few things?"

Yeah... but the way she said that... it was almost as though she was alluding to something more. Huffing a laugh, I let it go.

"I'm gonna go talk to Xander and Rome," Royce says, placing his hand on the base of my spine as he looks down at me. "You okay here?"

I give him a reassuring smile. "I'm good."

His stare lingers for a moment longer before he breaks it, striding toward the ring where Xander and Rome are still standing.

"How are you really?" Tara asks when he's out of earshot.

"Surviving."

She nods, and her expression says she knows exactly how that feels. "The guys taking care of you?"

"Yeah, they've been great."

She arches a disbelieving eyebrow. "Even the douchebag?"

I chuckle. "Shockingly, yes—even Grayson."

"Good," she says with authority, turning to link her arm with mine as we move toward an empty mat. "Because I'll happily junk punch him if need be."

"I was kinda hoping I'd be capable of doing that myself after this session," I tease.

Facing me, she flashes her white teeth in a vicious impersonation of a grin. "That's the spirit."

"You're sure you're okay with me taking some time off?" I ask awkwardly. Logan had informed her that I wouldn't be in for my shifts, but I never actually discussed it with her—mostly because I have no idea what's going to happen. "If you need to replace me with someone else, I understand."

"What are you even saying right now? Of course, it's fine!" She waves a dismissive hand. "I got your shifts covered, and I've taken you off the schedule for the foreseeable future. Take as long as you need, and I'll slot you back in when you're ready to return." Reaching out, she squeezes my hand. "Your focus is where it needs to be. Don't worry about Lux. We'll be here when you've got Aurora back."

I squeeze her fingers in return. "Thank you."

"Alright, ladies. I think we're ready to start," Xander calls out from the ring. His gaze scans the room, and glancing around, I realize all the mats are now occupied, everyone having teamed up.

Spotting Kelsey on the far side of the room, I wave at her. She waves back before Xander's commanding voice cuts through the murmurs, demanding our attention as I look back to where he, Rome, and Royce are standing.

"Welcome, everyone, to today's self-defense class. Today, we'll learn some basic moves that will enable you to break free of an attacker's hold so you can escape and call for help." With a clap of his hands, Xander leads us through a series of dynamic warm-up exercises designed to get the blood pumping and our muscles primed for action.

Lunges, jumping jacks, and high knees fill the air with the sound of exertion until we're all sufficiently warmed up, and Xander emits a piercing whistle to regain our attention.

"One common self-defense move for escaping an attacker's hold is the wrist grab escape," Xander explains, gesturing for Royce to step forward.

Royce grabs Xander's wrist aggressively but does not move to do anything else as Xander turns his head to face us. "In any self-defense situation, remaining as calm as possible is crucial. Panicking will only cloud your judgment and make it harder to execute the technique effectively."

Lifting his arm that Royce holds, he continues, "If an attacker grabs your wrist, focus on the grip. Determine whether the attacker's thumb is positioned on top of or under your wrist. This will influence the direction of your escape.

"Use your free hand to create space between your wrist and

the attacker's grip," he explains. "You can do this by pushing against the attacker's thumb or leveraging your hand against their fingers." He demonstrates exactly that. "With the space created, rotate your arm in the direction that weakens their hold on you. So, if the attacker's thumb is on top, rotate your arm downward. If their thumb is below, rotate your arm upward." He demonstrates both moves for our benefit.

"Then, once you've rotated your arm, pull your wrist away with a swift and decisive motion. Use your entire body to generate force if necessary." He pulls his arm from Royce's grip and faces us fully. "As soon as you break free, move away from the danger zone immediately. Utilize any nearby objects or obstacles to create additional barriers between you and your attacker. Once you're safely out of their reach, seek help from bystanders or authorities." His eyes run over each of us, a hint of a grin tugging at the corners of his lips. "Now, it's your turn."

"Do you want to be the attacker or attackee first?" Tara asks, grinning like she's having a blast.

"You're way too excited about this," I point out with a half-smile. "Attackee. I'm a little worried you might get carried away and kick my ass."

Laughing, she makes grabby hands for my wrist, which I hand over before systematically working through Xander's moves.

"Good," she praises when I break free. "Go again, but faster this time."

She has me repeat the action several times until I can complete the entire move without having to stop and think. From the corner of my eye, I spot Xander, Rome, and Royce walking around the room. Occasionally, one of them will stop to critique someone.

Once everyone has had a chance to practice the move, they return to the ring and work through another one. As the morning goes on, the moves become more engaging, and several hours later, I find myself facing off against Tara, my hands balled into fists in front of my face as I wait for her to throw a punch.

Her eyes gleam with excitement, and admittedly, I'm having more fun than I thought I would. Tara's fist swings toward my face, and I immediately block with a well-timed parry. Tara follows it with a powerful kick that I again block before throwing a counterattack.

Sweat dots my forehead and drips down my back, but a grin ignites my face as we work through the moves Xander showed us. Royce was right. There's something liberating about fighting back. About knowing I'm not solely surviving. My battle may not be physical, but this physical exertion feels *good*.

"Well done, Riley," Xander praises, crossing his arms as he stands at the edge of our mat and watches us.

"Hey, what about me, asshole?" Tara teases.

"Your footwork is off," her brother retorts with a wry smirk.

"Like fuck it is. Why don't you come over here, and I'll prove it to you," Tara throws back at him, all while continuing to block and counter my moves.

"Tara," Xander sighs. "You do remember this is a self-defense class, don't you? It wouldn't be a good look if I kicked your ass in front of all your employees."

Snorting, she flashes a glower his way. "You mean, it wouldn't look good for you to get beat up by a girl. Worried it'll hurt your chance with the ladies?" She smirks viciously.

Damn, I love their sibling spats.

Shaking his head, Xander walks toward the front of the group, whistling to call us to attention.

Hands on my hips, I suck in deep breaths as I glance around the room, noticing everyone else is sweaty and breathless too. However, there's a sense of accomplishment on everyone's face.

"I think that's plenty for today. You've all done great," Xander praises. "Remember, in any situation, remain calm, assess, escape and evade, and seek help."

Murmurs of thanks echo off the steel walls before everyone disperses, the other girls slowly filtering out of the warehouse. Tara bounces up to me, a bundle of energy despite the grueling workout.

"I've gotta bounce if I'm going to have time to shower before work." She gives me a quick hug. "Text me, yeah?" She's already walking away when she spins and points a finger at me. "And I want to be kept in the loop."

As the steel door slams shut behind her, Royce approaches. His eyes bore into me as if searching for answers to unasked questions.

"You were right," I tell him when he's close enough. "I do feel better." I feel stronger and more empowered, knowing that if I end up in a situation like I did with Ben, I'll be able to get myself out of it—or at the very least fight back.

"You did well today, Riley," Xander says, joining us with a soft smile pulling at the corners of his lips and sympathy warming his pale blue eyes. His attention slides to Royce, and he jerks his head toward the back of The Depot. "Dax is here. Wants to talk to you."

My hand squeezes Royce's, who glances down at me before nodding to Xander. Placing his palm at the base of my spine, he escorts me across the room and down the hallway to Xander's office.

I step into the cramped space with my heart lodged in my throat, barely registering the paperwork piled atop the desk or the two seats wedged between the desk and wall that occupy most of the space.

My entire focus is on Dax, sitting behind Xander's desk with a laptop open in front of him. He's impeccably dressed in a suit.

His jacket is neatly hanging over the back of his chair, allowing an unobstructed view of his crisp, white shirt as it stretches across his chest, the top two buttons undone and offering a glimpse at the tattoos visible beneath. More of the artwork inked into his skin can be seen along his muscular forearms, where his sleeves are rolled up to his elbows. He shifts in the chair, stretching, and I swear I hear the seams of his shirt tear as they're pulled to their limit.

There's the same ruthless edge about him that I recall from the time I briefly met him at Rogue. A savagery oozes from his pores, a brutality that makes your palms instantly sweat and urges you to flee.

This room is far too small for a man like him, who sucks all the oxygen from the air. Even sitting behind the desk, he dwarfs it, practically spilling out of the chair, which creaks beneath his weight.

"Have you been back here all morning?" Royce grunts. "Why didn't you join us for the self-defense class?"

Xander snorts from the doorway. "Idiot is scared of a certain five-foot-six, black-haired woman with psychotic tendencies who I have the misfortune of calling my sister."

Royce arches a brow as Dax glares at Xander. "You're one to talk—scared of your own sister," he drawls in that deep voice edged with menace. Honestly, everything about Dax is honed into a deadly weapon intended to cut you out at the knees on the first swing.

"She can be terrifying," Xander defends. "But I go out of my way to ingratiate myself to her." He pierces Dax with a meaningful look.

Dax merely grunts. "It was years ago. We were children."

I'm unable to participate in this conversation. Can barely even follow it, knowing he might have information that could help us find my daughter.

"Well, I'll leave ya's to talk," Xander says, rapping his knuckles against the doorframe before pushing off it. "Let me know if you need anything."

With that, he disappears, and Dax slides his penetrating gaze my way. "Riley," he greets, standing and flattening a hand down the front of his shirt before holding it out for me. "It's nice to see you again. I'm sorry it's not under better circumstances."

It's with a numb awareness that I shake his hand, searching his face for clues as to why he wants to speak to us before I finally just blurt it out. "Did you find anything?" I know Royce gave him a phone he and Logan found amongst Lydia's belongings at Bertram's new house, but that was only a few days ago, so it seems quick that he'd have something from that so soon.

Unless it gave up nothing.

He shakes his head, and something fundamental inside me shatters.

I'm distantly aware of Royce stepping up behind me as though fearful I might collapse. His heat engulfs my back as his hand moves to rest on my hip in a reassuring move.

"My guy is still working on the phone," Dax explains. "Other than that one message, it was clean. So far, he's traced the text to another burner phone, which has since been disconnected, but he's doing some tech mumbo-jumbo to trace where it was sent from. If we have a location, we might be able to narrow it down—check traffic cams for the area, that sort of thing."

Swallowing around the suffocating lump in my throat, I drop my gaze and nod in understanding.

"What did you want then?" Royce directs.

"I have to head back to New York. I put off my last fight, but I can't delay it any longer. However, I just wanted to let you know I'm still working on this. I'll be back as soon as I can."

"Understand, man," Royce answers, holding his hand out to shake Dax's. "Appreciate it."

With a curt nod, Dax gathers his laptop and moves to leave the office.

"Thank you," I blurt, my voice strangled with emotion. He stops at the threshold, turning to look at me. "For everything you've done. For what you're doing. I—I can never repay you, but *thank you* for helping me find my little girl."

Dax's hard, shuttered gaze bores into mine for a long moment. He merely nods before striding away.

"You're home!" Logan pounces on us as soon as we step into the house. "How was self-defense class?"

"Surprisingly cathartic," I tell him, although any adrenaline I had during class has waned, and I'm left exhausted—my permanent state of being these days. Even looking at Logan and his golden retriever energy is giving me a headache. "I think I need to lie down, though."

He nods enthusiastically, a sparkle in his eyes. "I've got the perfect place," he says cryptically, snatching my hand and hauling me up the stairs before I can protest. Glancing over my shoulder, I arch an eyebrow at Royce, who simply shrugs as he follows us at a more leisurely pace.

I'm assuming Logan means his bed, although I hope he realizes I really meant sleep when I mentioned going to bed. However, when we reach the top of the stairs, instead of moving toward his bedroom, Logan drags me toward the one I was held captive in all those months ago. The door has been closed ever since, and I make a firm point of darting past the room without casting it a glance any time I'm walking past.

"Logan," I hedge, pulling on his hand as he reaches for the door handle.

He doesn't pay heed to my warning as he swings the door open, and before I slam my eyes shut to avoid looking at that stupid stripper pole that I hate with my guts, I catch glimpses of pale pink and soft gray.

A gasp tumbles from my lips, and my feet are rooted on the floor. Gone are the stripper pole, the sofa, and the heavy drapes that covered the windows. Instead, a comfy-looking double bed takes up most of the room. Its pale pink covers, the white fluffy blanket spread across the end of the bed, and the multitude of cushions make it look warm and inviting. Wooden side tables frame it, and my gaze catches on a photo set on top.

My feet are moving before I realize it, taking me across the room until I'm looking down at the photo, a lump in my throat. It's one from my apartment—of me and Aurora. Aurora is grinning at the camera, blue frosting covering her mouth, and I'm smiling at her, a light dancing in my eyes that is distinctly missing these days.

My breath catches in my lungs, and my voice wobbles as, unable to take my eyes off the picture, I say, "I-I don't understand..." When no one responds, I rip my gaze away, turning to find Logan and Royce standing in the doorway. "You did this?"

Logan's gaze slides away, "Uh, no. It wasn't me."

"Wasn't me either, James," Royce states when I look his way.

"Then who?" They both give me a look. That *who the hell do you think* look that only confuses me further. "Grayson?" Brow furrowed, I do another sweep of the simple yet carefully thought out room, catching sight of other knick knacks from my apartment. It's so... me. There's no way Grayson did this. Not for me.

"He wanted you to have someplace that's yours," Logan

says softly, likely reading the skepticism written all over my face. "Somewhere you can go when you want to be alone. A room in this house that's entirely yours."

A room that's mine.

A room that has personal items from my apartment. Photos of me and my daughter. My clothes hanging in the closet.

A room *Grayson* made for me.

GRAYSON

CHAPTER SEVEN

"I look forward to doing business with you soon." I sign off on the video call. Rubbing at my temples, I sigh and lean back in my chair. I don't think I've ever been more tired. Of course, it would help if I was actually sleeping in my bed at night. Instead, I sit outside Royce or Logan's room and listen—a silent sentinel. Every bone in my body itches to go in there and join them every night, but Riley isn't there yet, and while I'm all for pushing her, now isn't the time.

Still, I can't leave her. Not when I know she wakes up with nightmares most nights. So, instead, I listen to one of the others soothe her back to sleep, and I remain as close as I can get to her —for now. I'm giving her space while we find Aurora, but once we do, I'm making it crystal fucking clear to her that she's mine. Even if I have to share her with my two best friends.

I grit my teeth, not liking that idea, yet I can't argue that it somehow works. I couldn't physically be here today if I didn't have the comfort of knowing they are both with her on campus. Knowing that they can soothe her demons in the middle of the night.

I might be a selfish asshole, but I know she needs them

both. She relies on them. Leans on them in a way she would never do with me.

So yeah, I've come to accept that the woman I've been obsessed with since I was seventeen will never be mine alone—now, I'll share her with my two best friends.

I suppose it could be worse…

My door abruptly opens as my secretary struts in. She stops in her heels when she sees me sitting there, a blush covering her cheeks. "Oh, Mr. Van Doren." She lifts the folder in her hands. "I was just going to leave this on your desk. What are you still doing here?"

"It's only ten in the morning. I've got eight more hours before I can get out of here."

"Uh, no." Her lips flatten, contrition flashing across her face. "I meant, your father scheduled a meeting with the board and execs for, eh, right now."

What the fuck? "When did he do that?" I demand, my headache intensifying as I stand from my chair and round the table.

"I'm not sure. I only just heard about it."

I'm already past my secretary and out the door, stalking down the hallway toward the conference rooms. I should have expected my father to pull an underhanded move like this. One fucking week since his release. That's all it took before he started interfering. I knew he would. Knew it was only a matter of time, but I expected him to want to be included in deals and meetings. I didn't think he'd schedule *his own fucking meeting*—with the board and all senior members of the company, no less.

Through the glass wall of the conference room, I can see my father standing in front of the gathered crowd, addressing them as I quietly open the door and slip inside.

"—Reassure everyone that, while I'm back, it's purely in an advisory role." Hands in the pockets of my suit pants, I lean against the back wall as I listen to my father's fake speech of remorse and how he's all about making amends for his past mistakes. "While I am mostly here to help my son adapt to the role of CEO," my father continues, fully aware of how every word undermines my position as everyone's fucking boss, "I want to remind you all that the transition from being an heir to a leader is a daunting one. Not everyone is equipped to handle such a monumental task, especially without a guiding hand. Any one of you is welcome to approach me if you have any questions or concerns—or if you feel the need for a more experienced perspective. After all, it's in everyone's best interest to ensure that the company remains on solid ground during this, shall we say, delicate phase."

My teeth grind, and I shoot lasers at him from across the room.

He pauses, his eyes scanning the crowd as he meets each person's gaze as if to solidify his position as the go-to authority. "Rest assured, my priority is, and always will be, the stability and prosperity of this company. Sometimes that means stepping in where I'm needed... whether or not my son realizes it." He gives the room a beaming, charismatic smile that I'm two seconds from punching off his face. "Anyway, I have taken up enough of your time. It's great to be back, and I look forward to catching up with old acquaintances and meeting the new faces I see today."

Everyone murmurs their acknowledgment of my presence as they file out of the conference room until only me and my father are left.

"I had already addressed all the employees and advised them of your new... *role*."

"Yes, well. I felt it was prudent that I make my own introductions."

"That went a little beyond *introductions*." It takes serious effort to keep the cool, calm facade he dons so well. I'm furious. Raging. I don't know why I'm shocked, but I'm *shocked* that he dared to pull a stunt like that. That he thinks he can just come back and undermine me and worm his way back into CEO of this company.

This company that *I* built after he destroyed it. The one I've nurtured and fostered until it became stronger and more profitable than it ever was under his care. I scoff to myself. I knew his pretty words at that parole board were bullshit. My father wants only one thing: control. Control over everyone and everything in his environment.

"This is not a new or *delicate* phase. I've been doing this job for a long time now. I've gotten pretty good at it, actually."

He makes a derisive noise of disagreement. "You're a child playing at being a grown-up. You might have kept the company afloat, but you have no idea what it takes to run a business of this size long-term." He runs a hand down the front of his impeccable, designer suit. It is one that I don't recall him having before his incarceration, so it must be new. "Now that I'm back, the board members will want a more experienced person to have a prominent say."

"You're back in an *advisory role*," I remind him. "One that does not require you to call last-minute board and exec meetings, especially without running it past your CEO first."

Bertram scoffs. "I presumed you had much more important business to attend to. God knows when I was in your shoes, I did."

"I do things a little differently," I retort stiffly. However, nothing I say will prevent this argument from going around in circles. Instead, I pivot. "You've just gotten your life back. I'm sure Lydia would love to spend time with you—rekindle your marriage. The two of you should take a few months—go to Europe or lounge on a beach on some Caribbean island."

Anywhere that gets the two of them the fuck away from here. "Enjoy the free life."

"Since when have you known me to *lounge on a beach*?" My father drawls, voice dripping with absolute disgust.

Sadly, never.

"You deserve time for yourself. To... acclimate," I hedge, softening my tone. My father has always responded better to submission. "You've always put me and this company first," I say, trying to seem like the caring son worried about his father.

"Last I checked, it still said Van Doren above the door. That means it is a *family* business." There's a tick in his jaw, and when the next words spew from his lips, I imagine they took great effort to phrase. "While you've done an adequate job in my absence, you're still just a kid. You haven't even graduated college, for Christ's sake. You can't seriously expect to be able to handle the rigorous demands and convoluted problems of a multi-million dollar company."

In the past, I'd have believed him. Believed he knew what he was talking about with all his many years of running the company. Believed he had my best interests at heart.

Now, I know he's incapable of caring about anyone other than himself.

I should feel *something* at that acknowledgment. Some sort of loss for the father I thought I knew. Instead, I feel absolutely nothing beyond cold detachment.

He's done so much to hurt me, to try and destroy Riley, that any vestige of the man I once respected is gone. All that's left is this empty shell. A manipulative, selfish bastard who only thinks of himself. The mask he always wears no longer works on me, and instead, when I look at him, all I see are the years of lies, deceit, and cruelty.

I want him out of my life, permanently. Out of *our* lives. He's a poison, a cancer that needs to be cut out so we can finally start to heal. I don't need his approval, his guidance, or his love. I never did. Maybe I wanted it, relied on it after I was left to sink or swim in the shitshow he left me to handle after his arrest. However, with crystal clear clarity, I realize I've accomplished everything I have on my own. He's never loved me, and any approval I obtained was a reflection on him. There was a time when I counted on his guidance, but those days are long gone. Despite what he believes, I have grown into my role as CEO. That's not to say I won't make mistakes, won't get things wrong, and fuck up. But I'll learn from them and do better in the future.

What I need now is to protect the people I care about. To protect Riley from whatever nefarious plans he's brewing and ultimately build a life free from his shadow. That's all that matters. That's all that's ever mattered.

"We should schedule a meeting to discuss your *advisory role*," I state, hating that I must deal with him at all. However, I'm done letting him call the shots. *I'm* the one in control here, and it's past time my father realized that. "I'll get Stacey to check my calendar and get back to you with a suitable date and time. Until then, I suggest you keep a low profile in the office while people adjust to your unexpected return."

Not giving him a chance to respond, I pull open the glass door and stride out of the conference room.

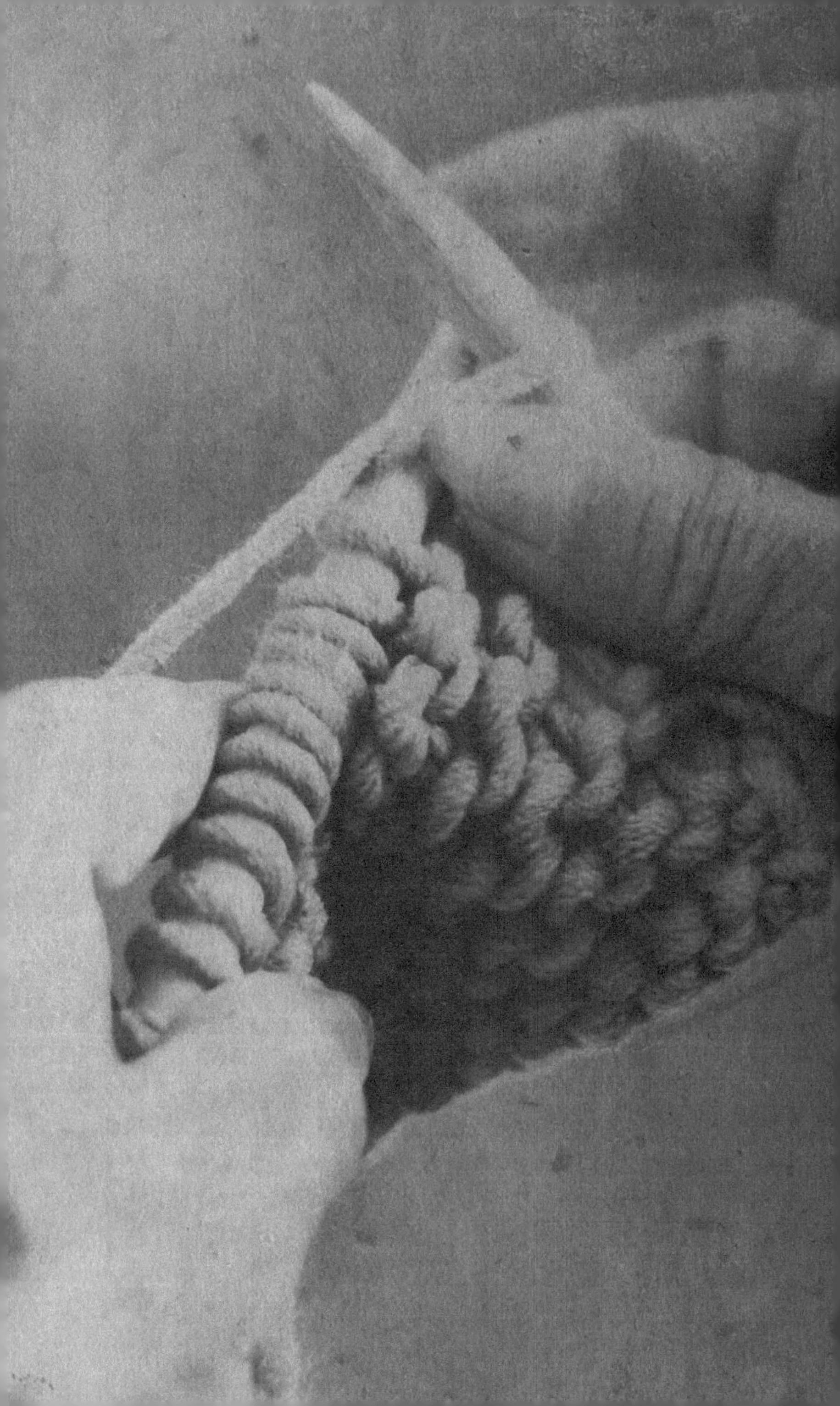

RILEY

CHAPTER EIGHT

The thump of a backpack hitting the seat beside me jolts me out of my daydreaming. Although, is it daydreaming when all your thoughts resemble a nightmare?

Blinking, I stare absently across the tables—some occupied but most empty—and book stacks that comprise the Halston U library. *Right, I came here to study.* Coming to campus had sounded like a good idea this morning. Anything to get out of that house, to distract myself...

Yeah, that plan failed.

All I've done is think. Think of her. Of what I could have done differently. Of how horrifically I've let my own daughter down.

A large palm is waved in front of my face, obstructing my view.

"Earth to Riley."

Tearing my gaze away, I look blankly at Grayson. Everything feels so distant... disconnected. I can barely keep my thoughts in line. I'd forgotten entirely that something—or some*one*—had distracted me. "What are you doing here?"

Even my voice sounds monotone and world-weary.

"You weren't answering your phone." His eyes narrow in a glare, but there isn't the usual warning behind the action. If anything, concern is the prevalent emotion shining through his dark brown orbs.

"Oh." I glance down at my phone, sitting on the table. I hadn't even heard it buzz or seen the screen light up.

"Pack your stuff." At Grayson's order, my face snaps up to his, and my features pull down in a frown. "Now, Riley." His tone is non-negotiable, and I obey without a word of protest because I have zero fight left in me.

The cadence of his sigh from behind hints at his disappointment at my lack of fight, but I pretend I don't hear it as I shove my things into my bag. Before I can swing it over my shoulder, though, he snatches it from my hand and strides away from the table, leaving me with no option but to chase after him. A faint flicker of irritation penetrates the numb shell I'm encased in.

Asshole.

I have to take two steps for each of his as he marches across campus.

"Hey," I bark as we approach his car, and he finally slows. "What are you doing? I have class in an hour."

Whirling on me, he cocks an arrogant eyebrow. It should make him look haughty. Correction, it *does* make him look haughty, but not in the way that grates on your nerves and screams *rich kid*. Instead, Grayson manages to make the entire stance appear... smoldering.

Haughty has never looked so *hot*.

It's infuriating.

He is infuriating.

"Don't try to tell me you're actually going to take in a word of what is said in that class," he drawls in a tone that *should* be insulting but instead is like a caress against my skin.

My lips purse because, no, I haven't managed to take in a word of what's been said in *any* of my classes all week. I'm here because I can't stand the thought of sitting in my apartment or at the guys' doing nothing.

Even if my being on campus is just as futile.

Not helping myself.

Not able to help my daughter.

Useless.

I'm completely. *Fucking.* Useless.

"Hey!" The snap of his tongue, along with the cold press of fingers as they wrap around my chin, wrenches me from my spiraling thoughts and dumps me firmly in the wasteland that has become my reality. "Where did you go?"

I stare up into Grayson's impenetrable eyes. They're always shielded, shuttered against the world. He keeps everything so carefully contained, putting on a front for everyone around him.

"Nowhere." I try to pull free from his grip, but he holds firm, preventing me from hiding.

"Don't lie to me." It's less of a chastisement and more of a plea. Which is the only reason I don't balk and snap at him as I typically do.

"Nowhere pleasant," I correct in the same tired tone.

"Tell me anyway."

My responding sigh is heavy, weighed down with the truth I don't want to admit aloud. However, Grayson's hard stare tells me I won't get away with another vague non-answer.

My teeth sink into the tip of my tongue, biting back the truth even as my gaze drops, unable to meet his as I confess, "I've never felt so helpless. There isn't a single thing I can do to help my daughter. To protect her. To bring her home. What am I supposed to do, Grayson?" I throw my hands out to my sides and gaze up at him imploringly. "What. Am. I. Supposed. To. Do? I'm genuinely asking because I don't have a fucking clue.

My baby girl is *missing*, and I'm going to class, taking self-defense, and having dinner with your fucking *dad* like nothing is wrong."

Releasing my chin, his fingers skate down the column of my throat until his hand rests at the base and his thumb rubs tight circles over my pulse point. His gentle yet domineering touch sears into my skin like a brand.

"Firstly." His rough voice is gravelly against my skin. "You are doing absolutely everything you need to be doing." My lips part in protest, but his eyes narrow in a silent warning not to interrupt. "You *are* helping your daughter. By looking after yourself, you are *helping*." His thumb continues to rub soothing strokes. "She needs you to take care of yourself right now so you can take care of her when we bring her home."

Eyes burning with unshed tears, I close them.

"Look at me." My eyes snap open at his demanding rasp, and I instantly fall into the dark pools of his irises. So stoic. So steady. Grayson's ability to hide his emotions has always grated on me, but now... Now, I stare into those depthless orbs, and instead of searching for answers to what he's thinking, I steal strength from his steady gaze. Strength that I use to tape, super glue, and staple all the shattered pieces of myself together. It's a temporary fix. A Band-Aid on a gaping wound. A belt to an amputated limb.

But at least I'm not freely bleeding.

"There she is."

I don't know when Grayson became someone who could soothe my jagged edges—at least, without the two of us attacking one another and ending up naked—but that's precisely what he's achieved.

And I'm too wrung out to question it. To worry about what it might mean. To throw up the mental roadblocks I usually do when I sense him inching closer to my heart.

"Come with me."

Although it's phrased as a demand, there is a hint of a question behind it. Just enough hesitation for me to know he'll leave it be if I refuse. Sucking my bottom lip between my teeth, I search his gaze before glancing around me. A few students hurry between buildings; otherwise, we're alone, the cold weather preventing anyone from dawdling outside.

"Okay," I acquiesce, turning back to face him in time to catch the flash of accomplishment that crosses his features before he turns away to open the back door. He places our backpacks inside before opening the passenger door and waving me into his sports car. The cold leather of the seat penetrates through my tights, chilling the backs of my legs, and I shiver as Grayson slides in behind the wheel.

With the press of a few buttons, heat blasts through the vents, and a moment later, my seat heats, and I sink deeper into it. Grayson fires off a text on his phone before he pulls out of the parking space, and as we drive out of campus, I stare out the window.

A moment later, the sound system in his car announces an incoming call from Logan. I turn to stare at the console as Grayson answers. "The whole point of messaging you was to avoid a phone call," he drawls.

Logan scoffs on the other end. "You tell me you're taking Shortcake off campus, and you expect me *not* to question if you're kidnapping her."

A semblance of a smile twitches at the corners of my lips, gaining momentum when Grayson huffs his irritation. He must see my response because he flicks his gaze my way, eyes narrowing in warning, however there's none of his typical hostility. Instead, his eyes are alight... almost as though he's amused. I find it intriguing—I find everything about Grayson intriguing. He's an enigma. A puzzle that, just when you think you've figured out how to solve, you realize it's more complex than you initially anticipated.

"Shortcake, you there?"

Logan's voice pulls my attention back to the console. "I'm here. Don't worry. There was no kidnapping involved. I came of my own free will."

"Are you sure?" he enquires, unconvinced. "Pizza is the code word. Say *pizza,* and I'll come rescue you."

"You realize I can hear you," Grayson drawls as I chuckle.

"I promise I'm fine," I assure Logan.

Logan makes a noise as though he still doesn't believe me but relents. "Fine, but if you change your mind, send me a pizza slice emoji, and I'll come and rescue you from Grayson's grumpy ass."

"I'm hanging up now," Grayson grumbles, pressing *end call* in the middle of Logan's protests.

With a smile still on my face, I relax into my seat and ask, "Where are we going anyway?" We ended up at the forgotten church the last time we were alone, and my blood heats at the memory, my core clenching at the idea of a repeat performance. Grayson and I may have our issues, but fucking is most definitely not one of them. And the way he manages to make me forget while he's chasing me… pinning me down… stretching me…

"To see Gran."

That instantly wrenches my thoughts from the filthy gutter they'd tumbled into.

"I go and sit with her every week," he continues. "She has advanced dementia, and most of the time, she doesn't know who I am." Tight lines form around his eyes, his knuckles whitening around the steering wheel as he stares steadfastly out the front windshield.

My hand moves to rest on his forearm, and I feel his muscles flex beneath my fingers. "You're a good grandson," I murmur.

His head whips in my direction, eyes flaring with so many fractured emotions—doubt, grief, weariness. It suddenly hits me, and I don't know why it didn't before... the weight of the responsibility that he carries on his shoulders. That he has *been* carrying... since when? Since he was eighteen?

It's not only his responsibility to his company but to his Gran... the only family member he has left. The only connection to his mom. Most likely the only woman he ever remembers loving him...

"You were seventeen when your dad was arrested. Did you stay with her?"

Focus back on the road, he nods. "It wasn't long after I went to live with her that I started seeing the signs. She'd forget to turn off the stove, leave lights on, and faucets running."

My heart clenches for a teenage Grayson, not only losing his dad and the life he'd grown up in but having to watch his Gran slowly disappear too.

"It was manageable when I lived with her in high school, but when I started at Halston... She lived too far away, and I couldn't be here and there at the same time. I paid for someone to come in and check on her, but I started getting calls from neighbors. Even a call from the police department once, saying they'd found her walking down the road in her slippers and nightgown." He sighs wearily. "It was then that I realized I couldn't let her stay there by herself. I packed up all her belongings—sold what I could and put the rest in storage—and registered her at Sunnyside Nursing Home."

"You did the right thing," I tell him, sensing he needs to hear it.

"Yeah," he sighs. "Maybe."

"Definitely. You did the right thing for her—and for you.

Even though it was probably a tough call to make." Staring absently out the windshield, I admit, "I very nearly turned down my admission to Halston. Although I'd been working toward the goal for an entire year, I knew what being accepted would mean. Being faced with the reality..." I sigh, twisting my fingers in the ends of my hair.

"Knowing you'd have to leave Aurora."

"Hardest decision I've ever had to make. When my—*Lydia*—found out I was pregnant, she insisted that I abort it. I didn't even have to think about it. In my mind, it wasn't a decision. I'd known since the moment the pink lines appeared on that stick that I was keeping the baby." I scoff, remembering that time. "Not that it stopped her from finding someone who would do it against my will. Thankfully, I was too far along by then." I shake my head, not wanting to think about how close I came to losing Aurora before I even really had her.

"My point is, sometimes we have to make the hard decisions. We have to do what we really don't want to do because it's ultimately in the best interests of everyone involved. The last thing I wanted to do was leave Aurora with Lydia for four more years, but I couldn't bring her with me. Even if Lydia had agreed, I didn't have the means to provide for her. If I wanted to give my daughter the future she deserves, I had to make the hard choice. It was *because* I love her that I left her."

Sighing heavily, my gaze drops to my knees. "I knew Lydia didn't give Aurora the love or attention she needs, but I never *ever* thought she'd be so callous as to do this." My throat closes over. "If I'd known..."

A large, smooth hand lands on my knee, squeezing.

"You're the one that told me regrets don't do us any good. You made the best decision for you and your daughter at the time. You couldn't have known how things would pan out. All we can do is look forward."

Grayson's words ring in my ear, and his hand remains on my knee for the rest of the drive to the nursing home.

"How are things going at the office?" I ask as we pull into the parking lot at the nursing home.

Sliding the car into an available space, Grayson's head falls back against the headrest as he groans. "Not good."

"Your dad still causing problems?" He'd mentioned earlier in the week how he'd made a surprise appearance in the office, strutting around like a peacock and acting as though he'd never been gone.

"Of course. He's doing his best to undermine me. To encourage people to go to him instead of me. It's pissing me the fuck off."

I nod thoughtfully. "It's like he's trying to reclaim the life he had before his arrest."

"I'm pretty certain that's exactly what he's trying to do." Grayson's head falls to the side, those steely eyes colliding with mine. "Except, I have this sick feeling that he wants more from you."

My brows furrow. "That doesn't make sense. He's still married to Lydia."

"Yeah, as a way to remain close to you." He lifts his head to stare out the windshield, running a hand through his hair and mussing it up. "Whatever it is, I don't like it."

Yeah, neither do I.

Grayson knocks on the door before popping his head into the room. "Gran? I have a friend with me today." Pushing it wider, he steps over the threshold, ushering for me to follow.

I look around the spacious room. Pale blue walls and light streaming through the large window give it a homey feel. A bed is pushed against one wall, and two armchairs are positioned by a window opposite a television, which is on but muted.

Rounding the chairs, a frail, elderly woman comes into view. A basket of yarn is placed by her feet, knitting needles in her hands as she glances between us with a friendly, if not bland, smile.

"Oh, hello. Are you here about the refrigerator? It keeps making that awful noise." She makes to get up, but Grayson places a hand over hers.

"No need to get up," he says with a reassuring smile. "Our colleagues are looking at the refrigerator as we speak. We thought we would keep you company while they did."

"Oh." His Gran relaxes back into her chair. "Well, isn't that sweet of you?" Her eyes scour his face for a drawn-out moment, eyebrows slightly furrowed as though she can't quite piece together what she's seeing. "What were your names again?"

With that amiable smile still in place, Grayson places a hand over his chest. "I'm Grayson." Gesturing to me, he says, "And this is Riley."

His Gran's gaze flits to mine, passing over my face and pausing on my auburn hair before returning to Grayson.

"Grayson and Riley. What lovely names."

Gesturing to the spare armchair, Grayson silently tells me to sit as he pulls over a stool and perches on it.

"What are you knitting there?" I ask, indicating her knitting needles.

A grin that reaches her eyes spreads across his Gran's face. "A baby blanket. My daughter is pregnant with our first grandchild." Grayson's inhale is audible, but the delight on his Gran's face is blinding.

"That's so exciting," I say, keeping up the conversation and giving Grayson a moment. "Do you know yet if it's a boy or a girl?"

"A sweet baby boy."

"How far along is your daughter?"

"She's just entered the second trimester and started showing a little baby bump."

I grin at her. "She'll be able to feel the baby kicking in no time. How was her morning sickness? I had a terrible time with my little one. Could barely keep anything down for the first twelve weeks."

Gran's eyes go wide as her gaze rakes over me. "You don't look nearly old enough to have a child."

Throwing my head back in laughter, I nod in agreement. "I have a three—nearly four—year old. A girl." Fishing my phone from the pocket of my coat that I shed when I sat down, I pull up a photo and show her.

"Oh, isn't she a sweetpea?" she coos.

"She's a stereotypical little girl. Obsessed with princesses and everything pink."

Gran chuckles, eyes still on the photo on my phone.

"My grandson was the same way at that age." It takes me a second to grasp that showing her a picture of Aurora must have shifted her reality slightly, and my gaze slides to Grayson, who is staring transfixed at his Gran.

"He was obsessed with princesses too?" I tease, keeping my focus on Grayson. His gaze snaps to mine, and he mouths *'haha'* even as the corners of his lips lift.

"Oh gosh, no." She chuckles. "Girls were gross. He was a typical boy, getting himself into all sorts of trouble. Had his mama constantly chasing after him, dragging him out of trees and cleaning up his cuts and scrapes." Amusement softens her features. "She even had to hose him down in the backyard one day after he crawled through a hole in the hedge after a rainstorm." She shakes her head. "He was covered head to toe in mud. Looked like a swamp monster."

A rough rasp rips from Grayson.

"I bet he's still a troublemaker," I tease Gran.

Some of the life in her eyes fades, and her shoulders sag. "I wish. That boy carries the weight of the world on his shoulders. He's been through so much. He tries not to let it show, but I see the strain, the toll it's taken on him. Losing his mother, enduring his father, and being forced to grow up too fast. It's changed him, hardened him. He never complains or speaks of the hardships, but I see it. I see how it's molded him into the man he is—for better or worse."

Throat thick, my gaze slides to Grayson. My breath catches at the utter, wretched heartbreak that fractures his features.

He's silent while I chat with his Gran for a bit longer, but I keep casting glances his way. He keeps his head buried in his hands, but I can tell his grandmother's admission has affected him.

When it's time for us to leave, I hold my hand out for her to shake. "It was a pleasure to meet you."

"You too, dear."

Grayson says his goodbyes before we leave her room, walking back to the reception in silence.

"How was she for you today?" a woman behind the desk asks when we approach.

"She was in good spirits." Grayson's response is terse, his features set into their typical impenetrable mask as he focuses on the visitor log before him.

"I'm sure she enjoyed having a new visitor," the woman says, giving me a warm smile as Grayson signs his name and sets down the pen. "Well, it's a beautiful day. You two should go and enjoy it. I've got your Gran, sweetie."

I roll my lips between my teeth, holding back my laughter as Grayson places a hand at the base of my spine and escorts me outside.

He walks beside me across the parking lot, and my shoulders begin to shake as we approach his car. He glances at me from the corner of his eyes, his gaze narrowing; however, there's a rare, mischievous spark illuminating his dark orbs. "What, pray tell, has you so amused?"

Lips still between my teeth, they slip free as I grin. "Oh, I don't know, *sweetie*."

His eyes flare, mirth dancing in their dark depths. "You little —" He dives for me, and I squeal, jumping backward and running around to the car's passenger side.

Except he follows, barricading me against the door with his long arms and solid body.

"Think you can tease me like that without punishment, Tempest?" He breathes into my ear before nipping the lobe with his teeth and sending shivers cascading down my spine.

"You like my teasing... *sweetie*."

A groan, followed by the bite of teeth on flesh, sends a tug straight to my core. "God help me, I do," he whispers against my skin as he trails his lips closer to the crook of my neck. "I like your teasing. I like your fight. I like it when you glare at me like you're envisioning stabbing me."

One hand leaves the car to glide down my side before resting on my hip. "I like that you're soft yet fierce. Caring yet cutting. I like your tears and the sound of your laugh. That when I challenge you, you challenge me right back."

He pulls back just enough for our eyes to collide. "But what I love the most about you, Tempest, is your pain." My brows dip in confusion. "It is the pain you have endured that makes the fact you *can* tease inspiring, that makes your fight so much more fearsome. Makes your ability to care so precious, your tears more potent, and your laugh fucking *musical*."

Leaning in, he presses his forehead against mine, our breaths tangling in the scant space between our lips. "That pain that should have destroyed you, yet you're still standing, still breathing. That strength with the courage—the resilience and sheer determination it must have taken... It's a flame teasing me closer when I'm lost in the dark and need a way out."

"Grayson." His name is barely a breath between us. Like a tug on a boat, his body leans into mine, a soul-deep sigh slipping from between his lips before he wrenches himself away.

"Don't say anything." He looks down at me with his usual stoic expression, except it's lacking some of its typical hardness. There's a rare softness around his eyes, a slight hitch to his lip. "Just do as you're told for once and get in the car."

Not moving, I stare up at him, searching. "Do you want to talk about it?"

He hesitates before shaking his head. "No."

"Okay," I readily agree. "I may not understand what pain you've endured, Grayson, but like you just pointed out, I do understand pain, and I know what it is to be forced to grow up too fast." I give him a small smile and a shrug of my shoulder. "In case you ever feel like talking."

Giving him my back, I slide into the car, feeling the intensity of his gaze boring into me before he strides around the front of the vehicle.

As he gets in, his phone buzzes in his pocket, and he pulls it out, frowning at the screen.

"What is it?" I ask, suddenly on alert.

He tilts the screen so I can see the text from Royce.

Get to The Depot now. We have a lead.

ROYCE

CHAPTER NINE

Leaning over the back of the desk chair in Xander's too-small office, I squint at the grainy picture on the screen.

"Dude, I swear, if your putrid breath hits my cheek one more time..." Dax growls. He raced back here after his fight in New York when Blue notified him of this possible lead.

"Fuck off." I smack the back of his head, but not hard enough to do any real damage—he is helping us, after all. "I popped a breath mint." Ignoring him, I lean in closer to the screen once more, scanning every pixel of the photo.

A photo that shows a brown-haired—is that a hint of red?—little girl. Her face is down, her hair falling forward, preventing us from getting a half-decent look. She's dressed in a worn, blue-green princess dress that looks a size too big for her, and beneath the picture is the name *Ariel*.

Definitely not her name. Still... my nose presses closer to the laptop screen. That is, without a doubt, a hint of red, right?

"I'm serious, man. I can't work if you're blocking my view." Dax shoves at my shoulder, and I grunt a half-hearted apology as I reluctantly lean back.

Crossing my arms over my chest, I scan the dozen other photos alongside *Ariel's*. All are little girls dressed up and renamed as Disney princesses. In each one, the dresses are a little torn or tattered, the girls are barefoot, and most aren't looking at the camera. The ones who are... they are the photos that scare me the most. While the images are grainy, making it impossible to discern individual features, there is no mistaking the fear in those kids' eyes—the red noses from endless tears.

A commotion in the hall is quickly followed by the door being thrown open, and Logan rushes in. Riley is on his heels, Gray bringing up the rear.

"You have a lead?" Riley asks, breathless and wide-eyed as she stares at me.

Fuck, there is so much hope in those eyes. This lead better pan out because the thought of getting her hopes up only to be crushed sickens me. I'm already in a state of constant agitation, made worse when Riley startles awake in the middle of the night from a nightmare. I can't bear the thought of adding even more disappointment to her plate.

"Maybe," I hedge.

"What the fuck do you mean, maybe?" Gray snarls. "You said you had a fucking lead."

I arch a warning brow at him. Now is most definitely not the time for his temper to get the better of him. This room is already suffocatingly small with all of us in it.

Teeth grinding, he sucks in a breath before slowly exhaling.

"What's the lead?" Logan asks, defusing the situation as he pulls Riley into his arms, holding her steady.

Dax turns the laptop to face them, giving them a second to take in what they are seeing before pointing to *Ariel's* picture. "Do you think that could be Aurora?"

My gaze remains glued on Riley's pale face as her eyes bounce over the screen, seeming to linger on every one of the twelve pictures before coming to rest on the one that may be of her daughter.

Her throat stretches around a swallow before she steps forward, coming closer to the screen as Logan's arms fall away. However, he doesn't let her go far, remaining right behind her in case she needs him. He's the source of comfort she has needed this past week. The only one of us who knows how to care for her while I do everything I can to track down the sick bastard who purchased Aurora, and Grayson... Grayson gives Riley an outlet for all those ugly emotions she's feeling and unable to process or give voice to. He has a knack for sensing when she needs that outlet— someone to explode on—and he's perfected the art of pissing her off.

"I—I don't know," Riley admits in a tight voice after staring at the photo for several long moments. "Maybe?" She shakes her head, eyes never leaving the screen as frustration creases her brow. "I can't be sure. The hair looks like hers, and the size and build look similar, but..." Her eyes lift to mine, the turmoil I find in her hazel depths slaying me. "Shouldn't I know what my own daughter looks like?" Her lips tremble, and my heart openly bleeds for her. It takes everything in me to remain in place. To not round the table and pull her into my arms so she can freely fall apart.

"It's a poor-quality photo, sweetheart," I try to soothe instead. "And you can't see her face. We didn't expect you to be able to discernibly identify her."

Tears rim the bottom of her lids as she holds my gaze. "But you're going to investigate anyway?"

I nod, holding her stare and hoping she can see that I won't stop until I find her little girl. She latches onto my gaze like it's a lifeline. A buoy in rough waters preventing her from being dragged under.

"What is this anyway?" Gray asks, stepping up beside Riley to get a closer look at the screen.

"We think it's some sort of auction," Dax explains.

"You *think*?" Grayson's harsh snap might have others jumping out of their skin, but Dax doesn't even miss a blink.

"As I was saying," Blue drawls, interrupting the stare-off between Gray and Dax—oh shit, I completely forgot he was on the phone—"That's all the info I can get without registering to attend the event. Whoever is organizing this has covered all their bases. They have everything locked down. I've been searching for hours but can't find a backdoor past their security."

"Keep trying," Dax tells him as he grabs his phone from the desk and ends the call. Pushing to his feet, he casts his eyes around the room. "This is a discussion between the four of you." Meeting my gaze, he adds, "Whatever you decide, you know you have my support. I'll get a team organized."

I nod, and without another word, he strides from the room, leaving oppressive silence, the stench of fear, and the tiniest amount of, dare I say, hope in his wake.

"What's he talking about?" Logan asks, glancing between the closed door and me.

"Along with the image Blue found, there's a link to a private room where you can get the event details—when, where, etc." My gaze drifts over each of them. "There's a price simply to get into the chat room—it's steep."

Riley's face drops as Logan scoffs. "Whatever it is, we'll pay it."

"Agreed," Grayson adds.

"I figured as much." Given how, between us, we had agreed to put a hell of a dent in our inheritances to get Aurora away from Lydia. However, since we don't know for certain that this *is* Aurora, I needed to run it past them first.

Riley glances between us with an open mouth and so much gratitude shining in those hazel eyes. However, she doesn't mount a word of protest—for once. I didn't expect she would, not when it comes to something so precious. She may feel guilty, but she won't object. Nor would we let her get her way, even if she did.

What is the point of having money if we can't spend it on making the woman we love happy? And nothing will make her happier than having her daughter back in her arms. Not that I'll let that stop me from spoiling her. I might not have the same bottomless pit of inheritance the others do. In fact, I have pennies in comparison—My dad all but disinherited me after I publicly *disgraced the family*. In other words, he didn't give two shits about what I'd supposedly done when he'd swept it under the rug, but once Halston got wind of the accusations, and the rumor mill started, he claimed he needed to 'distance' me from the King name. If he had another child, I'm confident I'd have been excommunicated. As it was, he settled for publicly disowning me and financially cutting me off *to teach me a lesson.*

The only lesson I learned was that I don't need my father's money to survive. I do just fine with what I make from my fights, plus a few well-placed bets on myself.

However, I do have a small inheritance from my grandfather that I have never been more grateful for than I am now. *That* is the money I plan on using to help get Aurora back, and I don't give a shit if I spend every penny achieving it.

As far as I'm concerned, it's the investment of a lifetime.

Knowing we're all in agreement, I sit in Dax's vacated chair and drag the laptop closer. Unlocking my phone, I pull up the username details Blue sent me for an account he's been warming up for the past couple of weeks. He reckons—and I'd agree—that if whoever runs this thing is so tight on security, they'll vet anyone who tries to join the group, regardless of how much they are willing to pay to get in.

Once I've logged into the account, I glance at the others crowded around me before requesting to join the private room. A message pops up on the screen. *Your request is pending approval.*

"What now?" Logan asks, his arm around Riley's waist as he flicks his gaze from the screen to me.

"Now, we wait."

Dinner is a quiet affair. The laptop sits open on the kitchen island, and I'm pretty sure we all spend more time glancing at it than at our plates.

"What's the plan when we have a time and location?" Gray asks when the scrape of cutlery against porcelain becomes cloying.

Riley abandons any pretense of eating—all she's done is push food around her plate since Logan set it in front of her—to look at me. It's the set of her jaw and the spark of determination in her eyes that gives away her intentions before she says, "Whatever the plan is, I'm coming."

"Absolutely not." Grayson's harsh tone cuts like a blade, earning him an incinerating look from Riley.

"Ry—" I try more tactfully before she shakes her head, cutting me off.

"No. You kept me out of the loop last time, and while I understand why you did, I'm not doing it again. I can't sit here and wait for you to return, wondering whether you have my daughter with you. It's not happening. *I'm coming with you.*"

Her declaration is met with a moment of silence as I exchange glances with the guys. Gray looks like he's about to mount another protest—*fucking idiot*. Thankfully, before he can incite World War Three, Logan interjects. "Alright, so looks like we need to find a way to get the four of us into this event."

"You can't be fucking serious?" Grayson growls.

Seriously? Dude needs to learn to recognize a losing battle. Do I want to put Riley in danger by bringing her with us? No. Do I want her exposed to the sick underbelly we're going into? Hell no. Do I recognize that wild horses won't stop her from coming? You can bet your ass.

Instead of trying to talk her out of coming—or knowing Grayson, devising ways to ensure she *can't*—my priority needs to be ensuring she is safe and protected at all times.

"Grayson," Riley snarls in a tone so vicious that I can't help but smirk. In a fight between Mama Bear vs. Grayson, my money is on Riley. Every. Single. Time. "If you so much as *think* about keeping me away from this, I will blend your balls into soup and force it down your throat."

Coughing to disguise his laugh, Logan not so subtly lifts his hand from the table to cover his balls.

Unperturbed, Grayson's dark eyes narrow on Riley. "While you're focused on your daughter and these two idiots are too pussy whipped to say no to you—"

"Hey!" Logan interjects with a scowl.

"—*I* am trying to keep *you* safe. You don't need to see the shit that goes down in a place like that."

"But my daughter does?" Riley spits back.

Pinching the bridge of his nose, Grayson's shoulders drop on an exhale. "Of course not." Bottling up his anger, an emotion I've never seen on him before flares from his eyes as they meet Riley's. "If I could prevent Aurora from stepping foot somewhere like that, I would." He swallows roughly. "But I can't."

"You can't stop me either, Grayson. And if you try, you will destroy any hope of there ever being anything between us."

Nostrils flaring, the grind of Grayson's teeth is the only sound in the otherwise silent room. Just when I think he's going to shoot himself in the foot and forever ruin whatever they might have, he manages to swallow back his protests. Sounding like he's chewing on nails, he spits a "Fine."

"It's not like we're going to let anything happen to her in there," I point out. "She'll always be with one of us, and Dax will have a team on standby."

Grayson's curt nod is the only response he seems capable of making as he sulks in his chair, looking like someone pissed in his cereal.

"Laptop," Logan barks as the screen lights up with a notification. Chair legs scrape against the floor as we all crowd around the island. Me in front of the laptop with Riley on my left, Logan looking over her head from right behind her, and Grayson on my right.

I can feel the tension coiling through the air around us as I type in my password and bring up the site. A notification pops up saying I have a new message. All it contains is an amount and a phone number. Probably a burner, and the bank account it's connected to is emptied as soon as the money hits and closed once the event is over.

Should the organizers check, we've already moved money into an account Blue set up that will link back to my dummy online account, so I quickly transfer it over.

This time, we only have to wait several minutes before we're sent a link to the private room.

Welcome to the Royal Ball, is written on a banner across the top, ***where you have the opportunity to find your perfect little princess.***

"Jesus, this is sick," Logan unnecessarily comments.

Beneath are profiles for each of the *princesses*. I scroll to the *Ariel* one. The pictures are all as grainy and out of focus as the initial one Blue found. However, the unhelpful photo includes details such as the girl's height, weight, eye and hair color, plus any unique features.

Riley's sharp inhale has us all straightening. "Aurora has a birthmark on her lower back," she exclaims with restrained hope, reading the unique feature mentioned for *Ariel*.

"Eye and hair color match," I point out.

"And the height and weight are about right. I hadn't checked her height since I started at Halston, but she's shot up several inches since last summer," Riley supplies. I notice her squeeze Logan's arm from the corner of my eye. "Oh my god, it really could be her."

"When is the event?" Grayson asks, his impatience audible.

Scrolling to the bottom of the page, I find the details we're looking for—date and time along with an image of a map with a circle indicating the general area of the event and a note that an entry pass and coordinates will be sent fifteen minutes before the start time.

Reading the date and time, my gaze snaps to the digital clock. "Shit, it's in two hours." I shouldn't be surprised that we're only finding out at the last minute. Why announce a highly illegal event days or weeks in advance and give the authorities time to find out about it and assemble a team.

"Where is it?" There's an urgency behind Logan's question. "Can we make it in time?"

Fuck, I hope so.

Typing the name of a nearby town into the browser brings up the location as close to three hours away. "It'll be tight, but we can make it if we leave right now." I'm already closing the laptop and grabbing my phone to call Dax. No way do I want to go into this without knowing we have backup ready outside.

"Hold on, we can't go like this." Grayson gestures at the

sweats Logan is wearing. "It's a ball. They're going to expect us to be dressed up."

"Shit, he's right." Logan swipes his hand through his hair. "I'll be ready in five."

Grayson has a point, though. "We all need to change. Full suits. Ry, you got a dress you can put on?"

She nods, pupils dilated with anxiety, leaving only a thin ring of hazel as she nibbles on her lip. "Are they going to let all of us in?" she asks nervously, glancing between us.

"You'll go in with Grayson. Logan and I will pretend to be his muscle. There to ensure the *cargo* is transported safely." Riley's nose isn't the only one that scrunches.

"Alright, so we have a plan," Logan states seriously.

"Yup, go get ready, and I'll call Dax."

"Got it," I state as coordinates, and a QR code appears on my phone. We broke every speed limit and took more than a few risks climbing the steep mountainside roads to get here on time, and I had pulled into a mostly empty gas station a few minutes ago to await this message.

Plugging the coordinates into the GPS of the unmarked SUV Dax lent us to protect our identities and help sell our aliases, I glance at Riley in the rearview mirror before I pull the car onto the road. She's sitting in the back with Grayson, the two of them finely dressed, as she stares out her passenger window and chews on her lip.

Leaving behind the small mountainside town, I follow the directions along a winding road. The SUV's tires glide over the asphalt, the hum of the engine the only sound as we draw nearer. My hands grip the steering wheel with white-knuckled intensity, my jaw set in a hard line as I navigate the treacherous curves. The headlights cut through the inky darkness, revealing the perilous drop just inches from the road's edge.

Beside me, Logan stares out the window, his thoughts a storm of fear and resolve. I can feel the tension radiating off him in waves, mirroring my own anxiety. I can't fail Riley again. I *need* this little girl to be Aurora, and this time I'm not fucking leaving without her.

Flicking my attention to the rearview mirror, my gaze catches on Grayson, his focus on the winding road ahead. His face is stoic, but a tightness around his lips and eyes belies his concern—not only for Riley but for Aurora. For all of us, really. Grayson's anger comes from a place of caring. He's a strategist. A planner. He despises how we've had to rush into this without knowing all the variables. I can't say I disagree.

The road twists and turns as we drive in silence, each lost in our thoughts. The gravity of the situation is a dense cloud surrounding us all. Finally, a faint light appears in the distance, our destination coming into view as the SUV's headlights sweep over a set of tall, imposing gates guarded by men in dark uniforms. The sight brings a mix of emotions—relief, anxiety, and a flicker of hope. Riley takes a deep breath, steeling herself for what's to come as she leans forward between the two front seats. I catch a whiff of her perfume and inhale deeply, breathing it into my lungs.

A short line of high-end cars forms a line in front of us, each vehicle inching forward, their occupants masked in shadow and secrecy. I pull the SUV into the line, my heart pounding louder with each passing second. Logan shifts beside me, his gaze sharp and alert as he scans our surroundings.

As we near the front of the line, my pulse quickens. "Remember your roles," I remind everyone as the first guard approaches, his expression stern and unyielding. He motions for me to lower the window, and I comply, feeling the cool mountain air rush in.

"Your QR code," he demands, holding out a scanner. He runs it over my phone screen, and the device pings in confirmation. With a nod, he signals to another guard, who approaches with a different device.

This one begins meticulously scanning our SUV, running the device over and under the vehicle. I grip the steering wheel tighter, every muscle in my body taut with anxiety.

"How many are in the car?" the first guard asks, pointing his flashlight into the backseat before I've had a chance to respond. In a panic, my gaze snaps to the rearview mirror, and I breathe a quiet sigh of relief when I see Grayson has pulled Riley in against him. Her face is hidden from view, his hand high on her exposed thigh as he nuzzles her neck.

As the flashlight glances off his face, he lifts his head, scowling at the guard. "Aren't we done already?" he drawls in that perfected haughty arrogance. "I want to get this party underway."

"Apologies, Sir. We're just doing a quick sweep of the car, and then you'll be on your way."

With a grunt, Grayson dismisses the guard as he buries his face in Riley's neck, eliciting a fake moan.

My fingers tap against the steering wheel, counting out each tense second until the second guard gives a curt nod to his colleague. The first guard steps back and gestures for us to proceed. "Enjoy your evening."

One hurdle down, I tell myself as I roll the SUV through the open gates. I swear the entire car releases a collective breath as we leave the guards behind and move down the driveway.

"Who knew your assholery could be used for good?" Logan taunts in a bid to break the cloying tension.

Riley's laugh is strained, and Grayson merely grunts in

response, any levity falling by the wayside as a mountain lodge comes into view, exuding timeless elegance and rustic charm. The car's headlights sweep across the exterior, illuminating the striking combination of natural stone and rich, dark wood, which blends seamlessly with the surrounding forest. Towering evergreens frame it, reminding me that we're a long way from Halston.

The lodge's exterior lights, positioned to highlight its architectural beauty, cast long, dramatic shadows across the front lawn and the surrounding forest, highlighting the number of parked cars.

I roll the SUV to a stop at the foot of a stone pathway that leads up to the front door. "Ready or not," Logan murmurs. The significance of what we're about to do crackles in the air as we all share a final, loaded glance before I push open my door and step out of the vehicle.

"Keep it nearby," I tell a valet as I hand him the car keys. "We won't be staying long after the event."

"Sir." With a nod, he hurries into the driver's seat, and I move to open the back door, maintaining my role of bodyguard as Grayson elegantly exits the car. His posture straightens as he takes in our surroundings with an air of indifference before turning to offer Riley his hand, helping her out.

Her heels clack against the stone as she clings to his arm. She smiles up at Grayson like he hung the moon as she plays the part of his alluring side piece. Her red dress shimmers in the dim light, highlighting her pale, creamy skin on display. My jaw tightens, and I have to rip my gaze away before I toss her back into the car and drive her the hell out of here.

Grayson keeps Riley tucked beneath his arm as they walk ahead of us along the stone pathway lined with softly glowing lanterns. The lanterns guide visitors to the set of heavy wooden doors wedged open, allowing bright light to spill into the night.

Logan and I fall into step behind them, our expressions stern and unyielding, embodying muscle and intimidation.

Two guards stand on either side of the entrance, their eyes cold and calculating as they skim over each of us before dismissing us as we step over the threshold and into the lodge filled with its sickening opulence.

"Looks like the lodge has been rented by a private corporation," Dax informs me via the tiny earpiece hidden in my ear as I glance around the lobby. High ceilings adorned with intricate chandeliers cast a warm glow over the marble floors and plush carpets. A soft, seductive melody plays in the background, enhancing the atmosphere of luxury and decadence. Guests mill about, their conversations a low murmur that adds to the air of exclusivity. Most of the attendees are men dressed in tailored suits, their eyes scanning the room with a mix of curiosity and predatory interest. Scantily clad women accompany them, their laughter ringing out like the tinkling of glass.

I'd sent Dax our coordinates before I climbed out of the car. He has a team stationed back at the village, should they be needed.

If all goes well, they won't be.

"Probably a shell corp."

Meaning, there's no way to trace it back to whoever is behind this sick sense of entertainment.

Grayson leads the way, his confidence unwavering as he navigates through the crowd with pretentious swagger. Riley stays close, her hand delicately resting on his arm, her eyes taking in the surroundings with feigned disinterest. She plays her role perfectly, the epitome of a woman who knows her place in this world of wealth and power. Logan and I flank them, our eyes constantly scanning for any sign of trouble, our presence a silent warning to anyone who might think of crossing our path.

As we move deeper into the lodge, we pass through a set of

heavy wooden doors into the main hall. This room is even more lavish, with rich draperies lining the walls and an elaborate stage at the far end. Tables covered in fine linens and adorned with crystal centerpieces fill the space, each occupied by men sipping expensive drinks and engaging in hushed conversations. The scent of expensive cigars and perfume hangs in the air, creating a heady mix that only adds to the sense of indulgence.

Grayson beelines for a vacant table near the front, a prime spot with an excellent view of the stage. He pulls out a chair for Riley, who sits with practiced grace, her eyes subtly scanning for any familiar faces. Logan and I take our positions behind them, our gazes sweeping over the room, noting exits and potential threats.

"There are more people here than I thought there would be," Logan says in a low voice, ensuring it doesn't carry to the nearby tables.

My hard gaze skims over them regardless, ensuring no one is paying us any attention.

"Pretty sure I just saw Senator Torrence over there," Grayson disguises behind his hand as he shifts closer to Riley. One arm goes across the back of her chair as his other lands on her exposed thigh. "Get us drinks," he orders in an arrogant tone that fits perfectly with this place. "A martini for the lady, and I'll take a whiskey."

"Coming right up, *sir*," Logan drawls before casting me a look that says he's already had enough of this performance before heading toward a bar at the back of the room.

"How long until..." Riley gestures toward the stage.

"Probably not long. They'll want to give everyone time to arrive and have a drink or two, but they won't want to wait too long and risk exposure," I tell her, keeping my face impassive and attention on the goings on in the room.

"You're doing great," Grayson assures her. "Just keep your focus on me. That can't be too much of a hardship."

I barely restrain my eye roll, my lips twitching ever so slightly when Riley doesn't bother to smother her snort.

Grayson's hand moves from the back of her chair, sliding into her hair and holding her captive as he nips at her jaw, working his way along it to her lips. I know it's mostly for show, but I don't pull my gaze away as I watch her reaction to every one of his touches—notably, the heat that builds in her eyes, how her skin flushes beneath his touch, and her breaths grow shallow.

Oh yeah, Riley might protest there being anything between them, but there is no denying that chemistry.

A presence appears out of nowhere, dropping into one of the empty seats at the large, round table and forcing them apart as we all stare at the unwelcome newcomer.

"Haven't seen you at one of these before?" the man drawls, eyeing Grayson before his gaze flits to Riley, and a salacious grin brightens his otherwise hard face. He looks as though he's not much older than us—late twenties to early thirties—and is as crisply dressed as Grayson. Unlike Grayson, though, he doesn't appear to have any security. Although, I have noticed that plenty of others do.

Leaning closer to Riley, he purrs, "I'd definitely remember if I'd seen *you* before. What's your name, sweetheart?"

"Since she's here with *me* tonight, her name is none of your concern," Grayson retorts in a manner that says he's bored with the entire conversation.

Unperturbed, the newcomer simply smirks. "I see how it is."

Logan chooses that moment to return with their drinks. Sending me a *who the fuck is this* arch of his brow as he sets them down on the table.

I shrug a *no fucking clue* in response.

"So, first time?" the newcomer enquires.

"What did you say your name was?" Grayson turns the conversation back on him as he glares suspiciously.

Taking a sip of the whiskey he brought, he smirks at Grayson over the top of the glass. "Didn't give you a name."

"I'm bored," Riley whines, leaning into Grayson and stretching so she can bring her lips to his ear. Loud enough for the rest of the table to hear, she says, "Want to take me to the coat closet and fuck me?"

Holy shit. There is no way I'm the only one at the table who got an immediate boner.

Although if new-guy's dick so much as twitched, he'll be going home without it.

I don't dare take my eyes off him as he studies Riley and Grayson, that playboy smirk of his firmly in place.

"Mm," Grayson hums, sliding his hand to the back of Riley's head and dragging her mouth to his for a hot and dirty kiss. "That does sound like a lot more fun."

"I wouldn't go running off," the newcomer states, finishing his drink and setting it on the table. "The auction will be starting soon." Getting to his feet, he rakes his eyes over Grayson, and there's an astuteness in his gaze that I don't like. Just as I'm about to step forward and tell him to beat it, he glances at Riley, offering her one of those signature smirks before he ducks his head. "Enjoy the rest of your evening."

"Douchebag," Logan hisses when he's out of earshot.

Riley sinks back into her seat, shoulders dropping as she takes a large sip of her martini.

"Please tell me not everyone is going to scrutinize us being here tonight."

"I'm sure he's not the only one who will be interested in potential new players on the field," I murmur.

"Great."

Thankfully, the room lights dim a moment later, and spotlights illuminate the stage as a man steps onto it. His voice is smooth and commanding as he looks around the room, welcoming everyone. "We have an extraordinary lineup for you this evening." His twitchy eyes practically dance with cold excitement, his slimy mouth curling into a vile smile that sends a noticeable shiver through Riley.

He quickly explains the rules and how to bid before ushering out the first princess of the night. "First up this evening is *Belle*," he announces as a ball of yellow is dragged onto the stage by a mountain of a man with dead eyes. Her straw-colored hair covers her face as she stands on trembling legs and bare feet. Before the bidding begins, the auctioneer rhymes off the facts available in the online private room. The entire ordeal is beyond sickening, and as the little girl is dragged off the stage, putting up zero fight, I realize we can't walk out of here with Aurora and leave the others behind.

It hadn't crossed my mind before. My focus was solely on getting Aurora. Even so, none of these kids deserve the fate they are being marched toward. If we could buy every single kid, we'd do it in a heartbeat, but not only would that draw too much attention, it would cost more than all of us have.

"Dax," I murmur into the earpiece, barely moving my lips.

"I know, Royce." His tone is bleak. "We're not leaving any of them behind. Focus on Aurora. I'll get the rest. I've got a safe house and a doctor set up and waiting for them."

The anvil that had been sitting on my chest lifts.

I do my best to detach myself from the situation as girl after girl, ranging in age from as young as three to preteens, is marched onto the stage. Some are forced to curtsy or twirl, while others merely stand there. Most keep their heads down, faces obscured, but occasionally, a spitfire of a kid emerges, and the excitement that strums through the crowd has my stomach revolting.

Dropping my gaze, Riley's hand is white as she tightens it around Grayson's arm beneath the table. However, none of her disgust is portrayed on her face as she astutely watches the stage as though memorizing every kid's features before they disappear from wherever they came.

I strain to listen as she leans closer to Grayson. "Ariel must be next. All the other princesses have gone." My spine straightens, and I share a look with Logan, a brief nod before our focus returns to the stage as a little girl in a sea-blue dress is hauled out.

"Our final princess of the night is the fiery-tempered, red-headed Ariel," the auctioneer announces as the little girl is shoved into the spotlight. Head down, her hair covers her face.

Come on, sweetheart, I urge. *Lift your head.*

Feet planted, she stares steadfastly at her toes as the announcer runs through her stats.

"Give us a wave, Ariel," the announcer encourages, crossing the stage to coax her forward. He pulls on her hair when she doesn't obey, forcing her head up as she yelps.

My nails dig into my palms, except as I take in her tear-streaked face...

"It's not her." Riley's voice cracks over the words, the mask she has perfected tonight crumbling as she ducks her head and closes her eyes.

Fuck.

Fuck.

It's not her. How the hell is it not her?

"I'm sorry, man," Dax says in my ear, making me realize I said that aloud. "We'll find her. She's the last kid tonight. You've got five minutes to get out."

"What are you going to do?" I ask as I watch *Ariel* being ushered off the stage.

"Better you don't know. Just get to your car and don't look back no matter what."

Catching Grayson's gaze, I gesture for us to leave. He pulls Riley into his arms, and Logan and I follow as we move through the lively crowd. Many are celebrating their new *possessions*, while others are simply enjoying the adrenaline rush that seemingly comes from participating in this sort of debauchery.

As we leave the auction room, my eyes lock on a set of familiar ones—the guy who made himself at home at our table earlier. Still smirking like a smarmy tool, he lifts a fresh glass of whiskey in salute before I rip my gaze away and follow the others out of the room. Thankfully, we make it across the lobby uninterrupted.

The fresh air hits my face as we step outside, careful not to appear as though we are rushing as we descend the steps toward the car. Catching the valet's eye, I lift my chin, and he hustles to grab the car keys, tossing them to me when I walk by. Just like I asked, the car is parked close to the entrance, and with eyes on us, Logan moves around Grayson to open the backseat door while I climb in behind the wheel. Riley hurries into the car, her makeup smeared and eyes red-rimmed as Grayson joins her. My foot is on the accelerator before Logan even has his door closed, and gravel kicks up as I shoot down the long driveway. I slow only long enough for the guards to open the gate before I slip through the gap.

"Stop," Logan barks as soon as we're out of sight of the gates. "Fucking stop," he snarls when I don't do it fast enough. Slamming on the brakes, the car is still coming to a stop when he shoves open his door and climbs into the backseat. He bundles Riley into his arms, and her sobs serve as the soundtrack of our failure as we tear away from the lodge.

The SUV's headlights carve a path through the expanding darkness. As I navigate the narrow, twisted mountain road, the adrenaline coursing through me makes every shadow seem like a potential threat. That is until the night sky lights up as if the sun itself has burst from the earth. It's followed a moment later by a deafening explosion behind us.

Easing my foot off the accelerator, I steal a glance in the rearview mirror, my heart pounding. The blast radiates a fiery glow and the lodge, once a distant silhouette, is now a blazing inferno.

"Shit!" Grayson mutters, his eyes wide as he twists to look out the back of the SUV. "What the fuck was that?"

Dax.

Flooring it, the SUV roars as it emerges from a tight bend, and we speed through the next curve and the next, the entire way down the mountain until there's nothing but open roads leading home.

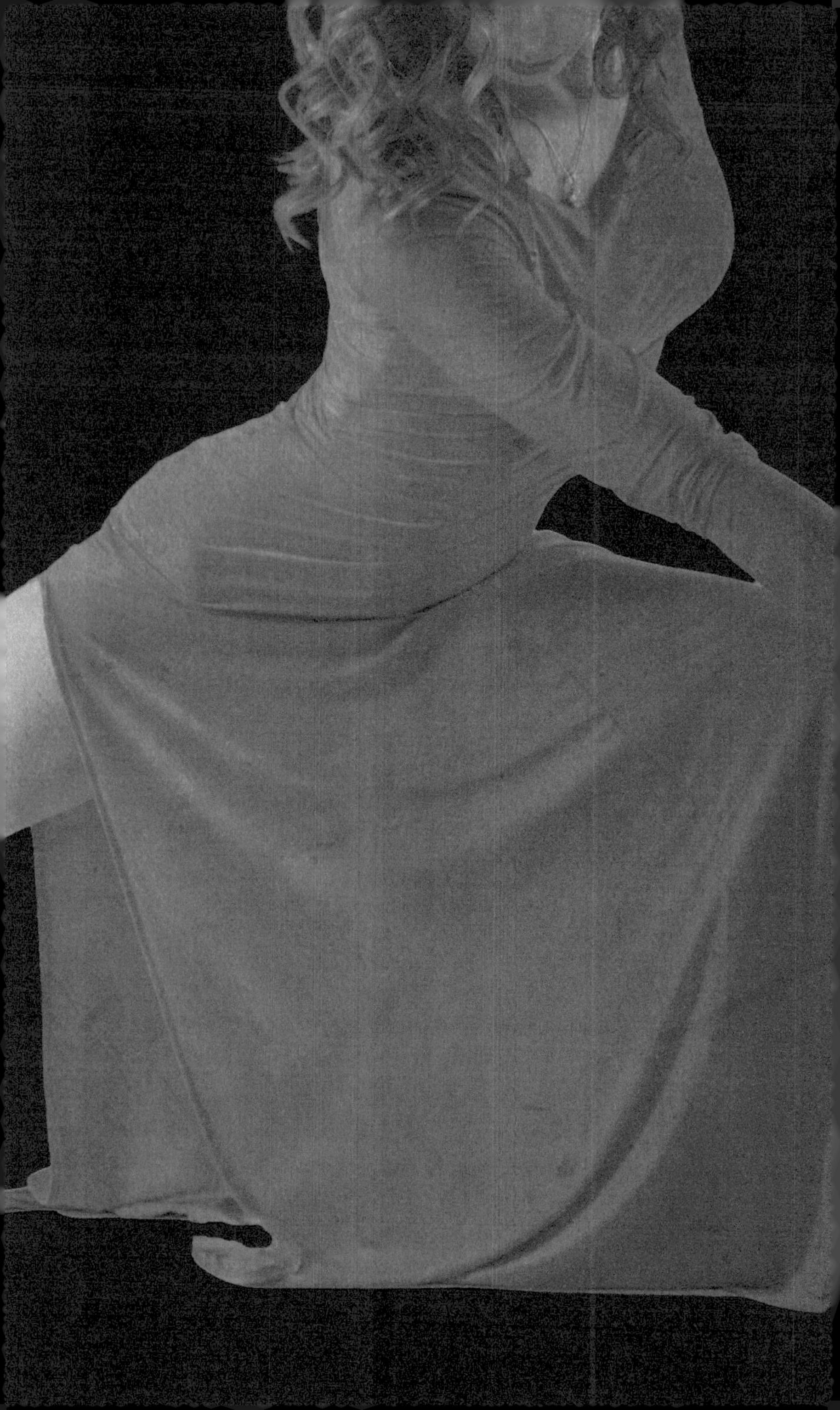

RILEY

CHAPTER TEN

At some point during the drive home, exhaustion must have pulled me under. When I wake, it's like emerging from the depths of a dark ocean. My eyelids are heavy and swollen from crying, and my throat is raw. The car's gentle hum and the rhythmic sound of the tires against the road lull me into a half-awake state. My body feels leaden, but my mind begins to stir, piecing together fragments of the evening.

We failed.

I failed.

Again.

Guilt threatens to drown me, and I shift slightly as strong arms give me a quick squeeze. Peeling open my eyes, I find Logan staring down at me with a fractured expression. I shift again, getting comfortable in his arms as I rest my head on his shoulder and turn to look out the window. The outside world is a blur of dark shadows and distant lights, a stark contrast to the blazing chaos we left behind.

Ducking my head to the jacket wrapped around me, I inhale the faint smell of Grayson's cologne, comforting yet bittersweet. Feeling eyes on me, I meet Royce's gaze in the rearview mirror. His expression is a mix of relief and concern, his usual hard mask cracked by the night's catastrophe. "Hey," he says softly, his voice a balm to my frazzled nerves. "You okay?"

I nod, though the word *okay* feels like a distant memory. "Yeah, just... processing."

Logan presses me tighter against him, his lips brushing my temple, and at the feel of fingers on my ankle, I glance over to find Grayson drawing soothing circles onto my skin.

The car's interior is dim, the dashboard lights casting a soft glow that feels almost soothing. Yet it does nothing to diminish the chaos ripping me apart inside. We were *this* close, except we weren't close at all.

We're no closer to finding my daughter than we were this morning.

And that thought threatens to destroy me.

"Shh," Logan soothes. "We're not giving up. We'll keep looking." He must feel the need to reiterate, "We aren't going to give up, Shortcake."

Sniffling, I ask the question I haven't even allowed myself to think until now. "What if we don't? What if we don't find her?"

"That's not a reality any of us are willing to consider, Tempest."

The absolute surety in Grayson's tone soothes some of the jagged pieces of my soul. Although his eyes are partially obscured in the dim interior, I latch onto his stare as it steadily hauls me out of the dark pit I fell into when I saw that little girl's face and realized she wasn't *my* little girl.

I burrow deeper into the jacket as I rest my head against Logan's chest, and as gravel crunches beneath the tires, I stare into Grayson's eyes, holding on to that lifeline the entire journey back to Halston.

"We're almost home," Royce says quietly, breaking the silence as we pass the *Welcome to Halston* sign.

Home.

Over the last few weeks, I've come to consider the guys' house *home* more so than my apartment. It seems ironic that not long ago, I fought with Grayson over going back to my place, and since then, I've only been there a handful of times to grab things.

I haven't wanted to be alone.

None of the guys have wanted me to be alone, and I'm under no illusion that even if I said I wanted to return to the apartment, they wouldn't all follow. However, my apartment is far too small for three grown-ass men, especially ones the size and breadth of Royce and Logan. As for Grayson? My apartment's square footage is *way* too little to share with him. Hell, even their house isn't big enough to contain the both of us at times.

Still, as we pull up to the curb outside their brownstone and I stare up at the front door, the last place I want to be is inside— where the guys will hover over me, wanting to do everything to make this better even though we all know there isn't anything they *can* do.

Grayson will poke and needle me to distract me from the gaping, empty hole in my chest. Royce will brood over what he considers another failure—even though I could never blame him—and Logan will convince me to cuddle in bed with him. But I won't be able to sleep, and I don't want to be distracted from this pain.

I need to bathe in it.

"Shortcake?"

Blinking out of my stupor, I tear my gaze away from the front door of the house toward Logan. He's standing in the open car door, when I hadn't even noticed him get out. His hand is stretching out for mine, and I stare at it before lifting my gaze, meeting Royce's watchful eyes in the rearview mirror.

"Guys, give us a bit."

"Bu—"

Logan's protest is cut off as Royce presses on the accelerator, and the car jumps forward, the door slamming shut.

"That's my car, you fucker!" Logan's yell is muted, and Royce responds with a middle finger before taking off down the street and leaving Logan and Grayson on the sidewalk. We'd switched cars at The Depot, leaving the unmarked SUV Dax arranged where we found it before climbing into Logan's.

Trusting Royce, I fall back against the warm leather seat as he navigates the streets of Halston. Only when we turn onto my street do I sit up. The car stops outside Ava's dance studio, and Royce gets out, rounding to my side before opening the door and helping me out.

"I don't have my keys on me," I tell him as he walks me to the door.

One side of his lips lifts. "I'm not about to let that stop us," he cryptically states before falling to one knee and pulling a set of tiny tools from his back pocket. Lifting two out, he maneuvers them into the lock.

"Do you carry lock-picking tools everywhere you go?" It feels good to tease, even if we both know it's hollow—merely a distraction.

Still, he huffs out a chuckle. "You never know when you might meet a locked door you want to peek behind."

A loud *click* sounds like a gunshot in the otherwise quiet street before the door swings inward, and Royce ushers me inside.

"Why are we here?" I ask, stepping into the dance studio.

Mirrors line the far wall, and I flick a glance over my red

dress and matching heels, not lingering on my blotchy face before I wrench my gaze away.

Royce strides straight for the sound system, fiddling with it as he connects his phone. Feeling my eyes on him, he lifts his head. His gaze rakes over my face before he answers my question. "This is where you go to bleed out your pain."

The slow opening notes of *Keep Your Head Up Princess* by Anson Seabra seep into the air, and still holding my gaze, Royce murmurs, "Bleed, baby."

That's all the encouragement I need to kick off my heels. Not looking at the mirror, I move into the center of the room. My bare feet press into the polished wooden floor, reflecting the street lights from outside since we didn't bother to turn on any lights in the studio. As the slow beat plays out, I stretch out each of my limbs, lifting my arms above my head and twisting my core as I point my toes and extend my legs until I'm warmed up and the music is wrapped protectively around me.

The song shifts to *Naked* by James Arthur. Another slow beat that enables me to turn inward as I close my eyes and allow all my pain and grief to press down on me.

I start to move, each step deliberate, each motion a desperate attempt to expel the anguish that's tearing me apart. The lyrics echo in the hollow ache of my chest, resonating with the raw, unfiltered pain of our failure tonight—of going another day without holding my daughter. Every beat of the song is another heartbeat I can't feel against mine, every note a reminder of the emptiness that consumes me.

My agony expands as the song bleeds into another, *Said So* by Alexander Stewart. I spin, the world blurring around me, even as the ache remains sharp and clear. I pour every ounce of sorrow into the dance, my body a conduit for the despair that words can't capture. My arms reach out as if trying to grasp the ghost of my daughter, finding nothing but air. As if running could bridge the unbearable distance between us, my legs carry me across the studio in frantic strides.

Tears stream down my face, hot and unrelenting, but I don't wipe them away. They're a testament to my pain, proof of the love I have for her, a love that's stronger than the torment but no less agonizing. I drop to my knees, the impact jarring but grounding. The floor is cool beneath my palms, a stark reminder of the reality I can't escape.

Empty by Letdown plays next, and all that pain, desperation, and anger swells. It crashes over me. My body trembles as I push myself up, the music guiding me through a fast-paced sequence of movements that cut through the air and slice through the plume of heartache.

With each song, the beat increases, and along with it, the speed at which I race across the floor, dipping and spinning until the world is a blur. Every movement is a plea, a prayer, a scream into the void.

My movements hit a crescendo with *Breath* by Breaking Benjamin. I'm drenched and gasping for breath as my feet slap against the hardwood floor. Every lift of my leg is a kick, my arms a sharp flick as I throw them out to my sides.

I dance for Aurora, for the moments I've missed, for the nights I've cried myself to sleep with her name on my lips. I dance for the fear that grips me every second she's gone, for the hope I can't let go of. My heart aches with every beat of the song, a painful rhythm that drives me to the edge of my endurance.

As the music fades into silence, I feel my body give out, the intensity of my emotions taking their toll. Strong arms catch me before I can hit the floor. Royce. I don't have to look to know it's him; his presence is as familiar to me as my own heartbeat.

He lifts me, cradling me against his chest, and for a

moment, I let myself fall into him, taking comfort in his strength.

The song changes, and *Confidence* by Steven Ryan begins to play. Royce doesn't say a word; just starts to move, guiding me in a slow, gentle dance. His hands are firm yet tender, one resting on the small of my back, the other holding mine. I let him lead, my body following his like we've done this a thousand times before.

As the music swells, Royce pulls me closer, his warmth seeping into my skin, grounding me. The lyrics speak of a man coaxing out a woman's confidence in the face of everything she has overcome, and that's exactly what it feels like Royce is doing. He's showing me that I can fall, I can bleed, but he'll always be here to help me up. He'll be at my side while I fight another round.

Sometimes you gotta bleed 'til the poison drains out.
You gotta believe when your heart's filled with doubt.
Let me see your confidence.

It's as though the song was written for us, for this moment.

His gaze meets mine, and I see the promise in his eyes: I've got you.

We move together, our steps in sync, and I let myself lean into him, letting go of some of the pain. His arms are a safe haven, his touch a balm for my raw wounds. I can feel the tension in my muscles slowly start to ease, the frantic rhythm of my heart calming as we sway to the music.

"Sometimes we have to let ourselves feel what we're feeling," Royce murmurs, his voice a steady anchor in the storm. "It does us no good to keep those feelings bottled inside. We have to let them out, let them consume us. Drown in the pain, baby. I'll be here to pull you back to the surface and hold you tight."

Tears gather in my eyes again, but this time they're different. They're tears of relief, of gratitude. I press my face into his shoulder, letting myself feel the safety he offers. With every step, every turn, he's there, holding me together, piece by piece.

His fingers trace soothing patterns on my back, and I cling to him, absorbing his strength. The music wraps around us, a cocoon of melody and emotion, and while my chest still aches and despair still clings to my skin, I no longer feel like I'm suffocating beneath the weight of it all.

However, with his heat seeping beneath my skin and the strength of his arms wrapped around me, I want to feel nothing but him... if only for a few moments.

With the melody of a song I don't recognize bleeding into the studio, I press onto my toes and seal my lips over Royce's, my body seeking solace in his embrace. His lips meet mine, and it's like a switch flips. All the pain, the anguish, the crushing despair—it all fades away. His kiss is a stopper on all those feelings, replacing them with heat, desire, warmth, and need. I melt into him, one hand on his shoulder to balance me while my other tangles with his hair.

The music swells, and for a moment, nothing else exists. It's just us, lost in each other, drowning out the world. His kiss is demanding and all-consuming. I let it take me over completely. I pour everything into it until all that's left is the fire between us.

Royce's hands roam over my back, pulling me tighter against him, and I can feel his heart pounding in sync with mine. We move together, and the dance of our lips and bodies becomes the only rhythm that matters. It's intoxicating, this escape we've found in each other, and I never want it to end.

"Riley," he rasps in a plea as he draws back.

"Royce." I drag his name out in vexation. Lifting my gaze to his, I say earnestly, "I need you."

He groans, face pinched in indecision. "You make it impossible to say no to you."

My lips lift in a coy smile as I wind my arms around his neck and press myself impossibly closer so I can whisper in his ear. "So don't. I want you." Hitching my leg over his hip, I drag my cunt over the obvious erection tenting his pants. "You want me. Let's lose ourselves in one another."

Ducking his head so his nose presses against my neck, he murmurs, "Leave the world behind."

"All of it," I agree, tilting my head to give him better access as he nips and sucks a path down my throat and across my collarbone. His hands slide to my hips as he traverses the valley between my breasts until he falls to his knees before me.

My chest heaves as he lifts his gaze, those ice-blue eyes smoldering as he stares up at me through thick eyelashes. "Are you wet for me, James?"

Lip trapped between my teeth and my gaze heavy, I nod, loving how his eyes flare with predatory pride.

"Show me."

The sheer desire in his eyes gives me the courage to slide my hand between the high slit in my dress and dip my fingers into my black lace panties. Pressing two fingers inside me, I coat them in my excitement before pulling them out to show him the shimmering wetness.

Smirking, he wraps his calloused fingers around my wrist, bringing my hand to his face as he dips my fingers inside his mouth. His lips wrap around the digits, his tongue lapping at the taste of me as he hums.

"Delicious," he declares with the smack of his lips. "However, it's not nearly enough. I want these gorgeous creamy thighs sticky with your mess before I bend you over and fuck you."

His filthy words have a fresh gush soaking my panties before he glides his hands up the outside of my thighs, hooking his fingers in my panties and dragging them down my legs until I can step out of them.

His touch is gentle, reverent, as he palms the back of my calf and lifts my leg over his shoulder. Pushing my dress aside, he brings his face to my pussy and inhales deeply. His chest vibrates with approval, sending me desperate with desire before he buries his face between my thighs.

My head falls back on a moan, my fingers tangling with his hair as I hold on while he licks and sucks through my folds and around my clit until nothing exists beyond his touch and the pleasure he's eliciting.

"Royce," I moan. "Yes. God, that feels so good."

My hips rock, and I grind against his face as his tongue does incredible things to me. He applies the perfect amount of pressure to my clit, wrenching my orgasm right to the edge before he pulls back, plunging his tongue into my channel and making me writhe.

"I need to come," I groan when I feel myself getting close for the third time before he eases up. I gasp when he delivers a sharp smack to my inner thigh before massaging the area, somehow only making me more desperate for him.

Lapping at my clit, he roughly shoves two fingers into my sopping channel. The music is nothing but background noise to my needy pants and the *squelch* of my desire as Royce forces me to come apart on his tongue in the middle of the dance studio.

The darkness casts our silhouettes in shadows as I fist his hair, and he squeezes my ass while rubbing that magical spot inside me and sucks on my clit until I *explode* with his name on my tongue.

My body is still trembling from the intensity of my release when his fingers slip from me. Covered in my release, he smears it over my inner thigh before licking it away.

Sliding his fingers back inside me, he scoops up more of my pleasure, doing the same to my other thigh. "Mmm," he hums. "I fucking love it when you're all messy like this."

Lowering my leg to the ground, he stands to his full height before me. "My filthy girl," he coos appreciatively before slamming his lips down on mine and forcing me to taste myself on him.

Strawberries and leather.

Complete intoxication.

"Put on your heels and go stand in front of the mirror for me, Babydoll."

I arch a brow at his bossy tone, which is more reminiscent of Grayson. Smirking, he swats me on the ass, and with a half-yelp half-giggle, I scurry to put on my shoes before standing in front of the mirror that runs the entire length of the studio.

My focus remains on his silhouette behind me. His stark blue eyes cut through the dimness, glowing in the yellow light cast by the streetlamp outside as his gaze rakes over me, taking in my flushed cheeks, the curve of my ass emphasized in the dress, and my toned calves in the heels I'm wearing.

His presence is a beacon in the night, pulling me in with its intensity.

Royce's dress shoes clack against the polished wood with a steady, deliberate rhythm as he crosses the dance studio floor toward me. Only then do I realize the music has cut off, leaving the room cloaked in a heavy, charged silence.

His gaze remains latched onto mine as he steps up behind me, the warmth of his body radiating through the thin fabric of my dress. Being the sole focus of his searing attention ignites a slow, simmering desire. The space between us is electric, humming with unspoken words and raw, shared emotions. His breath tickles the nape of my neck, sending shivers down my spine.

"Hands on the mirror, James. Rub that ass against my crotch."

Eyes on him, I slowly bend at the waist, pushing my hips back so my ass is firmly pressed against the bulge of his crotch as I place my hands against the cold mirror.

"So compliant for me," he purrs as he brushes a hand up my spine, forcing me into a deeper arch. "Does my dirty girl want to be fucked?"

I rock my hips along his length, wishing his pants weren't in the way. "Yes." There's no hiding the desire practically dripping from my tongue. "I need it. I need *you*."

One corner of his lips lifts in a smirk as he pushes my dress out of the way. A faint breeze dances across my bare ass cheeks as his fingers slide between my thighs. "You've got me, sweetheart."

He plunges three fingers into my wet heat, and I buck against him, groaning. "Always so ready for me," he appraises. "My needly little slut." I mewl. "You're going to take my cock like the filthy whore you are." I whimper at the loss of his fingers, my pussy clenching around nothing but air as the metallic teeth of his zipper slice through the air. "You're going to let me fill your wet little hole with my cum until it's dripping down your thighs," he rasps, his restraint fracturing as he presses his blunt head to my entrance. "Then you're going to let me eat it out of you, and when I kiss you, you're going to taste *us*."

Fuck, yes! I want all of that.

He slams into me in one mighty thrust that has me nearly smacking my head against the mirror. I stabilize myself in time for him to pull out before driving back in, somehow going deeper than he did before.

He fucks me hard. The entire time, his eyes remain on mine through the mirror. Through his stare, he tells me he loves me. He says how much he worships me while our bodies succumb to primal need, taking from one another with ruthless abandon until the telltale spindles of heat begin to sweep outward from my core.

My pussy flutters around his hard length, my legs trembling with the upcoming onslaught of my pleasure. Arms outstretched and toes curling around the cliff's edge, I'm ready to dive off it when Royce slows his relentless pace.

Hand fisting my hair, he wrenches my head back. My eyes snap open, connecting with his. "Look at yourself," he barks between pants, thrusting shallowly into me.

My gaze remains fixed on him, refusing to do what he says. To ruin this moment with the remnants of my devastation still staining my cheeks and darkening my eyes.

"Do it," he growls, forcing himself slower. "Do it if you want to come."

With a whimpered protest, I force my gaze forward. The harsh reality of my pain stares back at me, etched into the lines of my face. The vibrancy of my hazel eyes is gone, as though my irises have been leached of color these past weeks. The stains of tear tracks mark my face, my pale skin doing little to disguise the battle I've been fruitlessly fighting. Each tear shed, each sleepless night, they all leave their mark, a testament to the depth of my sorrow.

"You are beautiful," Royce murmurs, his voice low yet sure. "Don't shy away from your pain. Your heartache, your grief... They show how much you care. They tell me how deeply you love your daughter. How can that not be beautiful to look at?"

Leaning over me, he runs a finger over my flushed cheeks—

a sign of life in an otherwise desolate expanse. It forces me to look past the remnants of my devastation to the dilated pupils and shining eyes. The breaths fogging up the mirror with each shallow pant.

I see a mom desperate for the safe return of her daughter.

But more than that, I see a woman in the throes of passion.

A woman who is still fighting. Who hasn't completely given up.

"See the strength in your eyes, the resilience in your spirit," Royce continues. "You've been through so much, Ry, and yet you still stand tall."

With each shallow thrust and tender caress, Royce forces me to look at myself anew. To see myself not as broken, but as resilient. A survivor of love's most powerful trials.

Royce captures my gaze in the mirror before tilting his head to whisper in my ear, "Beauty lies not in perfection, but in the raw, unfiltered expression of our deepest emotions." Nipping my earlobe, his stare turns heated as he rasps, "Now, show me the most beautiful expression of all, and come for me."

Grasping my hips, he abandons all soft touches. Skin slaps against skin as he brings us barreling toward the release we both so desperately need, leaving me on unstable legs that won't hold me up as I sink to the floor.

The mirror is a cold relief against my heated skin as my head falls back against it, my eyelids closed as I catch my breath.

I swear I doze off for a second, and my head rolls to the side, eyelids cracking open at the press of hands spreading my legs.

"You didn't forget, did you?" Royce drawls with a teasing smirk and a hungry glint. "We're not done yet, baby."

Diving between my thighs, he laps at our combined release as it drips from my cunt like it's the forbidden fruit he can't get enough of.

He only lifts his head when his chin is damp, his lips shimmering in the low light with our pleasure as he brings them closer to mine. Flicking my tongue out, I taste us on his lips before they collide with my own, and he shoves his tongue into my mouth in a filthy, sloppy kiss that has nothing to do with piecing each other together and everything to do with the undeniable chemistry that will forever draw us to one another.

With a desire-ridden moan, I hook my legs around his waist. And his cock, invigorated with new life, easily finds its home.

Yeah, I'd readily hide from reality with this man any day.

RILEY

CHAPTER ELEVEN

"What is he doing?" I gasp from behind my hands, eyes wide with concern as I watch Logan tackle an opposing team member before taking off down the ice like it's melting beneath his skates. After getting reamed out by his coach for missing last week's game and now this... he'll be lucky not to get kicked from the team.

There are only fifteen minutes left of the game, and thank god, because Logan is out for blood tonight, and he doesn't seem to give a shit if it's his or someone else's. In fact, based on the number of fights he's started, I think he's *hoping* it'll be his blood spilled all over the ice before the final buzzer. The only reason he hasn't been benched is because the ref has missed most of his fouls. However, with the game nearly over, Logan is growing reckless.

What I can't understand is *why* he's behaving this way.

He had seemed fine when Royce and I finally dragged ourselves off the floor of the dance studio last night and crawled into Logan's bed. Logan left early this morning for a meeting with his coach, and since it was game day, I hadn't seen him all day.

Except the Logan on the ice right now is not the Logan who held me in his arms all night and whispered *I love you* before he slipped from the room this morning. He's a beast in a helmet and skates, barely paying attention to the puck, more focused on laying out anyone who dares go near him.

The question is, what happened?

Royce groans from beside me. "He's on the warpath."

He is. His hockey stick is a battle ax that he wields with deadly precision as he cuts his way across the rink, uncaring of who is in his way. Logan has a reputation for being ruthless on the ice, but this is on a whole other level. He's been sent to the sin bin multiple times, and I'm honestly shocked he hasn't been kicked from the game.

There's still time.

Even as I think it, Logan crashes into another player, sending him sprawling to the ice, and the whistle blows. The other guy gets up swinging. Logan fists the front of the guy's jersey, and then words are exchanged between them before Logan shoves at his chest, sending him backward so he can throw off his helmet and gloves.

"Oh shit," Grayson murmurs, leaning forward in his seat, elbows on his knees as tension radiates from him.

There's a moment where the entire stadium seems to stand still. The calm before the storm. Logan and the guy face off before Logan's lips quirk in a savage grin that promises violence and stalls the air in my lungs.

"For fuck's sake," Royce groans. However, I can't take my eyes away from the impending doom on the ice.

In the next second, the two of them are in the middle of a full-blown brawl. Fists fly as the ref's whistle blows, nothing but white noise amongst the hoots and cajoling of the riled crowd.

"Oh my god," I gasp from behind my hands.

"He's going to get himself suspended," Grayson sighs, shaking his head. Although, the tight press of his lips belies his concern for his friend.

The game is forgotten as players from both teams dive into the action—whether to pull the two fighters apart or to back them up, I'm not sure. It becomes chaos, and even standing on my seat, I can't spot Logan amongst the other black and gold jerseys.

"Where is he?" I ask in a panic.

Royce and Grayson are on their feet too. "I can't see him," Royce yells to be heard over the crowd. "Damn it, Logan," he growls, "What are you doing?"

Grayson is already moving down the aisle. Royce ushers me after him, and with a final look at the ice, I jump down from my seat. The crowd around us is just as wild as the fight on the ice, people yelling and shoving, caught up in the drama. We fight our way through the mass of bodies, each step a struggle against the tide of spectators craning their necks for a better view.

Grayson reaches back to grab my hand, tugging me until I fall into his back, while Royce shoves a man away when he moves to smack the plexiglass and nearly hits me instead. His beer spills over the rim of his cup, but we're moving before he can say anything.

Worry for Logan clogs my throat as the chaotic energy of the crowd makes everything feel even more out of control.

"This is insane," Grayson mutters when we finally reach the aisle. His eyes scan the ice, and I turn to follow, still unable to make out Logan amongst the other players. Refs are dragging apart players and sending them to their respective benches.

"Do you see him?" I ask frantically.

A tense moment before Royce points. "There!" My gaze bounces from player to player until I finally spot the familiar dirty blond hair of my husky. My breath catches as I watch him being escorted from the ice, his face a mask of fury and blood dripping from a cut above his eye.

"They're sending him off," Royce states, his voice tight with concern.

"Can we see him?" I ask, glancing between him and Grayson.

"We'll find out." Grayson's expression is a mask of determination as he grasps my hand again and marches us up the stairs and away from the ice.

Perhaps because of the fight or because there is still time on the clock, but there is no security in the hallway leading to the locker rooms.

Shoving the door open, the locker room is eerily quiet as we enter. With the team still on the ice, it is empty. "He's not here." I march over to his locker. His street clothes are still hanging up, so he hasn't left the stadium.

"Treatment room," Royce says, his words only increasing the churning in my stomach. They wouldn't have taken him there unless he needed to be seen by medical personnel, right?

Royce leads the way, probably knowing roughly where the treatment room is from his days on the football field. He pokes his head into several empty rooms before we find the right one. Inside, Logan sits on the examination table, a butterfly bandage applied to the cut above his eye. Ice packs rest on his knuckles, and his lip is split, a stark contrast to his usually composed demeanor.

"Logan," I breathe, relief flooding me at the sight of him, but it's mixed with a deep, gnawing worry.

Logan's head snaps up. His hair is damp with sweat sticking to his forehead, and his expression is a mix of exhaustion and frustration. His lips twist in an uncharacteristic frown. "I'm fine, Riley." Except his voice lacks any of its usual confidence, and he can't seem to look me in the eye. "Just a few cuts and bruises."

My lips purse. He never calls me Riley. It's always Shortcake, and I fucking *hate* hearing my name on his tongue.

I step closer, my eyes taking in the full extent of his injuries. His jersey and shoulder pads are tossed on a nearby chair, his bare chest revealing red splotches that will bruise. From the waist down, he's still clad in his hockey gear, skates discarded on the floor at the end of the bench.

My fingers itch to touch him, but I'm not sure if he wants me to. "Logan," I say his name softly and wait until he finally lifts his gaze to mine. "What happened out there?"

His face pinches, and he shakes his head. "Nothing."

Grayson scoffs behind me. "That wasn't nothing. You were on a rampage. You'll be lucky if you don't get suspended for the rest of the season."

Logan glowers at him over my shoulder until, unable to help myself, I touch his arm. His eyes snap back to mine, immediately softening. What looks like regret flashes across his chestnut hues.

"Tell me what happened," I plead. "Please."

Logan looks away, the muscles in his jaw working as he struggles to find the words. Royce steps forward, placing a hand on his shoulder. "We're all under a lot of stress, man. Whatever you're feeling, you know you can tell us."

Taking a deep breath, Logan's eyes meet mine. Whatever walls he'd erected when we walked in, crumble, leaving so much pain and unspoken turmoil in their wake.

"I'm sorry, Shortcake." Pulling me into him, I wrap my arms around his waist and breathe out a sigh of relief into his warm chest. *This* is my Logan. Folding over me, he presses a kiss to the top of my head. "Just... Last night. Letting you down again. Being back at square one..." He sighs, and it's such a defeated sound that I can't help but squeeze him tighter. "I'm sorry."

Face pressed against his chest, I shake my head. "You have nothing to be sorry for, Logan." Lifting my head back to see his face, I say, "You're always taking care of me, putting my needs first. You need a way to let out your frustration."

Brushing his thumb down my cheek, genuine regret is carved into his features as he murmurs, "I didn't mean to make you worry."

"I know."

"Maybe next time, though, you could find a way to let out your frustration that doesn't incite a riot and get you kicked from the game," Royce drawls.

Ignoring him, Logan gives me a cheeky grin, and my last bit of concern fades. With a wink, he lifts his face to look at Royce. "Guess I could beat on your pretty face instead."

Royce snorts. "If you think I won't hit you back just because you're gonna be a pro hockey player someday, you've got another thing coming."

"I might have an alternative to beating each other up..." When Logan's teasing brown eyes slide to mine, I press up on my toes and bring my lips to his. Stunned, his lips are unmoving against mine. However, it lasts all of a second before he relents, groaning as he kisses me back with fierce possession.

My lips part, the taste of copper sliding over my tongue and adding a primal edge to our heated kiss. There's the sound of his ice pack hitting the examination table before his hand slides into my hair, holding me still as he devours my mouth.

"Seriously?" I hear Grayson grumble from somewhere nearby, but I don't pay him any heed. Logan needs this.

We all do.

Climbing onto the table, my crotch slides over his as my knees fall on either side of the thick pads encasing his legs. The fact that Logan only hauls me closer shows just how badly he needs this release.

He's been setting his feelings aside to accommodate mine. To take care of me. To ensure *I'm* okay. But I want to take care of him, too. I don't want him to bottle things up until they explode out of him like they did tonight.

Just like how Royce knew I needed to dance last night.

I know Logan needs to lose himself in me.

And I want to lose myself in him too.

I've missed him. He's been at my side every time I've needed him, and we cuddle in bed every night, but he hasn't initiated anything sexual since that night.

"Fuck, I missed you," he rasps, verbalizing my internal thoughts.

"I'm right here," I assure him, stroking a hand through his hair. "I'm not going anywhere."

With an approving growl, he attacks my lips again. His hand slides down my spine before slipping beneath my top, and the press of his bare skin against mine is heaven. My hips rock against his in search of friction against the need stirring low in my belly.

"You can't be fucking serious?" Grayson snaps. "You can't do this here."

Wrenching his lips from mine, Logan glowers at Grayson over my shoulder. His hands continue to knead my skin as he steadily climbs his way up my ribs, bringing my top with him. "Since that's your stance, you can stand by the door and make sure no one comes in." Dropping his gaze to mine, he purrs, "You want to do this here, Shortcake?"

In case the grind of my pussy over his hard cock isn't enough of an answer, I rasp, "Yes."

He smirks, his eyes already dilated with desire as he pulls my top over my head. Before the chill of the room can hit me, I feel a warm presence at my back. Looking over my shoulder, my gaze connects with ice-blue eyes before sliding to Grayson's taut posture.

"Don't worry about him," Royce murmurs. "He's got a stick up his ass."

Grayson snarls his contempt, even as his hungry gaze is locked on me, cataloging every movement. Taking in every inch of exposed skin that Logan is making his mission to mark with his lips.

"He still doesn't understand what it means to *share*," Logan interjects before nipping at my throat. "But we can show him how you like to be shared, can't we, Shortcake."

"Mmhmm." Words are impossible with his lips leaving trails of flames all over my skin and Royce's rough hands like napalm as they skate along my spine while my eyes remain locked on Grayson's.

Despite his protests, without looking away, he flicks the lock on the door, the *click* resonating like the starting bell before a fight throughout the room—the starter gun giving us the go-ahead.

He steps forward before Logan's "Nu-uh" stops him in place. "You, with all your growled *mines*, you're going to stand there and watch us make *our* girl feel good." Logan turns me on his lap so I'm facing the other way, my back to his chest and Royce in front of me. Bending to kiss my neck, he says loud enough for Grayson to hear on the far side of the small room, "That is if our girl is okay with you watching." A kiss to the sensitive spot beneath my ear has me arching my spine. "What do you think, Shortcake? Should we kick the asshole out?"

Tilting my head to give Logan better access, I cast my heavy gaze over Grayson. His posture is rigid, his fingers digging into his palms at his side as he stares at the spot where Logan lavishes my skin.

"I vote for kicking him out," Royce deadpans. "He hasn't earned a spot in *this* yet."

While I agree, I do like the thought of torturing Grayson and giving him a taste of his own medicine.

"He can stay," I state authoritatively. "But he can only watch," I smirk. "And he can't come."

Logan barks out a laugh while Royce grins. Grayson glowers, even as his gaze smolders with need.

"Shortcake has spoken. No touching your dick, Gray, and don't think we're going to make this easy on you." As if to prove his point, Logan unclasps my bra, letting the straps fall down my arms until Royce pulls it away, dropping it on the floor nearby.

Logan palms my tits, kneading and squeezing while I writhe in his lap. My breaths become pants as he nips and tugs on my nipples, forcing them into stiff peaks.

"Fuck, I love your tits," he rasps in my ear. "You want Royce to suck on them, baby?"

"Yes." Eyes at half-mast, I lick my lips as Royce ducks, bringing a nipple to his lips and sucking it into his mouth. I moan as the sensation sends sparks straight to my core, and I shift on Logan's lap, desperate for friction.

"That's it, Shortcake, grind on me," he growls. His hand wraps around my jaw, fingers digging into my cheeks as he wrenches my head to the side, his lips capturing mine in an intoxicating kiss. He licks and bites at my mouth while Royce sucks on my tits, and I make a mess of my panties.

"More, please," I practically beg when they've descended me into a ball of aching need.

"Well, since you asked so nicely," Logan teases, already popping the button off my jeans. Royce releases my nipple with a pop as he moves to help me out of my jeans and panties.

"Bring your knees up, Shortcake. Show them that sweet pussy of yours."

Leaning back on Logan, I plant my feet on the examination table and spread my legs.

"Fuck," Grayson hisses, his hand swiping across his mouth as he stares unblinking at my pussy.

Logan's chest vibrates with a chuckle, and he murmurs in my ear. "I bet he's regretting all those times he chose to be an asshole right about now."

Bringing his fingers to my slit, he dips two inside me, pumping before pulling out and spreading my juices over my clit. Royce licks his lips, watching the erotic act. Noticing, Logan comments, "Royce looks like he's starving. You gonna let him feast on you, baby?"

He already *feasted* on me last night, but Logan is right. Royce looks like he'll fall to his knees at my say so.

"We need your words, Ry," Logan encourages when I merely nod.

"Yes," I say almost desperately. "I want you to eat me out, Royce."

With a groan, Royce's knees hit the floor with a soft thud before he buries his face between my thighs. The feel of his tongue on my heated core rips a moan from my throat, and my head falls to rest against Logan's chest as sensation after sensation is coaxed from my body until I'm a trembling mess in Logan's arms.

"Look at Grayson," Logan murmurs. I flick my eyes open, not remembering when I closed them, to find Grayson staring hungrily at where Royce is lapping at my folds. "See how badly he wants you?" Logan continues in a quiet voice. Not that I think Grayson is aware of anything else in the room right now. "How he's struggling to hold himself back?" Dropping my gaze over his body, I see how his feet are planted hip-width apart, his hands tight fists at his sides, even as his body leans forward, straining to get as close as possible without disobeying the rules laid out for him. "His brain might struggle with the concept of sharing you, but his body has no such reservations. He's as obsessed with you as we are."

As if he heard those words, Grayson's gaze snaps to mine, the dark depths of his eyes holding me hostage as an orgasm barrels through me, pressing beneath my skin and tearing me open until I'm screaming.

The aftershocks are still wracking my body, and my head is in the clouds, when I feel pressure at my entrance before Logan slides in with zero resistance.

"Fuck, you feel so good," he hisses, teeth gritted, as he pulls me down on top of him. Fingers firm on my hips, he lifts me before dragging me back down. Our breaths are nothing but pants as I move, getting my legs beneath me so I can fuck him. "You wanna ride me?"

"Yes," I say, looking back at him over my shoulder. "I want to make you feel good, too."

Logan's face is smoothed out in pleasure, displaying his sincere and loving smile. "I always feel good when I'm inside you, Shortcake, but if you want to fuck me, I'm not about to say no." Leaning back on his hands, he smirks. "I'm more than happy to watch that tight ass of yours bounce on my cock."

Grinning, I place my hands on his knees and ride him reverse cowgirl. "Fuck, that feels insane," Logan grinds, his hand stroking up and down my spine. The sound of a zipper renders through the air, and I lift my head to find Royce fisting his cock as he watches me ride his best friend.

"Hottest fucking thing I've seen," he agrees.

"Hotter than when she sucked your cock in front of us?" Logan teases, his voice strained.

"Yes," Grayson all but growls his input to the conversation from his position by the door.

Royce swipes his thumb over the bead of precum gathering at his tip, smearing it. His piercing glints in the light, and my pussy clenches, remembering how it felt scraping against my inner walls last night.

"Fuck, our girl needs more," Logan strains. "You want Royce too, Shortcake?"

I mewl my agreement, my nerve endings on fire from all the stimulation and how close I am to coming again.

"Royce, come here, take our girl," Logan dictates. He slides me off his cock, and I whimper at the loss of him.

"Shh, Shortcake. We're going to take care of you." He presses a quick kiss to my sweaty temple before passing me over to Royce. "Royce is going to impale you on that metal glittering dick of his," he says, fisting his engorged cock.

"I don't have a metal dick, fuckwit," Royce snarls, all while steadying me on my feet and pressing between my shoulder blades. My hands tighten around the edge of the examination table, and I lower my face to Logan's hard cock, standing sentinel like a red flag waving in the wind.

Pulling me back by my hips, he sinks effortlessly into me as I swipe my tongue out to taste myself on Logan's blunt head before lowering my mouth over his length.

The room fills with the sound of the three of us. Heavy pants, soft moans, and the slap of skin against skin. It's sexy. Heady. Intoxicating. And in no time at all, tingles erupt along my spine, heat expanding outward from my core.

"Fuck she's close," Royce grunts, picking up his pace as Logan buries himself deeper in my throat.

On the precipice, my orgasm dangles just out of reach for endless seconds until I feel an unfamiliar pressure at my backside.

"Has anyone ever fucked you here?" Royce asks in a low, desire-dripped tone.

I shake my head, mumbling a no around Logan's thick cock.

The pressure increases as Royce pushes the tip of his finger inside, but the pain has nothing on the pleasure wracking my body. The sting only heightens the sensation.

"Good," he purrs. "This hole is ours. One day, we're going to fill all of your holes. Have you so full that you'll feel like you're going to burst from your skin. We're going to fill you with our cum—all *three* of us."

As if he knew that was what I needed, my release rushes to the surface at the image of all *three* of them taking me at once. With another couple of pumps, Royce explodes in my cunt, and Logan grunts as he spills down my throat.

My legs give out, and Logan bundles me into his arms before I can collapse. Eyes narrowed, my hazy gaze lands on Grayson. More specifically, the blatantly obvious hard-on stretching the fabric of his jeans, before I slowly drag them up to his face.

The extent of the hunger, the possession burning in those dark depths, should terrify me.

It *should*.

But it doesn't.

It makes me excited for when I can have them *all*.

LYDIA

CHAPTER TWELVE

Dabbing at my lips with my cloth napkin, I glance at my husband seated at the far end of the table as I determine how to breach the subject in a way that will ensure I get what I want.

Something I'm accustomed to achieving... except when it comes to my obstinate husband. Of course, he gave me everything I expected when I married him—money, the lifestyle I wanted, lavish gifts. Our marriage was one of contractual obligation: He gave me the opulent life I'd always strived for, and in turn, I'm the pretty accessory on his arm and in his bed every night.

The problem is, as time went on, I wanted more.

I wanted *him*.

Yet, all he ever wanted was *her*.

I analyze him for another moment as I delicately slide my knife through the filet of poached salmon and place it in my mouth before setting my cutlery on my plate and lifting my chin, pinning him with my gaze.

"Bertram, we *are* going on this trip," I state assertively, disregarding his previous objections. My voice echoes in the large dining room, vibrating off the walls before reaching him. He lifts his gaze, chewing on his bite of steak. "The matter is not open for debate; it has been decided. People will be expecting us to take this time to reconnect. It will seem strange if we don't take time for ourselves." I pause, tapping my perfectly manicured nails on the table for emphasis. "I've arranged everything already. The pilot is on standby and ready to leave tonight."

My declaration is met with the scrape of his knife against the plate as he cuts another chunk of meat before soaking it in red wine au' jus and putting it in his mouth. The silence that follows is thick and oppressive, charged with the unspoken battle of wills that hangs in the air between us—two predators circling one another, each waiting for the other to show a moment of weakness—as he chews deliberately on his bite of steak as if savoring it more than he ever savored any moment with me.

He sets his fork down with meticulous care before finally deigning to respond.

"Lydia." His tone is measured and icy, as it often is with me. "I appreciate your enthusiasm, but I'm afraid your decision lacks the necessary consultation." His eyes meet mine, unflinching and cold. "A trip sounds charming, truly, but I have more pressing matters to attend to here. Matters that require my undivided attention and are, quite frankly, far more important than the gossip mill of bored housewives."

Irritation surges through me as he leans back in his chair, a faint, infuriating smile playing at the corners of his mouth. "Besides, you know my focus is on reconnecting with our family and re-familiarizing myself with my business." His stare is hard. "Your arrangements are noted, but they do not dictate my actions."

He pauses, letting the silence stretch, clearly enjoying the tension, the challenge in my eyes. "You can dismiss the pilot.

That plane won't be going anywhere tonight. Nevertheless, do feel free to go alone. It's not like your presence will be greatly missed."

I watch, seething internally as he dabs at the corners of his mouth with his napkin before dropping it onto his plate and rising. His oxfords squeak as he crosses the floor, pausing when he reaches my side. He stares down at me, a smugness twitching at the corners of his lips. "Perhaps you should invite Riley over to keep me company while you're away. We can catch up, father to daughter. You know how much I have *always* preferred her company to yours."

I see green.

He goes to move past me and I dart out of my chair, putting myself in his face. "You can't talk to me that way! How dare you bring her into this—say her name in my presence."

Bored. *That's* his expression while I scream in his face.

"*I* am your wife!"

Finally, I get a reaction from him. "Yes," he drawls. "You are." His lips are pursed in disappointment before he leans in and lowers his voice. "I wouldn't be getting too comfortable in that role, if I were you."

With that, he walks out, leaving me gaping at his back.

"Well, did you invite her?" Bertram snaps at me at dinner the following evening.

"Invite who?" I enquire, keeping my eyes fixed on the plate as I delicately slide my seared scallop through the cauliflower purée and beetroot reduction. I'm still mad at him for his callous remarks last night and his not apologizing.

"Riley."

My fingers tighten around the fork at the sound of *her* name in his mouth, and my appetite flees. I glare at the tabletop, and it takes everything in me to sound unaffected when I ask, "And what, exactly, am I supposed to have invited her to?"

He sighs, his frustration audible all the way on my end of the table. "We discussed this yesterday," he grits out.

Making my own exasperation known, I lift my head to look at him. "We discussed a lot of things yesterday." I wait, letting my words hang in the air. One minute. Two. By the time *five* minutes have passed, I'm squirming uncomfortably beneath his piercing stare. Eventually, I'm forced to admit defeat. "I'm delaying our trip," I say primly. It's not as though I had any other choice. Yes, I *need* to get away, but I refuse to lose my husband to *her*—again. I'd planned for both of us to leave the country once he was released from prison, but *she* is ruining all my carefully laid plans.

He hardly mentioned my slut of a daughter while he was in prison. Beyond the first couple of months of his sentence, any time I visited or we talked on the phone, her name was never brought up in conversation.

I'd assumed he'd moved on. That, with her out of the house, he'd be mine, but this obsession he has with reconnecting as a family is foiling all of my carefully laid plans.

It reaffirms my decision to remove Aurora from the chessboard. My so-called daughter is enough to contend with, but at least she can be controlled. However, with every day that passes, that control weakens. Riley, the perfect little bitch that she is, has been hounding me religiously, demanding to speak to and see her kid. Seriously, that girl needs to get a life. It's pathetic how involved she tries to be in that kid's life. Regardless, there is only so long I can delay the inevitable. I'd expected to be sipping champagne on a beach in Montenegro by the time she realized her snot-nosed kid was gone.

Except Bertram is making that far more challenging than I'd

anticipated. With the company in Grayson's hands and his ruined reputation amongst all his old friends and acquaintances, I'd assumed it would be easy to convince him to leave.

Obviously, I underestimated him.

He leans back in his chair, swirling his whiskey glass between his fingers as he holds my gaze. "So?" he retorts with a cool indifference that infuriates me. How dare he speak to me that way! I've stood by his side all these years, supporting him.

Despite trying to school my expression, he must catch a flash of my irritation as he smirks openly. "Invite her to dinner on Saturday."

"Will you be inviting Grayson to this little family soiree?" I snipe.

Tutting, Bertram shakes his head. "You'd think you'd *want* to spend time with your daughter, Lydia."

Lifting my napkin from my lap, I set it on the table and push back my chair as I rise before walking the length of the long dining room table that could easily seat a dozen people. My heels clack against the hard floor, and I add an extra sway to my hips, knowing I look absolutely killer in my low-cut, short-hemmed burgundy dress, with my makeup done perfectly and hair styled.

His eyes rake over me as I approach before returning to my face. When I'm close enough, I reach out and run a manicured finger along his shoulder before moving to stand behind him and gliding my hand over his chest. Leaning in, I bring my lips to his ear. "She's really not someone worth wasting your time over. Not when you have me, and I'm happy to play out whatever fantasy you wish. She's vanilla. Boring. Not worthy of a man with your... appetite." My hand sinks lower, over the defined ridges of his abdomen. Prison has kept him taut and lean, exactly as he was the day I met him. The only difference now in his appearance is the gray dusting along his temples, but I find it makes him appear more distinguished. Refined. *Sexier*. "Why obsess over *her* when you could be fucking me?"

I sink my teeth into his earlobe as I palm his growing erection through his slacks.

Chuckling darkly, he grabs the wrist of the hand resting on his shoulder and tugs me forward until I fall into his lap.

"You want to play out my fantasies, *wife*?" Pushing his empty plate away, he shoves me down onto the table. With one hand squeezing the back of my neck, he keeps my face pressed into the hard surface as he hikes up my dress and drags my lace panties down my thighs. Bending down, he growls in my ear, "Then be a good girl for Daddy and spread your legs."

I do, soaking up his harsh breaths. His eyes roam over my ass as he unzips himself and strokes his hard length.

"Please, Daddy," I plead. He groans in pure pleasure before slotting his blunt head at my entrance and driving in.

I moan, his groan mixing with mine as he fills me up. For a moment, he doesn't move, relishing our joining. "Did you miss me?" he rasps. "Did you miss your daddy?"

"Yes."

"Fuck," he hisses, his fingernails digging bruisingly into my hips. "Daddy missed you too." One hand strokes along the strands of my hair and down my back with a reverence I've never felt from him, right before he pulls out and slams back in.

The room is silent except for the sounds of our fucking. The slap of skin against skin mingled with our heavy breaths and low moans. "Show Daddy how much you missed him," he growls, pulling my ass back as he plows deeper. "Come all over my cock like a good little girl." With one final slam of his hips against mine, he buries himself deep inside me and groans out his release.

Still breathing heavily, he leans down to whisper in my ear. "You're right. As long as I don't have to look at your face, I can do a pretty decent job of pretending you're your daughter... At least, until I get a taste of the real thing again."

I bristle but bite back the words *over my dead body*. He's *mine*, and I won't let that little harlot steal him away from me this time. I listen as he tucks himself away, pulling up his zipper before he steps around the table. "Invite Riley to dinner," he dictates like he wasn't just dick-deep in my pussy two seconds ago. "And don't play dumb with me this time. If you fail at that simple task, I'll have to question whether I have any use for you at all."

Scoffing, I push myself upright and yank down my dress. I don't bother to pick up my discarded panties on the floor. Let the housekeeper deal with them. "Please, Bertram, we both know you *need* me to maintain your perfect image, to help curry favor with your used-to-be associates, and help weasel your way back into your own company. Despite your attempts to squash them, the whispers remain. *I'm* the only way to keep them at bay. You couldn't possibly have done what was rumored if you're still with the mother, right?" I taunt.

With his cum sticking to my thighs, I stalk toward him in my heels. When I'm directly in front of him, I slide a hand over his chest and peer into his dark, agitated eyes. "With time, they'll eventually move on. And you will, too. You'll realize the appeal she once held has gone, but I'll still be here." Pushing up onto my toes, I whisper into his ear, "I'll *always* be here," before stepping past him and walking away.

***

I recline on the chaise lounge, the sun lamps overhead casting a warm, golden glow over my flawless skin as I sip on a chilled glass of Chardonnay. The pool, heated to a perfect temperature, steams slightly in the crisp February air, creating an oasis of warmth in the meticulously manicured estate Bertram secured upon his release. The glass walls of the solarium enclose me, shielding me from the biting cold outside while letting in the winter sunlight.

It's quite an upgrade from the crapbox I was relegated to during the years of his incarceration. It's as if *I* was being punished too. It's not like *I* embezzled money. Not that the government cared about *my* welfare when they froze all of Bertram's accounts. Neither did his little shit of a son when he kicked me out of *Bertram's* house. Even after I stood by his father, providing the excuses necessary to ensure no further resources were spent determining the legitimacy of my daughter's so-called claims.

What little money Bertram could give me these last few years wasn't anywhere near enough to maintain the lifestyle I had become accustomed to before his arrest. Forcing me to make sacrifices I truly detest...

Regardless of what was, I finally have my life back now.

I refuse to lose it for a second time.

Glancing at my reflection in the water, I admire how my designer sunglasses perfectly frame my face. Everything here is pristine. I am once more the queen of my own domain with servants to order around and attend to my every whim.

I reach for my phone, my perfectly manicured nails tapping against the screen. It's time to make the call I've been putting off. As the phone rings, I idly swirl my wine, watching the liquid catch the light. Finally, she picks up.

"Riley," I say, my voice dripping with the false sweetness I've perfected over the years. "It's your mother. I'm calling to invite you to dinner."

"You and I have never once had a family meal together. Why the sudden fixation?" her tone is as flat and lifeless as ever. The fact she can't just agree so this interaction can be done with grates on my nerves.

"Aurora will be spending the night at a friend's, but I'll set up a video call for you on Sunday morning," I negotiate instead of answering her question, scanning my eyes over the nail job I had done today.

"Aurora is *three*; she doesn't have friends," Riley snaps. This newfound defiance of hers is really starting to irritate me. "And I know for a fact that she's not living with you. You'd never allow her to interfere in rekindling your marriage," she snarls in clear disgust. "So why don't you tell me what the hell is going on?"

I suck on my teeth as I debate my next words. "Come to dinner, and I'll tell you everything. Tonight. Seven o'clock. Don't be late." I hang up before she can respond, tossing the phone onto the lounge beside me.

Seriously, her voice is as grating as nails on a chalkboard. Popping two Advil, I down them with a glass of chardonnay as I mentally berate myself for not aborting her in the womb.

Biggest. Mistake. Of. My. Life.

Sighing, I lean back on my deck chair beside the pool and stare at the sky as I debate what to do. My infuriating thorn of a daughter isn't going to give up on her kid, and my husband, insistent on recreating the past, refuses to leave this god-awful country and start anew.

There is one common denominator between my two problems...

And with each sip of my wine, I become more and more certain that she needs to be gone from my life—permanently.

RILEY

CHAPTER THIRTEEN

"There's not a snowball's chance in hell that you're going to that dinner," Logan snarls like a rabid dog as he paces back and forth in front of the kitchen island. Grayson throws his hands up. "Finally, someone who's on the same page as me," Grayson rejoices, lifting his closed fist to Logan as he passes.

I roll my eyes as they bump knuckles. Ignoring them both, I shift all of my attention to Royce. At least he's still capable of thinking rationally. Planting my hands on my hips, I huff out a sigh. It's not that I want to go. It's the last place on earth I want to be. However... "She said if I came to dinner, she'd tell me everything."

The three of us are spread out in the kitchen, looking as exhausted and beaten as the next. To say it's been a long week and a half is an understatement. It's been *awful*. Words can't even describe what it's been like, existing without the knowledge that my daughter is safe, fed, and sleeping somewhere comfortable.

Fuck, not even knowing whether she's still breathing. If there is life left in her eyes.

My flimsy walls shake and begin to crumble before I wrench my thoughts in a different direction.

I can't think like that.

I can't allow myself to fall into that hopelessness.

It won't do me any good, and it won't help Aurora.

I need to be strong—for both of us.

Grayson scoffs, glaring at me with a questioning raise of his eyebrow. "You don't seriously believe her, do you?"

"Of course not," I snap. "But maybe if I play it right, she'll slip up. Give me a piece of information we can use." I shake my head, shoulders dropping. "I don't know, but if she knows anything, then I have to try." There have been no new developments since the false lead, and the burner phone Logan and Royce found was a dead end. Blue couldn't triangulate a location from the message left on it. Meaning, we've got nothing. "It's been eleven days, and we are no closer to finding her." My voice cracks over the words, and Logan is by my side instantly, pulling me into his strong frame.

Royce clears his throat, drawing my attention to where he's standing on the opposite side of the kitchen. He's leaning against the countertop, his bulky arms folded over his chest. Where Grayson and Logan immediately started in with their protests and straight-out objections to Lydia's dinner 'invitation', he's been silently contemplating.

"Say you go to this dinner..."

"She's not," Logan and Grayson immediately interject at the same time.

Royce huffs out a breath, piercing them both with a *shut the fuck up* glare while I roll my eyes and give Logan's arm around me a reassuring squeeze.

"*Hypothetically*," Royce tries again.

"Notice I've conveniently been left out of this invitation," Grayson points out after a moment.

"All the more reason why she's not going," Logan hisses, practically vibrating with anger despite me stroking my fingers over his arm in a bid to soothe his ruffled feathers. "It's a ploy to get her alone."

"Well, obviously, we wouldn't let her go on her own," Royce states, circling back to his train of thought.

"No," Grayson agrees with a sharp nod of his head. "*Hypothetically*, I'd go with her. That makes the most sense. I can say we ran into each other on campus, and Riley mentioned the dinner, assuming I'd been invited too. She asked for a ride since she doesn't have a car. It would be completely reasonable." Pinning me in place with his eyes, Grayson, for whatever reason, feels the need to emphasize, "I'd be coming with you."

Did he genuinely think I'd contest him being there? I'd assumed one of them would be, and Grayson is the obvious choice. Besides, I'd rather walk over hot coals than enter their house alone. Dinner at a public restaurant was one thing. Sitting across from *him* at that table drove me to the brink of what I could handle. A private meal—or ambush, or whatever the hell this actually is—is in another realm altogether. I'll do whatever it takes to find my daughter, but putting myself in a position of danger would just be reckless and stupid—which is exactly what going to their house alone would be: Dangerous.

"Actually," Royce hedges, "I was thinking one of us should go." His finger flicks back and forth between him and Logan. At the looks of shock his statement incites, he flashes me an apologetic look before he explains, "We all know Lydia isn't going to give up shit. She's extended this invite on Bertram's orders."

"Fuck, of course!" Grayson whirls, his expression haunted as his hand pulls on the ends of his hair until they stand upright.

"If they expect anyone to show up," Royce continues with a carefully blank expression, "It'll be Grayson, but they won't be expecting either of us. They won't be expecting *a boyfriend*. It could throw enough of a spanner into whatever fucked up plan Bertram is concocting." He lifts his shoulder in a casual gesture. "And while we're there, it can do no harm to push Lydia." His tone is unconvincing as he says, "Who knows, maybe she'll say something—give us a clue."

He doesn't believe she will. Hell, I don't believe she will, but all I hear is her promising to tell me where my daughter is if I do come, and despite knowing it will entail sitting across the table from *him* again, I *have* to go. For the slight chance my mother might actually do the decent thing. For the sliver of hope that she'll slip up. Because I'll do anything and everything it takes to get my daughter back—including believing in the impossible.

"It's the perfect way to make them realize Riley isn't as *alone* as they think she is," Logan muses. "That she's got support. Someone who would care if something were to happen."

Royce nods. "Exactly. I doubt it will be enough to make Bertram set aside whatever notions he has, but it would give us some breathing space where we don't have to worry about him on top of finding Aurora."

"It's not a terrible idea," Grayson admits, tapping his fingers against the island marble as he mulls it over.

"It'll certainly piss off Bertram," Logan states, his bubbling anger giving way to a mischievous smirk as he more than likely pictures Bertram's face when he opens the door to find a *boyfriend's* arm slung over my shoulder.

"You can't go," I point out, arching a brow at Royce. "Lydia knows who you are."

"I mean, that would be pretty fucking hilarious." Logan chuckles. "I'd love to see that bitch's face if you showed up tucked beneath Royce's arm."

"I had considered that myself," Royce states. The slight uptilt of his lips is the only hint of his amusement. "It could put the pressure on Lydia that we need. Cause her to panic." He wipes a hand over the scruff of his beard, thinking. "However, this dinner is about your dad." He gestures to Grayson. "He's deliberately creating scenarios that put him and Riley together, which will only escalate the longer he doesn't get what he wants." I full body shiver, and it doesn't go unnoticed by Logan whose firm palms rub up and down my arms. Royce pierces Grayson and Logan with his steely gaze. "We need to make it clear to him that it's not going to be as easy as he thinks to get to Riley."

"Okay, and how do we do that?" I ask, not quite catching his drift.

He lifts his chin to Logan. "You take Logan as your boyfriend. Act all lovey-dovey. Show them that you're in love."

"And I *inadvertently* make it clear to Bertram that Riley is *mine*," Logan smirks.

"Ours," Grayson immediately interjects, earning a side glower from me. *Yeah, I'm not touching that.* I should probably just be grateful he has upgraded from *mine*, although I'm not entirely sure how I feel about being all of theirs. Of including Grayson in *ours*. However, Grayson's insistence on our non-existent relationship is truly the least of my problems.

"We show Bertram that there are obstacles in his way he hadn't anticipated. That it won't be as simple as him manipulating Lydia or whatever the hell he's doing with her to get to Riley," Royce spells out.

"I dunno," Grayson sighs, scraping a hand up the back of his head. "That still means Riley is going into my father's house. I don't like it."

"You don't have to like it," I state, pinning him with a look before swiveling my focus to Royce. "I'll do it. It's time I confronted Lydia—that she knows *I know*. Besides, I'm on board with anything that puts roadblocks between me and

Bertram." Grayson snarls in disgust, but I ignore him as I twist my head to look at Logan. "Assuming you're okay coming with me?"

"Shortcake, there's nowhere else I'd rather be." Logan kisses the tip of my nose, squeezing his arms tighter around my waist. He grins down at me. "Is it fucked up that I'm kinda looking forward to it?"

My lips quirk in amusement, Logan's teasing smoothing out the jagged edges of my anxiety at this possibly insane plan. "No," I assure. At the same time, Grayson hisses, "Yes."

"You're there to protect her," he snarls, glaring at Logan like he's lost his mind. "Not to get your rocks off at pissing off my dad."

Logan rolls his eyes at him. "Yeah, I'm aware." He grins savagely, every bit the husky he plays on the ice. The split lip and bruise forming around his eye only add a dangerous edge to his demeanor. "Doesn't mean I can't have some fun while I'm at it."

The guys bicker back and forth for a bit longer before Royce and Logan leave the kitchen, and the conversation moves on to other things.

"Riley," Grayson calls when I move to follow after them. Stopping, I turn to face him. He's standing in the same spot he has been all morning, hands shoved in the pockets of his slacks and stern, angry gaze on mine.

"Grayson," I respond in the same tone when he doesn't speak.

His face is pulled tight as he stares at me, and I can see the thoughts churning behind his eyes.

"I don't like this."

"You've already said that." Standing to my full height, I cross my arms over my chest and lift my chin.

His gaze drops over me, noticing my defensive stance as his

nostrils flare. All of a sudden, he's striding toward me, eating up the space between us with his long legs until I'm forced to either back away or hold my ground. Refusing to be cowered by the likes of Grayson, I plant my feet and glare into his face as he towers over me.

Locked in a silent stand-off, the anger and frustration roll off of him in waves. "I hate the idea of you and him being in the same room," he finally spits out between gritted teeth.

Acting as unaffected as I can when I'm this close to a seething Grayson, I keep my voice bland as I retort, "I don't exactly love it either."

"The possibility that he could touch you..." He continues as though he doesn't hear me.

"Touch what's yours, you mean?" My retort has more attitude than the situation warrants, but fuck it. I'm strung out and exhausted, and perhaps I need to vent some of this nervous energy that's constantly buzzing through me. Who better to unleash this bubbling mess of emotions onto than Grayson? After everything he's put me through... the bullshit he *still* continues to pull...

The vein in his jaw pulses as he whips out a hand, wrapping his long fingers around my throat and dragging me against his hard body as he lowers his face to mine until our breaths tangle in the minuscule amount of space between our lips.

"You *are* mine," he snarls, practically vibrating with anger. "Whether you want to acknowledge it or not. You. Are. Mine, Riley." His fingers flex around my throat, reflecting the inner turmoil threatening to tear him apart as his eyes bore into mine, slicing through muscle until he's staring right into my soul. "I won't let him destroy someone else I care about. Won't let him *kill* another woman I love."

My lips part in a silent O, my brain struggling to make sense of what he just said as I stare into his eyes, searching for what,

I'm not even sure. Confirmation that he speaks the truth? Something that will dispute his feelings?

The problem is Grayson is so accustomed to being on guard that I can't get a read on anything beyond the resounding resentment that has been flooding his system since Aurora went missing and his dad was released.

Pressing my hand flat against his abdomen, I apply pressure until he loosens his hold around my throat and takes a half step back. Instead of letting my hand fall away, I keep it in place, not pushing him away but simply maintaining the contact, unwilling to sever it.

"I'm sorry for what he did to your mom," I say, my voice soft with sympathy, "but I have no intention of letting Bertram destroy me. I already survived him once, and this time, I have a hell of a lot more to live for. To fight for. He didn't break me when I was fifteen, and he's sure as hell not going to now." My eyes scan his, and I bite the inside of my cheek as I debate my next words. "I've already fought my way back from the darkness once. I have no intention of *ever* going back there. While I understand your concern, I'm not your mom, Grayson, and you can't expect me to sit at home while my daughter is out there somewhere and the likes of Bertram are threatening the life I've worked my ass off to build. I'm a survivor. It's all I know how to do." I search his gaze. "I won't allow your fear to chain me."

LOGAN

CHAPTER FOURTEEN

D*on't leave her alone.*
Sit between her and him.
Always keep her in your sight.
Don't let him touch her.

Grayson and Royce's obnoxiously long list of rules for dummies circles around in my head as I pull through the gates and drive my SUV up the tree-lined drive of Bertram's estate.

With one hand on Riley's knee, I draw soothing circles on her skin. Not that it seems to be doing anything. Her knee has been bouncing the entire journey. As pumped as I am to give Bertram a virtual *fuck you* when he realizes whatever plans he has have been foiled, I'm equally as concerned about Riley's mental state. I know she said she wanted to do this—that she needs to confront her mom, and I agree we need answers from her at this point—I worry about what the cost will be for my Shortcake. Every day without her daughter, she loses a piece of her soul. Now, she has to confront the Devil and his mistress?

There's no getting out of this unscathed, and I wish to fuck she didn't have to be here at all.

Bringing the SUV to a stop in the circular drive at the front door, Riley stares out the window, her gaze roaming over the expansive, plantation-style house before I draw her gaze my way with a gentle caress of my fingers along her jaw. Her face is pale even beneath the makeup she applied before we left, and her eyes are wide with the fear she's fighting to keep contained.

Everything in me demands I turn the car around and get her the fuck out of here. It was one thing her meeting them at a restaurant, but being behind a closed door with him again... it might be a different house, but the trauma is the same. No doubt, she'll have nightmares after this fiasco. Yet, she's still here. Ready to confront her greatest torment.

"You're not the same kid you once were," I tell her, sensing she needs to hear it. I could give her the out. Tell her we're leaving. It's what Grayson would do. However, I know nothing will stop my girl from entering that house. All I can do is ensure she goes in there confident and strong. "You've faced so much since then." I carefully stroke my fingers down her cheek, ensuring her focus remains on me. "This time, you're not alone. We're all in this together. You're stronger than you know, and you have the power to do this. Just remember why we're here."

"Aurora," she murmurs, her voice shaky before she takes a steadying breath.

I nod. "Aurora. We'll get the answers we need, and I'll be beside you every step of the way." Closing the distance, I press my lips to hers in a chaste kiss, reassured when the fear in her eyes steadily solidifies until all I can see is her strength and determination. "There she is," I murmur, tracing my fingers along her jaw one final time. "My warrior." I grin savagely, letting the wild, ruthless side of myself I typically keep contained to the ice come out to play. "Let's go cause some mayhem."

Her responding grin is music to my ears as I climb out of the SUV and round the front to open her door and help her down. With every step toward the front door, I feel her growing stronger, building her resolve and solidifying her defenses. By the time I knock on the door, she's an impenetrable fortress of fire and purpose.

"For Aurora," I whisper as I hear footsteps approaching from inside the house.

"For Aurora," she responds as the door is thrown open, and I finally face the Devil himself.

I've never met Grayson's dad before. Still, I instantly know it's him who answers the door, wearing an impeccable three-piece suit and looking like he's just returned from a day of business meetings at the office—which makes no fucking sense since he's no longer CEO, but whatever.

He's the spitting image of Grayson... or, I guess, Grayson is the spitting image of him. Their features are strikingly similar, from the dark brown of their hair and eyes to the curve of their cheekbones and the angle of their jaws. Even their facial expressions match, and it strikes me that Grayson has perfected his father's impassive mask. The difference is, with Grayson, it is exactly that... a mask—a cover to hide his true emotions.

I instantly know it's not the same for Bertram as I stare into those cold, dead eyes. There are no emotions *to* hide. A sick, twisted predator peers out from behind those frigid irises, one incapable of feeling human emotions. One entirely consumed with fulfilling their wants and desires.

As his gaze latches on to his ultimate desire and his eyes

flare with want, it takes everything in me not to drag Riley behind me and out of his exploitative view.

He doesn't even seem to see me standing there as his lips curl in triumph. "Riley." He practically purrs her name, and I swear on the Stanley Cup that one day I will rip his tongue from his mouth so I never have to hear her name on his lips ever again. "It's so good to see you again. I'm looking forward to our *intimate* meal together."

Yeah, I've had enough of this fucking bullshit.

Sliding my arm around Riley's waist, my hand rests dangerously low over her hip bone as I pull her into my side. All the while, I keep my focus on the monster in front of us as he finally sees me standing there. His gaze drops to where I'm touching Riley, nostrils flaring before his eyes snap to mine.

I don a charming, charismatic smile, ignoring the threats practically spilling from his glower. "So am I, Mr. Van Doren."

"Who are you?" His lips curl in a sneer. "And *why* are you touching my daughter?"

"Well, she *is* my girlfriend." Drawing Riley closer, I keep my gaze locked on Bertram's as I kiss her temple before holding out a hand toward him. I take great satisfaction in seeing him so murderous. "I'm Logan Astor. Boyfriend."

Teeth grinding, he ignores my outstretched hand as his gaze snaps to Riley. "Since when do you *date*?"

"Since me," I answer with a cocky smirk before Riley can form a response. "It's hard to resist this charm. Although this one really made me work for her attention."

Finally looking away from Bertram, my soft gaze rests on the side of Riley's head until she turns to face me. I coax her with my eyes to relax. To not let Bertram win by seeing that he has her on edge. She forces the tension from her muscles as she smiles lovingly at me. Her eyes shine with gratitude and a little bit of mischief as she retorts, "Well, what can I say? I needed to make sure you were serious."

"What part of me serenading you in front of the entire campus said I wasn't serious? Or the love poem I wrote for you. That was some of my best rhyming!"

Lips between her teeth, Riley is struggling to contain her laughter. "Your best rhyming, huh? Guess it's just as well you're not an English major." She taps a finger against her lips. "Although... are you sure marketing is where your strengths lie?"

I growl playfully at her, pretending I'm not entirely aware of Bertram glaring at us as I tickle her sides and nip at the flesh of her neck. She writhes against me, momentarily distracted from this awful night, as she squeals and giggles. "That's how it is, eh?" I torture her with my fingers until she's laughing uncontrollably, having wholly forgotten whose presence we are standing in. I, however, have not. "I'm deadly serious when it comes to you." I ensure those words are loud enough for Bertram to hear, but instead of looking to see his reaction, I focus on the angel in my arms as I squeeze her tighter and hold her gaze, hoping she knows that while all of this is just for show, I mean those words right down to my core.

We only break eye contact when the asshole coughs, probably done with the attention not being on him. "As... insightful as this is," he drawls, looking thoroughly unimpressed, "Tonight is a *family* dinner. You can see Riley another time."

My lackadaisical smile solidifies in place. *Fuck.*

"Oh." Riley frowns, her lower lip pushing out in a slight pout. "I already had plans with Logan when I got the last-minute call from Mom. I figured bringing him would be okay, but we can do dinner some other time." Grabbing my hand, she moves back toward the car.

We make it all of two steps before Bertram's irritated sigh

reaches my ears. "Don't be so dramatic. He can stay." Riley stiffens, the move barely perceptible if I wasn't watching her with a keen eye. My fist curls, my desire to deck the asshole potent, but when I turn back to face him, he's stepped out of the doorway. Although his intent gaze bores into mine with blatant distaste. "Will be good for all of us to get to know *Logan* better."

With a tense posture and alert eyes, I follow Riley into the house, keeping my hand at the base of her spine, just above the waistband of her jeans. The click of the door closing behind us echoes through the room like the resounding clang of a prison cell, a sharp, metallic finality that sends shivers skating down my spine. The heavy thud reverberates around the foyer, bouncing off the walls and sealing us in with an unnerving sense of permanence. If that's how it feels to me, I can't begin to imagine how trapped Riley feels right now. Her breath catches beside me, her eyes darting around the expansive, white-painted foyer as if searching for an escape route. The air grows thick with her trepidation, the anxiety of being locked up with a predator, and I brush the backs of my fingers along her arm in a subtle *I'm right here.*

Her eyes lock with mine, and she takes a fortifying breath, forcing herself to calm before we follow Bertram through to a grand dining room. The table is set for three, and as we enter the room, a maid sets a fourth place setting before scurrying away.

The room is eerily empty, our footsteps echoing as we cross to the table. Bertram claims a seat at the head of the table and gestures to the seat on his right for Riley to sit. Ignoring him, I pull out the chair on the newly set place setting, getting Riley settled before taking the spot beside her, placing myself between them.

Bertram's face contorts, and smoothing his tie, he clears his throat. "So." He drags out the word, glaring at me with contempt. "How did you two... meet?"

He doesn't sound the least bit interested in the story, which is exactly why I regale him with every minute detail of how Riley tutored me and I flirted my way into her heart, winning her over with my persistent charm and endearing smile. He peppers me with more questions about our relationship and me, and any time he tries to include Riley in the conversation by directing a question her way, I answer it for her.

"Where is my mother?" Riley asks when the fake politeness grows strained.

Bertram waves a dismissive hand toward the doorway. "Running late, as usual."

Plates of steaming food are placed before us, and I'm beginning to wonder if Lydia even intends to make an appearance when I hear the clack of heels against tiles before she enters the room.

"Apologies for my tardiness," she states, not sounding the slightest bit sorry about potentially leaving her daughter alone with her abuser. She scans the room, and when she spots me sitting beside her daughter, a coy smile curls her lips, and her steps slow, her hips swaying in what I can only presume is meant to be a seductive swagger. It only makes me grateful I hadn't eaten anything yet. It would be incredibly rude to barf at the dinner table in front of my future in-laws.

Well damn. Now, I wish I had eaten so I could see their faces when I ruined their pristine tablecloth. What a first impression that would be!

Riley digs her elbow into my ribs, giving me a quizzical look, and I realize I'm smiling.

"This is Riley's *boyfriend,*" Bertram informs her, presumably answering a question I missed.

"Boyfriend?" Lydia muses, grinning far too lasciviously.

Instead of moving around the table to shake my hand, she leans across it, shoving her tits right in front of my face. Despite the inappropriateness, there's an astuteness to her gaze as it rakes over me. "Who knew my daughter had such good taste in men," she practically purrs before her gaze snaps to Riley. "Riley, you never told me you had a boyfriend." While she goes for teasing, there's an unmistakable chastisement beneath her tone that makes me wonder if she suspects I'm the one responsible for the lawyer's letter she received. Of course, she can't blatantly say as much—not with Bertram in the room.

"It all sounds very... *new*," Bertram states, appearing unperturbed by his wife's promiscuous behavior as he sips his wine. "Logan is a senior at Halston, so I doubt it will go anywhere beyond his graduation."

Ha. You shitstain, I plan on marrying this girl one day, so fuck you.

Instead, I give him another one of my classic cocky smirks as I lean my arm over the back of Riley's chair. My fingers play with a loose strand of her hair, and my smirk grows when Bertram's focus zeros in on that little bit of contact.

"I dunno. Riley's a pretty special girl."

His smile definitely resembles more of a grimace as he tears his eyes away from where I'm entwining Riley's hair around my finger while she delicately picks at her meal, like touching her is something I do all the time. I mean, it is, but I fucking love seeing that realization settle in Bertram's eyes.

"That she is," he agrees between gritted teeth. "But you're an Astor, right? I assume you'll be joining your family's marketing business."

"Actually, I'll be staying right here in Springview. I've got a spot on the Timberwolves ice hockey team, and I'm looking forward to seeing my girl in the front row of every game."

Riley's head whips to mine, questions dancing in her eyes.

Yup, baby, I will be right here for the next three years while you finish college. Except, that's a conversation best had in private, so for now, I merely wink at her before returning my focus to the two pythons in the room.

"A hockey player." Bertram scoffs, seeming to relax for the first time all evening. "You'll barely be here for half the year, and even when you are, you'll have those... what do they call them? Puck bunnies? Climbing all over you after every game. You're young, believe me, you'll realize there's an entire world of opportunities out there. No need to tie yourself down so quickly."

Riley tenses beneath my arm, but I merely shrug. Not seeing the point in arguing with him—'cause I truly don't give a fuck what this guy thinks, and despite whatever insecurities he might have poked at in Riley, she knows how much I love her— I take a bite of my food.

The first course is soon replaced with the second. Bertram seems to have checked out of the conversation, his attention either on his glass of wine or Riley while his wife asks me various verging-on-inappropriate questions about me and the Halston U hockey team. When she suggests joining Riley at our next home game, I merely give her a tight-lipped smile and make a mental note to ensure security never grants this viper access to the stadium.

It's only when the plates have been cleared from the table that Bertram leans forward, interlocking his fingers and pinning Riley with a stare that has her squirming in her chair.

"Riley." His sharp tone demands her attention, even as he flicks his gaze to mine. A flash of what looks like sympathy enters his eyes before he reverts his attention to Riley. I know this asshole isn't capable of feeling fucking sympathy, and I'm instantly on edge, wondering what's about to come next. Riley, who has been mostly silent throughout the entire meal, goes

eerily still. "The whole point of this dinner is because, well"—
another apologetic glance my way that has my hackles rising—
"we're worried about you."

"Worried about me?" Riley queries, sounding as confused as
I feel. "Why?"

"I have spoken with your advisor, who has informed me
that your grades have slipped this semester. That, and your
landlord tells me you haven't been staying at your apartment."
Bertram's features crease in faux concern. *Damn, this guy is good!*
"I don't know how much you've told Logan, but given your
history..." Riley physically flinches, and my teeth grind, hating
how this fucking pissant is getting to her. "We're worried you
might be slipping back into... unhealthy habits."

"Unhealthy habits?" I've never heard Riley's voice so small,
and it snaps the end of my restraint.

"What the hell are you talking about?" I demand, moving
my arm to rest on Riley's shoulders so my fingers graze her arm.

Sighing in a way that makes it seem like this is the last thing
he wants to be doing, Bertram shifts to face me. "I don't know
what Riley has told you, but she is a very troubled child." His
face is the perfect blend of sympathy and grief. "She has a
history of attention-seeking behavior, and I fear she's heading
down that path again."

"Because her grades have slipped slightly, and she's been
spending her nights with me?" My eyes narrow, ensuring he
knows I'm not buying his bullshit. Unfortunately, there's
nothing I can do to counter her lowered grades this semester.
What the fuck else would one expect when their daughter is
effectively missing? Of course, he can't fucking know that...
"Everyone's grades slip during the second semester," I counter
instead. "First semester eases you in, then they up the ante.
Plus, students can take a while to settle into an effective
routine."

Shaking his head, Bertram all but dismisses me, focusing his attention back on Riley. His eyes flare with something that looks uncannily like triumph. "Regardless, we have decided it's in Riley's best interest to move back home."

If I thought Riley was tense before, she turns to fucking stone beneath my arm, and my first thought is to get her the *fuck* out of this house before Bertram literally locks her up in a room.

My gaze flicks to Lydia's, catching the shock on her face before she disguises it. *Interesting, so she wasn't aware of her husband's plan. Not that that means she's innocent in any of this. She's far from fucking innocent!*

Focusing back on Bertram, I scoff. "That's absurd. Riley's a grown woman."

"Son," Bertram says in the most condescending tone I've ever heard. "With all due respect, you have no idea what you've gotten yourself involved in. You seem like a nice guy, but Riley is unstable." I swear steam blows from my nostrils. "She has self-harmed in the past and even tried to commit suicide."

"I'm fully aware of the trials Riley has overcome in her past," I snap before I've thought through what I'm saying. *Fuck.*

"Then you'll understand our concerns," Bertram presses. However, his lips are pursed, and his tone is less sympathetic and more wary now.

"I understand that you've been in prison the last four years, and she has no relationship with her mother, so as far as I can see, *neither* of you are in a position to speak to Riley's best inter-ests." I pin both fucking parasites with my furious gaze. "*Riley* is the only one who gets to determine what she does with her life."

At some point, Riley's hand finds mine under the table, and I squeeze her fingers. She returns the gesture before her soft voice joins the conversation. "He's right." I can hear the nerves in her voice, but I'm pretty sure I'm the only one. The rest of her oozes pure strength as she lifts her head to face her mom and stepdad. "I'm done with the pretenses. I want no part in this game, and I'd sooner die than live under the same roof as either of you." Pushing back her chair, she gets to her feet, and I join her. "I believe that's the end of dinner. We won't be doing this again—ever."

With that, she strides away, and with a smirk on my face, I wiggle my fingers in farewell before striding after her.

The second we're out of view, I pull her in against me and push her against the wall. "That was so fucking hot," I murmur against her lips. Her eyes are wide, and there's a slight tremble to her limbs, even as she gives a nervous laugh. "Are you okay?"

Sagging against me, she nods. "It felt good to stand up to him. If it hadn't been for Aurora, I wouldn't have played along at all."

I brush hair out of her face. "I know, Shortcake."

The sound of arguing reaches our ears, and we fall silent as we both strain to listen.

"You wanted her to *live* here?!" Lydia screeches.

Bertram's retort is too low to hear, but the vitriol behind the words is impossible to miss before we hear the clip of his shoes as he walks away.

"Trouble in paradise already," I whisper.

"We knew they only got back together because they were using each other," Riley says, her voice just as quiet.

I nod, searching her eyes. "What do you want to do now?"

Sighing as though she's carrying the weight of the world, Riley rests her forehead against my chest. "We can't leave until I speak to my mother," she murmurs after a moment. "That was the whole point of enduring this disaster."

I rub soothing circles up and down her spine. "Alright. Do you want me to come with you?"

With another exhausted sigh, she straightens, debating my question before shaking her head. "I'm more likely to get something useful from her if it's just us."

Grayson's rule to not leave her alone filters through my head, and I give it—and him—a mental middle finger. This is Riley's call, and if this is how she wants to play it, then that's what we'll do. Besides, it's not like I'm going to walk outside and leave her alone in here.

"I'll be right here," I promise her.

"Thank you," she murmurs gratefully, pressing up on her toes to bring her lips to mine in a too-quick kiss before she strides back into the dining room for the night's second battle.

While I wait, I get comfortable leaning against the wall at the entrance to the dining room, just out of Lydia's sight, and pull my phone from my pocket. I've got a plethora of messages from the guys on the team.

GAVIN

Tonight's win wasn't the same without you.

RICKMAN

Win, baby!

BARNES

You coming to the after party?

There are even more in the group chat with the team, with everyone congratulating themselves and going back and forth as they argue over where to go. Coach was so furious after last week's game that he didn't even want me sitting on the bench tonight. I already knew I wouldn't be playing before he called me into his office to ream me out. I was already on a warning after missing a game, so I completely understood Coach's decision to bench me after my antics last week.

Hell, I don't even care. My head's not in the game, just like Riley's focus isn't on studying. None of us can steer our attention to anything besides getting Aurora back.

That's partly why I never told anyone about the phone call I got last week from the owner of the Timberwolves. The excitement I thought I'd feel at getting that call wasn't there. The only reason I even brought it up tonight was to shove it in Bertram's face. I grimace, knowing Riley is going to be *pissed*. She should have been the first person I told—not that asswipe who doesn't even matter.

My head falls back against the wall, and pushing aside my own problems, I listen in on the whooping Riley is hopefully giving her mom...

RILEY

CHAPTER FIFTEEN

A headache pounds behind my eyes as I step back into a dining room that I hope to never set foot in again after tonight.

Hearing me, my mother looks up from where she's sipping on her glass of white wine. A look of disdain crosses her face. "You're still here."

"I believe we have some things to discuss."

Flicking her gaze toward a door that I'm assuming Bertram disappeared through since he didn't re-enter the foyer when he stormed off, she says, "Now hardly seems like the time."

"Now seems like exactly the time," I immediately counter. "Where is my daughter?"

I doubt Bertram is listening in on our conversation, but I keep my voice low, nonetheless. My mother casts another glance toward the door, appearing equally intent that Bertram doesn't hear what we are discussing.

Lydia places her glass on the table with an exorbitantly long sigh, followed by an excessive gulp of her wine. Still staring at her nails, she says, "I've sent Aurora away to a boarding school."

What. The Actual. Fuck?

Certain I must have heard her wrong, I repeat, "You sent her to boarding school?"

My mother's attitude is gratingly nonchalant as she shrugs a shoulder. "It was the best thing for her. I wish I had been able to do the same with you."

Of course she does, but that is neither here nor there.

"What boarding school?" I demand, beyond confused. This is not what I expected her to say, and it's thrown me for a loop. Is it possible she changed her mind at the last second, and instead of selling her, she sent my daughter to boarding school? I mean, we don't have any proof she *actually* sold her. Just that she refused to sell her to *Ruthless*. But why would she change her mind? Why would she go to all that effort to find Ruthless if she was going to back out at the last second? Maybe she got scared…

As far-fetched as it seems, hope flickers in my chest.

She waves a dismissive hand. "I forget the name. One of those expensive European ones. France? Switzerland? It had a fancy name I can't pronounce."

"Why would you do that? Why would you send her away?"

She scoffs like I'm some sort of idiot. "My husband was being released from prison." Her hand lifts to rest over her heart, and she looks at me, appalled. "We needed time to ourselves without some sticky-fingered kid getting in the way."

"So give her to me," I argue. "You don't send her away without consulting me."

Again, she waves away my protests, and I swear, if she does it one more time, I'm going to snap the bones in her wrist.

Folding my arms over my chest, I tap my foot. "You know what I think? I think you found out your husband was getting out of prison, and you knew if he found out you were raising his kid, who he knew nothing about, he'd take the child and leave you. After all, it's never been *you* he wanted, has it?"

"You spiteful child," my mother hisses.

"My daughter is not in some European fucking boarding school, is she?" Hoping that she is, is futile. My mother is too selfish. Even if she got cold feet, she wouldn't pass up the money. Or risk losing her husband. Vibrating with rage as I advance on her, where she lounges in her chair like she's in-fucking-vincible. Standing over her, I practically spit in her face. "Tell me where the fuck she is!"

Malice glints in her hazel eyes, which are so similar to mine and yet nothing alike, as she gracefully rises to her feet. Leaning in, the overwhelming floral scent of her perfume threatens to choke me as she brings her poisonous lips to my ear. "You'll never find her."

She's already halfway across the room before her words truly penetrate, and I whirl, yelling, "You bitch!"

Stopping, she slowly turns in her heels to face me, a victorious grin stretching her red lips. "Maybe it will teach you not to take what isn't yours."

"I did *not* take your husband," I practically snarl. "You're sick, twisted, vile husband *raped* me. He impregnated me."

"Perhaps if you hadn't flaunted yourself in front of him, he wouldn't have." I flinch at the verbal slap, my mouth dropping open in a silent O. "Flouncing around in your bikini and short skirts." My mother's face has contorted into one of pure hatred. "You wanted it, so stop lying to yourself." I don't notice the tear burning a track down my cheek until she sneers at the display of emotion. "And stop playing the sympathy card. It's pathetic." She runs her eyes over me, disgust curling the corners of her lips. You'd think I'd strutted in here in heels and sexy lingerie instead of a long-sleeved, high-necked top, jeans, and sneakers. "For trying to steal my husband, you can live the rest of your life knowing your daughter is chained in some basement and being passed around for the amusement of men who get off on making her scream in agony."

More tears chase the first one down my face, and my throat closes over as I bring a hand to my mouth.

Knowing she's won, my mother smirks before striding off with a swing of her hips. No sooner has she left the room than Logan appears. I don't know how she didn't see him in the foyer, but I don't question it as my knees give out beneath me.

"Hey, there." He lurches forward, catching me just in time. With a hand on the back of my head, he presses my face into his chest. "For the record, Shortcake, your mom is one heinous bitch."

Despite the numbness taking over me, a strangled chuckle makes its way up my throat before it turns into a choking sob.

"Shh," Logan soothes, stroking my hair. "Nothing she said is true. She's a hateful, spiteful woman who gets off on seeing you being cut out at the knees. Don't give her the satisfaction."

"But what if she's right about Aurora?" I hiccup.

"She's not," he states with conviction. "Whatever she's done with her, we'll find her. You know none of us will give up until we do."

"Except it's been nearly two full weeks, and we have no leads." My heart is an anvil in my chest, dragging me down.

"Don't give up hope yet, Shortcake." He maneuvers my head back so he can press his forehead to mine. "Keep fighting. We *will* find her."

He waits until I give a slight nod in agreement before he pulls away, interlocking our fingers. "Let's get the fuck out of here, and *please,* let's never come back."

"Agreed." His cheeky grin brings a reluctant one to my own lips, and I wait until we're safely ensconced in his car before I ask, "The Timberwolves... were you just saying that?"

His entire face brightens in pure delight. "Nope. Got the call last week."

I smack him across the chest. "And you didn't say anything?!" I exclaim in mock outrage.

"Baby, you've had so much going on. It wasn't the right time to bring it up." He shakes his head. "It's still not the right time."

"I don't care, Logan." Reaching over, I clasp his hand in mine and squeeze. "I don't care what else is going on in my life, I *always* want to hear about what's going on in yours. Especially when it's good news, and this is *amazing* news!"

His responding smile is soft and full of so much love.

"We should celebrate!"

He shakes his head. "Shortcake, you've been through hell tonight. We should go home and cuddle on the sofa while we force the others to watch rom-coms."

I grin. *Okay, that does sound highly amusing.*

"I will absolutely take you up on that... tomorrow night. But tonight, we need to celebrate." He goes to protest once more, and I cut him off with the shake of my head. "There's nothing more we can do tonight." While somber, my voice is firm. "There's nothing we can do for Aurora tonight. And after that dinner, I could use the distraction."

Lips pursed into a flat line, he reluctantly agrees with me. Reaching across the console, I kiss his cheek quickly before pulling my phone out of my pocket to message the guys in our group chat that I'm relatively certain Grayson only set up because I repeatedly ignored his texts.

ME

Did you guys know Logan got accepted into the Timberwolves?

We need to celebrate.

They make it obvious they've been waiting for a message from one of us by responding immediately.

ROYCE

No. Any ideas?

GRAYSON

Are you okay?

I roll my eyes at Grayson's response and his completely ignoring what I said, even as my traitorous heart flutters at his concern.

Eh, no. I was kinda hoping you might have something.

I respond to Royce, choosing to ignore Grayson's message.

ROYCE

Leave it with me. Meet us at the diner.

GRAYSON

Riley, answer me!

"Royce says to meet them at Leon's," I tell Logan, pocketing my phone without responding to Grayson. That will earn me grief from him, but a part of me enjoys the thrill of riling him—of pushing him to that edge and seeing what he'll do when he snaps.

Like chase me through an abandoned church.

"Milkshakes!" Logan groans the word, earning a laugh from me. "I'm fucking starving."

"Same," I admit.

"You didn't eat a bite of your dinner, so no wonder."

"Hard to swallow in the presence of pure evil," I comment.

Logan gives an undignified snort. "Sing it, sister! The few bites I managed to swallow were ash in my mouth. I can't get over what massive piles of steaming shit yours and Grayson's parents are. I mean, I knew, obviously. But seeing it, holy fuck." He glances my way, the dark road and infrequent streetlights casting his face in shadow. "Did Bertram seriously try to keep you in his house against your will?"

I shudder, my throat instantly drying at the reminder. What the hell would I have done if Logan hadn't been there? Would he even have let me leave? My gut tells me no, and that's terrifying as fuck!

"How the fuck did he think that was going to go down? Did he seriously think he could just hold you hostage inside that house?" Logan shakes his head, his shoulders tense and hands twisting the leather of his steering wheel as he seethes.

"He must have thought he'd be able to; otherwise, he wouldn't have tried." I chew on the inside of my cheek, frowning out the windshield. "If he's been sending me cards, perhaps he's had someone keeping an eye on me. Enough to know that I'm a loner on campus. Enough to ensure that I could disappear and not be missed."

"But not enough to know you have a boyfriend," Logan

tacks on correctly because Bertram definitely was *not* expecting Logan tonight.

"Or that I'm spending all my time at his son's house."

"Yet, he knew you weren't staying at your apartment." Logan frowns in thought.

"He said the landlord told him that." I shiver. "How long do you think he's been reporting my comings and goings to him?"

With a look of resigned disgust, Logan says my worst fears aloud, "Probably since you moved in."

I sigh heavily, the two of us falling silent for the remainder of the journey to Leon's diner. Only when we've pulled into the gravel lot, and Logan has shut off the engine does he turn to me. Leaning across the center console, he effortlessly lifts me into his arms, depositing me in his lap so I'm straddling him.

My gaze latches onto his, and I can feel the rapid thump of his heart beneath my palm, the warmth of his chest seeping into my skin. Through the small amount of light seeping in from a distant streetlamp and the glow from the diner, I can see the tension in his clenched jaw, the muscle ticking just beneath the surface. His eyes are intense, almost glowing in the darkness. There's a storm of emotions there—anger, frustration, but most of all, a fierce, unyielding need to protect me.

His arms are wrapped around me, holding me close as if he's afraid I'll disappear if he loosens his grip even a little. The silence between us is heavy, charged with everything we've been through and all that's still to come.

"You would absolutely be fucking missed, Shortcake." There's so much pain in those words. A desperate need for me to believe them. "Not just by me—by us. You know Tara would tear the world apart to find you if you just disappeared on her. That woman is utterly terrifying." Sniffling a little at the senti- mental moment, I chuckle. "And Ava cares about you too. I don't believe she'd just sit back and do nothing if you disappeared, either." His hands climb my body until he cups my face. "However, the point is that you will *not* be disappearing. None of us will let Bertram get his hands on you. I won't let anything happen to you." That last part is said in a whisper, his voice rough and full of conviction.

I reach up and gently trace the lines of his face, trying to soothe the tempest within him. His gaze softens slightly at my touch, but the underlying determination remains. He presses his forehead against mine, his breath warm on my skin.

"I love you," he vows. "You're everything I ever wanted and never thought I'd find. You are my breath, my blood, my life. One day, we're going to get married. The four of us will raise Aurora together, along with her future siblings." A mischievous twinkle enters his eyes. "We're going to have a happy, beautiful life."

The conviction behind his words leaves no room for argument. Nor do I want to argue. I *want* everything he's saying— even the parts I have yet to fully accept.

I bring my lips to his, and he tightens his arms around me. In the cab of his SUV, Logan is my fortress, my shield against the world. And though the night is filled with uncertainties, I feel a flicker of hope. We might be in the middle of nowhere, but with him, I'll never be lost.

We break apart at the bright glare of headlights slicing through the cab before Royce's truck pulls into the space beside us. It hasn't even fully stopped before Grayson jumps out, practically ripping Logan's door from its hinges as he flings it open.

"My car never did anything to you," Logan grouses. "There's no need to be such a caveman."

Grayson doesn't acknowledge him as, eyes glowing in the low light, his gaze rakes over me. "You're okay."

The sheer relief in his voice makes me feel bad for not answering his question, especially given his earlier confession. His hand stretches out for me before pausing, his fingers twitching with the need to touch me before he reluctantly withdraws.

An awkward silence fills the space between us, and swallowing, I assure him, "I'm okay." My voice sounds small in the cab. Or perhaps it's Grayson's tension suppressing the volume and making everything muted. That's the thing about Grayson. One minute, he's all growly and *mine* and invading my personal space, and the next, it's like he's afraid to touch me. It's almost like he's two people and can't decide which version of himself to be from one minute to the next.

It doesn't help that there are still unresolved emotions from our implosion in the classroom when I held a plastic knife to his throat while I fucked him and he confessed.

"Your confidence in my ability to keep our girl safe is insulting," Logan gripes, rolling his eyes to show he's teasing as he helps me out of the SUV. Grayson is forced to step aside, and Royce immediately envelops me in his arms.

"I'm okay," I assure him.

The relaxing of his posture gives away his relief, even as he murmurs for only me to hear, "I never doubted you wouldn't be. Doesn't mean I liked letting you go in there without me."

"I know." I give him a brief smile. I knew he struggled with the idea as much as Grayson did. The difference is, where Grayson would readily wrap me up in bubble wrap and ensure I never needed to leave the house, Royce understands there are things I have to do, even if none of us likes them. He *respects* my decisions enough to support me, even if he wishes he didn't have to.

"I want all the details," he says, louder this time so the others hear.

"And we'll tell you, but this is a celebration." Despite the tiredness tugging at my limbs, I turn in Royce's hold to grin at Logan.

Grayson smacks him lightly on the shoulder. "How could you not tell us you got a spot on the Timberwolves?"

Logan shrugs a shoulder, but he grins smugly—and he fucking deserves to! "There's been a lot going on."

"There's never too much going on," I tell him, extracting myself from Royce. He instantly opens his arms for a hug. "This is a big deal. We want to hear about your successes, regardless of whatever else is happening."

"She's right, man." Royce's heat envelops my back as he claps Logan on the shoulder. "Congrats. I think this deserves burgers and milkshakes."

"Thank god! I could literally eat all of you right now," Logan groans as we move as one toward the diner. "Safe to say, dinner was a disaster. Neither of us ate anything."

The broken bell hangs listlessly above our heads as Grayson pushes open the door to the diner, and I'm instantly hit with the smell of fried food and burned coffee. A few tables are occupied, and a couple of guys sit on stools at the counter. A few people look our way as we enter, but for the most part, we're ignored as Grayson leads us to an empty booth at the far end of the retro-fitted diner along the window overlooking the parking lot.

He slides into the booth as Logan gestures for me to sit opposite him, claiming the seat beside me as Royce sits beside Grayson. After glancing briefly out the window, I focus on the menu in front of me. Despite not having eaten anything at dinner, I'm not hungry. Couldn't actually tell you the last time I had an appetite. Still, I know the guys won't let me get away with not ordering anything.

Spotting a grilled cheese sandwich on the menu, I settle on that.

"What can I get ya's?" the waitress asks when she approaches our table.

"Milkshakes all round," Logan declares before anyone else can speak. "Oh, and fries for dunking."

Grayson's face scrunches while Royce groans, "Seriously, man?"

"What? Everyone knows milkshakes are a cure-all. Plus, only a heathen would order a milkshake without fries."

They both shake their heads, more than used to Logan's antics, before everyone orders their actual meals.

"It was twisted as fuck," Logan continues once the waitress is out of earshot.

"He was surprised to see you?" Royce asks.

"Oh yeah." Logan chortles. "He was not happy *at all*. Tried to get me to leave until Riley made it clear she would be leaving with me." He pauses as our milkshakes and drinks are delivered, waiting until we're alone again before continuing. "Her mom wasn't even ready when we went inside. If I hadn't been there, she would have been left alone with that sicko." He practically rips the paper cover off the top of his straw in his agitation. "Then, when she finally did show up, she was like a granny on the prowl. It was twisted as fuck. Serious MINWF vibes."

"MINWF?" Grayson repeats. I'm glad I'm not the only one confused.

"Mother I *Never* Want to Fuck," Logan clarifies in a *duh* tone. "Or more accurately, but it's got too many words for a good acronym, 'Mother I'd Rather Scratch My Own Eyes Out Than Fuck'."

Despite the situation, I snort into my drink.

"I warned you she'd probably hit on you," Royce points out. "Although I didn't think she'd do it in front of Riley or Bertram."

"Yeah, it was some weird ass shit." Logan fake—or maybe not so fake—shivers. "I need a shower just from the greasy feel of her eyes on me. Seriously, man, you deserve props for letting her touch you. You must have an iron-clad gag reflex."

"What do you mean she *touched* you?" My shocked gaze jumps between Logan and Royce, certain I must have misunderstood.

Sighing, Royce levels Logan with a *thanks man* glower, to which Logan simply shrugs a *sorry* before Royce focuses on me.

"After we found your mom's post on Craigslist, I met her to find out what she was up to." As he says it, I vaguely recall them explaining this to me when they got home that night...

Understandably, the details of what they'd done were forgotten amongst everything else.

"And that involved her touching you?"

What am I saying? This *is* my mother, and I mean, look at Royce... *Of course, she hit on him.* Imagining it, a wave of nausea hits me, and I close my eyes. Of course, that makes the images sharper, and I quickly snap them open as I stare into Royce's suddenly pale face.

"I didn't want her to, Babydoll." He shudders in disgust at the reminder, showing exactly how much he didn't want Lydia touching him, and anger ignites at the thought of my mom draping herself over him against his will. My nostrils flare, and my eyes harden. I have half a mind to drive back to her house and snap her fingers one by one so she can't touch any of my men or anyone else ever again.

"James." Royce tries to get my attention. "As hot as this murderous look is, I'd readily endure it all again. We never would have had a chance of getting Aurora if I hadn't."

"We would never have known what happened to her," Grayson adds softly.

"Doesn't mean I like it," I reluctantly grumble, focusing on those steel-blue eyes boring into mine as though asking for forgiveness. Except there's nothing to forgive. "You should never have had to put yourself in that position," I tell him. Hating that he had to while simultaneously loving him all the more for it.

"There isn't a situation I wouldn't put myself in for you—for Aurora."

I have the overwhelming urge to climb into his lap, but I settle for sliding my foot from my sneaker and stretching it toward his under the table. Grasping it, he squeezes my calf before tucking my foot beneath his thigh. His hand remains on the exposed skin of my ankle as he draws soothing patterns with his finger.

He maintains eye contact with me the entire time, and it's like everything around us falls away. We're the only ones in the booth. In the diner.

I love you, I mouth.

I've never said the words aloud to him before, and now isn't the time, but I need him to know how I feel. Need him to know I appreciate everything he has done and will undoubtedly do for me more than words can ever describe.

The corners of his lips hitch up in a faint smile, his finger outlining a heart on my ankle as the worry bleeds from his posture.

The waitress chooses that moment to return with our meals. As soon as his plate is set in front of him, Logan dives into his burger. *I guess he wasn't exaggerating when he said he was starving.*

We lapse into silence while we eat. Royce keeps one hand on my ankle while I nibble on my grilled cheese sandwich. I make a solid attempt at eating half of it before pushing the rest away and ignoring Grayson's disapproving frown.

"You need to eat."

My eyes flick to Grayson's narrowed ones before dropping to the table when he pushes my plate back in front of me.

"I did. Now I'm full." I push the plate away. *Again.*

"You're not eating enough," he grouses.

"Since when did you become a nutritionist?" I snap.

He growls in frustration. "Don't think none of us have noticed how you only eat a few bites at every meal."

"Yeah, well, I'm not exactly hungry."

"I don't care if you're not hungry. You need to eat!"

My hand smacks the top of the table. "Dammit, Grayson. I'm not hungry! How many times do I have to say it before the words penetrate your thick skull?"

As some sort of peace offering, Logan pushes my untouched milkshake in front of me. "How about you sip on this instead? Then you can share some celebratory dessert with me after."

Loosening a breath, I reluctantly agree and take an acquiescent pull on my straw. The sweetness of strawberries floods my mouth. *Damn, there is no denying that milkshake is gooood.*

Grayson throws his hands up in exasperation, and I hear him grumbling under his breath about how sugar isn't food. Still, we all promptly ignore him, and thankfully, Royce redirects the conversation by saying, "Lydia making googly eyes at Logan can't have been the highlight of dinner..."

"Ha," Logan barks humorlessly. "That was the warm-up act. Your father followed it up by basically dictating that Riley move in with them."

"*What?!*" Grayson roars before glancing at the tables around us and lowering his voice. "He did *what?!*"

"How did he think that would go over?" Royce adds, his brows creased in thought.

"I'm pretty sure he thought he was just going to lay down the law, and Riley would oblige," Logan practically snarls. "He went on and on about how she was fucking *unstable* and *attention-seeking*. He's fucking lucky I didn't stab him with my fork."

Cheeks heated, my gaze drops to the table, feeling just as embarrassed as I had when Bertram said all that shit at the dinner table. With the exception of being attention-seeking, nothing else he said was a lie. But hearing him say it all in that fake-as-fuck sympathetic tone made me feel like I was that fractured fifteen-year-old again.

Every word out of his mouth had been a slice of a blade to my skin, cutting me open. Flaying me until I couldn't find the strength to stand up for myself.

If it hadn't been for Logan...

God, I can't even bear to imagine.

"Hey." Smooth fingers that don't belong to my husky or my bad boy fighter wrap gently around my chin, lifting my face until I'm staring into dark brown eyes that leave me feeling like I'm falling into the depths of a warm, endless night. For the first time, I notice subtle flecks of gold and amber buried deep, like the last embers of a dying fire inviting me closer.

Grayson's fingers stroke tenderly over the angle of my jaw. "Don't let him get in your head. It's what he wants. To control you. To break you down piece by piece until you no longer recognize yourself."

I latch onto his bolstering words, letting them push out the insidious voice of his father, whispering that I'm damaged. Staring into his eyes is like falling head-first into a pool of melted chocolate: Deep and inviting, and in their warmth, I find the strength to silence the tormenting echoes of my past.

"I'm no longer that little girl," I say aloud in a small yet steady voice.

"No, you're not," Grayson agrees, his tone a blend of

strength and tenderness. "You've transformed your pain into power, your trauma into resilience. You've become this incredible, strong woman who stands tall despite everything that tried to break you."

He pauses, his gaze unwavering, allowing his words to sink in. "You're a testament to what it means to rise above, to overcome. Your strength isn't just in surviving; it's in thriving, in becoming the woman you are today. Don't let anyone, especially him, make you forget that."

His words wash over me, along with Royce's affectionate touches and Logan's steadying warmth, filling the cracks in my armor with renewed strength until I don't need Grayson to hold my head high anymore.

The instant I sit straight in my chair, Logan pulls me onto his lap and kisses my temple. Somehow, Royce manages to keep a hold of my foot and shifts it to rest on his thigh as he continues his ministrations, and I melt into their comfort as I rest my head on Logan's chest.

"Bertram has been speaking with her advisor and landlord," Logan informs them. "He knew her grades had dropped this semester and that she hadn't been staying at her apartment."

"Shit," Grayson curses. "I should have expected him to do that. It's just like him to stick his nose where it doesn't belong."

"I told him she's been staying with me, but we suspect he might have someone watching her. Not all the time, but enough..."

"I mean, we knew he had to have eyes on her with the cards he's been sending. How else would he have known Riley had started at Halston unless Lydia told him?"

I shake my head. "I don't think she did. I just... I can't see her giving him any information about me that she doesn't have to. It's clear that whatever the reasons for their marriage, she *wants* him, and she views me as an obstacle standing in her way." My heart clenches as her hate-filled words try to tear me apart.

For trying to steal my husband, you can live the rest of your life knowing your daughter is chained in some basement and being passed around for the amusement of men who get off on making her scream in agony.

Who the hell says that to their daughter? What sort of person *sells* their grandchild, then holds it over their daughter's head? I always knew Lydia was a self-involved bitch, but this is on a whole other level. She truly *hates* me. Hell, hate isn't a strong enough word for the pure malice she leveled at me.

Loathes.

Detests.

Abhors.

Words all more befitting.

"Then we need to be on our guard." Grayson's tone is severe. "Whoever has been watching Riley might have been watching us too. And if they haven't, they'll be on the lookout." Focusing on Logan, he says, "I'm sure my dad will be digging up everything he can find on you."

Logan shrugs easily. "I figured he would. Let him look; there's nothing for him to find. Another reason why it was better for me to go tonight instead of Royce."

My eyes go wide, and I sit up straighter as I realize going in Logan's place tonight would have put Royce in the firing line—where Bertram would have found out about the fake rape accusation. I hadn't even considered that he'd go digging for dirt on any of them.

"Shit, Royce. You *have* to stay out of his line of sight. He can't know you're involved in any of this."

"Sweetheart, he's going to put it together sooner or later. I agree, it's better not to hand him the ammunition by walking in his front door, but sooner or later, he'll realize Logan lives with his son and that you've been staying at our house. Even if I'm simply *the roommate* in his eyes, it'll be enough."

My stomach sinks as I scramble to think of a way to protect him, the way he's always protecting me.

"What if I go back to staying in the apartment? Logan can visit me there, and we can just... I don't know. See each other on campus?" I wince, hating the idea even as the words leave my mouth.

The corner of Royce's eyes soften with affection. "Not happening, James. You can go back to staying in your apartment if that's what you want, but there's no way I'm letting Logan steal all your nights."

"She's not going back to her apartment," Grayson all but growls, ruining the tender moment. "Even with the security cameras, I don't trust my dad. Not if he's paying off the landlord. He could have gotten a key to her place or anything."

Fuck.

I shiver at the notion, not having considered that. At least Grayson's cameras have been in place since before his release, so we know he hasn't been inside the apartment, but Grayson is right. He could have a key and is just waiting for me to be home alone. *Fuck that!*

Grayson pins me in place with a look that clearly shows he expects me to argue, but for once, I hold my hands up in surrender. "You'll hear no argument from me. Now that we know his intentions, I have no plans on making it easy for him to lock me inside his house."

A war plays out on Grayson's face before he finally settles on a self-satisfied smirk. "See, it's not so difficult to comply with me. Perhaps you'll be more inclined to do so in the future."

I snort. "Don't hold your breath." Bringing my finger to my lips in contemplation, my eyes widen. "Or maybe you should.

Save us all the two dozen headaches you're bound to give us in the future."

Our typical back and forth is enough to break the heaviness that had descended over the table. "Burn!" Logan jests, cackling like an idiot and holding his hand up for a high-five while Grayson huffs in annoyance, and Royce smothers a smile behind his hand. "Enough of this depressing talk. Did someone say something about celebrating?"

Dropping his hand, there's a genuine smile on Royce's face and a glint in his eyes that promises trouble—hopefully not the violent kind—as he sets a handful of bills on the table and slides out of the booth. "If you'll all follow me, we'll get the celebrations underway."

RILEY

CHAPTER SIXTEEN

"Breaking and entering wasn't exactly what I had in mind when I asked if you had any ideas," I hiss as Royce leads the way along the deserted corridor of the Timberwolves stadium. Despite trying to keep my weight on my toes, the echo of our footsteps bounces off the concrete walls, and the air is thick with the musty scent of damp cement and the faint remnants of popcorn and hot dogs.

"I don't know what you mean, James," he responds with a roguish quirk of his lips. "We're just celebrating."

Logan is too busy practically jumping on the spot as he takes everything in like he hasn't been to the Timberwolves stadium before when I know for a fact he has. It's cute to see him so excited. He deserves that. Deserves to be *here*. Playing for the team of his choice, even if it's not the best team in the league. I have no doubt he will *make* it the best team.

Since it's after hours, the crowd, players, and staff are long gone. The corridor is dimly lit, with just a few emergency lights casting long shadows that dance along the walls. I run my fingers along the cool surface, feeling the rough texture beneath my fingertips. The quiet is almost oppressive, broken only by the soft hum of distant machinery and the occasional creak of the building settling.

As we approach the end of the corridor, I can see the faint glow of the stadium lights ahead, spilling through the open doorway. Excitement billows in the air as we all hasten our steps until we're stepping through the threshold. The vast expanse of the empty hockey arena opens up before us. Usually filled with the excitement of the crowd and the thunder of skates on ice, it now stands silent, a giant monument to the thrill of competition and the passion of the game.

Rows upon rows of empty seats stretch out around us, a midnight blue and silver sea of plastic and metal. Each is a silent witness to the countless games and cheers held here. More blue and silver banners hang from the rafters, each proudly displaying the fierce Timberwolf logo—a symbol of strength and tenacity.

The rink below is a perfect rectangle of pristine ice, illuminated by the overhead lights that cast an ethereal glow over the howling wolf painted at center ice, announcing this as the home stadium for the Timberwolves—in case the team's colors everywhere didn't give it away. My gaze slowly wanders over the arena as I take a deep breath, the cool air filling my lungs. I let the moment wash over me as I envision it full of people, with Logan skating in his new colors alongside his teammates to the crowd's roar.

Banners are proudly displayed on the walls, showcasing past victories and retired numbers. It adds a sense of history and tradition, and a smile lifts my lips, knowing one day soon, Logan will be contributing to those victories. To the history of this arena. This team. It's pretty monumental when you stop and think about it.

Logan isn't simply joining a team. He's making history.

"It's something, isn't it?" Logan murmurs, awed by the

sight before him. Stepping forward, his eyes scan the expanse as a wide grin slowly stretches across his face. His voice is barely more than a whisper in the cavernous space, yet it carries the reverence one often hears inside a church.

I shake my head, unable to find words to describe the awe and wonder I feel. For a moment, we all simply stand there, soaking in the atmosphere, each of us lost to our thoughts.

Logan descends the stairs toward the rink, and quietly, we follow. Our footsteps echo in the expansive arena until we reach the plexiglass separating us from the ice. Logan simply stands there, staring out across the rink like he can't believe he'll be playing here one day soon. Grayson and Royce claim seats at the end of the closest aisle, but I step up beside Logan, threading my fingers through his.

"I can't wait to come to every home game," I say after a moment.

As though blinking out of a trance, Logan looks down at me, and a lascivious grin takes over his face. "I can't wait to see you in silver and blue."

"Hey, what about us?" Royce interjects, having clearly overheard us. "Are you excited to see us in silver and blue, too?"

"Since when have you ever worn a Huskies jersey to a game?" Logan teases, draping an arm around me as he faces the others.

"I've worn a beanie before," Royce counters. "It gets cold sitting in the stands."

"Not the same thing, and no, I would not be nearly half as excited if you showed up in a silver and blue jersey," Logan smirks. "I have no interest in peeling it off you after I win."

Royce's eyes flash with heat. "Touché. I certainly have no interest in you peeling *anything* off of me."

"Hmm, maybe not, but it sounds like an image I could get behind," I tease as I try to smother my smirk.

Logan's chest rumbles with silent laughter. "It's an image that will only ever occur in your dreams, Shortcake."

"I told you, Babydoll, that was a one-time thing," Royce adds.

"Wait, what was a one-time thing?" Grayson asks, gaze darting between us. "What did I miss?"

"Oh, only these two kissing." I don't even try to hide my cheesy grin as Grayson gapes at his two best friends.

"You two *kissed?!*"

"It wasn't like that," Logan grouses.

"Yeah," Royce supplies with a wink in my direction. "I was only sharing the taste of our girl with him."

Grayson's eyes snap my way, raking over my skin as his pupils dilate until only a thin ring of brown exists. "*Fuck,*" he hisses, and I can tell he's picturing the entire scene. My skin blushes beneath his heated stare, and my thighs clench. Logan's warmth at my back feels like it's melting through my clothes, incinerating them until I swear I'm standing there naked.

"Too bad you were being an asshole and missed it." I don't have to look up to see the smirk on Logan's face. His smugness is imbued in every word. Despite Grayson being one of his closest friends, I swear he gets as much enjoyment from tormenting him for his past grievances as I do. "Wanna check out the locker rooms?" he asks me, a dirty gleam in his eyes.

"Oh, hell no. You're not going to fuck in the locker rooms," Grayson gripes. "We're not even supposed to be here. We should at least stick together."

I smile innocently up at Logan, ignoring the angry bull. "I'd love to check out the locker room with you."

"You can't be serious?" Grayson spouts as Logan takes my hand and leads me away from him and Royce.

"Leave them be, man," I hear Royce trying to placate him.

"Yeah, man. Leave us alone." Of course, Logan just has to

poke needles. "Maybe when you make it onto an NHL team, our girl will want to spend time alone with you." He glances down at me before looking over his shoulder again. "Then again, maybe not. Sucks to be you." With a two-finger salute, he hustles me into a tunnel that must lead to the locker rooms.

"Shortcake," he asks almost hesitantly when we're out of sight of the others. "Can I ask what the deal is with you and Grayson? Things seem different, but you're still keeping him at arm's length—not that I'm judging if you're still not ready to forgive him."

I sigh, snuggling closer into his side. "I don't know," I admit honestly. "That day..." I don't need to say which one. He knows. We all do. "We... both got some things off our chest. I feel like I got some resolution for what he did, but I still hadn't figured out what that meant when..."

"When we came home without Aurora," Logan finishes dejectedly.

I simply shrug because what else is there to say to that? "And I haven't exactly had a chance to piece it together since." I shake my head, at a loss. "Grayson is a mess over everything. I don't even know..."

"He seems like he's trying," Logan supplies.

"He does," I agree with a weighted sigh.

"He wants to find Aurora as desperately as the rest of us. Even though he's never actually met her, he considers her his sister. She's family—to all of us."

"Isn't that part of the problem, though?" I argue. "He's my daughter's brother, but if I start something with him and it goes somewhere..." Because that's the problem. I *know* if I give in to this thing between me and Grayson, it will consume us in an eternal flame. There will be no ending it. No walking away.

Logan snorts softly. "There are far more twisted things than Aurora's half-brother being her mom's boyfriend."

Pulling me to a stop outside a door, he spins me so I face him. "You don't need to figure out anything right now. Grayson isn't going anywhere. Now, serious question time." He wags his eyebrows, the action so contrasting with his tone that I burst out laughing. "Are you ready to witness the inner sanctum of the Timberwolves?"

"I think a better question is, are you?"

Logan's mischievous smile softens. "Baby, with you at my side, I'm ready for anything."

Grinning, I press up on my toes until our faces are inches apart. "Then let's go check it out." Grabbing his hand, I push against the heavy door, and we sneak inside.

The Timberwolves locker room is bathed in the soft glow of overhead lights, casting shadows that dance along the walls adorned with Timberwolves insignia. The home colors, a midnight blue and shimmering silver, are everywhere – from the large logo on the polished floor to the banners hanging with pride.

Wooden benches line the room, sturdy and smooth, ready to support the weight of dreams and the burden of losses. Each locker is meticulously organized, with nameplates gleaming under the lights, some of them bearing the names of legends. Soon, Logan's name will join them. The thought sends a thrill through me. I can almost picture him here, suiting up, lacing his skates, sharing a laugh or a motivational word with his teammates.

Logan steps ahead of me, his eyes scanning the room with a mix of awe and determination. He walks over to one of the lockers, stopping in front of a nameplate that reads "Markus Lindstrom." His fingers trace the engraved letters, and he turns to me with a smile that barely contains his excitement.

"Markus Lindstrom," he says, almost reverently. "This guy is a legend. Three-time MVP, two Stanley Cups, and over 500 career goals. One of the best to ever play the game." He shares some of Lindstrom's stats, his voice filled with admiration.

I nod, feeling the weight of the history and achievements that have passed through this room. Knowing Logan will soon share this space with such greatness is inspiring and a little daunting.

Logan moves on, but I linger, my eyes drawn to the empty locker beside Lindstrom's. I step forward, examining the smooth surface and imagining the possibilities. This could be Logan's space, where he'll prepare for battle and become part of something bigger than himself. The room feels alive with possibility, buzzing with the energy of games won and lost, of sweat and effort left on the ice. I can almost hear the echoes of past games, the roar of the crowd, the thud of skates on ice. My heart swells with pride for him, knowing this is where he belongs, where he'll carve out his legacy.

From across the room, I catch Logan's eye, and he smiles, the kind of smile that reaches his eyes and lights up his whole face. "This feels like a dream," he admits, slowly making his way back to me.

I smile back, feeling the warmth of his excitement. "You were born for this, Logan. I can't wait to see you out there, showing everyone what you're made of."

Closing the distance between us, I stretch up to wrap my arms around his neck. His hands automatically go to my hips, and I love the casual touch of possession. "I'm so proud of you," I tell him earnestly. "You could have played for any team you wanted, and I know this wasn't your first choice. That you settled—"

He cuts me off with his fingers over my lips.

"Choosing to be where you are is *not* settling. *You* are my first choice. Whatever team makes that possible is my first choice. Always. I'm not settling with the Timberwolves, and I'm sure as fuck not settling when it comes to you.

"The Pacific Penguins might be a better team, though that's not worth losing time with you. It's not worth giving up my nights cuddled up with you or not being there for Aurora's first day at kindergarten. Or watching her effortlessly wrap Grayson around her finger and weasel Royce into a princess dress while they have high tea."

Tears blur my vision as I sniffle, and despite my heartache, a wobbly grin breaks across my face. "I don't know how I got so lucky to find you," I murmur.

"Flunking statistics was all part of my master plan to meet the smartest, most beautiful girl on campus." He winks at me, making me laugh.

"Guess we're both lucky you wore me down with your relentless begging."

"Hey!" He frowns in mock offense. "The way I remember it, you fell for my dazzling charm."

"Dazzling charm, huh?" Sliding my fingers through his hair, I let my nails scrape along his scalp. "I think you're misremembering. You sure you're not concussed from that stupid fight you got yourself into last night?"

"You know," he begins on a low groan. "I'm not so sure. You should probably check."

Smirking, I repeat the action, relishing how his head falls back, and he sighs at my intimate touch. His fingers press into the skin of my hips, and I feel the press of his erection against my stomach before he parts my legs with his thigh.

"Fuck it," he says with a desirous sigh. "I don't care if I *did* beg you to tutor me. I'd happily beg for your attention any day of the week."

He has my legs around his waist in a flash of movement as

he spins us before lowering to the bench beside Markus Lind-strom's locker.

Logan's arms tighten around me, and his words echo in my mind. All those desperate study sessions, late—night cramming, jokes, and shared frustrations were about more than just passing a class. They were about us, about finding each other in the chaos of our lives.

Straddling his hips, with his hand cupping the back of my head, he drags my face to his. The first touch of his lips against mine ignites a fire in my core and incinerates my soul.

I go up in flames, fisting his t-shirt and pressing myself infinitely closer in a need to feel all of him. Everywhere. Despite only having him yesterday, there is something so intoxicating about having Logan all to myself. This man, this hockey god who could have any woman he wanted, chose me. He sees me, truly sees me in a way no one else ever has. The thought sends a thrill through me, a rush of empowerment that's almost dizzying.

When he looks at me with those affectionate eyes, I feel wanted and cherished—like I'm the only woman in the world. Knowing that this incredible athlete, this future star of the NHL, is mine is a heady feeling. It makes me feel sexy and confident like I can conquer anything with him by my side.

Taking control, his hand moves to one side of my throat, holding me in place as he bites and sucks and nibbles his way along my jaw and down my neck.

Each brush of his lips against my skin has my hips rocking against his in desperate need of friction.

"You're all I'll ever want, Riley. I won't ever get enough of this—of you." My heart warms at the sentimentality of his words, even as my thighs clench at the husky rasp of his voice.

"I need you," I whimper, grinding against his hard erection and wishing I could vaporize his jeans with just a thought.

"You have me. I'm yours."

I scramble from his lap, hurriedly stripping out of my jeans as he scrambles to undo his belt and lower his zipper. Our movements are frantic, both of us desperate to collide in a display of fireworks. A bead of precum glistens in the low lighting of the room as he pulls his hard, angry cock from his boxers, and I hover above him, watching as he pumps his hand up and down his erection while his eyes drink in the flush of my cheeks and glaze in my eyes.

"Can't wait any longer," he rasps before shoving my panties aside and wrapping his arm around my waist, forcing me downward and onto his awaiting cock.

I sigh, and he groans as we come together in perfect symphony. Fully seated inside me, his hand slides into my hair, and he captures my lips in the kiss of all kisses. He devours me, sucks my soul from my body, and steals it for himself until we're both breathless and delirious with the need to move.

We might be fucking in a locker room where anyone could walk in, but what we're doing is so much more than that.

"Fuck, Riley," he mutters, chasing every roll of my hips like a drug addict in need of his next fix.

"Logan," I babble, eyes closed as my breathless pants fill the air and my pussy flutters.

"Look at me, Shortcake. I want to see those pretty eyes when you come."

Peeling them open, I latch onto Logan's warm chestnut hues. The intensity and depth of our connection send me spiraling, and keeping my eyes on him, I come on a low moan.

Logan follows me over the edge until we're left breathless and sated, sagging against one another. My eyes are heavy as I lean into him, and I can almost comfortably fall asleep when I hear the clip of approaching footsteps.

Logan must hear them, too, as he snaps upright. "Shit," he hisses.

"It might just be Royce or Grayson," I whisper. Even though I know it's not. Whoever it is doesn't feel the need to quieten their steps, suggesting it's a security guard or someone else who works here. My heart leaps into my throat as panic surges through me, my breath hitching as my eyes dart frantically around the room in search of somewhere to hide.

Thankfully, Logan has already grabbed my discarded jeans and sneakers. His hand grasps mine as he tugs me through a door at the opposite end of the room from where we entered.

I barely catch a glimpse of a shower room before Logan rips open the door to a utility closet and ushers me inside. We press ourselves against the far wall, amongst shelves stacked with towels and equipment.

The space is cramped, and I can feel Logan's breath on my neck, his cum soaking my panties and drying on my inner thighs. It would be hilarious if I weren't terrified of getting caught and how that might ruin Logan's Timberwolf career before it gets off the ground.

In the dark, all I can make out is Logan's outline. As the door to the locker room creaks open, he presses a finger to my lips in a gesture to keep quiet. I squeeze my lips together, acutely aware of how loud our breathing sounds in the confined space. My pulse races at the squeak of a shoe against the shower room floor, and my eyes go wide when I see a flashlight beam from beneath the door.

Straining my ears to hear through the wood, the guard's footsteps are slow and deliberate as he inspects the room. I squeeze Logan's hand, silently praying he doesn't think to check the closet. It feels as if he stands in the shower room for ages, and I'm beginning to wonder what he's doing. Does he know we're here? Is he waiting for us to show ourselves?

After what feels like an eternity, the footsteps retreat. I distantly hear the sound of the locker room door swinging shut, and I let out a shaky breath, my body trembling with the release of adrenaline. Logan squeezes my hand, and we wait a few more moments to be sure the coast is clear.

A crazy-sounding laugh bubbles out of me when we're certain we're alone, a mixture of relief and exhilaration. A moment later, Logan joins me. My legs feel weak, and I lean against him for support as he stares at me with a mischievous grin tugging at his lips.

"That was close," he whispers as we creep out of the closet. Despite the close call, his eyes twinkle with excitement.

"Too close." I barely dare to breathe the words in case the security guard somehow hears them.

Logan pulls me into a tight embrace, and I feel the tension drain from my body. "You okay?" he asks, his voice soft and reassuring.

I nod, looking up at him with a grin. "Yeah, I'm okay. That was... terrifying."

He chuckles, his breath warm against my cheek. "Definitely one for the books. Here." He passes me my jeans and shoes. "We better go find the others and get out of here before we push our luck."

"Good idea." I hurry back into my jeans, face scrunching at the wetness of my panties.

No time to worry about that right now.

Once I'm ready, Logan moves to the locker room door, cracking it open and peering into the hall before waving for me to follow him. Thankfully, we don't run into anyone as we hurry back to the others, and together, we sneak out to Royce's awaiting truck.

GRAYSON

The conference room at Van Doren Holdings is all polished mahogany and cold glass, a space designed to impress with floor-to-ceiling windows overlooking the Springview skyline. Our senior executives are currently seated around the long table, their faces a mix of anticipation and guarded caution. I can feel their eyes on me, but it's *his* presence at the end of the table—in the seat that should be *mine*, but he deliberately arrived before the meeting began to claim it as his own—that commands the room, no matter how much I hate it.

Despite the fact I'm not sitting at the head of the table, I take charge of the meeting as though I own the room—because I *do* own the room. Leaning forward, my hands are clasped on the table as I stare down each one of my employees. "I've reviewed the terms of the merger, and I believe the deal is sound. However, I think we should negotiate a better price before proceeding." My voice is steady and confident, but inside, there's a simmering frustration I'm fighting to keep in check.

Before I can continue, Bertram speaks up, unaware of how

his unwanted input makes my teeth grind. "That's an interesting point, Son." His voice, smooth and calm, slices through the air, and my nostrils flare at the subtle undermining of calling me *son* instead of using my name when we're at work. "But in my experience, pushing too hard on price can sometimes make us appear… desperate." He pauses, letting the words hang in the air, a faint smile curling at the edges of his lips. "I'm not sure if you've had the chance to fully grasp the nuances of these types of negotiations yet."

I grit my teeth, my jaw tightening as I force myself to remain composed. He's cutting me down in front of everyone, chipping away at the authority I've worked so hard to build since he was locked away. But that's his game—always has been. Undermine, manipulate, take control without ever making it obvious.

He continues, looking past me to address the rest of the room as if I'm not even here. "I've been through dozens of these deals, and I know when to push and when to show restraint. Perhaps we should move forward with the current offer rather than risk losing the deal entirely. After all, we wouldn't want our partners to question our commitment, would we?"

I see heads around the table nodding, some of them barely masking their doubt. They're buying into his bullshit, just like they always have. My frustration deepens, a slow-burning anger that I have to swallow down. He's not just questioning my judgment—he's painting me as inexperienced, unqualified, like I'm some fucking intern who hasn't earned his seat at this table.

He leans back in his chair, all smug confidence, as he glances around the room. "I'm sure everyone here understands the importance of maintaining our reputation in the market, especially during such a transitional period for our leadership."

Transitional period. As if I'm just a placeholder, biding time until he can swoop back in and take over. The weight of his words presses down on me, the subtle insinuation that I'm not enough—that I'll never be enough.

The silence stretches, the executives waiting for my response. I can feel the frustration knotting tighter in my chest, but I can't let it show. Not here. Not in front of them. I take a breath, forcing the tension out of my shoulders as I meet his gaze, trying to match his calm with my own.

"We'll take all perspectives into account," I say, my voice steady, even though inside I'm raging. "But I believe it's worth revisiting the terms before we make any final decisions. This deal is too important to rush."

There's a murmur of agreement, but it's faint, lacking the conviction I'd hoped for. They're uncertain—about the deal and about me—and he knows it. He's planted the seeds of doubt and is waiting to see how deep they'll take root.

I lean back in my chair, feeling the heavy weight of the room's gaze. He's sitting there, looking every bit the concerned father, the wise advisor, but I know better. He's playing his game, and no matter how much I want to call him out, I can't. Not yet. I need them to see me as the leader, not just the son trying to fill shoes too big for him.

But with every word he says, every sideways glance, he's making that more challenging. And for all my frustration, all my anger, I know this is just the beginning. He won't stop until he's back in control, and I'm just another pawn on his chessboard.

But I won't let that happen. Not again.

As has become a regular occurrence since my father's unwanted return, I take to the hallways that afternoon, eaves-dropping on water cooler gossip. My father has supporters among the employees, but many remember what he did. Plus, the facts speak for themselves, and there's no denying that I've grown this business more in the past five years than he did the entire *twenty years* he was in charge.

It's during one of these walks, shortly before the end of the day, when I spot David glancing the opposite way down the hall before slipping into an empty office.

David is a weasely bitch. One my father has trained well. A junior employee at the firm, he worked his way up to a position well beyond his capabilities under my father's tenure. Firing him is something I've had on my *to-do* list for quite some time, but with all the other shit I've had going on, I haven't gotten around to it.

Curious as to what he's up to, I move closer. Unlike the offices on the higher exec floors, this one has no glass offering a view into the hallway, so I can get right up to the ajar door without being seen by David or anyone else in the room.

The hushed murmur of voices stops me at the door, my ear straining toward the room as I listen.

"Why are you bringing this to me *here?*" That infuriated growl most definitely belongs to my father. "I told you not to bother me with issues like this at work."

"My apologies, sir." That voice is familiar, too. "You've been ignoring my calls, and I—well, I didn't know what to do. It's... a lot. All the time. S—"

"Deal with it, David," my father snaps. "That's what I pay you for."

There's a tense pause before David's meek response. "Yes, sir. Of course, sir."

Fearing that is the end of their behind-closed-doors scheming, I slip away. The entire walk back to my office, I replay the conversation, wondering what the hell they were discussing. I wouldn't be surprised to hear my father using David to garner control of the other executives and board members. Using him to do his dirty work. But this sounded more... personal. Closing the office door behind me, I make a mental note to get Dax to keep an eye on my father and David. Whatever it is they're up to, I want to know.

"How can there be no new leads?" I demand several days later as I pace back and forth across Xander's shoebox of an office. "A child doesn't just disappear."

"Children disappear without a trace every day of the week," Dax unhelpfully points out.

Whirling toward where he's sitting, laptop open in front of him, I smack my hand down on the desk. *"Not my sister!"* Not Riley's fucking kid!

The way Dax pierces me with his stark blue eyes would have lesser men pissing themselves. Dax is the type of man who walks into a room and you instantly know he's in charge, not by words but by sheer aura. His eyes, cold and calculating, miss nothing. Even now, as he sizes me up, a predator assessing his prey. I'm not Royce. I'm not a fighter and don't have his build, even though I work out religiously in our home gym. Regardless, Dax could undoubtedly knock me out with one punch if he wanted to.

Right now, I don't give a damn. I don't give two fucks if I piss him off. Between my father fucking everything up for me at work and messing with Riley, Aurora being missing, and the fact we have *no fucking leads*, plus having to see Riley's heartbroken face every single day, I'm *this* close to snapping. I'm at my limit, and the next person who gets in my face will get my fist in theirs.

"Are you even looking?" I snap. My frustration simmers, boiling just beneath the surface. We haven't heard a goddamn thing from him since that stupid fucking false lead that only served to destroy the fragile strands of hope Riley has been clinging to. There are no leads, no sign of Aurora—nothing but dead ends and empty promises. And at the center of it all is Dax, sitting there with that infuriating calmness, like he has all the time in the world, while *my world* is falling apart.

I'll do whatever I must to bring Aurora home, to have a chance at a relationship with her, and to have any *hope* of a relationship with her mother.

"Yes, I'm fucking looking." His calm composure snaps in an instant as violence bleeds into the air around him. "I have Blue working day and night, and my team is still tidying up loose ends from that auction."

"I don't care about the fucking auction," I practically yell, vibrating with all this pent-up anger. It presses against my skin, making it impossible to stand still. "Aurora is out there somewhere, scared and alone!"

Dax's eyes flash with the promise of bloodshed, and the temperature in the room heats by several degrees, the air turning thick with the taste of savagery as he slowly stands. He takes controlled, deliberate steps around the desk until he faces off against me.

"Dax," Royce warns.

"You think this is easy?" Dax's voice is low, dangerous. "You think you can just snap your fingers and everything falls into place? This isn't a movie, Grayson. This is real life; it's messy and complicated."

I clench my fists, my knuckles white with the effort. "Don't patronize me, Dax. I know exactly how messy life is. But all we've done is sit around and wait. I'm *done* waiting."

He takes another step, now close enough that I can feel the heat of his presence. "You want to do something? Fine. Let's go a round in the ring." His lips quirk in a cruel smirk. "Let's see if you have the guts to channel that anger into something useful."

The challenge hangs in the air, heavy and electric. My heart pounds in my chest, a mix of fear and exhilaration coursing through me. I've seen the brutality Dax brings to the ring, the ruthless efficiency with which he dismantles his opponents.

"Gray." Wariness lines Royce's tone. He, more than anyone, knows what Dax is capable of. I won't be coming out of this unscathed, but the thought of an outlet for all this rage and frustration is too tempting to pass up.

"Fine," I spit out, my voice shaking with barely restrained fury. "Let's do it."

A flicker of something dark and satisfied crosses Dax's face. "Hope you're ready to bleed, pretty boy."

I scoff. "I might not live for the taste of blood in my mouth like you two, but I can hold my own in a fight."

Dax's grin only turns more savage as he wags his eyebrows in a weird mix of mischievous violence. *Dude is clearly a little unhinged.*

"This is a bad idea," Royce groans as we follow Dax out of the office and down the hall. Being the middle of the day on a Sunday, The Depot is closed. Xander is our only audience, and he's doing inventory behind the bar when we emerge into the main bar area and stalk toward the ring in the center of the room.

Tension crackles like static electricity as I shed my top, thankful I was feeling lazy and put on sweats today. Rolling my shoulders, I duck to step through the ropes. Dax has already dressed down to a pair of loose shorts, his chest bare and displaying the patchwork of tattoos covering every inch of exposed skin. *Jeez, I thought Royce was addicted to pain.*

With a cocky smirk, he tosses me a pair of gloves. "Better put these on. Wouldn't want you to damage those pretty boy hands of yours."

I catch the gloves and slip them on, ignoring the jibe. I

already know I'm going to hurt like a bitch by the time we're done. If I can get away without fucking my hands up, then I'm not about to turn down the opportunity out of fucking stubbornness.

"Ready when you are," I inform him once I've stuck the Velcro straps in place. I knock my glove-covered knuckles together as I jump up and down on the spot, getting my blood pumping. Not that I need to. I can already feel the adrenaline rushing through my body, desperate for release. I need this. I need an outlet. I need to feel something other than this helplessness consuming me.

Dax cracks his neck and rolls his shoulders, his eyes locked onto mine. "Alright then. Show me what you've got, Desk Jockey. I'll even give you the first shot."

Bouncing on the balls of my feet, I don't bother playing games or trying to suss him out. I charge straight at him, putting my weight behind my first punch as I drive it into his face. There's the satisfying crack of leather on flesh as his head whips to the side.

He chuckles, his fingers swiping the corner of his mouth and coming away bloodstained before he turns to face me. Blood stains his teeth as the crazy asshole grins at me. Already, the adrenaline of the fight has a manic gleam in his eyes. "Come on, Grayson, is that all you've got?"

Nostrils flaring, I slam my fist into his gut. I become enraged when he barely moves, laughing like I'm an annoying fucking gnat buzzing around him. Letting loose, I unleash on him. Jab. Uppercut. Cross. Hook.

Over and over.

The pent-up frustration of not finding Aurora, the anger at my father, the self-hatred for how I treated Riley—all of it pours out with each punch. But it's not enough. I need more. I need to feel *more*.

I grit my teeth and throw a combination of punches, my fists flying with all the anger I've been bottling up. Memories flash through my mind—my father's harsh words, Riley's voice trembling when she disclosed her dark secret, the sickening fear when Royce and Logan came home without Aurora.

The entire time, Dax takes every hit I deliver until my arms are heavy, and I begin to fear that I'll run out of steam before I sort through the shit in my head.

Eventually, Dax has enough. He moves. His fist shoots out, catching me in the ribs. Pain explodes through my side, and I stagger back, gasping for breath. He's not holding back anymore. He's giving me what I asked for.

"You think this will help?" he growls, his eyes cold and calculating. "You think beating me will find her?"

I charge at him, my vision red. "Shut up!" I roar, swinging wildly. He sidesteps and delivers a punishing blow to my ribs that sends me to one knee.

Pain radiates through my body, but I push it aside and get back up. "You don't get it," I spit out, gasping for breath. "I have to find her. I can't just sit around and wait."

Dax's eyes narrow, and for a moment, I see something in them—a flicker of understanding, maybe even respect. "Then get up," he says quietly. "And keep fighting."

I do. I launch myself at him again, driven by a need to prove myself, to show that I'm not broken. The fight becomes a blur of fists and fury, each punch a release of the emotions that have been tearing me apart.

His blows are relentless, each one a reminder of my failures. My failure to recognize the monster that is my father. To see the hurt and pain he was causing Riley all those years ago. To stop him. To save her. To rescue Aurora.

Failure.

Failure.

Failure.

A punch to my jaw snaps my head to the side, but I barely feel the physical pain beyond the emotional one. Riley's face flashes in my mind, the reservation in her eyes when she looks at me, the uncertainty of whether she can ever forgive me, ever trust me, ever rely on me.

The fight has become less about the catharsis of unleashing my fury and more about the punishment I deserve. With each hit Dax lands, the pain radiates through me, burning away the self-disgust, the self-hatred. I deserve this pain for my failures, for not protecting Aurora, for hurting Riley. Each blow is a penance for my mistakes, a reminder of how I've fallen short.

Another hit to my ribs, and I swear something cracks, threatening to take me to my knees. Dax's fists are like sledgehammers, but I deserve every hit. Every stab of pain. Every punch of air from my lungs and bruise to my bones.

Poor little Grayson with his confusing feelings that are too big for him to control. It's far easier to hate on me than actually confront how you're feeling, right, Grayson?

My anger has always been my crutch, my way of avoiding the deeper, more painful emotions buried within. It's easier to be angry, to lash out, to build walls that keep everyone at a distance. But in doing so, I've only pushed Riley away, and that's the last thing I want.

This anger of mine—it's been a shield, a way to protect myself from the vulnerability that comes with confronting my true feelings. But that shield has become a prison, keeping me locked in a cycle of rage and isolation. And it's cost me. It's cost *us*.

I can't keep using my anger as a crutch. Not when all it ever does is alienate me. It was because my anger blinded me that I didn't see the truth of what my dad did to Riley. That I didn't just fucking listen to her. I might have seen the clues earlier if I hadn't been so hellbent on revenge, so consumed by my anger. We could have gotten Aurora away from Lydia before it was too late. My obsession blinded me, made me miss the signs, and now we're paying the price for my stubbornness.

With every one of Dax's brutal hits, I feel a piece of that weight lifting until he finally steps back, breathing heavily. A look of respect mingles with the disdain in his eyes. "You're tougher than I thought, Suit Slicker."

The metallic taste of blood is sharp on my tongue, and every inhale hurts. It's taking everything in me to stay on my feet.

Shaking his head and frowning, Royce approaches. "Hope you feel better for that," he drawls. "Here, drink this." He shoves a water bottle into my hands, and I down half of it before pouring the rest over my face, letting it run down my neck and mingle with the sweat on my chest.

Dax moves directly into my line of sight, and amidst the pain occupying ninety percent of my body, a faint spark of satisfaction ignites when I see the cut on his lip and eye, along with the red marks over his chest and the sweat coating his skin.

"You've got fire, Grayson. Use it. But don't let it consume you."

I'm breathing hard, swaying on my feet where I stand. My body aches, but there's a clarity in my mind that wasn't there before.

With Royce's help, I hobble over to a stool at the bar, practically collapsing into it as Xander sets a cold beer in front of me.

"So why haven't we found any trace of Aurora?" Royce asks, immediately getting back to business. Now that my mind isn't polluted with anger, I can think straighter and focus better on the task at hand.

"'Cause we reckon whoever has her isn't selling her."

"They bought her to keep for themselves?" I clarify, taking a sip of my beer as I process what that might mean.

"That or they sold her to someone they know. Off the books, no digital trail."

Dax sighs, knocking back a gulp of his own drink. "I'm sorry, but we're at a dead end until we find out who the buyer was."

I sigh as Royce rubs his hand over the scruff covering his chin. "That's not going to be easy," he admits. "Lydia's not just going to give us a name—assuming she even has one."

Nodding as if he expected as much, Dax offers, "I could have a couple of guys pick her up. Scare her into giving up whatever information she has."

Honestly, not a bad idea.

"Word would likely get back to my father, and we can't have him finding out about Aurora's existence," I reluctantly admit.

"Besides, I'm honestly not even sure Lydia would give us a name—even under torture. She *hates* her daughter," Royce adds. I nod in agreement.

"That's fucked up," Dax comments before shrugging off his offer like it's no big deal. It probably isn't to him. Tapping his knuckles against the top of the bar, he says, "Well, let me know if you change your mind. I can get some guys to pick her up."

With that, he walks off, and I tuck his offer into my back pocket. Not because I think resorting to torture will get us any answers, but because, once we finally get Aurora back, I plan on eliminating every threat against her from the board—starting with the bitch who sold her.

RILEY

CHAPTER EIGHTEEN

S lamming the lid of my laptop shut, I yank my earbuds from my ears as I full-body shiver. *I can't take another minute of that.* We're currently covering criminal psychology in my psych class, and the professor assigned us an essay on understanding the minds behind various criminal activities. Of course, he selected *which* criminal activity each of us would write about. Then, because the universe truly despises me, I was assigned the task of understanding the twisted minds of people who kidnap others.

Yup, my life is some cosmic joke, apparently.

I've been trying to watch psychological interviews of various kidnappers, but I've yet to make it more than several minutes into a video before I have to stop.

I just... can't.

All of it rings too close to home.

"Can we get out of here?" I ask Royce.

He looks up from where he had been sketching something for an assignment, eyes searching my face. "Everything okay?"

"I just need a break." I'm already packing up my things, and he follows without question.

"Do you want to head home?" he asks as we leave the library.

I shake my head. "Can't. I've got my advisor meeting in an hour." Which I am *not* looking forward to.

"I can bring you back to campus."

Again, I turn him down. Brooding on campus feels marginally better than brooding in the deafening silence of the house. I'm less likely to fall so deep into the pit of depression that I can't claw my way back out if I'm on campus, surrounded by the constant buzz of life happening around me. Students living out the *typical* college experience.

The cold February air nips at my cheeks, and I snuggle into Royce's side, stealing his heat as he drapes his heavy arm over my shoulder. "The Coffee Hut is on the way to the administration building; let's just go there." He stiffens, his stride slowing slightly before he catches himself. "Or we can—"

"No." His tone is curt. "Coffee sounds good."

My teeth gnaw on my lower lip, having forgotten Royce's aversion to public places on campus. He's become more comfortable eating in the food court, never missing a lunch if he's on campus, although I can tell he's never entirely at ease, even when it's all of us sitting together.

"We can just go to the food court."

"It's fine." His voice still sounds strained, but I drop any argument I was going to make, and we walk to The Coffee Hut in silence. I'd have preferred the coffee cart, but it's too cold to sit outside. Maybe in another month or so, I'll be able to return to sitting on a bench while sipping on a steaming-hot drink. When winter officially hit Halston, I was forced to seek out a coffee shop with actual walls and a roof. Thankfully, there are several on campus.

Reaching the coffee shop, Royce pulls open the door. A small bell jingles as he ushers me in ahead of him. The warmth immediately wraps around me as I look around the interior, along with the rich, comforting aroma of freshly brewed coffee. The walls are painted a warm, earthy brown, with cream and green accents interspersed around the room to give a chilled vibe.

The place is busy but not packed. Students and faculty alike taking advantage of the good coffee and warm respite from the cold. Some are hunched over laptops, while others are chatting animatedly, creating a low hum of conversation that blends with the occasional hiss of the espresso machine.

A few people glance up as we walk past, but most are engrossed in their own worlds. We join the back of the line, which moves steadily as people order their midday caffeine fix. The baristas behind the counter work with practiced efficiency, quickly calling out orders and steaming milk.

While we wait, I glance at Royce. He's scanning the room with a stern glare, his *fuck off* face firmly in place. Pinching his side, that hard expression snaps to mine, and I can't help but giggle. It's so rare that I see this side of him now. Sure, he's not a fluffy kitten, but I almost forget how acerbic he used to be—how he still is around anyone who isn't me, Logan, Grayson, or the guys at The Depot.

"If you're trying to scare everyone else out of here, you're doing an excellent job."

He manages to force the muscles in his face to relax—a little. "Sorry." That one word is a grunt.

"You don't need to apologize." I glance around us, teeth firmly embedded in my lower lip. "Maybe we should…"

"Next," the barista calls.

"Just order your drink, James." With a firm hand on the base of my spine, Royce pushes me in front of the barista. I ask for a caramel latte while Royce orders a black coffee before we wait at the end of the counter.

Several minutes later, with our drinks in hand, we look

around for a place to sit. "Oh, over there." I point in the direction where a group of guys are leaving a booth, and we weave our way through the tables, sliding into the newly vacant booth before someone else can claim it.

The seat is cushioned and pleasantly comfortable, and I sink into it as I sip my latte, the sweet, creamy flavor instantly lifting my spirits. We sit in companionable silence while we sip on our drinks, and I people-watch. The hustle and bustle of the coffee shop is a welcome relief from the morbid arena that has become my mind, and I go from table to table, creating stories for each person sitting there, all to avoid my own mess of a life.

Lost in my own world, I notice Royce stiffen from the corner of my eye. My head whips in his direction, gaze raking over him as I try to figure out what's wrong. His hand is clenched tightly around his cup, and if it had been a disposable one, he'd have crushed it, likely burning himself in the process. His expression has turned to stone. He's completely shut down.

This is more than just being pissed off.

Something has gotten to him.

Frantic, I scan our surroundings, not understanding.

"It's definitely him."

Another voice adds, "I can't believe he's allowed to just walk around campus."

"Right? Like, how has he not been expelled? He's a menace to society."

My focus zeros in on the girls sitting in the booth behind him. They aren't even trying to keep their voices low, talking so loudly that I can hear them over the din of other customers.

Clearly, Royce hears them, too, and based on the furtive glances they keep flicking his way, I can hazard a guess as to who they're talking about.

Sitting opposite each other, the brunette has her back to me, so I can't see her face, but I recognize the other girl as the one who was talking about Royce that day in the library—the blonde who said her cousin knew Royce. Does that make her cousin Melissa?

"I'm going to say something to my parents," the blonde states snootily. "I don't feel safe walking around campus with him on the prowl. What if we ran into him when it was dark out?" She gapes scandalously at her friend.

"Do you think the girl with him *knows?*" her friend asks, and I quickly avert my gaze in case either of them looks my way.

"Maybe we should tell her," the blonde suggests. "It's our civic duty, after all. What if he does the same thing to her? I mean, who knows how many other girls have fallen victim to those good looks."

Aaaand I've had enough.

Teeth gritted and fury burning a path through my veins, I get to my feet.

"Riley," Royce hisses. "Don't—"

I shut him up with a lethal glare before stomping over to the booth behind him. Towering over the table, I fold my arms across my chest and stare down at the two girls. They fall silent, blinking up at me.

"Uh, can we help you?" the brunette asks, frowning. I realize she's the other library buddy, and for some reason, that only pisses me off more. Do these two just spend their day talking shit about my boyfriend?

"I couldn't help but overhear your conversation," I begin curtly.

"Oh, good." The relief in the blonde's expression is palpable. "We wanted to say something—"

"Do you realize slander is a prosecutable offense?"

My question is met with a moment of confused silence. The two girls share a glance.

"Uh, it's not slander if it's true," the brunette snipes.

"Except the bullshit you two are spewing is *not* the truth." I pin my searing gaze on the blonde. "Your cousin is the one you heard this from, yes?"

Her mouth opens and closes, making her look like a fish. I'm done listening to her talk, so I don't wait for her to find her voice. I lean in, ensuring they're the only ones who hear my next words.

"I suggest you go back to your cousin, and this time, ask her to tell you the truth of what happened that night." I cast my gaze toward her friend, including her in my next sentiment. "In the meantime, the two of you should shut your pie holes, focus on your own lives, and leave the rest of us alone."

A warmth envelops my back as I stand upright.

"Ry," Royce pleads in a low voice.

The girls' focus shifts to the threatening presence at my back, their throats bobbing.

Grabbing Royce's hand in mine, I squeeze it. I just have one more thing to say, then we can leave.

"Royce is the most respectful, loyal, honest man I have ever met. Whatever you *think* you know, I can guarantee you, it's all lies. Maybe you should think about the harm spreading such unfounded gossip can do to a person before any more bullshit spews from your mouths."

Spinning on my heel, I keep Royce's hand tucked in mine as I march out of the coffee shop. The smack of cold air only seems to fan the flames of my anger as I stalk down the path, visibly fuming.

How dare they talk about him so openly like that.

Even worse, he was within hearing distance. They had to have known that.

Bitches.

I rarely use that word, but it's fitting in this instant.

"Ry." Royce pulls me to a stop, and I blink out of my murderous rage, finally seeing him for the first time.

"Royce." Stepping into him, I press my forehead to his chest. "I'm so sorry. I should never have taken you in there."

His hand comes up to cup the back of my head. "Not your fault, sweetheart."

"You shouldn't have to deal with that."

His blasé shrug somehow makes it worse. "It is what it is. The rumors have been around since last year. No one has any real idea of what happened to get me kicked off the football team, but everyone speculates."

I frown up at him. "They were the same girls I overheard talking about you in the library last semester. The blonde said it was her cousin..."

His gaze darts back and forth between mine. "She might be. I didn't recognize her, but for all I know, she could be Melissa's cousin."

My lips tug down in a pout. "I don't like it if she is. They shouldn't be talking about you like that."

His chest vibrates with a contained chuckle. "Yeah, I saw that. Got worried for a moment that you were going to drag them out of their seats by the hair."

"Now that you say it, that's not a bad idea." I make as though I'm going back there, and he tightens his hold on me.

"Hold on there, Tiger. I think you've done enough for one day."

"Well, if you change your mind, just let me know." I give his chest a condescending pat. "Don't you worry, Royce. I'll be your bodyguard."

My teasing earns me a rare smirk, and I totally take that as a win as he tucks me into his side, and we walk aimlessly down the campus path.

"Did you really just say pie hole?" He does a poor job of hiding the laughter in his voice.

I groan, burying my face in my hands. "It just came out in the heat of the moment. I don't even know where it came from!"

He gives up the fight and laughs out loud. "Well, it gave me flashbacks to fifth grade."

"Can I ask," I hedge, glancing up at him through my eyelashes. "You told me your dad paid her family off, along with the school, last year, but you never really talk about your dad... or your family."

He blows out a long breath, and we walk in silence for a moment before he responds. "That's because he only did those things for himself."

Not understanding, I frown up at him.

"All that truly matters to my dad—to my family—is the *King* reputation. The accusations against me... not exactly the kind of press they want to be associated with. *That's* the reason my dad paid off the family. He didn't even care enough to hear my side of the story. He received word of a scandal and immediately went into damage control. It was the same last year when the Ellingtons sabotaged any potential I had at going pro by contacting Halston and trying to get me expelled.

"After that, he pulled me aside and said he was done with me. He can't actually disinherit me. Well, he could, but he won't. I'm his only heir, so for the continuation of the King line, he wouldn't. But I'm essentially a King on paper only. None of the benefits—which basically just means no money. Which is fine. I make plenty from the fights at The Depot, and I have an inheritance from my grandparents that I can dip into when needed."

"What about your mom? Doesn't she have anything to say about all of this?"

He snorts. "My mom is drinking the same Kool-Aid as my dad. All that matters to either of them is their reputation and amassing even more wealth, which they don't need. Anything that stands in the way of that, including their own son, is a threat."

"That's... messed up." That is about the only way I can think to sum that up.

"Yeah." He sounds more indifferent than sad about it. "I mean, it's not like we were a close, loving family before. They've always been disinterested. According to them, they've done their job by producing an heir to continue the family line. They never really gave a crap about me beyond that."

"You don't sound like it bothers you all that much?"

"Because it doesn't." He shrugs. "Maybe when I was younger, but now... I prefer it this way. For as much as they don't want anything to do with me, *I* don't want anything to do with *them*." He looks down at me, a softness in his gaze. "As far as I'm concerned, I've found my family. They're the only ones I care about."

Uncaring of the fact we're on a public path in the middle of campus, I spin, bringing us face to face as I loop my arms around his neck. "Mm, I like the sound of that."

His hands rest possessively on my hips, focus intent on me. "Good. 'Cause that's what you are. What Aurora is. Family."

"Family," I murmur, as though testing the weight of the word on my lips. My gaze drops to his lips, and he groans.

"James, you can't do that here."

"Do what?" I blink innocently up at him.

His gaze narrows, his hands squeezing my waist as though attempting to hold me at bay. "You *know* what."

"Oh, you mean kiss you."

"Yes," he hisses. "That."

I push my lower lip out in a pout. "Well, can I tell you I love you?"

"Fucking hell, Ry." He sounds like he's in literal agony.

"What? *You* were the one that so casually threw it out there before you fled out the door. I didn't get to say it to you, too."

"And you're choosing this moment to reciprocate?"

I glance around as though only now realizing our location. "Seems like as good a time as any."

With a grin tugging at the corner of his lips, he rolls his eyes, still holding me possessively. "Well, get on with it then."

I flash him a full grin. "I, Riley James, am in love with you, Royce King."

"So formal," he teases, eyes shining.

"And I don't care what any of them say. If I hear anyone talking smack about you, I *will* beat them up."

"My hero."

"You better believe it."

"Are you about done now?" He arches an eyebrow.

"Why?"

"So I can kiss you."

My mouth drops open, and I gasp scandalously as I flick my gaze around our immediate area. "*Here?!*"

"Yes." That one word is a growl. "Here."

In the next instant, his lips are on mine, and any thoughts about being in public cease to exist.

RILEY

CHAPTER NINETEEN

"Ah, Miss James. Nice of you to join us." I'm too busy cussing Dr. Whitaker out in my head for making it sound like I'm late when, in fact, I'm five minutes early to pick up on his phrasing. It's only as I step over the threshold and see the absolute last person I want to be confined in a room with, sitting in a chair opposite my advisor's desk, that I realize he said *us*.

Him and Bertram.

The air stalls in my lungs, and I can't look away. His dark hair is meticulously groomed, not a strand out of place. Those cold, dark eyes that used to haunt my nightmares are now filled with a sickening gleam of triumph. As always, he's well-dressed in a tailored suit that screams power and control. He's the very image of sophistication, a mask hiding the monster beneath.

His lips curl into a smile, charming and disarming to anyone else but me. I know what lies beneath that facade: cruel manipulations and twisted games. My heart pounds in my chest, each beat a reminder of the fear and pain he inflicted.

His presence exudes a nauseating confidence, the kind that

turns my stomach and makes my skin crawl. He's exactly the same as he always has been—not a hint of remorse or change in his demeanor. Just the same polished exterior, the same air of superiority. And as I stand there rooted to the spot without Grayson or Logan to ground me, memories flood back with a ferocity that threatens to bring me to my knees.

"Have a seat, and we'll get this meeting underway." Dr. Whitaker's voice rips me out of my spiral, and I swivel to leave, but he's already closed the door behind me. With that look of disapproval permanently stuck on his face in my presence, he gestures toward the only available chair—the one right beside Bertram.

"W-what is he doing here?" I demand, feet cemented to the floor. There is absolutely no way I am sitting beside that sick bastard. The fact I'm breathing the same air as him is too much already.

"Your stepfather felt it was prudent that he be a part of this conversation," Dr. Whitaker states in a no-nonsense tone, which makes it clear there is no getting out of this. "Given the circumstances."

"Now, Riley." Bertram's tone is falsely sweet as he slowly rises to his feet, hands held up as though he's trying to calm a wild animal. "I only want what's best for you. Together, I'm confident that the three of us can come to some agreement on what that is."

"What are you talking about?" I'm physically shaking now.

I might not be a wild animal, but I feel cornered between these two predators. Trapped. My gaze darts back and forth between them, my palms sweaty as I fist my hands at my side.

Bertram's head tilts in a mimic of sympathy that I know is bullshit. "We talked about this the other night, remember? How you've been struggling to keep up with the course load. How you were considering dropping out to focus on your mental health—maybe try community college in the fall."

My teeth grind, pure molten rage flaring hot through my veins. "I never said that. I'm not dropping out. Halston is where I belong."

"Your grades would suggest otherwise," Dr. Whitaker drawls, and fuck me, I truly despise this man. Of course, even if I had wanted to explain my slipped grades to him, I can't with Bertram here.

"I'm working on improving them," is all I say, but it sounds weak even to my ears. Mainly because I know I'll struggle to give my studies the attention needed until Aurora is safely back in my arms.

Dr. Whitaker hums in disagreement, but I'm too busy eyeing down Bertram to look at him. "In my experience, students rarely come back from this. The academic rigor at Halston is such that once you fall behind, it's near impossible to catch up."

Tongue in cheek, I don't respond. I can't, because deep down, I know he's right. While it's perfectly understandable that my grades have slipped, and one lousy semester isn't going to derail my academics or future career, there's no arguing with the fact that every day I fall farther behind creates a deeper hole for me to climb my way out of.

Obtaining Bs or Cs now could result in me struggling to achieve anything higher for the rest of my academic career. A subpar transcript could follow me into my working life and prevent me from being chosen for jobs or result in me getting paid less than someone else because I'm deemed not as *competent.*

The entire point of working my ass off to get in here and leaving Aurora with Lydia was so I could do everything within my power to ensure I could provide for her. That she'd have the life she deserves. A mother she can respect and look up to.

While focusing on my studies feels impossible right now, I *have* to give them the attention they require. I *have* to keep working toward that future, regardless of its implausibility.

"I'll do better." This time, the conviction in my voice rings true, and I lift my chin, staring down Bertram. No way am I letting him convince this old dickbag to kick me out.

"Dr. Whitaker and I feel community college would be more at your... level."

This fucking asshole.

"No." I refuse to even stand here and listen to him spout such bullshit. Turning my back on Bertram and ignoring the cold sweat that gathers along my spine, I focus purely on my mentor. He's the only one who matters. "Give me until the end of the year. If I can't prove to you that I can get my grades back up, *then* we can discuss alternatives."

It's a daring move, especially given how volatile my life outside of Halston is, but it's all I can do.

Dr. Whitaker's lips purse in displeasure. The arrogant dickhead probably has the paperwork to have me stricken from the school register tucked in his top drawer, just waiting for his signature.

"My inability to hack it at Halston could be perceived as a reflection on you," I hedge, aware I'm walking a fine line. "Whereas if I can pull my grades up and pass the year, everyone will credit you with helping me turn things around."

His eyes flash, and I know I've got him. He clearly hates scholarship students, but he wants to be admired and recognized by his peers.

"You have until the end of the year, Miss James." I stand straighter with triumph. "*But* I will accept nothing less than a

4.0 GPA." *Well, shit.* "I have no faith you will actually achieve that, but if you want to enjoy one last semester at this school, then I'll be keeping a close eye on your progress."

I give him a curt nod, refusing to let his words stick to me. I'm not getting kicked out today, and that's all that matters. He dismisses me, and I scurry from the room. My pace is quick, my footsteps echoing off the walls as I march down the hall.

"Riley."

Nope. My footsteps quicken.

"Riley. Stop this instant!"

My heart trips over itself at the blatant command in his tone, but I don't even dare glance back at him over my shoulder as I continue toward the exit. The very last thing I want to do is get into a conversation with Bertram in an empty corridor.

Except he catches up to me as I step outside. His fingers wrap around my wrist, squeezing so the bones grind together. It's a warning. A threat. Whirling, I tug on my arm, but he only tightens his hold.

My gaze darts around us, noting that no one else is nearby. Other than two students conversing as they walk across campus and a professor sitting on a bench, talking into her phone on the opposite side of the green, we're alone.

So very *alone.*

"I—" My throat goes dry, my breathing growing erratic as I fixate on the point where his fingers burn into my skin. With the amount of force he's using, he's going to leave bruises. "I have class."

He chuckles, a self-deprecating sound that feels like claws dragging down my spine. "You have *Introduction to Psychological Theories* with Dr. Martin in classroom 202 of the Social Sciences building at three-thirty. Until then, you're free."

The knowledge that he is so familiar with my schedule that

he can recite it sits like lead in my stomach. I remain frozen on the spot, with no idea how to escape this situation.

He can't do anything to you here, I tell myself. We might be alone, but there are other people around. All I have to do is scream.

Feeling marginally more confident, I demand, "What do you want?"

"I was hoping we could have a civil conversation—without that... *hockey player* interfering." He says hockey player like it's a disgusting word.

"You mean Logan, *my boyfriend.*" I don't know why I'm baiting him, and I regret it a moment later when I whimper in agony as he comes within an inch of snapping my wrist.

"I'm trying to be tolerant of your insolence; you don't want to piss me off, Riley." His grip loosens on my wrist as he strokes a finger lightly over my pulse point. "Where's my good little girl? I haven't seen much of her since my release, and I have to say, I miss her."

Bile floods my mouth, and it takes everything in me not to vomit all over his designer shoes.

"Now, like I said, I just want to talk—father to daughter. I only want to catch up on everything I've missed."

I'm honestly not sure which part of that fucked-up sentence gets to me, but a spark of anger fizzles away enough of my fear and disgust to have me finally lifting my head to hold his complacent gaze.

"Why do you do that?" I demand. "Why do you continue to pretend you didn't sneak into my bedroom and rape me every night for months?"

Eyes flashing in warning, his posture stiffens as he casts a quick glance around us. His gaze drops to where he's holding my wrist hostage, and as if realizing how it looks, he lets go. Instead, he steps into me, lowering his voice as he hisses, "It wasn't that, and you know it! It still isn't." His nostrils flare. "You *know* where you belong."

Shaking my head, I stumble back a step. "I'm not going anywhere with you. Not today. Not *ever*."

Finally free, I go to stride away, but I only make it a couple of steps when he says my name. There's something implied in it. A threat? Or perhaps it's the fact he sounds far too calm, considering I just thwarted his plans—again. *Something* has me turning to face him.

With that twisted, amicable smile in place, he stalks closer. With controlled, steady strides, he eliminates what little space I'd just put between us. There's something about his swagger. The cockiness behind it. The gleam of victory in his eyes. It *terrifies* me. Roots me in place until not even a strong wind could move me.

Leaning in, goosebumps pebble along my arms as his breath dances over my skin.

"You were always such a good girl for me. It's disappointing to see such defiance." My breathing is nothing but shallow whisps as his voice drops. "Every day you defy me will be a punishment I don't want to deliver, but I will." Pulling back just enough to meet my eyes, he cocks his head. "And sweet little Aurora will be the one who pays the price."

My blood goes cold.

My entire body buzzes with awareness, and his words ring in my ear.

Aurora. Aurora. Aurora.

Her name is all I can hear as the ground beneath my feet tilts, my surroundings blurring. It feels like I'm on some hellish carnival ride with no way off.

My hand clamps over my mouth, and I think I garble some sort of nonsense.

"I didn't want to resort to this; you forced my hand. I've

been obliging you, but I'm out of patience. Either you come to me, or that sweet little girl of yours will have to fill *your* shoes."

I think he touches me, but I'm so removed from my surroundings, so disconnected from my own body, that I can't be sure. I'm vaguely aware of him walking away before I stumble to a nearby bush and empty the entire contents of my stomach.

With Bertram's menacing threat reverberating in my ears, pulsating through my skull, and seeping deep into my marrow, I'm left feeling not just numb but utterly disoriented. Swiping at the spittle on my chin, I stumble blindly away from the administration building, my only instinct to escape his looming presence.

To find the guys.

To tell them.

Bertram has Aurora.

That knowledge circles on repeat in my head until fear blinds me, and guilt over just how greatly I've let my daughter down drives my actions. I stagger and stumble as though drunk as I race across campus, the once familiar landscape now blurring around me. The urgency of my escape is palpable.

Flee.

Find the guys.

Bertram has Aurora!

I should have known it wouldn't be as easy as putting him in his place at dinner. With Logan at my side and knowing Grayson and Royce had my back, I felt empowered. Emboldened. In that moment, I felt like I could take Bertram on. A strangled laugh crawls up my throat.

How naive could I be?!

Bertram has made it crystal clear, even from his prison cell, that he doesn't intend to simply let me go—that I'm his. By standing up to him at that dinner, I didn't put down a rabid dog. Instead, I waved a red flag in front of a rampaging bull.

I just didn't realize that he's been one step ahead of us all this time.

While I thought we were playing Go Fish, he was playing poker and holding the winning hand.

Now, I'm left running for my life with no clue how to get my daughter away from him without sacrificing myself in the process.

The guys will know what to do. They have to.

I flee across the campus, my steps quick and erratic, my breath coming in short, ragged gasps. My heart is pounding so hard it feels like it's going to burst through my chest. Saliva floods my mouth, and I force myself to swallow as panic clouds my vision, turning familiar pathways into a dizzying maze. I'm trapped in my own body, unable to think straight. To figure out what I should do. Every shadow feels like it's hiding him, and every passerby looks like they're watching and judging me. I keep glancing over my shoulder, unable to escape the feeling that he's right behind me, ready to reach out and drag me back. Force me to go with him.

Either you come to me, or that sweet little girl of yours will have to fill your shoes.

If he catches me... I'll die. Aurora and I will both be dead.

Yet, what alternative do I truly have?

That thought alone pushes out what little air is in my lungs, and I whip my head forward, picking up my pace until I'm running, uncaring of what anyone watching me must think.

I can't go back there. I just... *can't.*

Back to his house.

Back to that time.

Back to that helpless, hopeless girl.

I can't stop the flood of memories: the feeling of his hands on me and his soft, caressing voice as he whispered in my ear. *Good girl.* A sob wrenches from my throat, and I claw at my skin. I'm shaking all over, my legs threatening to give out beneath me.

My vision blurs as tears fill my eyes, but I blink them away, refusing to let them fall. I won't break down. Not here, not now. The fear is like a vise around my chest, tightening with every step. I need the guys. I need Logan's safe embrace. Royce's threatening stance. Even Grayson's murderous rage. They'll know what to do.

Except I can't make my mind focus long enough to figure out where each of them is on campus right now. Is Grayson even on campus today? I can't remember.

I round a corner, my steps faltering as I trip over a loose stone. My ankle twists painfully, but I barely register it. Pain is better than fear. Pain is something I can handle. But this... this overwhelming terror, not only for myself but for my daughter, is suffocating.

I'm trapped in a nightmare I can't wake up from.

I reach for my usual mantra to pull me back from the edge of hysteria. Except, it no longer works. I'm *not* safe. He *is* here. He *can* hurt me.

He *is* hurting me.

"Riley!"

My gaze whips over my shoulder, slamming into dark hair and dark eyes *chasing* me. Eyes wide with terror, I scream. Dropping my backpack, I break into a full-out sprint.

"*Riley!*"

There's an emotion in that one word that has an itch scratching at the back of my mind, but I'm too terror-stricken to register it. My name is called again, but this time, it is drowned out by the roar of an engine.

Unyielding bands of steel wrap around me. A scream rips from my throat, imagining it's Bertram before the world tilts. The air is pushed from my lungs as I hit something hard. A blinding pain radiates across my skull before the world dims.

Like a dying flame, my panic slips into the darkness until everything ceases to exist.

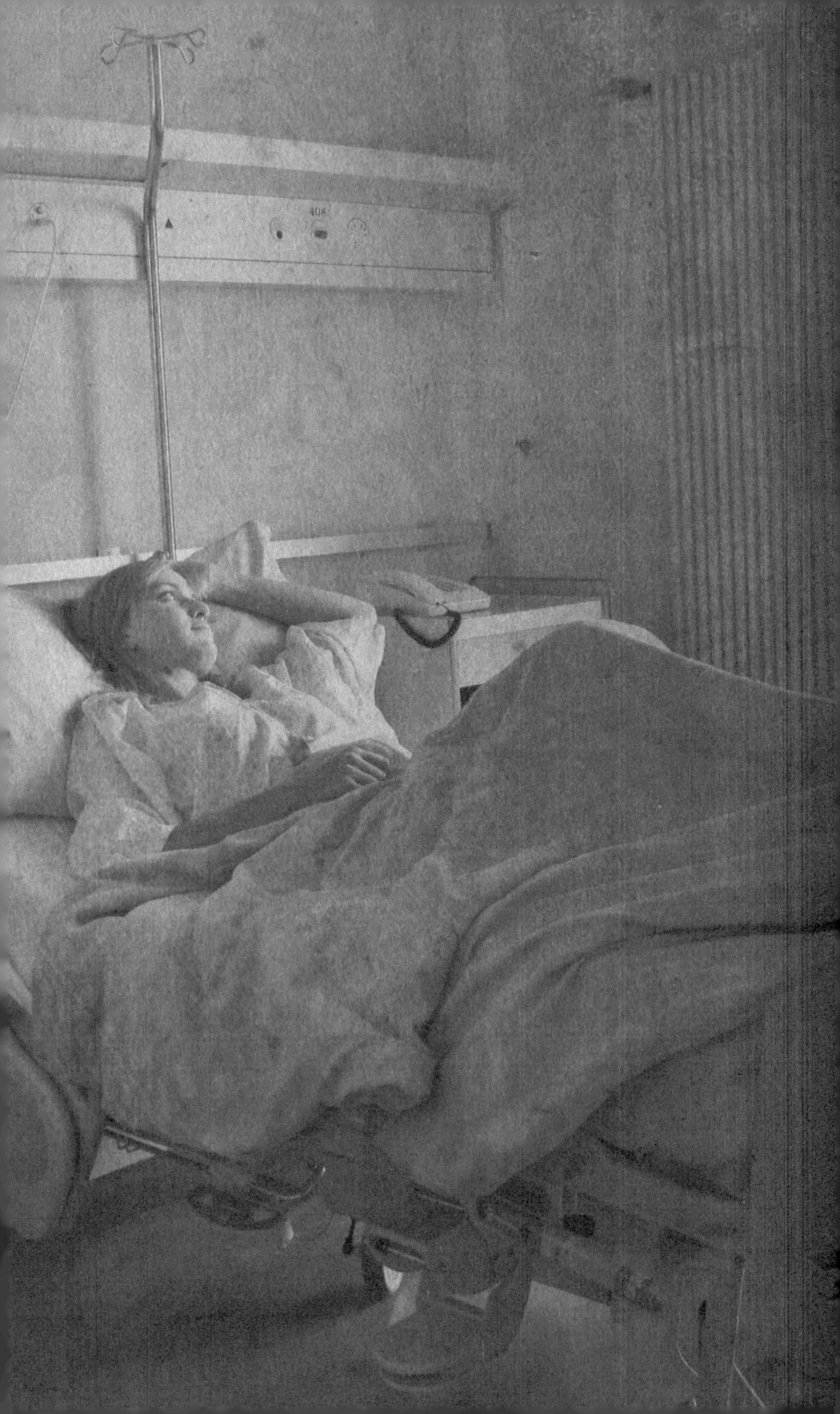

GRAYSON

CHAPTER TWENTY

"What are you doing?" I demand, leaning over the paramedic's shoulder as he flashes a light in Riley's eyes. I pull at my hair, nausea twisting my insides into knots as I stare at her bleary-eyed form. She's so pale. So fragile looking.

What the hell was she doing, running across campus like a bat out of hell?

I'll never forget the look on her face when she saw me. The blind terror. The suffocating fear.

"Sir," the paramedic huffs, glaring at me over his shoulder in a clear *back-off.* Scowling at him, I reluctantly step aside to give him room to move. Instead, I snatch up Riley's limp hand as I watch him work. She gives my fingers a slight squeeze, and I drop my gaze to where she's lying on the stretcher.

"Aurora," she mumbles, slurring slightly. Her gaze is unfocused, her eyes drifting shut before she snaps them open, only for the weight to drag them back down again. She was unconscious for several terrifying seconds after we hit the ground. I'll never unhear the sickening crack as her head bounced off the asphalt. Even now, a fresh shudder wracks my body.

Thankfully, she came around before the paramedics arrived, although she was groggy and out of it. Confused, and worst of all—completely fucking terrified, shoving at my shoulders and clawing at my face until I had to restrain her so she wouldn't hurt herself any further.

"Shh," I soothe, brushing a strand of hair out of her face as I lower my head to hers. "Focus on you right now."

She gives a minute shake of her head before whimpering in pain.

"Don't move," I chastise, struggling and failing to keep the snarl out of my voice.

"Grayson!"

Recognizing Logan's panicked voice, I look away from Riley for the first time since I caught her in my arms. Logan and Royce are both racing toward us, Logan in his practice gear. I'd messaged both of them once the paramedics arrived. Logan wouldn't have had his phone during practice, so Royce must have gotten him on his way here.

"What the hell happened?" Royce demands, pausing at the back door of the ambulance. Logan has no such intentions as he barrels into the cramped space, practically shoving me out the door as he moves straight to Riley's side.

Her eyes are once again closed, her face pinched.

"Shortcake," he murmurs, his tone gentle even as anguish strains his face. He reaches out to touch her but hesitates, leveling a glare on the paramedic, who is thoroughly unim-pressed with our presence. "What's wrong with her?" he demands, channeling the Logan his rivals meet on the ice.

"She's got a concussion," the paramedic states succinctly as he bustles about. "I'm checking her vitals, and then we'll take her to the hospital." Leveling each of us with a long stare, he dictates, "I need all of you to step outside and give me room to work."

Logan looks like he's about to argue when Riley's weak voice penetrates the tension-riddled ambulance.

"Bertram."

I go rigid, and I'm not the only one.

"Here..." *Fuck.* "Aurora."

My brows furrow, and I meet Royce's confused stare.

She grows agitated, attempting to push herself upright on the stretcher until Logan gently pushes her back down. "Easy now," he soothes, pressing a gentle kiss to her forehead. "You're alright. The paramedic here is going to check you out, but we'll be right here." He points to where Royce and I are standing before the paramedic nudges him aside, and reluctantly, he moves to join us.

"What do you think she meant?" he asks with a frown, eyes glued to her while the paramedic moves around, taking her vitals. His gaze snaps to mine. "Was your dad here?"

I shrug, not having an answer for that. "No clue. I just saw her running across campus. She has a concussion, so it's hard to know..."

Logan and Royce level me with a *tell us what the fuck happened* glare, and sighing, I lift a hand to rub at the back of my neck. My shoulder is already stiffening up, and stinging along my arm has me glancing down. For the first time, I notice the rips in my shirt, dotted with blood from scrapes I must have gotten from the asphalt.

Staring at the dried blood on my skin, I go back to the moment I got out of my car and saw Riley dashing toward the parking lot like the hounds of hell were on her ass.

"I'd just arrived on campus..."

Distracted by my father's new tactic to undermine me at the office, I wasn't paying any attention to my surroundings until I caught sight of a streak of familiar auburn hair from the corner of my eye.

Looking up, I stared in confusion as Riley raced blindly toward the parking lot. At first, I thought she knew I was there and was coming toward me, but then she veered off. Concern pricked at my skin, and I called out her name.

She heard me. She looked right at me, but instead of stopping, whatever she saw only urged her on. I didn't catch a good glimpse at her expression, but her glazed eyes had me running after her before I'd thought twice about it.

Her foot hit the sidewalk before she raced between parked cars and onto the road... right into the path of a car that I swear appeared out of fucking nowhere.

One minute, the parking lot had been empty, and the next, this car was racing right at her... right for my Tempest.

I'd screamed her name, the tendons in my throat tearing as I pushed my legs to go faster. With no thought for my own safety, I ran in front of the car, wrapped my arms around her, and threw us to the side as the vehicle roared past.

My shoulder took the brunt of our impact, but with my arms around her waist, I had no way to protect her head as it smacked off the ground. I might have stopped her from getting hit by a car, but in that moment, I failed her.

The panic that flooded me when her eyes closed and didn't open, no matter how much I begged and pleaded for her to...

I'd known this woman was embedded beneath my skin, but I hadn't realized how truly deeply until that moment. Until I feared I'd lose her.

Blinking out of my stupor, my head snaps toward where she's lying in the ambulance as if needing to assure myself she is okay. Hurt, but alive. My throat is tight, my chest pinched as I watch the paramedic fuss over her.

"She was supposed to be in a meeting with her advisor," Royce states, rubbing at his chin as he thinks. "Do you think your father ambushed her when she got out?"

His question forces my attention away from the entire reason my heart beats. "It would explain why she was running... why she seemed almost afraid of me."

"There's no brake marks." We both turn, finding Logan has stalked off and is looking up and down the parking lot. He turns his face toward us. "You said she ran out in front of a car, but there are no brake marks."

I walk over to join him. My gaze roams over the asphalt, realizing that he's right.

"The car was there." I point to where Riley had run out from between parked cars before walking over and doing a more thorough inspection of the area.

"If someone runs out in front of you, you slam on the brakes," Logan presses as I wrack my brain, trying to remember more than the sheer terror that lodged in my throat when I saw that car barreling right for Riley.

"I don't remember hearing the screech of brakes," I state with a frown. "Or the smell of burning rubber." I'd been too fixated on Riley then. However, no one else came to see if she was okay. That's what any decent person would do, right? In fact, I don't even remember seeing the car stop. One minute, it was there, and the next, I was alone with a concussed Riley in my arms.

The sound of a throat clearing has all three of us whirling toward the ambulance. The paramedic pales at whatever he sees in our expressions. "We're taking her to the hospital now. *One* of you can join us. The other two can follow."

Logan and I both step forward.

"I'm going with her," I hiss, my tone non-negotiable.

"Like fuck—"

Royce claps a hand on Logan's shoulder. "Let Gray go with her. He'll keep her safe. You need to go smooth over things with Coach since you just raced out of there without an explanation, and I wanna get CCTV footage and talk to Blue—get him to track Bertram's whereabouts. Then we'll go check on Riley." Logan's teeth grind, and I can see the refusal on the tip of his tongue before Royce says softly, "Trust him with her."

"Fine," Logan hisses. He jams a finger in my chest. "You better not let her out of your sight until we get there." Not waiting for a response, he stomps off back to the hockey arena.

Royce remains, leveling me with a hard stare. "Look after our girl."

"Always," I vow before turning away and climbing into the back of the ambulance.

My heart hasn't slowed down since we arrived at the hospital. I sit in the uncomfortable plastic chair beside Riley's bed, every muscle in my body tense, my eyes never leaving her face. The sterile smell of antiseptic and the low hum of hospital equipment surround us, but all I can focus on is her. The stark white sheets are a harsh contrast to the bruises forming on her pale skin.

She's resting now, her breathing even, but I can't shake the image of her lying on that pavement, unconscious. It replays in my mind on an endless loop, a constant reminder of how close I came to losing her. The moment I saw that car speeding toward her, instinct took over. Pushing her out of the way was the only thing I could think of. The sickening thud of her head hitting the ground still echoes in my ears.

I reach out, my hand trembling slightly, and gently brush a strand of hair away from her forehead. Her face is peaceful, almost serene, yet I can't shake the terror in her eyes when they'd connected with mine in that parking lot.

The room is quiet, except for the heart monitor's steady beeping. It's a sound I've come to rely on, a constant reassurance that she's still here with me. Royce and Logan are on their way, and they'll bring their own brand of support and reassurance that I know Riley needs, but right now, it's just me and her.

A rare occurrence.

Rarer still that we're in the same room without sniping at one another.

Ironic how I'd give anything to have her ripping me a new one right now. How I'd love nothing more than to poke and prod at her until she erupts and unleashes all that hot-as-fuck fury onto me.

Nothing gets my blood pumping more than seeing her fire, than reminding her that life may be doing its damndest to snuff it out, but her flames burn eternal.

Clutching her hand in mine, I brush my finger along the back of her hand as I stare at her face. I know she needs rest, but I want nothing more than to see those hazel eyes latch onto mine. I need them to anchor me to this chair so I don't give into the undeniable urge to storm out of this room and find whoever was behind the wheel of that car and make them pay.

As much as I want time alone with my Tempest, I need Royce to hurry his ass up and get here so he can fill me in on what he's found.

The door creaks open slightly, and I straighten in my chair, thinking it's them. A nurse peeks in, offering a reassuring smile before closing it softly. I exhale a breath, slumping back in my seat as my eyes once again return to Riley.

I startle when I find her heavily lidded gaze on mine.

"Hey."

She licks her dry lips. "Hi."

Grabbing the jug of water on her table, I fill a glass and help her sit up before bringing it to her lips. She takes several long gulps before relaxing back against her pillows.

"How are you feeling?"

Her brows furrow, a twinge of pain flashing across her features before she lifts her hand to touch her scalp. I capture it before she can prod the welt on the side of her head and hurt herself. "What happened?" she asks, seeming confused. The doctor had said that was expected, so I am trying not to worry.

"You ran out in front of a car." It takes effort to keep the chastisement out of my tone.

"I... don't remember that," she murmurs, voice sounding far off.

"What *do* you remember?" I hedge, not wanting to push her too soon but needing to know what happened before I caught sight of her. Is my father responsible for this? Is he what drove her to race across campus like a maniac and eventually run out in front of that car?

"I..." Creases form between her brows before her eyes widen, fear bleeding into those off-green irises and dulling them as they meet mine. "Your dad." She swallows, her hand squeezing mine to the point of pain. "Your dad has Aurora." There's an edge of panic in her voice that bleeds into her expression. Clearly not in her right mind yet, she throws back the cover and tries to sit upright.

"Whoa. You have a concussion. You need to take it easy," I tell her, attempting to push her back onto the bed. Except she fights me. Was I just saying I wanted her to wake up and give me hell? I change my mind.

"Grayson," she grinds, exasperated. "Did you not hear me? Bertram has Aurora! We need to go!"

"I heard you just fine, Tempest. However, *you* are not going anywhere, so how about you lie back there and tell me what exactly happened."

She glares murderously at me, and something loosens in my chest at that spark of fire in her eyes. *There's my girl.*

"What if he's—" Her eyes are wide as saucers, skin sickly pale as she shakes her head. "I can't let him—"

I squeeze her hand, capturing her attention. "If Bertram has Aurora, he's using her to get to you. I don't think he'd... touch her."

Her eyes bore into mine, and I can tell she's not entirely there. That a part of her mind is elsewhere—on the past, on the possibilities. "She's too young for him," I say softly, watching as those words sink in and she finally relaxes—marginally.

"She still shouldn't be alone with him." Her voice is so tiny, almost defeated, as she sags against the pillows.

"We'll get her away from him, Tempest," I promise her. "But we can't do anything until you explain everything to me," I tell her. She nods slowly, sitting stiffly in the bed as she stares at me with an absent look that I absolutely detest. "Bertram was on campus..." I start her off.

She nods, wincing when the movement causes her pain. "H-he was in my advisor meeting." That fucking bastard. "Afterward, he caught up to me." Her gaze lowers to her wrist sitting in her lap. I'd noticed the redness and bloom of fresh bruises, but I'd assumed she landed on it awkwardly when we hit the ground. However, now that I look closer, I see the distinct impression of fingerprints. *That fucking bastard!* I'll kill him for laying a hand on her.

Her lower lip trembles and her voice begins to shake. "H-he said every day I defy him, he'll punish her." Tear-stained eyes lift to mine. "That either I come to him or she has t-to fill my shoes." Big fat tears spill over, streaming down her cheeks.

"Grayson," she sobs, keeling over as though she no longer has the energy to remain upright. Her shoulder falls into my chest, her face burying into the crook of my neck, and I hold her like I'm the only thing keeping her together. "What am I going to do? *He has her.*" Her entire body shakes with the force of her sobs. "He has my little girl. He's had her this entire time! What if he destroys her just like he did me?"

Murderous rampage blazes through my veins.

Fuck going after the driver of that damn car, I'm going to *murder* my father. My teeth grind so forcefully that I'm shocked I don't crack a tooth, and it's only the blatant fear in Riley's eyes, the trembling of her shoulders, that stops me from marching out of here in search of my shitstain of a sperm donor.

My mind whirs, trying to put the pieces together and figure out what we missed, how he could have had her this whole time, and we had no idea. We didn't even know he knew of her existence!

"I will *never* let that happen, Tempest," I vow, my voice a dark and violent rasp. "*We* will never let that happen."

Cradling her head in my hands, I lift her face to mine. Despite the storm raging inside me, my gaze holds steady on hers. Unwavering. Confident. Sure.

"He did not destroy you, and we won't give him the opportunity to *touch* her."

"How?" Her voice is hoarse. Broken. "How can we stop him? If I don't do what he wants—"

"You are *not* giving yourself to him. You know that's not the right thing to do. It's why you didn't go with him there and then."

"*What* then?" she cries. "What are we going to do to get her away from him?"

I tighten my hands around her face to get her attention and implore her with my eyes. "Trust me. Trust *us.*"

She holds my gaze, and I can see the hope buried in her fear. She wants to believe me, but life experience has taught her not to have such expectations.

Well, fuck life! I'll show her that her past experience has no bearing on her future. Everyone has let her down, but not any longer. Logan and Royce have been working to show her she can depend on them, and slowly but surely, she's been opening up. Leaning on them. Trusting them.

But I want her to lean on me, too. Trust me, too.

"We will do whatever it takes to get her away from him. I swear it to you, Tempest."

Her throat bobs, the brown and green swirl of her hazel eyes holding me captive. I can see her desire to believe in what I'm saying, but she's not quite there yet, and that's okay. I'll prove to her that she is right to put her faith in me.

She sniffles, wiping at the tear tracks beneath her eyes. "Why do you call me that?" she asks after a moment.

Her question hangs in the air between us as I take her in, trying to find the right words. I could give her a dismissive explanation. Something vague and insignificant, but I can't keep holding her at arm's length. I need to let her in if I want any hope of a future with this woman. I need to be vulnerable with her, even if it's the hardest thing I've ever done.

She deserves the truth. The raw, unfiltered truth.

"Tempest," I begin, my voice low and steady, "because you're a storm. You've been through so much, more than anyone should have to endure, yet here you are, standing tall. You've faced trauma and pain head-on, and you've survived. But it's more than that."

I pause, gathering my thoughts and feeling the intensity of the moment. "You stand up to me, Riley. You don't let me get away with anything. You call me out, argue with me, and you never back down. You give me hell, and I respect you so much for it. You're fierce, and you fight for what you believe in, for the people you love. You don't let anyone, not even me, push you around."

I can see the emotions swirling in her eyes, which spurs me on. "You're my tempest because you've shaken up my world. You've made me confront parts of myself I didn't want to face. You've challenged me and made me better. And through all of it, you've shown me what real strength looks like. You've shown me that it's okay to be vulnerable, to let someone in."

My voice softens, and I lean in closer, my gaze never leaving hers. "You're my tempest, Riley, because you're a force of nature. You're wild, unpredictable, and incredibly beautiful in your strength and resilience. And I wouldn't want you any other way."

As the words leave my lips, I feel a weight lift from my shoulders. It's terrifying, letting her see this side of me, but it's also liberating. Riley looks at me like she's seeing me for the first time. And perhaps she is. It's the first time I've permitted myself to drop my walls, to show her the damaged parts of me that I usually keep buried deep. The damage that has been heavily impacted upon in these last few months as I've been forced to face each horrifying truth: The actual reason for my mother's death. The reality of the man I've called father. The existence of a sister I never knew about. The hurt I allowed to happen to this woman who has become my whole world. Who forces me to be better. To see the world through a new lens. To confront every complex emotion that I'm so used to burying.

Her lips part, and I lean forward, desperate to hear what she has to say.

"Shortcake!"

The door bursts open, and Logan rushes in, going straight to Riley's side and pulling her in for a hug. She returns the embrace while her eyes remain on mine, the softest expression on her face I've ever seen when she looks at me.

"How are you?" Logan pulls back, cupping her face and forcing her attention to him.

"I'm okay," she assures, giving his shoulders a gentle squeeze.

I snort. "She is *not* okay. She has a minor concussion. Doctors are waiting on scan results. We should hopefully hear more soon."

As if nothing had just transpired between us, Riley pins me with that fierce glare of hers. For the first time since I saw her in that parking lot, I feel calm. The tension bleeds out of me, and my muscles relax, making me feel like everything will be okay—that *she* will be okay.

Logan goes to make himself comfortable on the bed beside her, but he's dragged away by Royce's tight fist on the back of his hoodie.

Logan lets out a stream of curses that has Riley smiling. The sight is the most beautiful thing I've seen before Royce replaces him at her bedside. Leaning down, he cups the side of her neck, his fingers brushing along the underside of her jaw as he presses his forehead to hers. They communicate with nothing but their eyes, the world around them entirely forgotten. I watch unabashedly, irrationally jealous of my best friend and their ease of connection.

It's ridiculous. I'm happy for Royce, especially given how difficult he finds it to talk to others. Yet, I'm still jealous as fuck that he has what I want.

I catch Logan watching me from the corner of my eye. Giving him my attention, he smirks knowingly. I scowl. "We have a problem."

"Like that's anything new," Logan huffs, collapsing onto the end of the bed so his back is slouched against the footboard.

"My dad is the one who has Aurora."

That gets the idiot's attention as he pings upright, mouth dropping open. "How?"

I shake my head. "He was on campus today. Showed up at Riley's advisor meeting and told her Aurora would pay if she didn't do what he wanted."

Royce's forehead creases. "That doesn't mean he has her," he muses aloud. "Just that he knows of her existence."

"And the fact that she's missing," Logan adds.

Riley's shoulders climb up to her ears, her eyes darting back and forth at the realization Bertram could have been playing her. I wouldn't put it past him to not have Aurora for the mere fact of using the knowledge that *we* don't have her to fuck with Riley's head.

Royce already has his phone in his hand. "I'll update Dax. If Bertram has her, there has to be something we can find to confirm it—shopping receipts, CCTV."

"I already asked him to look into my dad and David. Although it was more just to keep an eye on them. I wanted to know what they were up to."

Royce nods. "Well, they've just become Blue's top job to investigate."

Rubbing at the back of his neck, Logan confesses, "We've got more problems than just your dad."

I perk up at that, my gaze swiveling to Royce's. "The car. What did you find out?"

"Got a make and model. There was no license plate, and the driver was wearing a cap, so you can't see his face. Regardless, I've sent the footage to Blue. Hopefully he can work his magic and ID the fucker."

"The car I ran out in front of?" Riley asks with a frown, looking between us. "Is that what you're talking about? Why would you be looking into the driver? I'm the one who ran out in front of him. None of this is his fault."

"Ry, baby," Royce says softly, lowering so he's eye level with her. "You might have run out in front of that car, but he had no intention of stopping. He *wanted* to hit you."

"What?" Riley asks, expression incredulous as she sits up straighter. "Why would he want to do that?"

Royce shakes his head while Logan watches on from the bottom of the bed, furious murder blazing from his chestnut eyes.

"I don't know, sweetheart. However, there were no brake marks, and he sped out of there as if his life depended on it after Grayson pushed you out of the way."

Riley's eyes meet mine. "Are you sure?" she asks, voice small.

I give a helpless shrug, but it's Royce who answers. "I saw the CCTV footage. He was *flying* through that parking lot."

"That doesn't mean he wanted to hit me," she argues, but I can see the thin thread of hope she's clinging to.

"Either way, we have some questions for whoever he is." The silent threat in Royce's words promises more than words will be exchanged before the end of that encounter.

The doctor, a man in his mid-forties, chooses that moment to enter the room. Pausing in the threshold, his sharp gaze rakes over each of us, likely picking up on the underlying tension and violence, before resting on Riley. He gives her a reassuring smile.

"Miss James, I'm Dr. Beaumont. I'd like to discuss your condition." He glances warily at the rest of us. "Would you prefer to discuss it in private?"

Riley waves a tired hand. "It's fine. You can talk in front of them."

With a curt nod, he adjusts the chart in his hands and says,

"I have good news for you. The scans are clear. There are no signs of any bleeding in the brain or fracture to the skull, two issues we were particularly concerned about. However, you do still have a minor concussion. Therefore, it is important that you take it easy for the next few days."

I let out a breath I didn't realize I was holding, the tight knot in my chest loosening just a bit.

"You are free to be discharged," Dr. Beaumont glances between us, sizing each of us up, "but only if there is someone at home who can keep an eye on you for the next twenty-four hours. It's crucial to monitor for any changes."

"We'll take care of her." Royce's voice is firm, his protective nature evident.

The doctor nods, satisfied. "Good. You'll need to watch out for persistent vomiting, severe headaches that don't go away, confusion or difficulty waking her, weakness or numbness in her limbs, slurred speech, or any unusual behavior. If any of these symptoms occur, bring her back to the hospital immediately."

Riley looks slightly overwhelmed by the list, but Logan moves to her side, giving her hand a reassuring squeeze. "Got it," he states confidently to the doctor.

"Make sure she gets plenty of rest," the doctor continues. "No strenuous activities."

Logan, always the practical one, asks, "Is there anything specific we should do?"

"Keep the environment calm and quiet," Dr. Beaumont advises. "Dim lights are better; she should avoid reading or looking at screens. Hydration is important, and small, light meals are best. If she has any pain, over-the-counter acetaminophen can be used, but avoid ibuprofen or aspirin as they can increase the risk of bleeding."

"Thank you, doctor," I say, unable to hide my relief.

He gives us a tight, although reassuring, smile. "You're welcome. Riley, if you have any concerns or if anything feels off, don't hesitate to come back. Take care, and I hope you feel better soon."

With that, he leaves the room, and I return my attention to Riley. There's relief in her eyes, but it's overshadowed by concern for her daughter. I know we're going to have a hell of a job getting her to relax and recuperate until we have Aurora home safe and sound.

"We've got you, Tempest," I say softly. "We've got both of you." *I swear it.*

RILEY

CHAPTER TWENTY-ONE

*L*aughter peels through the air—familiar laughter, so pure and joyful that it tugs at my heart. With quick steps, I follow the sound of my daughter's laughter through the house.

I find her in the living room, and I freeze in the doorway, my eyes raking over her long, dark hair and delicate features. She looks exactly as I remember from the last time I saw her.

She's playing on the soft rug, her tiny hands gripping a toy as she runs around in circles, her pigtails bouncing with each step. Sunlight streams through the windows, glinting off her hair and highlighting her auburn strands. Mesmerized, I can't take my eyes off her. I memorize that smile. The sparkle in her hazel eyes. God, she looks so happy. This is how I always want her to be. Safe. Carefree. Untroubled.

Logan is sprawled on the floor beside her, making exaggerated faces as he pretends to be a monster. "Roar! I'm gonna get you, Aurora!" he growls playfully, crawling toward her. She squeals in delight, darting away only to circle back and touch his nose with a giggle.

Royce is on the couch, his usually stern face softened with a rare smile as he watches my little girl playing with Logan. "Daddy!"

Aurora squeals, Logan chasing her. "Save me!" Her little legs race toward Royce, who holds out his arms, and she runs into them without a second thought before he lifts her onto his lap.

He holds her close like she's something precious, and the look on his face—on all their faces is one of pure love, unwavering affection. "Daddy," Aurora says again, and my heart clenches at hearing her say that word. At her calling my men that. Her eyes are heavy now as she snuggles closer to Royce. "Tell me a story."

Logan drops onto the sofa beside them, and Aurora shuffles over so she's nestled between them. She's blinking furiously, fighting sleep as Logan weaves a tale about brave knights and dragons.

Grayson's in the kitchen, but he's not far from us. He keeps glancing over, his eyes filled with love and contentment. Occasionally, he joins in the fun, tossing out comments or laughing at Royce's ridiculous story.

He finishes whatever he's doing in the kitchen and walks over, carrying a plate of freshly baked cookies. "Who wants a treat?" he calls, and Aurora's eyes light up, any notion of sleep forgotten as she scrambles off the sofa and rushes to Grayson.

"Me! Me!" she chants, bouncing on her feet as she reaches up with eager hands.

Grayson hands her a cookie, and she takes a big bite, her face lighting up with pure joy. "Ah-ah," he chastises with a smile when she goes to snag a second one. "I think we should see if Mommy wants one first."

Aurora nods, whirling on the spot to search for me. Spotting me in the doorway, she gives me a gap-toothed grin. "Mommy! Daddy made cookies!"

Grayson is already crossing the room toward me. He holds out the plate, offering me a cookie. I take it, our fingers brushing, and I feel a spark of something more profound. Something that grounds me in this moment and has me praying it never ends.

Aurora grabs my hand, dragging me to the sofa, and Logan and

Royce make room for me between them. Royce clasps my hand, and Logan kisses my cheek as the three of them settle around me, their presence a protective barrier against any harm. Grayson moves to sit on the floor at my feet while Aurora dances on the rug before us, the very picture of happiness and innocence.

Tears sting my eyes as I savor this impossible moment of peace and happiness, knowing that when I wake, this is what I'll fight for.

My daughter.

My family.

Our happiness.

This is my sanctuary, my hope, and I'll do anything to make it our reality.

ROYCE

I take off as soon as Riley is safely home and in Logan's care. I can't sit around and wait. Can't stare into her face, torn with anguish. I need to move. To do something—anything that helps. Which is how I end up in Dax's office at Rogue, hovering over him and driving him insane.

"Dude," he growls. "Back the fuck off before I hit you."

"How do you not have anything yet?" I snap. "You've been looking into Bertram for days now."

"It's not like that's all I do. In case you forgot, I'm also dealing with the auction aftermath, and I have my own fucking businesses to run. My own life to lead. I'm doing the best I can. Now that we know Bertram has her, I've devoted all the resources I can spare. These things take time, Royce. I promise you. We will get him. Just back the fuck off."

Huffing out a frustrated breath, I reluctantly step away.

"Blue is the only man we have on this," Dax continues. "But he's the best. I assure you, he will find what we need. He will find *her*." His phone pings, and I'm back across the room in the blink of an eye, once again hovering over him.

He gives me a death glare that would have most grown

men's hearts giving out. But I don't give a fuck. Sighing, he shakes his head at me and focuses on his phone.

"Blue has an ID on your driver." He tilts the screen so I can see the details. One glance at the photo, and I snort. "You recognize him?"

"Yeah. He goes by Knuckles, although his real name is Vincent. I've seen him around here sometimes. He likes to get in on the fights but has no real skill or talent."

"Why don't you go talk to him and let Blue do his job of finding Aurora?"

Gritting my teeth, I hesitate, reluctant to leave. But no, I need to burn off this frustration and hopelessness, this anger that's eating away at me.

"Fine," I hiss. Seething but knowing this is the best thing to do. It's *all* I can do for right now. Dax just better pray that by the time I'm finished with this guy, he's got some real fucking answers for me. 'Cause I'm done sitting back. I'm done letting Bertram call the shots. Knowing that he has Aurora, that he has Riley's little girl. That he's had her this. Entire. Fucking. Time pisses me the hell off. How could we not have known? It makes me feel like even more of a failure. Like letting Aurora slip through my fingers that night wasn't enough. Fucking karma had to laugh in my face with the knowledge that the buyer was Grayson's fucking dad.

Turning on my heel, I storm toward the door, but Dax calls after me. "Don't go alone. You'll probably fucking kill the guy. Take one of your buddies with you—Grayson. I'm sure he could do with the outlet if he's recovered from his last fight. Fuck knows, with the amount of work you lot are adding to my plate, I don't have the time to get back in the ring with that Suit Slicker."

I dismiss him without a word, marching out of Rogue and onto the Springview sidewalk. As I head for my truck parked just down the road, my phone vibrates in my pocket. Checking it, I find Dax has sent me the details on this fucking idiot who thought he could mess with our girl. I take one look at his douchey fucking face before scrolling through the rest of the info Blue sent through on him. He's got a criminal record—mostly petty crimes, assault—a few stints in the county jail but nothing significant enough to keep him locked up for long.

Shaking my head, I navigate to his home address, unsurprised that it's a trailer park in Boxum. Memorizing it, I dial Grayson.

Dax is probably right. Grayson will be as in need of this outlet as I am. Logan, too, but he's far better than either of us at setting his anger aside to meet Riley's needs. He's the best one of us to stay and comfort her, and Grayson and I are the best men for *this*.

"Got something?" Grayson asks when he answers.

"Not what you want, but we've got an address for the driver. Want to come with?"

"Fuck yes, I do." Despite the absolute shitstorm that has been this day, my lips twitch in a semblance of a smile.

"I'll stop by to pick you up. Be ready to jump in the car."

"Sure thing."

Instead of hanging up, I hesitate. "How is she?"

"Sleeping, finally. Logan convinced her to eat some food, but she was a strung-out mess. We need to find out where my dad is keeping Aurora, and we need to find out now."

"We will," I assure him. "Let's get some answers from this fucking asshole, then we're going to deal with your dad."

Hanging up, I climb into the car. It doesn't take long to make it back to Halston, and by the time I reach the house, Grayson is standing on the sidewalk waiting for me. He jumps in, and I'm away again, following the directions on the Satnav to Timberline Trailer Park.

"Tell me about this guy."

"Not much to tell. He's a thug, a street brawler," I tell him. "I've seen him hanging around The Depot, but I don't know much about him."

"He's a fighter?" Grayson asks, turning to look at me.

I snort. "A shitty one, but he's a dirty fighter. From what little Blue sent through, he's a petty criminal. Still lives in the same rough neighborhood he grew up in. He's not smart, but he's street-smart."

"So what the fuck is he doing trying to run over our girl then?" Grayson growls, hands forming fists as his anger gets the better of him.

"Fuck if I know." My finger taps against the steering wheel, the road disappearing beneath my wheels as we leave Halston behind. "Going after her isn't something he'd do on his own," I muse. "He has no reason to target her."

"You mean someone paid him," Grayson deduces with a cold calculation.

I lift a shoulder in a shrug. It's my best guess, but what the fuck do I know? We'll get answers when we talk to him. It's a tense ride to Timberline Trailer Park on the outskirts of Boxum County. The farther from Halston we drive, the more apparent the neglect becomes until we're bumping along roads that are more pothole than asphalt. Glancing skyward, I can see that most of the streetlights have been smashed out.

"This place is a shit hole," Grayson mumbles as we pass trailers that are packed together tightly. "Which one is his?" I jut my chin out the windshield, indicating the trailer in the far corner of the lot. It's the worst one in the park—a single-wide relic from the 70s that's seen better days. The paint is chipped and peeling, revealing the bare metal underneath, and the roof sags in the middle, threatening to cave in with the next heavy rain. A couple of junk cars sit on cinder blocks in the front yard, the parts slowly being cannibalized for cash.

Slowing the car to a stop, we both lean forward to look at the rust bucket through the windshield. "Looks... homie," Grayson drawls, lip curled up in disgust before he throws open the door. "Well, what the fuck are we waiting for?"

Getting out of the car, I follow him up the rotted steps. We share a glance before he bangs his fist against the flimsy door. Immediately, we hear footsteps approach from the other side before the door swings open. A muscular man in his mid-thirties with a barrel chest fills the doorframe. "Who the fuck are you?" Vincent sneers.

He looks down his nose at us like we're shit on his grimy boots, and I let my focus slide past him and into the trailer. The inside is worse than I imagined—filthy dishes piled in the sink, an ashtray overflowing on a rickety coffee table, and the stench of stale beer and sweat permeating the air. The carpet is stained, with patches worn down to the floorboards, and the walls are yellowed from years of smoke. The main piece of furniture is an old, threadbare couch, and trash is scattered across the floor. What I don't see is anyone else in there.

Perfect.

There's no holding back. I shove at his shoulders, sending him stumbling back into the trailer as I barge my way in. Grayson is right behind me, slamming the door to keep any unwanted eyes out. Although, I imagine people are plenty used to turning a blind eye to trouble here. The walls creak as the door shuts, and dust particles float in the stale air, catching the dim light from the single, flickering bulb overhead.

Vincent's eyes go wide as he holds his hands up. "What the fuck? Who are you guys? What do you want?"

"We want to know why you were in Halston today," Grayson demands, standing over him.

"Halston?" Vincent attempts to laugh. "Why the fuck would I be in that preppy shithole town?"

"Well, we have CCTV footage that says you were," I snap, crossing my arms over my chest and staring him down. "So let's try this again, Vincent."

His eyes widen. "Hey—" He points a finger at me. "I know you. You're Ruthless!" His lips twitch into a smile. The dumb fuck must've forgotten that we just barged into his house because he looks at me like we're fucking friends. "Yo, man, I'm a big fan. Holy shit, I can't believe you're in my house!"

"Yeah, no." I'm not having any of that. I grab him by the front of his stained T-shirt and slam him backward. The entire trailer rattles with the force. "Answer my fucking question, Vincent. What the fuck were you doing on Halston University's campus today?"

"Whoa, man, whoa." He's still giving me that stupid fucking smile, but his eyes are wide with wariness as he holds his hands up placatingly. "I was just there for a job, man. It was nothing."

Grabbing the half-full bottle of whiskey on the countertop, Grayson throws it at the wall. "You call trying to kill our fucking girl *nothing*," he screams. His jaw tightens, and his fists clench, his knuckles turning white. His eyes blaze with barely contained fury, rage simmering just beneath the surface.

For the first time since we barged our way in here, Vincent has the good sense to look fucking afraid. His Adam's apple bobs, and the color drains from his face. "What? Nah, man, no way. It was just some chick. Some rich bitch. This lady paid me to get rid of her. There's no way that pretentious bitch was Ruthless' girl—y-your girl."

I tilt my head, my cool, calm facade to Grayson's incinerating one. Which only terrifies the fuckwit more. "Auburn hair, hazel eyes," I drawl. "That ringing any fucking bells?"

"Oh god. Oh god. Oh god," he stammers on repeat, trembling like a fucking leaf in my hold. My nose twitches, and it takes a second for me to realize the dumb fuck has pissed himself.

"Jesus." Grayson's face crunches in disgust. "Have some fucking dignity, man. That's disgusting."

I snap. Expression twisted in fury, I land a punch square on Vincent's jaw. He cries out, and if it weren't for my firm hold on him, he'd have crumpled to the floor like the spineless piece of shit he is.

"I didn't know she was your girl," he sobs pathetically. "I had no idea. I would never have gone near her if I'd known. You gotta believe me, Ruthless," Vincent pleads, his voice shaking.

With my hold still on the front of his shirt, I yank him toward me before slamming him back. He cries out, but neither of us has any sympathy for the rat. Grayson holds up his phone in front of Vincent's face with a picture of Lydia on it. "Is this the woman who paid you?" he demands.

Vincent barely looks at it before nodding in alarm. "Yeah, yeah, that was her. She paid me ten grand to get rid of this chick. I had no idea. I just needed the money, man, you know?"

My lips curl into a sneer. "You agreed to kill another human being for a measly fucking ten grand? You're fucking scum."

Weirdly, that's what seems to enrage him, and in a surprising turn, Vincent locates his ballsack long enough to snarl, "We can't all be lucky enough to be born into fucking riches, can we? Ten grand might be nothing to you, but it's a fucked ton to me."

"Yeah, I bet that buys you a whole lot of booze, drugs, and hookers," I seethe.

"You're a fucking piece of shit!" Grayson growls, his voice low and dangerous. He kicks Vincent in the ribs hard enough that a snap renders the air, and he doubles over, wheezing.

"Please."

Grayson kicks him again, harder this time. The trailer shakes with the impact, and I let go. Vincent slides down the wall as I drive my fist into his gut. Spittle flies from his lips and dribbles down his chin as he sags onto the filthy floor, curling up on his side to try and shield himself. But it's no use. Both me and Grayson are relentless, our fury boiling over as we beat the shit out of him.

There's a catharsis in the violence. It won't solve anything, but it's a much-needed distraction.

When we finally slow down, breathing hard, Vincent is a bloody, unrecognizable mess on the floor. Grayson plants his hands on his knees, bent over as he catches his breath.

Vincent moans and I grab a fistful of his hair, wrenching his face to mine. "You're done with The Depot. I don't ever want to see your fucking face again."

"Let's get the fuck out of here," Grayson says, spitting on Vincent's unconscious form. "This place fucking reeks."

"You don't need to tell me twice." I'm already heading for the door. The worst of the fury has drained, leaving only a deep need to get back to Riley, to ensure she's safe.

The first step in doing that is eliminating Lydia once and for all.

That bitch is a dead fucking corpse walking.

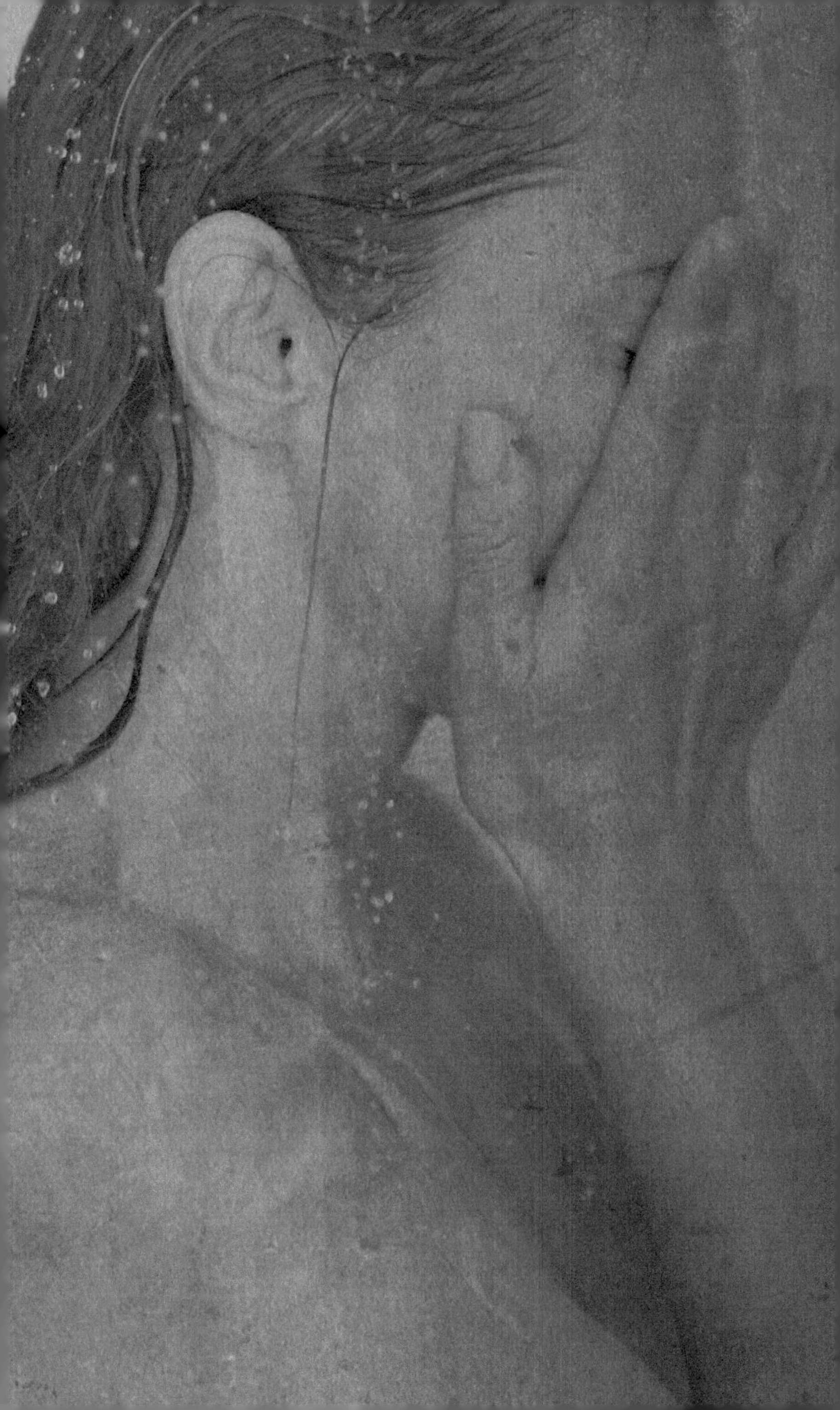

RILEY

CHAPTER TWENTY-THREE

The sound of the front door snicking shut wakes me from sleep. I stir in Logan's arms, which tighten around me as he groans into my shoulder. A makeshift bed had been constructed on the living room floor when I arrived home from the hospital, piled high with pillows and blankets. I've been cocooned in it all day while Logan plied me with food and distractions. When none of that worked to make me relax, I'm pretty sure he dosed my juice with pain meds because I don't remember falling asleep.

"Five more minutes," he mumbles, making me smile despite the heavy weight that has been wrapped around my throat, choking me as it sits painfully on my chest since Bertram dropped the bomb that *he* has Aurora.

That weight making it impossible to breathe? It's fear.

Terror over what Bertram has been doing with my daughter all these weeks. Dread over what he *wants*. What his end game is. Trepidation over how I get her back... how *we* get her back.

Bertram might be Aurora's father, but that little girl is *mine*.

If Aurora's going to call anyone *Daddy*, it won't be him. It'll be the three men who were as knocked off their feet as I was to discover the truth. The three men who have vowed to do whatever it takes to get her away from him. To bring her home.

I'm failing to untangle myself from Logan's octopus arms when Royce and Grayson walk in, expressions carefully blank. Too blank. It immediately has my shoulders bunching and my earlier headache reappearing with a vengeance.

Royce comes straight to my side, crouching on the mattress as he reaches for me. "How are you feeling?"

My eyes search his.

"She's still got a headache, but she ate and drank and has been resting," Logan fills him in, wiping the sleep from his eyes as he sits up. The sheet falls to his waist, exposing his chest, and my gaze lingers momentarily on those hard planes before I glance away, watching as Grayson collapses into a chair. His knuckles are split and raw-looking, and my attention snaps back to Royce, noticing his are the same. "What happened?" I demand.

He sighs this long, weary sound that tells me nothing good. My heart sinks.

Grayson emits an equally exhausted groan, swiping a hand down his face, but not before I notice the dark bags under his eyes, despite the still prominent bruising from his stupid fight with Dax.

"I think we need coffee for this conversation," Logan groans, climbing out from beneath the sheets.

"And you need more clothes." My gaze snaps to Grayson, finding him staring at the exposed skin of my shoulder, where the oversized T-shirt I'm wearing has fallen, with a feral sort of possession that liquifies my insides.

I shift, catching a whiff of myself. "What I need is a shower." And a moment to prepare.

"Go shower, Ry. Take as long as you need." Royce helps me to my feet, and feeling Grayson's heated stare on my bare legs, I pull down the hem of my T-shirt before Royce escorts me from the room.

In the shower, the hot water cascades over my skin, a temporary balm to my frayed nerves. Bertram has my daughter. It's a terrifying sentence I never thought I'd hear. What is he doing with her? Where is he keeping her? They are questions I barely dare to ask myself.

Hands trembling, I force my eyes closed and let the steam envelop me. Flashes of another life... no, a dream, play out behind my eyelids.

Aurora's laughter.

Royce's smile.

Logan's light.

The love in Grayson's eyes when he looked at my daughter... and when he looked at me.

My heart clenches, and a sob rips from my throat. I can feel it, right there, at the tips of my fingers. It's practically within reach, yet every time I grab for it, it slinks away. How can everything I ever wanted but never thought I'd find be so close yet so far? When I gave birth to Aurora, my life became all about her. Every breath. Every thought. Everything I did was for her. I never thought I'd find a man who would want *us*. Figured, I'd wait until she was grown, finishing high school, if not in college, before I considered a serious relationship with anyone.

Yet somehow, I've found not one but *three* men who accept us, who accept my little girl without even having met her.

I feel like the luckiest woman in the world.

And the unluckiest.

How much more can I take? How many more blows before I shatter completely? I've been barely holding on, clinging to the hope that we'll find Aurora and that everything will be okay. But with each piece of bad news, that hope feels more like a delusion. This final one... knowing Bertram not only knows of Aurora's existence but that he *has* her... I fear that it will be my undoing.

My body shakes with silent sobs, the sound of the water masking my despair.

Leaning against the cool tile, I allow myself to feel the fear that I've been holding at bay. It surges up, a tidal wave of anxiety and exhaustion that threatens to drown me.

Closing my eyes, I think of Aurora, her sweet face, and the way she laughs, and a fresh wave of fear grips my heart. I must be strong for her, but what if I can't? What if this is the hit that sends me over the edge? My mind spins with the what-ifs, the terrifying possibilities that keep me awake at night.

Hidden from the rest of the world, the sound of my openly bleeding wounds masked by the rushing of water, I allow myself this moment of weakness, these precious few minutes where I can break down and feel every ounce of my fear and pain. Then, slowly, I start to pull myself back together. I take a deep breath, feeling the steam fill my lungs, and I force myself to stand tall. I can't give in to despair. This life will *not* beat me down. Bertram *will not* destroy me.

Aurora needs me, and for her, I'll be strong.

The water washes away my tears, and with them, some of my fear. I start to rebuild my walls, brick by brick, fortifying myself against the onslaught of emotions that threaten to over-whelm me. I can do this. I *have* to do this.

I turn off the shower and open the steamed-up door. Royce stands there with a towel already in his hands.

"Wanted to check on you," he says at my look of surprise. I hadn't even heard him come in. His gaze drops to my thighs, shadows swimming in his eyes, and I realize he was worried I would do something stupid like I did when I found out about Bertram's release.

I step into the open towel and continue until I'm pressed against him, my cheek resting against the hard lines of his muscles. "That was a moment of terror-fueled stupidity," I tell him. "I'm... I'm not okay. I'm so far from being okay, but I don't want to hurt myself. I haven't truly wanted to hurt myself for a long time. Since I found out I was pregnant with Aurora." I shake my head. "It was a moment of weakness that I regret."

His large, calloused hand slides between the wet, heavy strands of my hair. "Don't regret a moment of weakness, James." His voice is deep and earnest. "Showing weakness isn't a failure. It's a necessary part of the journey. Those moments of vulnerability allow us to grow and find our true strength. Without them, we'd never know the full extent of our resilience. It's in those cracks that our light shines through the brightest."

His words hit me hard, resonating deep within. Tears prick at the corners of my eyes, but I blink them back, refusing to let them fall. "I just... I don't want to let anyone down. Especially not Aurora."

"You won't," he assures me, his grip tightening on the back of my head and tilting it so I'm looking into his face. "You've already shown more strength and resilience than most people ever do. The fact that you can admit to feeling weak and then find the courage to move forward, that's what makes you truly strong."

His breath dances across my lips before he seals it with a kiss, one that infuses me with more strength than I thought possible. I feel the cracks in my armor sealing over, melding together.

"And in those moments where you can't be strong," he whispers when he pulls back, still holding me. "I'll be strong for you."

"Thank you," I whisper, my voice filled with gratitude.

His responding smile is a thing of beauty before he helps me change into a pair of leggings and a long-sleeved top of his. Before we exit the bathroom, though, he places a hand on my arm. "I want to show you something."

I glance up at him, searching his eyes. "Okay."

With a small smile at my display of trust, he trails his fingers down my arm before slotting them through mine and leading me out of the bathroom.

We cross the hall to his room before he drops my hand, moving to flick on the bedside lamp before opening a drawer in his dresser. "I don't think I ever told you I snuck into Lydia's house once."

"You did?" My eyebrows hitch in surprise. "Why?"

Back still turned to me, he shrugs those broad shoulders of his. "I didn't like the things you said about her—how she was withholding Aurora from you. So, I went to do a little digging."

I huff humorlessly. "Of course you did. Wait, is that how you found out she was up to something?"

He nods. Lifting something out of his dresser drawer, he turns to face me. "I went there to better understand Lydia... but also because I was curious about Aurora."

I go still, hanging on his every word as he takes a step toward me.

"I saw the effort you'd put into her room." Step. "Ensuring she felt at home in that house." Step. "That she was loved."

The light from the bedside table glints off the box in his hand, a sparkle of glitter catching my eye. My gaze snaps to the pink box he's holding, a hand flying to cover my mouth as a gasp rips free. "Royce."

His name is choked. Strangled.

"I found this hidden under her bed."

My gulp is audible as I swallow, throat thick and dry. "H-how do you have that?"

Hands shaking, I drag my finger over the writing on the lid, scrawled in glitter pen: *Aurora and Mommy's box of memories.*

"I went back to her house the day after... She had the house packed up already. Her room..." Something in his tone has me lifting my eyes. He merely shakes his head and frowns. I focus back on the box. "I paid the movers to deliver everything she didn't want here. It's taken me a while to go through it all. I hadn't wanted to say anything until I found it."

Throat constricting around nothing, I croak, "Have you looked inside?"

One side of his lips tilts in a mischievous smile like he's been caught doing something naughty. Despite the chaotic storm of emotions raging inside, I can't help but laugh at his expression. "I might have peeked inside when I was in her room that night."

I slowly take the box from him, holding it carefully in my arms as I sit on the edge of his bed. I pat the space beside me, waiting until he sits before reaching for the lid. "We made this when I found out I'd gotten into Halston. I wanted her to have keepsakes." I swallow roughly. "I was worried my mother would toss out any nicknacks or reminders of me, so we put them all in here. Along with all the memories we made last summer."

Breathing shallowly, I delicately lift the lid, setting it gently on the bedside table before I look down at the contents of the box. My lips tremble with the onslaught of memories. Craft days spent together. Birthdays. Movie dates. Our trip to the carnival last summer.

"There's so much happiness in this box," I murmur, taking my time as I flick through the stack of photos. In every single one, Aurora is smiling up at the camera. *Happy.*

"So much love, too," Royce adds, leaning in to peer at the pictures.

"Yeah," I agree.

"You're obviously a great mom."

I make a noise of self-deprecation. "I dunno about that. There's a lot I've done wrong."

"Yeah, but there's also a lot you've done right, and the way your daughter looks at you in these photos, I'd say you've done a hell of a lot more right than you have wrong."

"I feel like I'm always failing her," I admit aloud. "Like, no matter what I do, I always make the wrong decision."

"I don't think that's true. Every decision you make, you do it with her best interests in mind. Sure, they might not always work out the way you intended." I snort derisively. "*But*, they were decisions made with love, which is all any kid really needs." Royce is silent for a moment before he confesses. "I'd readily give up every dollar to the King name if it meant having parents who loved me. Who *cared*."

"Yeah," I agree. "I'd give up anything to have that too."

Noticing something, he leans closer, dipping his hand into the box. "What's this?" he asks, beads dangling from his fingertips.

Smiling fondly, I take the bracelet from him. *Riley* is spelled out on white beads, each letter brightly colored in a different vibrant hue. At either end are tiny, shiny gold beads that add a pretty sparkle to the bracelet, while the rest is filled with shades of pink from soft pastels to deep rose, creating a beautiful gradient. It's playful and eye-catching, and I remember being so delighted when Grayson gave it to me.

"This is the only gift I've ever received from Grayson," I share with Royce.

"No way, Gray got you this?"

I nod my head. "For my fifteenth birthday. We'd only been

living in his house for a month or so. We hardly knew each other, but I was already crushing on him," I chuckle, remembering. "My mom hated it. She said it was cheap. I mean, it was a kid's bracelet; of course, it was cheap, but I loved it. She refused to let me wear it, so I kept it hidden in my jewelry box, scared that if she saw it, she'd throw it in the trash.

"This bracelet was my lifeline. When I was feeling so desperately alone and isolated, I'd hide in my closet, clutching this in my hand, and I'd think about Grayson and whatever stupid thing he'd done that day to make me smile."

I stroke my finger reverently over the beads spelling out my name. "It gave me hope that there was someone out there who cared, who saw me. It made me feel like I wasn't entirely alone in the world."

My lips are bone dry as I continue. "When I left for Halston, I gave it to Aurora, hoping it would offer her the same comfort —that when she was missing me or felt alone, she could lift it out and know that I was always with her."

"How about you keep it safe until you can give it back to her." Royce carefully takes the bracelet from me, before sliding it over my hand. "Now, she can always be with you. And Grayson, too, which I'm sure he'll get a kick out of."

My responding laugh is wet as I swipe at my eyes. "He's totally going to see this as a sign of possession."

Smirking, Royce teases, "Hey, it could be worse. It *could* be a choker."

"Oh my god!" I smack him in the chest with the back of my hand, even though I'm laughing, the moment of levity broken. "Wait, do you think that's what he was doing with this? Claiming me?"

Royce snorts. "I have no doubt."

"I don't understand," I say, barely feeling the heat from my scalding coffee as it sears into my palms. I can feel the coolness of the bracelet against my wrist, hidden beneath Royce's top, and thank goodness for its inherent powers because I am in need of its strength after that bomb drop—something Royce somehow knew.

Taking a steadying breath, I look into each of their faces. The four of us are seated around the kitchen table for this discussion.

I'm not sure if I'm in a state of shock or denial.

Both.

I'm definitely experiencing both.

Or perhaps that concussion was more severe than the doctor thought, and this is all some sort of twisted hallucination.

"My mother paid this guy, this… Vincent, to kill me?"

There's no way I heard that right.

Except, the mixture of outright hostile and sympathetic expressions they are each sporting says that's exactly what Grayson just said.

"Why?"

Okay, that's probably a stupid question. There is no love lost between me and Lydia. Still, outright murdering me sounds… ridiculous. *Yeah, so did finding out she sold your daughter…*

…To fucking Bertram!

The three of them share an uneasy look. It's Grayson who spells it out for me. "You're an… inconvenience. A problem. A… nuisance." Logan growls in warning, one leg bouncing erratically under the table. Grayson's hard stare slides his way. "Obviously, none of us think that," he drawls, glowering at Logan. "But I imagine it's what your mo—" It's my turn to glare at him, and he quickly corrects himself. "*Lydia* is thinking." He sighs. "I don't know what her plans were after she offloaded

Aurora"—Cue another furious hiss from Logan—"but I'm guessing she knows she can't put you off indefinitely. At some point, you'll go to the police and become a problem she can't handle."

"Now, with Bertram going after you..." Royce adds with a grimace.

I bark out a cold, caustic laugh that doesn't even sound like it comes from me. "She's jealous." Another arctic snort that doesn't feel like mine. "My mother tried to kill me because she's fucking jealous."

It would be hilarious if it wasn't fucking *insane*.

Except I'm now bent over the table, laughing hysterically. Because obviously, *this* is what breaks me. *This* is the line from which I won't return.

"My mother tried to kill me," I wheeze out.

"Uhh." Logan. "Is she okay?"

"Does she look fucking okay to you?" Grayson grinds out.

"Riley?" A hand rests against my upper arm.

My entire body continues to shake with laughter. The kind that signifies to those around them that you have fucking snapped. Spilled your marbles all over the floor. *Warning! Warning! Get the straitjacket!*

"I mean, who can say they were nearly murdered by their own mother?" Tears overflow and stream down my face. "What is that called? There must be a name for that. Like patricide but..."

"Filicide."

Blinking through the film covering my eyes, I stare at Royce.

"That's what it's called—Filicide. Although technically, since she didn't succeed, it doesn't apply."

"Yet. She didn't succeed *yet*." Because Lydia James—or Van Doren, I guess—is anything if not persistent.

It's that acknowledgment that zaps the energy from me. My

shoulders slump. I deflate, and those cackles of laughter turn into sobs. Heavy, heart-wrenching sobs.

I shouldn't be this upset, not after everything.

I'm not even sure that I am that upset. It's more the shock of it all. The realization—not that I needed it—that I mean so little to my own mother. The woman who carried me in her womb for nine months. Who gave birth to me. Who raised me.

I would lay down my life for Aurora. Would willingly have done so from the moment those pink lines showed up on the pregnancy test.

So why could my mother never do the same for me?

What is so inherently wrong with me that my own mother would hate me so much that she would steal every ounce of happiness I try to obtain for myself?

"Hey, shush." I'm wrapped up in strong arms as I'm carried from the room before being deposited on someone's lap on the sofa. I inhale, breathing in the crisp scent of Logan's body wash. The others settle around us while I sob quietly into Logan's t-shirt—one he put on while I was showering. The entire time, Logan murmurs soothingly into my ear while Royce's grounding presence presses in on my left side as he rubs calming circles up and down my back, and a smooth hand that can only belong to Grayson holds tightly onto mine, anchoring me.

Slowly, my wracking sobs turn to hiccupped whimpers until there is nothing but silence. The four of us sit in that silence. Words feel inadequate and unnecessary at this moment. They understand that nothing they can say will change what's happened or make the pain disappear. All they can do is be here, and that's precisely what they're doing. Their unspoken support fills the room, making it clear that I'm not alone. And that's all I truly need right now.

"She's got no idea she sold my daughter to Bertram, does

she?" My voice is hoarse, cracking over the syllables when I finally speak.

"I wouldn't think so," Royce answers softly.

"What a messed up twist of fate, that is."

Logan snorts, still holding me firmly against him.

"How are we going to get her back?" I ask the room. While discussing how my mother paid some thug to hit me with his car, they haven't once mentioned locating Aurora's whereabouts, so I'm assuming we still don't know.

That knowledge leaves me cold and empty. Perhaps I'd cry if I had any more tears left in me. As it stands, all I feel is hollow.

"Dax and Blue are working on it," Royce assures me, his voice strong and steady. "They'll have something for us soon."

He sounds so sure, but I'm too numb to feel... anything.

"Dax had offered to... question Lydia." Grayson's statement rings like a bell in the otherwise quiet room. I shuffle so I'm looking directly at him. "We'd said no 'cause we were worried about my father finding out about Aurora..."

"We don't need to question her anymore, do we?" My voice is small. Flat. Dead.

"I wasn't thinking about questioning her."

Pushing upright, I meet Grayson's hard, unwavering stare. There's no uncertainty there—only cold, hard determination.

Determination to keep me safe. To get revenge.

"Do it."

Was that my voice, so sharp and deadly?

"Do it," I repeat, pushing up from Logan's chest. I don't bother to wipe away the tears. I'm not ashamed of them. They aren't a sign of weakness. They're healing tears. Acceptance tears. Ones that needed to be shed to give way for strength. "But not Dax's guys." I glance at each of them. "Us. *We* do it. *We* go after Lydia. I want her to see that she failed. That she'll continue to fail. That I'm fucking done yielding to her. We can use the video footage from campus and the driver she paid to keep her quiet."

"Are you sure this is what you want to do?" Royce asks softly, even as determination blazes in the cold depths of those ice-blue eyes.

I hold his stare, letting him see the volition burning in mine. Then, I answer his question for all three of them to hear. "Yes."

RILEY

CHAPTER TWENTY-FOUR

The next day, I go to Ava's dance studio. I feel bad that, bar the odd text, we've barely talked, and honestly, I need to dance out this maelstrom of emotion threatening to swallow me whole. Between discovering Bertram has had my daughter this entire time and the fact my own mother tried to have me killed, it's safe to say that my head is a mess.

Grayson's acknowledgment that Aurora is too young for Bertram is the only thing getting me through. I was fifteen when we moved into his house. Even if his preferences went a bit younger... Three is too young! That's what I'll keep believing until the universe tells me otherwise.

I can't sit around that house while we wait for a call from Dax or his men to round up Lydia, and I'm incapable of focusing on my studies right now. Dancing has always been my escape, my sanctuary. The world could crumble around me, but in those moments when my body moves to the rhythm, I find solace. Today, I need that solace.

Unfortunately, I'm apparently unable to obtain it alone.

"After you," Grayson grunts as he pulls open the door to the dance studio and gestures for me to go in. He volunteered as tribute when I said I was coming here. Unfortunately, Logan has hockey practice, and Royce said he was going to The Depot to discuss plans to kidnap my mother—isn't it funny how fate works itself out?—with Dax and his team.

Meanwhile, Grayson has been hovering like a mother hen since I was released from the hospital, despite me telling him—and the other two—that I'm perfectly fine. Pissed off and a little shaken up, but *fine.* I could tell he didn't even want me coming here today, but for what must be the first time in his life, he learned how to keep quiet when I sent him a cutting glare after informing him and Royce what my plans were for the day.

"You can stay in here," I tell him as I drop my bag inside the door of the empty studio.

"Why? Where are you going?"

I point up the stairs to where Ava's office is. "To talk to Ava."

"Then I'll come with you."

Before he can step forward, I plant a hand on his chest. "No. You won't. Ava is my *friend*, and I need to talk to her alone."

The angle of his jaw pulses, and I fold my lips between my teeth to suppress my laugh at seeing him so easily riled. I definitely get a kick out of it.

"You're not supposed to be alone."

"Good thing I won't be alone, then."

"Riley." He growls my name between clenched teeth.

"Grayson." I pin him with a look. "That's how this works: compromise. Do you understand that word? Does it exist in your dictionary?" I flick my finger back and forth between us. "There has to be both give and take between us if this is ever going to work."

He seems to somehow grow in size as he inhales before slowly letting it all out, including his frustration. "You're right."

I'm... what?

"I'm sorry. I must have misheard you. Can you repeat that?"

"You're right," he says again, this time with a dramatic roll of his eyes.

"I'm sorry." I fish in the pocket of my oversized hoodie for my phone. "One more time for the camera."

He snatches it from me before I can record anything. "Don't be a brat."

Instead, I grin at him. "Now, where would the fun in that be?"

"Are you going or what?" he huffs.

I raise my hands in a fake show of surrender. "I'm going, I'm going." Ducking out of the room, I climb the stairs to the first floor where Ava's office is located, along with some storage space and a smaller studio she hasn't had the chance to fit out yet.

Tapping my knuckles against the door, I wait for her to call out before ducking my head in. "Hey, you got a moment?"

"Riley!" She's already waving me into the room as she moves out from behind her desk. The second I'm through the door, she pulls me in for a hug. "I've been worried about you."

"How's Izzy?" I deflect before she can ask me anything about the shitstorm that is my life.

The look Ava gives me says she knows exactly what I'm doing before she moves to sit on the narrow sofa stuffed into one corner of her small office. It's intended for Isabella to have somewhere to sit and work while she's here, but we've had a number of in-depth conversations here before and after a session in the studio.

"She's good. She's absolutely loving Hot Shot Huskies, although I've noticed a certain hockey player has been MIA recently." I can tell from the bumping of her eyebrows that she's teasing. "Is that the *friend* you've been staying with?"

"Yeah. Him, Royce, and Grayson."

"That sounds... cozy." I give her a weak smile, fiddling with the strings of my hoodie. Noticing, Ava tilts her head, watching me. "You wanna talk about it?"

"Not really," I admit, grateful when she accepts that answer without question. "There is something I do need to tell you, though. I, uh, have a daughter. She's three—well, nearly four now. She's been... She, erm, doesn't live with me at the minute, and honestly, it's been hard being away from her, which is why I never said anything, but I'm, uh, trying to get her back, and well, I thought you should know."

It all comes out as a rambling mess, but somehow, Ava manages to piece her way through it. By the time I'm done, her eyebrows practically hit her hairline as she gapes at me.

"That's... a lot." Leaning forward, she rests her hand on my knee. "I'm so sorry you're going through all of that. While I don't know exactly what you're going through—and I don't need to—I know I'd be a mess if Izzy's dad decided to fight for custody." Her other hand claps her chest, over her heart. "Not seeing her every day would kill me."

"Yeah," I agree. "That's what it feels like."

"Oh, Ry, I'm so sorry!" She's hugging me a moment later, and it feels as though a weight has been lifted off my chest. Even though I haven't shared half of what's actually going on, just sharing my daughter's existence with someone who has become a friend feels freeing.

"Anyway," I say, sniffling. "I thought I'd come to work out some of those feelings in the dance studio, if that's alright with you?"

"Absolutely! I have a class in an hour, but the studio is all yours until then."

She's already ushering me out the door, and I call a thank you before descending the stairs, feeling a million times lighter than I did when I arrived.

Standing in a simple black leotard and flowing, sheer skirt that sways with my every move, I can feel Grayson's eyes on me. Leg warmers hug my calves, while ballet slippers allow my feet to glide effortlessly across the floor.

The opening notes of *Elastic Heart* by Sia reverberate through the air and infuse my skin before I gracefully extend my arms, letting the music guide me.

My movements are fluid yet purposeful, each a cathartic release as I glide across the floor. The fabric of my skirt flows around me as I execute a pirouette. My body spins as if trying to shed the confusion and betrayal that cling to me. As devastating as it is knowing Aurora is trapped with Bertram, at least I understand his actions. However, my mother—the woman who should have protected me—tried to end my life. It's a fact I won't ever wrap my mind around, and the thought alone makes my heart ache. Yet here, in this moment, I can face it.

Still, the reality of her actions leaves me reeling, struggling to comprehend how any mother could harbor such malice toward her own child. I leap into the air, my legs splitting in a *grand jeté*, feeling the freedom in the height and the fall, the temporary escape from the weight of reality. Landing softly, I transition into a series of graceful arabesques, my arms reaching out as if trying to touch the peace I find elusive.

I feel the conflict within me, the love and hate intertwined. My mother's selfishness, her narcissism, is a poison I've been desperate to purge for years. I spin again, faster this time, my arms wrapping around myself, a shield against the world. How could she? The woman who gave me life trying to take it away? Knowing she actually went *out of her way* to end my life—it's a bitter pill to swallow.

Abandoning ballet's rigidity, I let my body fall into a series of controlled rolls and spirals, embracing chaos. Each movement is a conversation with my pain, my anger, and my grief.

My steps become more frantic, reflecting the turmoil inside. I slide into a deep lunge, my fingers brushing the floor, grounding me, reminding me that I'm still here, still fighting.

As I dance, the bracelet on my wrist—a string of pink and white beads spelling out my name—jingles softly, a comforting reminder of why I'm here, of who I'm fighting for. Bertram having Aurora is where my focus needs to be, and to face the battle ahead, I need to expunge my mother from my life and my soul once and for all.

My feet pound the floor in rhythm with my heartbeat as the song builds. I let my emotions pour into my movements, my body a conduit for everything I feel. I perform a series of turns, my arms lifting me into a *fouetté en tournant*. Each spin is a testament to my resilience and refusal to be defeated.

Stretching upwards, my body elongates in a perfect *arabesque penchée*, reaching for hope, for the light at the end of this dark tunnel. The bracelet remains my anchor, a symbol of the past and the strength it gives me to face the present.

Finally, the music begins to fade, and I slow, my breathing heavy and my body glistening with sweat. My eyes fall closed as I move into an elegant arabesque. I hold that final pose, my chest heaving, my body glistening with sweat, and slowly let my leg down, grounding myself back into reality. My eyes are closed, the echo of the music still reverberating in my soul. I feel the room around me, the weight of my emotions now lighter, the burden somewhat lifted.

When I finally open my eyes, Grayson is standing right in front of me so close I can feel his presence and warmth. His expression is one of awe, admiration, and something more profound—something that makes my heart skip a beat.

This is the first time he's seen me dance like this—seen me

so vulnerable, so open. I can see in his eyes that he understands the significance—that he's witnessed a private part of my soul. And in that moment, I see a reflection of his openness, a mirror to my own rawness.

His eyes are soft, filled with tender emotion. He looks at me as if he's seeing me for the first time, truly seeing me, and my breath catches. There's a depth in his gaze, a silent promise, a recognition of our shared past and pain.

"I've never seen anything so beautiful."

His words are simple, but they hold so much weight. He's seen me at my most exposed, and instead of retreating, he's stepping closer, showing me his own vulnerability. The love in his eyes is unmistakable, a silent confession that tugs at my heartstrings.

In the next moment, his lips are on mine, my head craning back as we collide in a vortex of inevitability. He walks me backward, and I gasp as my back connects with the mirror's cold surface.

He takes advantage of the opening to slide his tongue between my teeth, entwining it around mine and sucking until I'm putty in his hands. My hands clamp his face, dragging him impossibly closer until I can feel him everywhere.

His hand comes up to cover mine, but when his fingers nudge my bracelet, he breaks the kiss, turning slightly to investigate. With his hand covering mine, he pulls it away from his face for a better look. I hear the gasp fall from his lips as he brings my wrist closer, turning it this way and that to further inspect the bracelet.

"How do you still have this?" The question is asked in an awed murmur, Grayson seemingly unable to wrench his eyes from the bracelet... from the reminder of our past.

"Why would I get rid of it? You bought it for me."

Finally, he looks up, eyes meeting mine. "I *made* it for you."

Oh my god. No, he didn't!

"Purchased one of those bead kits online and strung it all together."

Well, damn.

"Why?" I search those dark, unyielding orbs. "Why would you go to all that effort for a girl you hardly knew?"

With his free hand, he reaches out, his fingers brushing my cheek and sending shivers down my spine. "Because I knew enough to know I wanted you to feel special."

Which is exactly what he achieved with this gift. I *did* feel special.

"I gave it to Aurora," I tell him. "Before I left for college. But it's too big for her wrist, so she keeps it in a shoebox. Royce found it amongst the items he rescued from Lydia's and returned it."

Gaze still resting on my face, he asks, "So you're keeping it safe?"

"It's giving me hope," I counter.

We're standing so close. There is not an inch of space between us. I slide the hand he's not holding captive up his chest until it comes to rest over the erratic thumping of his heart.

"I don't know what to do with you," I confess.

For some reason, that makes him smile. Leaning in, he nips teasingly at my lips. "Most of the time, I don't know what to do with you either." He drags his nose over the rise of my cheekbone; his next words whispered in my ear, "But I think I'm figuring it out."

"Oh?" My voice is shaky, breath uneven.

"Love you."

He says it so simply that his lips are already on mine by the time my brain has caught up to the words. Somehow, my leg ends up hitched over his hip, and I'm grinding shamelessly against him when a throat clears, and we practically jump apart.

Face blooming, I peer around Grayson's large frame, meeting Ava's amused eyes. "Sorry to interrupt. I just wanted to let you know my next class is in fifteen minutes."

"Uh, right." I clear my throat, looking anywhere and everywhere but at her. "Thanks. We'll, erm, get out of your hair."

Her tinkling laugh has my focus snapping back to her, eyes narrowed in a deathly glare. "Uh-huh. Good to know what you get up to when you're dancing *alone*."

She's gone before I can correct her, and instead, I bury my face in my hands, groaning. "Let's get out of here before we traumatize any children."

When I finally dare to glance in Grayson's direction, he doesn't look the least bit chagrined. In fact, the asshole is fucking smirking as he leads me out to his awaiting car.

Royce and Logan open the front door as soon as we pull up. One look at them, and I'm throwing open the car door. "What?" I demand, jogging up the front steps. Hope threatens to choke me. "Did Dax find Aurora?"

Royce's eyes are hard, and as they connect with mine, I know we're finally on the right track to bringing my daughter home.

RILEY

CHAPTER TWENTY-FIVE

Royce frowns at the sat-nav as he punches in Dax's address. "I recognize this street," he mutters.

"Well, yeah," Logan states in a droll tone. "Because it's two fucking minutes away—"

Royce shakes his head, cutting him off even as he starts the engine and pulls the car onto the road. "It's not that."

He's still obsessing about it when we pull to a stop outside the apartment building.

"Is this it?" I question, peering out the window at the red-brick building. There's nothing untoward about it, nothing that particularly stands out. It's a building like any other in Halston. There are lights on inside, illuminating various apartments, giving them a warm glow and a soft ambiance. Is this really where Bertram has been keeping my daughter?

According to Dax, Bertram and David have both been making frequent visits to this address. It doesn't necessarily mean my daughter's here, but it's something. *Something's* happening here.

Royce smacks his hand against the steering wheel, and I'm guessing the pieces have finally slotted together for him. "I knew it! This was the fucking address from Bertram's computer —from the night we snuck into his house while you and Gray were at that restaurant with them." He shakes his head, face twisted in anguish. "I'd dismissed it, assuming he was just stopping at a shop or to grab a coffee."

He looks so put out, so frustrated as he beats himself up, that I lean forward from the back seat to squeeze his shoulder.

"Don't do that. This is not on you. Until the other day, we didn't even know he had Aurora, so why would we ever think...? Even Blue didn't suspect anything, and he must have seen Bertram make other stops here. We're in the middle of a town," I plead with him. "Please don't take this on. Let's just go inside and see what's in there."

He sighs but nods. We all climb out of the car, and I follow the rest as they head inside. We enter a simple but functional lobby. Grayson heads straight to the wall of mailboxes, the rest of us lining up beside him, forming an impenetrable wall as we scan each box.

"I don't recognize any of the names," Royce growls.

"Same," Logan agrees.

Neither do I. What the hell do we do now?

"That son of a bitch," Grayson snarls so loud that I jump. Whirling, he marches toward the stairs, cursing up a storm. I dart after him, the others following.

"What is it?" I demand.

"David," he hisses viciously. "Apartment 8 is under his fucking lackey's name. Took me a moment to piece together his last name."

My eyebrows hitch, and a flicker of hope ignites in my chest. After everything I've been through, everything *we've* been through, is it going to be this simple? We'll just storm in, Aurora will be there, and we'll take her home.

As one, we hurry up the stairs, following Grayson down a

bland hallway until he reaches what must be Bertram's apartment. He glares at the door like it personally offended him before stepping back. Lifting his leg, he drives his foot into the wood above the handle. It splinters, the door flying inward and embedding itself in the opposite wall.

The four of us surge forward, spreading out as we search the sparsely furnished apartment. A figure appears at the end of the hallway, and I go still, my eyes raking over him. I don't recognize him—I don't know who he is—but Grayson clearly does.

"You disgusting piece of shit," Grayson snarls, stomping toward the guy and fisting the front of his top. "Where is she? Where the fuck is Aurora?!" He drags him away from the hallway, and that's when I realize Royce has a gun pointed at his head.

I didn't even realize he was carrying.

"Is there anyone else here?" he demands in an icy-cold voice that matches the brutal savagery in his eyes.

The guy stutters out a quick *no,* and I waste no time. I take off, shouting, "Aurora? Aurora, sweetie, are you here? It's Mommy!" I race down the hallway, throwing open closed doors, until I stall in the doorway of the last room.

My heart leaps into my chest. My legs go weak. I can't quite believe what I'm seeing. Is this real? A strangled sort of noise escapes my lips, and I bring my hand up to cover my mouth, not wanting to wake her. With quiet steps, I creep into the room, not so much as daring to blink in case the sight before me vanishes.

There, tucked into a bed beneath pale pink covers, is my little girl. My pride and joy. The entire reason for my being. I don't even realize I'm crying until tears hit the back of my hand. I fall to my knees at her bedside and reach out a trembling hand but stop inches away from her head, too scared to touch her in case none of this is real—in case it's some figment of my imagination, another dream. I don't think I could handle that.

Finally, slowly, I let my fingers brush her hair. Air rushes past my dry lips as my fingers stroke the soft strands. "It's you," I cry, sobbing quietly. "I can't believe it's really you."

She shifts beneath the covers, rolling over and making all my dreams come true as her sleepy eyes crack open. She blinks at me for a moment, as if equally unsure whether what she's seeing is real. Her voice is laden with sleep as she croaks, "Mommy?"

"Hi, baby." Despite my sniffles, my voice is soft and reassuring.

"Mommy, you're here."

"Yeah, baby. Mommy's here." She shuffles right to the end of the bed, wrapping her arms around me and squeezing with all her strength.

"Mommy, can we go home now?"

I half-laugh, half-cry, my emotions a messy, indecipherable whirlpool. "Yeah, baby. We're gonna go home now."

Grabbing a blanket from the end of her bed, I wrap it around her before hauling her into my arms. Some hollowed-out part of me comes back to life at feeling her beating heart against my chest. Her breath on my neck. The weight of her in my arms.

I might never let her go again.

I do a quick sweep of the room, noting the couple of toys and books and scattered clothing. I have no intention of taking any of it with us. Everything else in the room can burn for all I care.

"Keep your head down and eyes closed," I whisper to her before leaving the room. I have no idea what to expect when we reach the living room. I haven't heard any sounds of fighting or a struggle, but just in case, I don't want her to see anything she shouldn't.

Logan's at my side the second I re-enter the living room, hands clasped to the back of Aurora's head. I keep my gaze focused on the door, not daring to glance toward where Grayson and Royce stand over David, who's now sitting on the sofa, pale and sweaty.

"Come on, Shortcake," Logan encourages, one hand at my back and the other protectively on Aurora as he escorts us from the apartment. "I'll take you home and come back for those two."

Once we're in the hallway and I've lifted my hand from Aurora's head, he coos at her. "Hello, sweetheart. Long time no see. Tell me this: is pink still the best color?" I could kiss him right there for bringing a heartbreaking smile to my little girl's face.

"Duh," she says in a voice that assures me everything will be okay. "Pink's always the best."

The way Logan smiles at her, the sparkle in his eyes, it's clear he's already head over heels in love with my little girl. "Truer words have never been spoken," he agrees.

I wait until she is settled on my knee in the car before asking, "Are you okay, baby?" What I want to know is if either of them touched her. Hurt her in any way, but I can't be that direct.

She nods, her head resting against me and eyes droopy.

I give Logan a worried look, but he merely smiles reassuringly back at me, squeezing my knee before starting the car and driving us home.

"Home?" Aurora mumbles.

"Yeah, baby. We're going home. You and I are going to climb into bed and sleep; how does that sound?"

She gives another tired nod, burying deeper into me. Her fist hasn't let go of my top since I lifted her out of bed, and it messes me up to see how afraid she is that I'll just disappear on her.

"I'm not going anywhere," I whisper into her ear. "I won't ever leave you." Tears burn in my eyes, but I refuse to let them fall.

This is good. Regardless of everything else, I'm holding my daughter in my arms.

It's surreal.

I'm still half expecting to wake up and find it was all a dream.

God, please don't let me wake up.

"It's real." At the sound of Logan's voice, I glance up, realizing I've been staring down at Aurora with a look of disbelief that mirrors my thoughts.

"It's real." My voice lacks Logan's strength, the words shaky and uneven. I'm emotional and wrung out, running on adrenaline alone. Truthfully, I could climb into bed and sleep for a week straight. However, I don't give a single shit about the fact I'll be dog-tired when Aurora likely wakes me up in a couple of hours.

Logan helps me out of the car; Aurora is now asleep in my arms as I carry her into the house. I head straight upstairs to the bedroom Grayson put together for me so I'd have my own space in their house—somewhere to go if I wanted to be alone—and lay my daughter down in the center of the bed.

Standing over her sleeping form, my throat is tight. A warmth envelops my back before Logan's strong arms wrap around me. "She looks so peaceful," he murmurs, careful not to wake her.

"I don't know how she can sleep like that," I say aloud. "After everything..."

"Kids are resilient." Isn't that the truth. "And she appears unharmed. Maybe a little scared and lonely, but it doesn't look like they did anything to her." He's got no idea just how much of a relief his words are to hear. I'd been telling myself the same thing, but I honestly couldn't tell if it was just what I wanted to hear or the actual truth. "I think she was a means of getting to you. Otherwise, Bertram wasn't interested in her."

That doesn't mean he wouldn't have done something if I'd continued to defy him, but I take great comfort from knowing she's safely out of his reach now.

"You're dead on your feet," Logan murmurs, his lips brushing my temple. "Get into bed with her and sleep for a few hours."

I glance up at him over my shoulder. "What about the others?"

"Don't worry about them. They'll get whatever info they need from David and do whatever they must to keep you both safe."

I swallow but simply nod. I know Royce and Grayson won't go easy on him, and perhaps I should feel bad about whatever they'll do, but I just can't bring myself to care. He might not have physically hurt my child, but he kept her from me. No human who has any *inkling* of the agony being involuntarily separated from your child causes would commit such a heinous act.

Frankly, he can burn in hell alongside Bertram for all I care.

So tired that I'm swaying on my feet, I simply nod. Logan helps me out of my clothes and into a T-shirt and boxers of his, and as though I'm a child myself, he lifts the covers and tucks me in as I curl my body around Auroras.

I'm out before he's even left the room.

I'm woken sometime later to the hard press of a foot on my straining bladder. Despite my urgent need to pee, I smile before I even open my eyes because I *know* that foot. I *know* when I open my eyes, I will find my little girl in bed beside me.

It's like waking from a dream—well, more like waking from a nightmare. Slowly, I peel my eyes open, finding the pillow beside me decorated with long, auburn-brown strands of hair not dissimilar to mine. My smile only grows, and for the first time in weeks, my heart is whole. I could lie here all day and watch her, but unfortunately, nature calls. So I slip silently from the bed and patter barefoot to the bathroom.

I hear the murmur of voices downstairs as I step back into the hall after relieving myself. It's early—not long past dawn. I had expected them all to be asleep in their beds by now.

Curious, I creep down the stairs, following the sound of voices and the delicious smell of eggs and bacon into the kitchen. My smile turns into a full-blown grin as I stop in the doorway to admire the glorious sight that is Logan Astor wearing an apron and shaking his hips as he dances to non-existent music in front of the stove while turning bacon and flipping eggs like those strong, firm hands of his weren't made for slapshots and breakaways.

Royce sits at the island. With a coffee in one hand, he's deep in thought as he taps a pencil against the edge of the counter and frowns at whatever is in front of him. Grayson hovers over his shoulder, occasionally pointing at whatever they're working on and mumbling too quietly for me to hear. There's no hint on either of their faces as to what happened after I left that apartment last night. No signs at all that either of them is affected by whatever they did.

It eases the last remnants of tension that had been clinging to me.

"Shortcake!" Logan rejoices, catching sight of me in the

doorway. Spatula in hand, he throws his arms in the air. "Where's the little one?"

"She's still passed out in bed."

He nods. "She okay?"

I smile up at him. "She's perfect."

He grins back at me, agreeing, "That she is," before his eyes slowly lower to rake over me. It's not a heated or sensual perusal. More like he's checking to make sure *I'm* okay.

Reaching out, I squeeze his hand. "I'm perfect, too."

His expression turns saucy. "That you are, baby."

Rolling my eyes, I point to where he left eggs cooking on the stove. "You're going to burn that."

His eyes go comically wide as he darts back to flip them, and smiling to myself, I saunter over to Royce and Grayson. "What's this?" I ask, staring in confusion at the family calendar spread out on the kitchen island. It has been filled with each of our various class times, along with Logan's hockey schedule, Royce's fights, and Grayson's work meetings.

"We're putting together a schedule," Logan explains as if it's obvious, joining us as he pushes a cup of freshly brewed coffee into my hand.

"A schedule? For what?"

"So we can ensure one of us is always available to watch Aurora and do the daycare drop-offs and pick-ups." Again, there's that *duh* tone, and I'm not sure if I'm being particularly dense this morning or if these guys keep blowing through every expectation I have of them.

"She's not in daycare," I tell him because, apparently, that's the best response I can come up with.

"Well, no, she doesn't start for another two weeks. That's the soonest I could get her booked in for, but we figured that worked well since we all agreed we weren't happy letting her out of our sights until we decide what we're doing with

Bertram, and we've dealt with your mother." He gives a flippant shrug of his shoulder. "Besides, between us, we can totally handle it for a couple of weeks."

All I can do is blink stupidly at Logan. He's talking gibberish, right? Please tell me I'm not the only one who didn't understand a word of what he just said.

"I think you broke her brain," Royce whispers.

"Logan," I croak. "What are you talking about? Aurora isn't enrolled in daycare. I can't afford it."

"Actually, she's enrolled at Maplewood Preschool and Daycare."

"What? When…"

"I called them this morning," he explains, pushing a fresh mug of coffee into my hands before resting both of his on my shoulders and rubbing the tense muscles. *This morning?* My gaze flicks to the clock on the wall. It's not long after seven in the morning. *How the hell did he get talking to anyone on the phone this early?* He bulldozes over me before I can ask. "She's enrolled, and I've paid for her to attend for the rest of the year, so just say thank you and drink your coffee, okay? Let me do this for you."

"You didn't have to do that." I step back out of his hold, flicking my gaze to Royce and Grayson before my focus returns to the schedule. "You don't have to do any of this. I—we—are not your responsibility. You've already done enough."

"Shortcake, we *want* to. Aurora is all yours, but that doesn't mean you have to do this alone. We want to help."

"That is, if you want our help," Royce tacks on, drawing my attention his way, and immediately I know, if I say I don't want their help, he'll back off, and he'll drag Logan with him, kicking and screaming if need be.

I mean, we hadn't blatantly discussed what would happen once we got Aurora back. They've all, at one point or another, told me that they want to be involved in her life—to help out, to get to know her. But it's one thing for them to say that and another to see them planning it out as if our lives are intertwined.

As if... As if we're a family.

There's a lump in my throat and tears sting my eyes. My heart is full of so much love that it feels like it's about to explode. Still, I'm nervous. What if it's too much for them? What if looking after a kid is more work than they anticipated? What if, one day, they feel like it's too much? Like she's not worth it? Like *we're* not worth it?

"Whatever cynical thoughts are circling through that pretty little head of yours, stop it." There's an edge to Logan's tone as he wags a finger in my face. "We're here. We *want* to help, so let us."

"Fucking hell, Logan, you made her cry," Grayson snarls, smacking Logan in the arm none too gently when he sees my face.

"Shit. Fuck. I'm sorry, Shortcake. I didn't mean to make you cry. We'll do whatever you want. You want us to help, great, we're here. You want us to leave you alone, fine, we'll do that too."

Sniffling, I swipe angrily at the tears, but they keep coming.

"I'm not crying," I bite angrily, trying and failing to get the steady stream to stop.

"Uhh, yeah, Shortcake, you kinda—oh. *Oohhh.* Nooo, you're not crying." Logan pulls me in against his chest as Royce carefully takes the piping hot mug from my hand before I spill it. I go effortlessly into Logan's embrace, burying my face in his t-shirt and inhaling deeply. *God, how does he always smell so good?* "Definitely not crying," he continues, rubbing soothing circles on my back. "Those are allergy tears."

"It's only February," I point out, the words muffled by his shirt.

He continues with his soothing circles. "Mhm. But we're practically into March, and I hear the pollen is particularly potent this year." Despite my overwhelming emotions, I find myself laughing into Logan's t-shirt. I have no idea how he does that; he makes me laugh when I'm on the verge of crumbling.

"So what do you say?" Logan murmurs softly. "You gonna let us help you out, mama? They do say it takes a village. Let us be your village, Riley."

With tears clinging to my eyelashes, my face buried in Logan's top, I nod. "Okay, but only if you're sure." Pulling back, I stare up at him before turning to face Royce, then finally shifting my gaze to Grayson. "All of you—only if you're sure."

"We're sure," Royce states firmly, and Grayson nods.

"Fantastic." Stepping back, Logan claps his hands. "Now that's sorted, what is on the agenda for today? It's our first day all together. I feel like we should do something special to commemorate."

Shaking my head, I'm smiling as I finally take my first sip of coffee. "I need to take Aurora shopping. She has nothing here, but she needs clothes, food, and maybe diapers." I bury my face in my hands, already feeling overwhelmed. "I don't even know if she's potty trained fully. She was nearly there when I left for Halston, but I dunno if Lydia continued to put in the work with her."

"Take a deep breath, Shortcake." Logan steps up behind me, his large hands kneading my shoulders until they relax. "There you go. Don't worry about all that. We can go out with her today and get everything she needs. Anything we overlook can be gotten tomorrow or ordered online."

"Plus, don't forget we have her stuff from your mom's," Royce interjects.

"See!" Logan grins. "We essentially have everything already."

I groan, my eyes closing as I remember, "I have a test this afternoon." I'll have to skip it. Which isn't ideal, but it's not like I've studied for it anyway. "I'll email. Let the professor know I won't be there."

"You absolutely will not," Logan states in a firm tone that sounds so at odds coming from him. "You're already in trouble over your grades. Skipping a test will just give your advisor and Bertram the excuse they need to get you kicked out."

"Logan," I argue. "I haven't even studied for it."

He crosses his arms over his chest, looking absolutely ridiculous in his red apron and sweats. "Good thing you have all day to study then." I open my mouth to protest, but he holds up a hand. He's strangely hot when he's being all bossy and demanding, and a filthy shiver creeps down my spine. "*I'll* take Aurora shopping. Royce will stay home with you and—"

"I need to go to the office to keep an eye on my dad," Grayson interrupts.

My shoulders tense at the mention of his dad, and I worry on my bottom lip before asking, "That man... David... what did you—"

"Don't worry about that, Ry," Royce says softly.

My gaze bounces between him and Grayson. "Is he...?"

"No," Grayson confirms. He clearly doesn't feel the same need to protect me from whatever they did as he continues, "We got the answers we needed from him before beating him to within an inch of his life, but we left him alive."

My throat bobs as I swallow, my gaze anchored on Grayson. "But if he talks to your dad, then..."

He nods. "Yeah. My father will know that I know about Aurora. That I'm on your side."

I suck in a breath. Letting his father realize that says more than words ever could about where Grayson's loyalties lie.

"Was that the right move?" I ask hesitantly, trying to deduce the possible ramifications of that move. "What if your dad tries to get back at you through the company?"

"It's not like he's not already trying to get me ousted from the CEO position so he can reclaim it for himself. This way, David can let him know you've both got people on your side— people who won't hesitate to do whatever is necessary to protect you both."

He steps forward, tucking a wayward strand of hair behind my ear. "My father thought you were isolated. Alone. He thought it would be easy to manipulate or coerce you under his roof. We've just proven to him that it won't be."

I... have no words. What Grayson just did. Everything he's been doing recently to be there for me... he's stepped up in a way I never expected, and it leaves me speechless.

"Oh, we also have a surprise for you, Shortcake."

"A surprise?" I choke out.

Logan grins cheekily, and even Royce has a smug little smirk.

"You gotta wait until tonight for it, though," he teases.

I open my mouth to say something—perhaps that they don't need to get me anything. However, before I can say anything, a tentative voice breaks through the silence, and *god,* if it isn't the best sound I've ever heard. "Mommy?"

Spinning, I find Aurora standing at the bottom of the stairs, looking adorable with her hair all over the place as she rubs the sleep from her eyes.

I smile brightly at her, crouching as she races into my arms. Standing, I spin in a circle, making her giggle. The sound is infectious, infusing the kitchen with a warmth I hadn't even noticed was missing.

When I'm dizzy, I squeeze her to me. I know I spent all night cuddling up against her, but I can't get enough. If I thought she'd let me get away with it, I'd strap her to my chest like I did when she was a baby and carry her everywhere with me. I'd never let her out of my sight. "Morning, sweetie."

She peeks over my shoulder at the three silent statues, watching us with equal expressions of awe and nerves. Logan is the only one who doesn't appear uneasy. He's like an excitable puppy, bouncing on the balls of his feet, and I can tell he's just waiting for Aurora to feel at ease before he scoops her out of my arms.

"Baby, you remember my friends?" I point first at Logan. "This is Logan." Next, I gesture to Royce. "And this is Royce."

"I've been waiting a long time to meet you in person, sweetheart," he says, and I'm momentarily caught off guard. What happened to the one-word grump I first bumped into on campus?

Smothering a smile, I shift so she can see Grayson. I don't think he's blinked once since Aurora entered the kitchen. He stares at her the same way I imagine I did last night—like he can't believe she's real.

I kiss the top of her head. "Sweetheart, this is Grayson." I want to say more. To tell her he's her brother, but she's already been through enough change. Now isn't the time. Biting on his lip, Grayson gives her a soft smile.

"It's nice to meet you, Aurora."

She stares at him with wide eyes, nerves keeping her quiet until Logan jumps in. "What do you want for breakfast, Aurora? We've got pancakes, bacon, eggs. Or if you want all of the above, I can make you a pancake smiley face with bacon and eggs."

A slow smile steadily grows across her face. "Smiley face," she declares in a small voice.

Logan beams at her. "I knew you had good taste. That's what I would have picked, too." He points at Royce. "Mr. Grump over here never chooses the smiley face option."

Aurora stares at Royce curiously as he glowers at Logan before realizing she's watching, and that glare dissolves into a chagrined smile.

The guys plate up the food, and the five of us sit around the table. We keep the conversation light while we eat, the guys filling the silence with random chatter deliberately aimed to set Aurora at ease. Royce discusses an upcoming match of his. Grayson gripes about balancing work and his senior year course load while Logan discusses the team's travel plans for their away games next weekend.

Aurora's eyes bounce between them the entire time, drinking everything in, even if she doesn't understand what they're discussing.

Only when everyone is finished eating, and she's had time to relax do they bring her into the conversation, and the topic switches to her favorite TV show, her gymnastics class, and something called a Sparkle Squirt—whatever that is.

Nursing my coffee, I watch the entire scene unfold with a serene smile.

It's peaceful. Homey.

The sort of breakfast I could get used to having every morning for the rest of my life.

"You wanna come shopping with me today?" Logan asks while the others begin clearing away the plates.

Aurora's eyes narrow on him from across the table, and she stares at him suspiciously. I'm fully expecting her to say no. Logan is so easy to get along with, but she's barely spent any time with him.

"Can I get the new Princess Barbie?"

Logan chuckles. "You can get anything you want, Pumpkin."

"Logan," I groan as Aurora's face lights up like Christmas morning. "You can't say things like that to her."

"Why not?" He pouts at me, and I'm not sure whether to roll my eyes or laugh.

"Because she's three. She'll pick out everything in the store."

"So?"

Okay, now I do roll my eyes. "Logan, you can't buy her everything in the store."

With a smirk that makes me believe everything I just said went in one ear and out the other, he responds, "Whatever you say, mama."

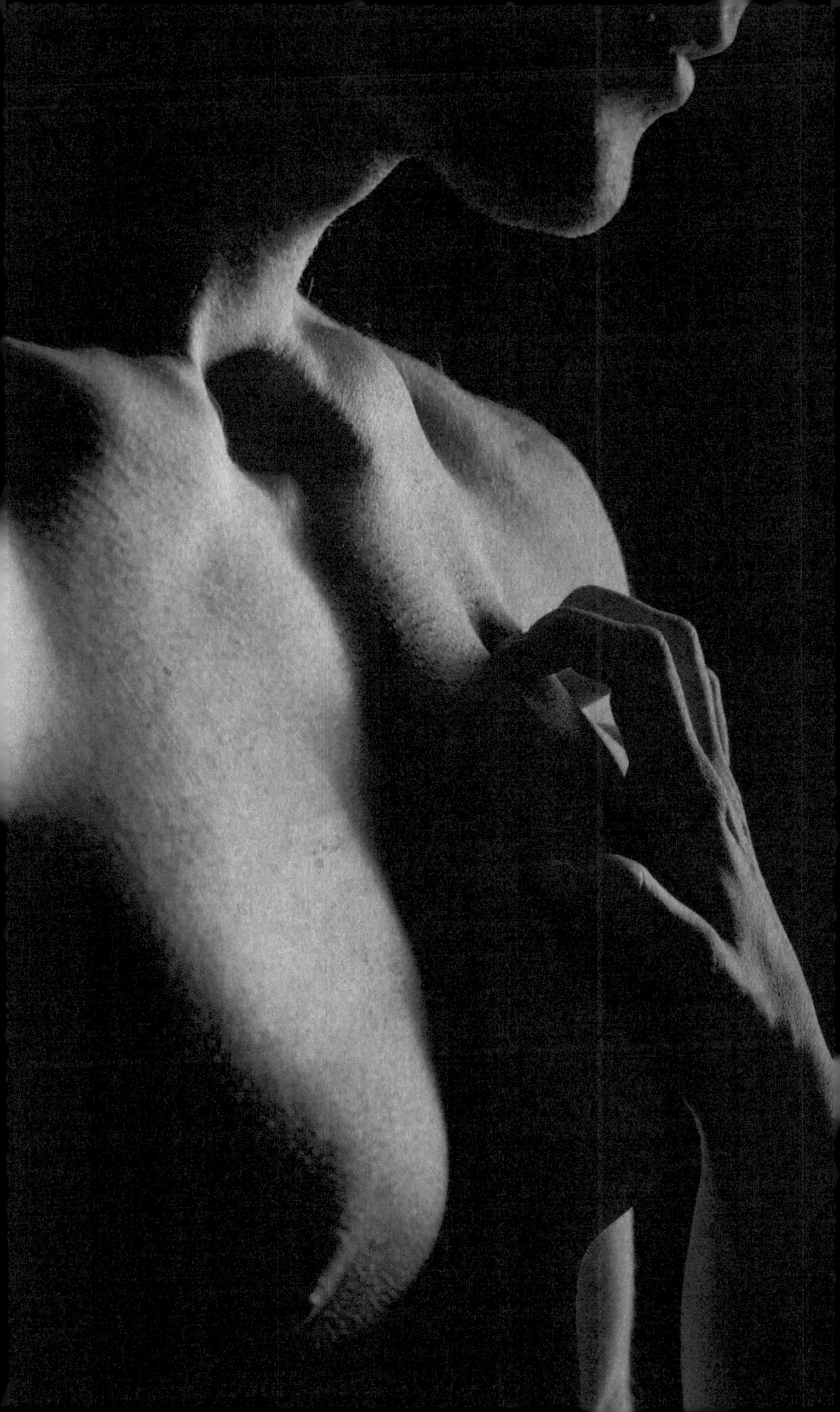

LOGAN

CHAPTER TWENTY-SIX

I. Am. In. Love.

So freaking *in love* with this little girl sitting opposite me, face covered in ice cream as she talks my ear off, just like she has been all day.

She is just the cutest thing. We've had the best day together. She hasn't asked me to buy her a single thing. Of course, she hasn't had to. If she so much as glanced at it, it miraculously found its way into the shopping cart.

If Riley asks, I have no idea how it got there!

"No shopping day is complete without an ice cream reward," I tell Aurora around my mouthful of chocolate chip.

She nods, face serious as though I imparted a priceless gem of wisdom.

Have I mentioned how head over heels in love I am with this kid?

Pulling out the list Riley stuffed in my hand before we left the house, I go through it, ensuring we have everything we need.

"Can you think of anything we might have missed?" I ask Aurora.

She taps her spoon against her lips, nose scrunching as she thinks. The whole thing is cute as hell.

"Jammies?"

"Got that."

"Night light?"

"Yup."

"Pancake mix?"

I chuckle. "And chocolate and bananas to go on top."

"I fink that's everyfing."

My list is much longer than three items, but it's good to know what Aurora considers *the essentials*.

"Good thing I didn't listen to you about not needing a toothbrush, eh?" I tease, pointing at her chocolate-covered mouth.

Her eyes narrow adorably, but she doesn't slow down as she shovels another spoonful into her mouth.

"Wouldn't want all your teeth to fall out. Otherwise, how would you eat the delicious pancakes we're going to make?"

We're silent as I finish my ice cream and watch Aurora devour hers like someone's going to snatch it away at any second. "Am I going to live wif you now?" she asks with an innocent tilt of her head, large eyes watching me over the tall glass of ice cream.

"Well, that's where your mommy lives, so yup." I give her an easy smile. I have no idea what she's thinking, but it must be confusing for her. "Royce and Grayson live there, too, so it will be the five of us."

She nods thoughtfully, but she's worrying on her bottom lip, so I know something is bothering her. Instead of pressing her, I wait until she's worked it through in her head. "What about those men..."

Fucking Bertram and David. Reaching across the table, I cover her hand with mine. "Sweetheart, those men will never take you away again, and they most definitely won't be living with us." My throat is tight, and *god*, I just hope I'm tackling this okay—the way Riley would if she were in my shoes. "Did, uh..." *God*, this is hard. "Did either of those men hurt you?" *Damn*, I really have to work at keeping my voice calm.

Staring at a spot on the table, she gives the slightest shrug of her shoulder, and my thoughts instantly spin out in a hundred different directions imagining all sorts of scenarios, quickly followed by various other ways in which I'm going to make Bertram pay for whatever the fuck he did to this little girl. *My* little girl.

"Aurora." Although my voice is soft, the tone is firm, and I wait until she flicks her eyes up to mine. "Did they hurt you? Did they hit you or say mean things?"

Her lower lip trembles. *Oh. My. God.* I just found my very own personal kryptonite. Before I know it, I'm out of my side of the booth and sliding into hers. She's so tiny and breakable as I pull her into my arms.

"It's okay, sweetheart," I whisper in her ear. "Whatever they did, it's okay. You can tell me."

Settling her on my knee, I fix her hair, giving her time to work through her feelings. "The mean one would shout at me," she begins, and suddenly, I'm not so sure that I want to hear anymore. I'm already barely keeping a lid on my murderous rage. "And they never wanted to play wif me."

I only got a brief look at David, but he seemed more of the sweat-it-and-stress type, so I'm guessing *the mean one* is Bertram. Her fucking father. I scoff at my own internal thoughts. That man is *not* her father.

My teeth grind. "Did either of them ever touch you?" Fuck only knows how that question doesn't come out as an indecipherable snarl.

She shakes her head, and I swear, waiting for that answer

took ten years off my life. I bet if I look in the mirror when I get home, I'll find a gray hair.

"The mean one said hugs were for babies."

I scoff. "He clearly has no idea what he's talking about because hugs are *the best*." Her eyes light up, and I promise to do everything in my power to ensure she only ever looks at me like that. "They literally cure everything. Bad day? Hug it out. Tired? Hug it out. Tummy ache from too much ice cream? Hug it out."

She giggles at that, and the tension uncoils from inside me.

"You wanna hug it out, Pumpkin?"

Flashing me that toothy grin, she launches herself at my chest. Her tiny arms barely fit around my neck as I squeeze her against me before tickling her sides until she's squealing with laughter.

Fuck, if I could get used to doing this for the rest of my life.

Aurora sits on my lap as she finishes her ice cream, and I watch her with awed fascination as snapshots of how life will look going forward fill my mind and flood my chest.

Aurora and Riley curled up in bed together.

Riley slipping out after Aurora has fallen asleep and sneaking into my bed instead.

Waking up beside my girl before getting up to make pancakes for everyone for breakfast.

Yeah, if I'd doubted it before, I know for certain now that here is where I'm supposed to be. I never would have lasted if I'd taken that offer to join the Pacific Penguins. Playing for the Timberwolves, I can be home for dinner most nights, we can watch movies together, and I can tuck her into bed. I want to be there for as much of it as I can.

"Riley's going to kill you."

"It's not that bad," I counter, staring at the mountain of bags covering every inch of floor in the living room. Gray's just gotten home from work, and Riley and Royce should be home any minute. They just called to say they were grabbing takeout on their way back from campus. "Is it?"

I'm starting to have second thoughts about some of my purchases.

"You're a dead man walking."

Shit. I swear it didn't look like this much when it was in my car. However, the fact I had to start asking shops to hold the items because I ran out of trunk space probably should have been a clue. This isn't even all of it. Some shops offered a delivery, which I gladly took them up on when I started running out of space in the car.

"It'll be fine." I'm not sure if I'm trying to convince Grayson or myself.

The asshole makes a grunt of disagreement, and when I turn to look at him, I find him staring at a passed-out Aurora. A sugar crash is a real thing. By the time we made our last few stops and got home, she was passed out in her car seat. I brought her in and put her on the sofa, creating a pillow wall around her so she couldn't accidentally roll off onto the floor.

I study him for a moment longer. His expression is part terror, part awe as he drinks in the sleeping child like he simultaneously can't believe she's here and doesn't have the first clue what to actually do with her.

"She's pretty spectacular." My voice is low so as not to wake her, although considering she hasn't so much as stirred as I've carried in bag after bag and box upon box, it makes me think it would take something close to the apocalypse to wake her from her coma.

Still not taking his eyes off the sleeping girl, he grunts. I don't speak Grayson, so I don't have the first fucking clue what he's saying. Does he even know?

"It's okay if this is weird for you."

"Weird's not the right word," he muses. "...Surreal?" Tearing his gaze from her, he finally looks at me. "Is it fucked up that I wish she were mine?"

"I don't think so. Is it weird that I already consider her mine? That I'd protect her with my life? That I've already decided no guy will ever be good enough for her?"

His lips twitch. "I think we can all agree she won't be dating until she's at least thirty."

I make a noise in the back of my throat like a dying cat. "I was thinking more like forty. She's already given me gray hairs. I don't want to be bald, too."

He's fully smiling now as he shakes his head before the sound of the front door unlocking has us both turning in time to see Riley and Royce stepping into the house.

Riley's eyes meet mine as she unzips her coat before darting around the hall, searching.

"She's sleeping," I explain before she can ask, indicating the living room where the little girl is passed out. "She tired herself out."

Riley's gaze shifts to the living room, her eyes going wide as her mouth drops open. Coat forgotten, Grayson takes it from her limp hands and hangs it up by the door while Royce stalks into the kitchen with the takeout bag.

I hear him return a moment later, but my eyes are stuck on Riley. I tense, nerves fluttering in my belly. "I may have gone a little overboard..."

"You think, Logan?" Riley retorts, still staring dumbfounded at the mountain of stuff.

"Dude, did you buy out the entire store?" Royce chuckles.

Rubbing at the back of my neck, I'm starting to feel uncomfortable as fuck. "We were having such a good time. I just wanted to make her smile."

Riley finally tears her eyes away to look at me, her mouth closing as an empathetic smile graces her lips. She wraps her arms around my waist, and unable to resist touching this woman, I envelop her in a hug.

She simply breathes me in for a second before looking up, her chin resting on my chest. "Thank you. I'm sure she had a blast with you today, and it means so much to me. The stuff is... a lot. And she definitely doesn't need it, but I'm sure it made her day. She's used to my mom not caring and me having to say no 'cause I can't afford it." Tears sting her eyes, and I squeeze her tighter. "I hated seeing her smile dim every time I disappointed her, and while I don't want her to become spoiled, I equally want her to have everything she's missed out on."

Bending my head, I kiss the top of her head. "I don't believe for one second that you've ever disappointed that girl. She loves you. You're all she truly needs. That, ice cream, and something called a princess castle doll house that I promised Grayson would help her build."

"Great," Grayson grouses in a low voice. "Exactly what I wanted to do." He's complaining, but there's no real annoyance in his tone. Dude just has issues showing his softer emotions. I'm hoping Aurora will be able to help him with that.

Riley's shoulders shake with silent laughter. Pressing onto her toes, she lifts her head and plants her lips on mine. It's intended as a quick peck, but not giving two shits about the two assholes watching us, I slide my hand to the back of her head and hold her there as I deepen it.

As my tongue parts her lips and I fall into her essence, I know I could do this for the rest of my life. Shopping with Aurora. Roping my best friends into girly shit they want no part of. Coming home to Riley every night.

"Thank you for looking after her today," Riley murmurs when she pulls back.

"Anytime, Shortcake. I loved hanging out with her and getting to know her better. You've raised one hell of a kid." I stroke my thumb over her heated cheek as she ducks her head before pulling away.

"Please tell me what's in the living room is everything you bought," she teases.

"Uhh..."

"Logan!" she chastises, but she's grinning too brightly to be truly annoyed. "Where are we even going to put all of this?" she asks, facing the mountain of bags and boxes. I don't even remember what's in half of them.

"We'll figure it out," Royce assures her.

She glances back at him over her shoulder before flicking her gaze to Grayson and arching an eyebrow. "Are you sure you still want us to live here, now that you've seen how much baggage a three-year-old comes with?"

Royce merely smirks. "I'm ninety-nine percent certain most of this is *Logan's* baggage."

Undeterred, Riley waves in the general direction of the living room before turning her back on it. Arms folded across her chest, she's a warrior as she stands tall against the three of us. "It's not just the *stuff*. Three-year-olds are hard work *and* exhausting. You're all in your senior year. You should be out partying and enjoying your last few months of freedom."

Eliminating the bit of space between them, Royce's chest bumps against Riley's, effectively pushing her back into me. Grayson steps up beside him, so the three of us crowd her. My hands fall to her hips, steadying her, and I like the feel of her sandwiched between us. She's so much smaller than us that she has to tilt her head back, and something about the sight gets all my blood pumping due south.

Grayson's voice is gravel as he drawls indifferently, "What has given you the idea any of us want to go out and party?"

"What about studying? How are you going to study with a screaming kid running around?" She's grasping at straws, and based on the way her hands shake with anxiety, she knows it. She's scared. Looking for any reason to push us away, but what Riley has yet to comprehend fully is that we're not fucking leaving.

None of us.

Not now.

Not in five years.

Not *ever*.

We're all in when it comes to her and her kid.

And in due time, she'll realize that.

"Probably the same way you're going to study," Royce counters unwaveringly. "We have the schedule and factored in everyone's extracurriculars. We can study at the library if we need to. Got any more excuses you want to try, Babydoll?"

She glares at him, and I have to bite back my laugh.

After a moment, her gaze flickers to Grayson. "What about you?" She doesn't sound as fierce now, but I understand that she needs to be sure. That she needs to hear it to believe it.

Smirking like an asshole, Gray's eyes shine with amusement as he raises a questioning eyebrow. "What about me?"

Ducking my head, I bring my lips to the shell of her ear. She shivers, and I grin at her reaction to me. "He's as invested as we are, Shortcake. Moreso, even."

"The schedule was *his* idea," Royce adds. "*He* was the one who said he'd look after her on weekends when you're working, and Logan has hockey."

"Assuming returning to Lux is something you're considering," I murmur.

She swallows but nods. "I want to—but maybe after we're

sure Bertram is no longer a problem." Her lips purse. "I don't want to leave Aurora if I don't have to."

Grayson makes a low growl of discontent at the mention of her returning to work—or maybe at the thought of his dad touching either of them. Either way, we all ignore him. Otherwise, the two of them will spend the rest of the night bickering.

When he doesn't say anything, Royce jams his elbow in his side, and with a grunt and a death glare, Grayson exhales and meets Riley's wide-eyed stare. "I might not know how to show it or what to do with a little kid, but I *want* Aurora here. We all do." His tone is soft as velvet as his hand moves to cup Riley's cheek. "So stop doubting us, and let us help."

Her throat bobs. "I'm not used to having help." Her voice is soft, vulnerable.

"I know, baby," Royce soothes, and Riley practically melts against me. She's protesting, but she doesn't want to win. It's painfully obvious.

"I'm scared I'll let you all the way in, and you'll change your mind. I couldn't handle it if you broke her heart. I-it would break mine."

Boxing her in so we're a solid ring of muscle around her and all she can see is us, Royce soothes, "No one is changing their minds, Ry. There's nothing you can do or say that will scare us away. We're all in. All the way when it comes to you *and* when it comes to Aurora."

He presses a kiss to her lips and the last of the tension drains from her body. "You don't have to do this alone." Another peck. "Not anymore." Kiss. "Not ever again." This time, his tongue slips into her mouth, and she moans into his touch.

The sound goes straight to my dick, and I pull her against me, bending to kiss the juncture between her neck and shoulder. "What do you say, Shortcake? You going to let us take care of the both of you?"

Her only response is another moan, followed by a soft whimper when Royce pulls back, staring down at her with piercing eyes that burn with desire. "Answer his question, James."

"Yes."

"Yes, what?" he pushes as I continue to pepper her skin with kisses that have her shifting against me.

She takes a moment, holding her gaze with each of us before nodding her head in defeat. "Yes, you can take care of us both." A bite to her tone has me glancing up, chuckling at the defiant glare she's giving Royce.

Royce simply smirks, his hand sliding to the back of Riley's head and tugging on the strands, forcing her face upward. "So much attitude in such a tiny body." His gaze slides to Grayson's and then mine. "What do you think we should do about that?"

"Hmm." I blow a breath along the bare skin of Riley's shoulder, grinning when she shivers. "I've always found orgasms are a good way to release some of that tension."

Riley chokes. "We can't do that. Aurora's *right there*." She waves toward the living room.

"Logan fed her enough sugar that an atomic bomb could go off, and she'd sleep through it," Grayson drawls, his dark eyes blown with lust as he rakes his gaze over her. Lifting a finger, he drags it down the center of her chest, between her breasts, to the top of her jeans, where he lingers with the tip of his finger just beneath the waistband. Leaning in, he nips at her lower lip. "Do you think you can be quiet for us, Tempest?"

Her gulp is audible, and a predatory smirk flashes across Grayson's face. "Hmm?" he presses when she doesn't answer.

"I-I don't know."

"Guess we'll find out." I need this woman so badly that the words come out as a growl when I haul her flush against me.

Lifting her off her feet, I walk backward until we're in the kitchen.

Royce and Grayson follow, practically incinerating her clothing as they mentally undress her with their eyes. Closing the kitchen door behind us, Royce reaches forward and tugs Riley from my grip, spinning her so her back is to his chest, and I have the perfect view of her flushed cheeks and glazed eyes.

Fuck, she's so beautiful like this, all wild and wanton.

Royce's hands slip beneath the hem of her long-sleeved top. His fingers stroke along her abdomen, causing her breathing to hitch and drawing my attention to the rapid rise and fall of her breasts. I can only see a glimpse of them through the V-shaped neckline, and my teeth grind, wanting to rip the damn thing from her so I can watch the way her rose-pink nipples would pebble beneath my gaze.

Royce works his hands up to cover her breasts, squeezing them until her eyes fall closed and she moans, arching into him. My dick is so hard that it's painful, and it's taking all my restraint not to steal her back and strip her naked.

"You see the way Logan's looking at you, Babydoll," Royce purrs in her ear. Her eyes snap open, pupils blown wide as she drinks me in. "See what you do to him. I think he deserves a proper thank you after today, don't you?"

Licking her lips and utterly oblivious to how fucking tempting she looks right now, Riley nods. Reaching down, I squeeze my painfully stiff shaft through my jeans.

"I need your words, Ry."

"Yes."

With a gentle nudge, Royce whispers loud enough for me to hear, "Go show Logan just how much you appreciate him taking care of Aurora today."

Stepping forward, Riley falls to her knees before me, and I

groan aloud as she tilts her head back and stares up at me with wide, lust-blown eyes.

"Not this again," Grayson groans under his breath. "I'm not fucking *watching* this time."

I don't give a shit what he does. I only have eyes for the red-haired goddess in front of me. "Fuck, Shortcake, you look so good on your knees for me."

She knocks my hand aside as she slides her smaller one up and down the front of my jeans. "I want to take care of you, too."

Fuuuuck. This woman is perfect for me. For us.

With steady hands, she undoes the button of my jeans and tugs the zipper down, sliding them over my hips until they fall to the floor. My boxers are next, and I toss my head back and groan as her dainty fingers wrap around my length.

"Shortcake," I rasp, looking down at her as her hand moves up and down, working me over. Those beautiful hazel eyes lift to mine, holding as her mouth opens and she slowly threads my head past her lips.

She feels like heaven wrapped around me, her mouth warm and wet, her tongue driving me wild as it circles my sensitive slit.

Coming up behind her, Royce strokes a hand down her hair. She stiffens for a brief second, her movements stuttering, but Royce calms her, getting on his knees behind her and murmuring, "Look how good you're taking Logan's cock. Such a filthy little slut for us."

She moans around my shaft, causing my hips to buck and pushing me to the back of her throat. Her fingers dig into my thighs, and I can't wait to stare at the half-moon marks later and recall this moment. This fierce queen on her knees for me.

"Look at you, sucking Logan's dick like a pro," Royce continues to purr, his fingers undoing Riley's jeans before sliding into her panties. "You love it when we fuck your face, don't you, Babydoll?"

She moans around my cock, and unable to hold back, I slide my hand into her hair, pulling on the strands until I can fist them in one hand. My hips thrust forward, her throat constricting around me until I feel as though I'm about to explode.

I force it back, not yet ready for this to be over. Not until I feel her constricting around me while she comes.

"You like the taste of Logan's cum, James?"

Fuck. I've never been one for dirty talk, but listening to Royce and watching the way Riley responds, her chest blooming red and her body rocking with her need for friction.

"Fucking soaked for us."

I groan, the base of my spine tingling and my toes curling in my sneakers as I fight off the urge to come down her throat.

Royce chuckles, and I force my focus away from my aching ballsack, watching as he finger fucks Riley.

"I think Logan's about to explode. You going to come on my fingers Babydoll so Logan can fuck your throat?"

Another vibration around my shaft has my knees threatening to buckle, and I let out a slew of curses.

One of Riley's hands twists around her back, and she must stroke Royce through his pants because he smirks. "Such a greedy girl. Not satisfied with Logan, are you? You need my cum too?"

At her whimpered vibration, I bark out a strangled laugh. "I think that's a yes."

Her eyes flick to Grayson, who, despite his protestations, has remained a silent participant, watching from the sidelines. At the heat darkening her hazel eyes, I purr, "You want all of our cum tonight, Shortcake? Want all three of us to fill you up until you're dripping?"

Her entire body shudders, and Royce groans as she likely constricts around his fingers. Her throat is tight as fuck, and it's a miracle that I haven't lost my battle against her hot wet mouth yet.

Royce grins, but it's feral. "Let Logan fill your belly with his cum, and maybe I'll consider filling that sweet cunt of yours."

"Come with me," I rasp, seconds from exploding down her throat. Her gaze flicks to Grayson again, and with a snarl, I snap at him, "Stop hovering and get the fuck over here. Give our girl what she needs."

"Don't tell me what to do," he snaps. Still, he drops to his knees beside her and pulls up her top before yanking down her bra, sucking her nipple into his mouth. She fucking loves it— having all three of us worshipping her. Writhing on Royce's fingers, she arches into Grayson's touch as she hums around my shaft.

I can feel the stabbing of her nails in my thighs, probably breaking the skin, but I don't fucking care. Nothing matters at this moment other than the four of us—our connection.

I hold off through sheer force of will until Riley comes on Royce's fingers. As her moans vibrate along my shaft and her throat constricts, I shove myself deep inside, blocking her airway as I shoot jets of ejaculate down her throat.

Fuck, that's the best blowjob I've ever received.

Royce barely lets me finish before he pushes Riley forward onto all fours, shoving her jeans and panties down her thighs. His pants are unbuckled, and he lines up at her entrance before driving into her.

"Oh god," she whimpers, her body vibrating as Royce fucks her ruthlessly. "Yes. Please. There. Please, Royce. *Please.* I need to come."

His breathing is ragged, his hair a mess as he fists the back of her head, forcing her back to arch and take him deeper. "Oh shit. Come for me, Ry," he rasps, pumping into her twice more before his thrusts stutter. She comes with him, and Grayson hauls her into his arms before she can collapse.

"My turn," he growls possessively. She's as limp as a noodle as he lays her on the floor, splaying her out for him to admire as he peels off every inch of her clothing.

As her bra falls away, I notice the teeth marks around her nipple before he covers her with his body, already leaving love bites all over her. *Possessive bastard.*

It takes no time at all before he's wound her so tight that she's begging him for more.

"Please, Grayson," she pleads as he strokes along her inner thighs, so close but not quite where she needs him most. Her hips rock, seeking the friction he denies.

"Please, what? What do you need, Riley?"

"You," she whimpers.

Removing his lips from where he was planting open-mouthed kisses along her navel, he leans over her, arching a brow as he waits.

She huffs a frustrated breath, and I swear, if she were a dragon, steam would come out her nose. "I need you to fuck me."

Oh Jesus, now I'm hard again.

Smirking like the arrogant ass he is, Grayson lines the head of his cock up with her entrance. "Fuck," he hisses as he pushes inside her. "So wet for me."

She moans, and I stare transfixed as Royce's cum squeezes out of her cunt while Grayson bottoms out. Why is that so fucking hot? *Our* girl dripping with *our* cum. Fuck, I need to add my own to the mix.

I fist my already hardening cock as I watch Grayson roughly and thoroughly fuck Riley into the floor. Her head falls to the side, gaze zeroing in on my dick as I work it over. My heated stare roams over her face before dropping to her bouncing breasts. They're covered in love bites, her nipples peaked and pointing toward the ceiling as they move in time to Grayson's hard thrusts.

"I want to come on your tits. Can I?"

She hums in approval, kneading the soft flesh of her breasts as she brings them together. I shift onto my knees as I shuffle closer, pumping myself harder.

Her eyes are glazed over, her breathing rapid.

"You gonna come for them, Babydoll?"

She nods at Royce's question.

"Words, Ry."

"Yes."

"Eyes on me," Grayson rasps. His muscles are tight, and the veins along his neck are palpable as he restrains himself. "It's you and me."

"It's us," she moans before her head falls back and her spine arches, and she comes for the third fucking time.

"Yes," I hiss, pumping faster until I spill all over her chest. I wait until Grayson slides free before gathering my cum on my fingers and pushing it inside her, twisting my hand to mix it in. Then I sit back on my haunches and stare at the creamy mess spilling out of her.

Hottest. Fucking. Thing. *Ever.*

"I should take Aurora shopping every week if this is the reward."

Safe to say, we have all thoroughly worked up an appetite as I sag to the floor and haul her into my arms, pressing a kiss to her temple. I rest my head against the cupboard door while I catch my breath. We can reheat the takeout in a bit once we've recovered. Maybe after a dirty shower followed by a clean one because I cannot get *enough* of this girl.

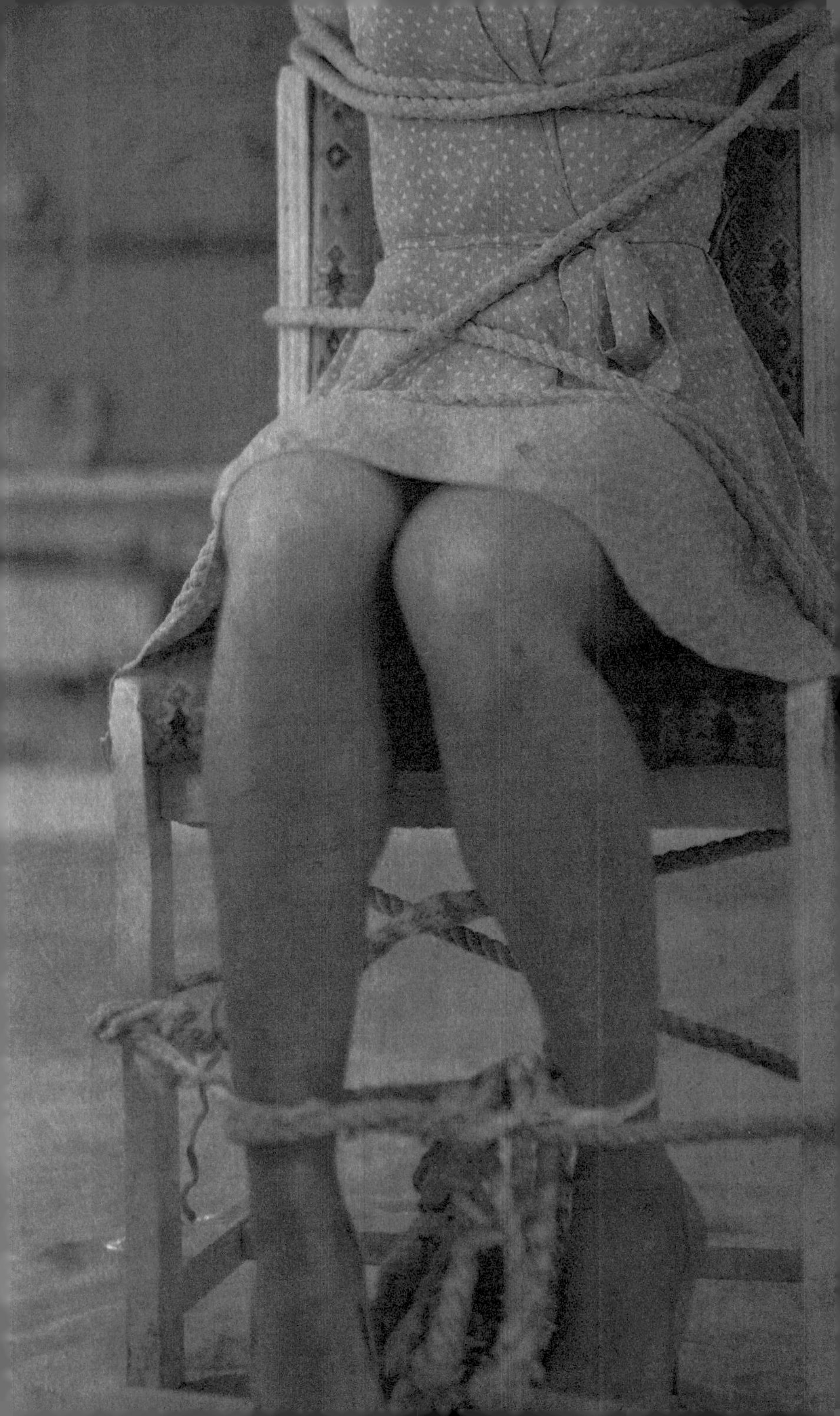

ROYCE

"Rogue?" Riley questions in confusion when she notices the neon pink sign above the club door before Logan navigates the SUV into an alley that runs up the side of the building. "Eh, you realize we can't go clubbing with a kid, right?"

My gaze flicks down to where Aurora is passed out in her booster seat.

"We're not exactly here to grind on you on the dance floor," Logan retorts with a wag of his eyebrows.

Riley swats his shoulder, and I'm thankful the lack of light in the alley means none of them see my smile. It's only been one day, but already Riley is more relaxed. She smiles and laughs more. It's fascinating to watch.

"What are we doing here then?" She glances warily around the alley, and considering we have Aurora in the car, I can't blame her, but she's safe here. Dax wouldn't dare let anything happen to one of us outside his own club.

"Dax owns the building," I explain to her.

She arches a brow. "Ooookay... Good for him."

That sarcasm. Makes me want to bend her over and fuck the

attitude out of her until she's begging for me to let her come. She must see the feral intent on my face because her cheeks blush—something I notice despite the poor lighting.

"*So*, it's suitable for more than getting drunk and dancing to shitty music..."

I stare at her intently, but it's Grayson who spells it out. "Say, like having a little tête-à-tête with your dear mother."

Riley's eyebrows hit her hairline, her focus moving to the back of the club as she runs her tongue along her lower lip. "She's in there?"

"Yup." Her eyes snap to mine. "It's up to you whether you want to go in there. You can sit out here, or Logan can drive you both home if you want to leave it to us."

She mulls it over, her focus shifting back to the building before dropping to stare at Aurora's sleeping face. "Dax's men will be out here, watching her and the car. If she so much as stirs, they know they're to get one of us immediately," I tell her, in case that's what's holding her back.

Thinking about it for a moment longer, she eventually gives a slow, steady nod. Her eyes lift to mine. I see the determination blazing in their hazel depths before she says a word. "I want to do this." She rolls her shoulders as if preparing for a fight. The action is cuter than it has any right to be. "I have a few things I need to get off my chest when it comes to that woman, and when I'm done, I don't want to think about her ever again."

There's my fierce girl.

Unable to help myself, I slam my lips on hers. Her fire, her resilience, it's so fucking hot. I rasp those exact words against her lips, making her moan before the sound of the others climbing out of the car jolts me out of my lusty thoughts.

I get out, helping Riley slide out behind me. She spares Aurora a final, worried glance but doesn't waiver. Simply closes the door and turns her back on the car, trusting us to ensure

she's safe. I don't know if she realizes how much that means—
that she's placing that much trust in us, especially given we've
just got Aurora back.

I'm desperate to touch her, so I thread my fingers through
hers as I search the shadows for Dax's men. Spotting one, I
jut my chin out, and he nods in acknowledgment, a silent
reassurance that enables me to focus solely on why we're
here.

All four of us are dressed in dark clothing as we approach a
set of concrete steps that lead to a large metal door typically
used for deliveries. It's good that this was able to come together
tonight. While we weren't sure if Riley would want to be
involved, the three of us agreed we all wanted to be present for
this. We all have our issues to address with Lydia, and Logan
has away games all weekend. With only a few weeks until
regionals, he can't afford to skip any more games, not after his
display of aggression last week. He's lucky enough that the
Timberwolves agreed to let him play for the Huskies for the
remainder of the season. The last thing he wants is to get
himself suspended for breaking NCAA rules. Despite everything
going on, I know he's buzzing about Riley being in the stands to
watch the Huskies take home that championship cup for the
fourth year running.

Grabbing the handle, I wrench open the heavy door. I'm
instantly met with the scent of stale beer and damp concrete.
Stepping inside, the dim lighting casts long, eerie shadows that
dance across the walls and emphasize the low ceiling, making
the space feel claustrophobic.

Our footsteps echo as we step further into the space, the
metal door slamming shut behind us with a resounding *thunk*.
Dax appears at the top of a set of short, wooden steps that must
lead up to the club's main floor. He's dressed in his typical attire
—an expensive, tailored suit that makes his muscles strain

against the fabric and his tattoos stand out against his white, ironed shirt.

"Any issues?" I ask.

"No. You sure you want to be the ones to do this?"

Riley huffs out a breath at my side while I answer, "We're certain. You've done more than enough, and we appreciate it, but this needs to be us." It needs to be Riley.

She needs this.

She needs to look her mother in the eye after what she did.

Selling Aurora. Trying to kill her own daughter... just the thought has my blood boiling. I need to keep a lid on my anger, or I'm liable to snap Lydia's neck before we truly make her suffer. Her death has been written in the stars since the moment she decided to sell Aurora, but after everything she's done, she needs to pay before the life drains from her eyes.

With a curt nod, Dax's gaze slides to a large, metal, heavy-set door on the far side of the basement. "She's in there. Room is soundproof. Do whatever you want; my guys will deal with the cleanup."

His inference is clear, and Riley shivers at my side. Still, she doesn't contradict him, which says everything about where her head is at. The same blood-soaked place as mine, apparently.

Dax leaves us to it as we turn to face the door he pointed out. Before I can take a step toward it, Riley is striding forward. Shoulders squared, her head is held high as she steps between crates and boxes piled haphazardly. Fierce determination gleams in her eyes, a fire that refuses to be extinguished despite everything she's been through. *In spite* of everything, she's survived.

This world might try to break her, but my girl is un-fucking-breakable.

I can't help but admire her strength and bravery as I walk behind her, sporting a hard-on. *Not exactly the time,* I tell my dick. Not that he's listening. Riley's courage is hot as fuck. Her iron will to keep going is the sexiest thing I've ever seen. That fight. That strength to get up and throw another punch when all you want to do is tap out.

Riley pauses at the entrance, just for a second, her grim determination unwavering. She's ready for this confrontation, even if it means facing some of her darkest fears. I step closer, my heat enveloping her in a silent reminder that she's not alone. That I'm here—*we're* here. No matter what happens in there. She glances over her shoulder, those captivating eyes meeting mine as a small smile lifts her lips. I nod, and she faces the door, which looks like it leads to a walk-in freezer once more. It is with a sense of pride that I watch her take a deep breath before pulling on the handle.

We follow her into the room, purpose-built for precisely this reason. Why Dax needs a soundproofed interrogation room is none of my business. I'm certainly not about to complain about the convenience. Unlike the rest of the basement, the light is startlingly bright, and I blink as black spots dance across my vision. When they finally clear, I look around the tiled room, the stench of bleach and an underlying hint of rust assaulting my nostrils.

Lydia is sitting on a metal chair in the center of the room, her wrists bound in front of her and a blindfold over her eyes. A drain sits beneath her seat. Her head is slightly tilted, and her ear is strained in our direction. Goosebumps pebble her exposed skin—of which there is plenty since her short dress fails to cover her—and the chair rattles from her shaking so hard.

"W-who's there?"

"I don't think you're in a position to ask questions," I drawl. We decided before we got here that I would take the lead, at least initially.

Her lips purse, a crease forming along her forehead before she asks, voice shaking even more than before, "R-ruthless? I-is that you?"

"I see you're just as useless at taking orders as the last time we spoke." My voice is rough and harsh, my tone like the crack of a whip that has Lydia cringing in her seat.

Standing over her, I stare down at her pathetic form, unfeeling. I don't have an ounce of sympathy for this piece of shit as I recall everything she's done, everything she allowed to happen. My gaze strains toward Riley, but I keep my attention focused on the sniveling woman before me, knowing if I catch sight of Riley's expression, I'll likely murder this bitch before Riley gets what she needs off her chest.

"I-I haven't done anything," she whines.

Leaning down, I bring my lips to her ear. "Haven't you?" She shuffles on her seat, trying to put as much distance between us until she's perched right on the edge of the chair. Her lips part, likely with another protest, but I cut her off before more bullshit can spew from her mouth. "I'd think real hard about your answer because I can't tolerate any more lies from you."

Her lips snap shut.

"Does the name Vincent *Knuckles* Fisher ring any bells?" Lydia's entire posture stiffens. "Ah, I'll take that as a yes." My voice is a velvet purr dripping with malintent.

"I-if he was one of y-yours, I-I didn't know!" Her panicked, shrill grates on my ears.

"Oh no, he wasn't one of mine," I state with a malicious chuckle. "But the girl you sent him after?" I snarl. "She's *mine*."

I whip off her blindfold. She blinks in the stark light, her wide-eyed, frenzied gaze darting around the room as what little color remained in her cheeks drains. Finally, she spots the others standing behind me. Recognition flashes across her face, quickly followed by confusion and a fresh wave of terror. "G-Grayson? R-Riley? I don't—What's going on?"

"What's going on, Lydia, is that you thought you could hire some amateur dipshit to take out *my girl*."

"*Our* girl," Grayson corrects automatically—possessive jerk.

At the sound of his voice, Lydia's attention snaps to where he is standing with his arms crossed, looking bored as all hell. What he is is furious. It's there in the tick of his jaw and the tense way he holds himself, as though he's fighting to keep from coming over here and slapping the bitch. *I can totally relate.* "G-Grayson." There's a pleading in Lydia's voice as she repeats his name. "H-help me. I don't know what he's talking about. This has all been some sort of mistake! A-an attempt to e-extort money from your father."

Grayson snorts, his arms crossed over his lean chest. "Believe me, Lydia. None of us are interested in my dad's dirty money."

A soft touch at my back has me stepping aside so Riley can take my place in front of her mother.

"What we want is retribution." Her voice is steel, and I'm so fucking proud of her.

"Riley." For the first time, Lydia's tone has a haughty snap. "This is absurd. What have you roped these boys into?"

Grayson and Logan bristle while I clear my throat in a clear warning. Lydia's shoulders curve in, her wary gaze flashing to mine before darting back to her daughter. "R-ruthless is a dangerous man. You shouldn't be associating with the likes of him."

Riley throws her head back in a caustic laugh that feels like broken glass embedding beneath my skin. Dropping her gaze back to her mother, she tilts her head to one side. "Says the woman who hired him to *sell my daughter!*" Her last words come out in a scream that bounces off the white tiles.

Lydia's face drains of color. Riley notices, her cackle at the turn of events something deranged yet cathartic. "Oh yeah. We know all about how you sold your only fucking grandchild on the black-fucking-market because you're a heartless, twisted bitch."

Every ounce of pent-up aggression pours out of Riley and hits her mother square in the face. Not that Lydia so much as flinches. If anything, a spark of malice ignites in her muddy brown eyes, and she lifts her chin in a show of defiance. Of silence.

Seeing it, Riley sneers. "I *hate* you," she spits in her mother's face. "What the fuck did I ever do to you?" Smacking a hand over her heart, her voice cracks with fury and despair. "*I'm your daughter.* All I wanted was for you to love me."

Unmoved by Riley's words, Lydia's lip curls in disgust. "You wanted to suck me dry! *Mommy* this. *Mommy* that. Always needing something. Even when I ensured you had everything you could ever want, it wasn't enough. You just had to keep taking. Taking what wasn't yours."

"*Oh my god.*" Riley paces away before marching forward, pointing a finger into Lydia's chest. "For the last fucking time," she snarls, "I did not *take* your husband. Your sick slimeball of a husband *raped* me, but of course, you're too self-involved to see it that way." It's Riley's turn to curl her lip as she glares down at her mother in disgust. "You were *never* a mother."

In a move so shocking I don't see it coming, Riley's hand whips out and slaps her mother across the face. Lydia's head whips to the side, a bright red palm print crawling across her cheek.

"*You* might not be a mother, but I am," she hisses. Bending down, she gets right in Lydia's face. Fisting her hair, Lydia screeches and writhes in the chair. Logan steps up, keeping her in place as Riley snarls in her face, spittle hitting the woman's cheek. "A mother goes to the ends of the earth for their child. They'll do *anything* for them. They never give up. They *never* stop looking." A slow and truly malicious grin spreads across Riley's face. "I found her." Lydia goes stock still, eyes wide as she stops fighting Logan's hold, and stares wide-eyed at her daughter. "Yeah," Riley smirks. "Bet you didn't expect that. You lose, Lydia."

"No," the bitch whimpers.

"It's over. You're done. I'm going to walk out of here, and my daughter and I will be living our best lives. We'll never speak your name again. You're dead to us."

I'm not sure if Riley realizes her mother will *literally* be dead by the end of this night, but I don't think she's too bothered either way. Like she said, once she leaves this room, it will be like her mom no longer exists. That's as much permission as I need to finish the job.

Sensing that she's done, I step forward. Aware of the sudden threat, Lydia's eyes snap to me, her body trembling. Flexing my muscles, I crack my knuckles. As each *crack* whips through the air, she flinches, her trembling growing stronger until the entire chair rattles. I take great pleasure in her terror. While I'm usually anti-violence against women, and I'm sure Grayson and Logan would agree, for this bitch, I'm more than willing to set that aside. Given that I haven't been to The Depot for an actual fight in weeks, and I'm a pent-up ball of aggression ready to unleash.

Lucky for Lydia, she's going to face the full ferocity of my wrath.

She begins to thrash furiously in the chair, and Logan's firm grip on her is the only thing keeping her from flopping onto the floor. "No! Please!" She screams bloody murder, the sound a waste of energy since it does nothing but vibrate around the room before swirling meaninglessly down the drain. "I-I'll talk. I-I'll tell you anything you want to know."

My chuckle is sharp and deadly. "Lydia, Lydia," I tut. "Don't you see by now that you have nothing of use to us?"

"I-it wasn't just me." She practically shrieks the words, pressing herself so deep into the chair she's practically rubbing up on Logan.

"Oh, you mean your little fuck buddy, David?" Even her lips drain of color. "Don't worry, we already had a chat with him. He was very informative. Told us all about how the two of you concocted this plan to sell Aurora to make a quick buck and get back at your daughter and husband."

"I-I can tell you about the buyer."

I shake my head. "No, you can't. You don't know shit about the buyer. Your buddy filled us in on that, too. How, the night you were supposed to hand Aurora over to me, you abandoned her in a fucking playpark while she was *sleeping*."

Riley stiffens. She wasn't aware of any of this. When I'd told her David had given us all the sordid details, she said she'd prefer not to know—all that mattered was that Aurora was safe and home.

I smirk down at the snot-nosed bitch. Crouching in front of her, I reach up to push a strand of bleach-blonde hair out of her face. "There's something David didn't tell you, though. Something I'm going to take great pleasure in informing you before we—" I point to Grayson and Logan—"take our pound of flesh."

She looks pathetic. Nothing like the pretentious bitch who walked into that speakeasy all those months ago and tried to get me to sleep with her in exchange for selling her granddaughter.

"Shit." Grayson curses, and I whip toward him. His face has lost its color, and when he glances at me, alarm has darkened his already dark irises. He twists his phone toward me, showing me the numerous missed calls from the nursing home. *Shit.*

He marches out of the room to call them back, but after sharing a look with the others, we know we need to leave now.

None of us bother to spare Lydia a glance—she's not worth our time—as we follow Grayson out of the room. "What's wrong?" Logan demands.

"It's Gran," Grayson chokes. "She's taken a turn. The home says I need to get there *now*."

"Then let's go." I'm already messaging Dax to let him know we'll be back and not to take out the trash just yet. I wasn't speaking metaphorically when I told Lydia I wanted her pound of flesh. I'm going to take it—all of it. For Riley. For Aurora. For our family.

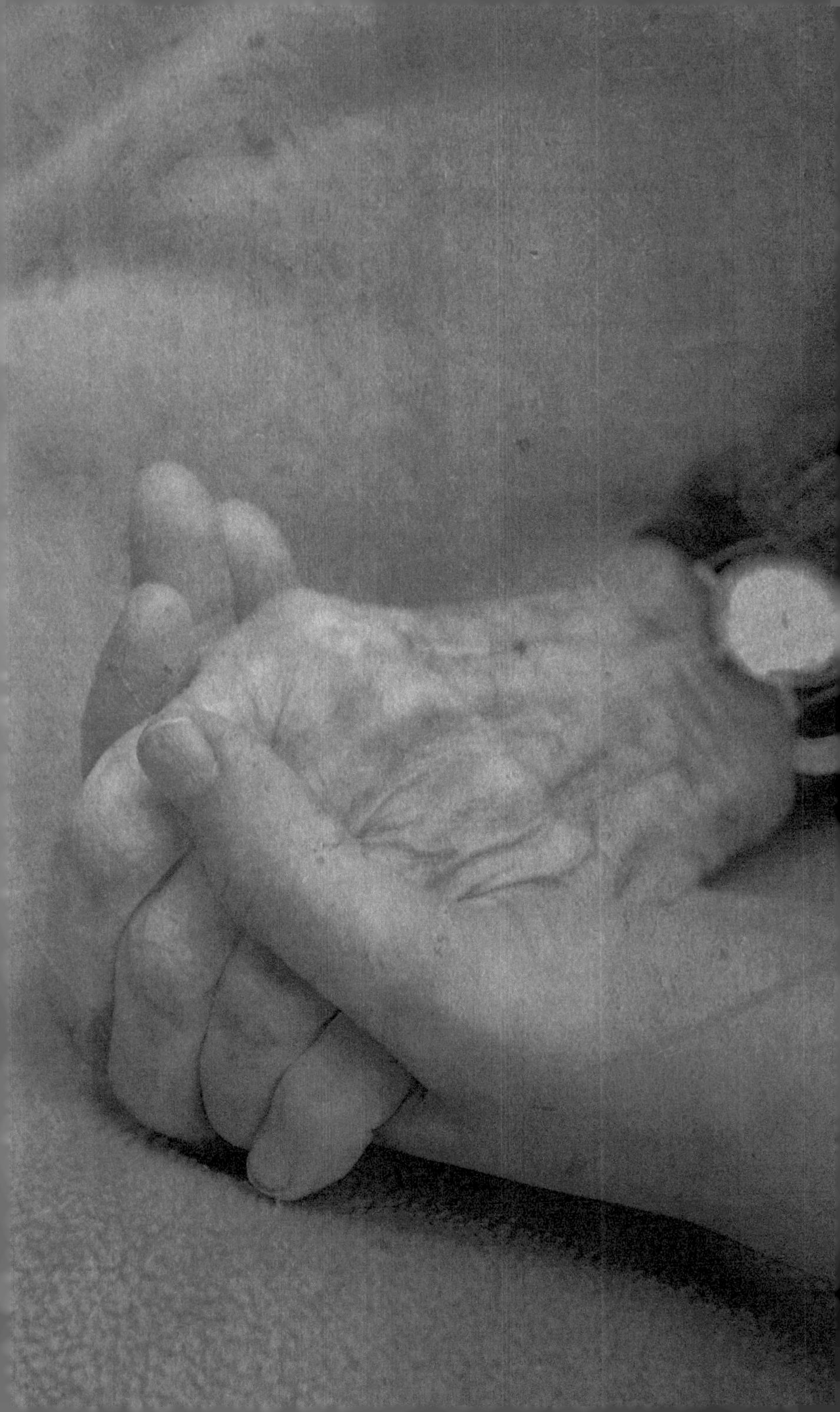

RILEY

CHAPTER TWENTY-EIGHT

We arrive at Sunnyside Nursing Home in record time. "Go," Logan urges as he pulls up to the curb. "I'll stay with Aurora."

I only hesitate for a second, but I trust him with her—I trust all of them with her. When he gives me his reassured, confident smile, I chase after Grayson. Rushing through the sterile hallways, the fluorescent lights flicker overhead as if sensing our urgency. The scent of antiseptic and faintly wilted flowers fills the air, clashing with the adrenaline coursing through my veins from tonight's activities. I pick up my pace, practically jogging to meet the guys' long strides as we hurry toward Gran's room.

Grayson's face is a mask of devastation, his eyes hollow and haunted. He hasn't spoken a word since we jumped in the car, and I can tell he's barely holding it together. We all can. The weight of his grief is visible in the set of his jaw and the tightness of his shoulders. It shatters my heart to see him like this.

I *hurt* for him.

It makes me realize he's been hurting for me too.

With Aurora. With Bertram.

He's been feeling that pain, too.

It makes all the shit that happened at the beginning of the school year seem petty. Childish.

Yeah, he fucked up. Yeah, he never apologized, but honestly, I wouldn't expect him to. He might regret what he did, but he's not sorry. He did what he felt he had to, and shouldn't that be something I value in a person? That they're willing to do what needs to be done regardless of whether it's right or wrong?

Besides, knowing Grayson, he'd probably use the excuse as some twisted logic that if he hadn't done that, the four of us wouldn't be what we are now. Which, admittedly, I'm not entirely sure what we are, but it feels like it's something significant. Something bigger than each of us individually.

It feels like family.

Grayson and I may be volatile, like oil and gasoline, but I'm ready to light that match and go up in flames with him.

When we reach the door, Royce slows, hesitating. "I'll wait here." His voice is a low rumble. "Let me know if you need anything."

I move to join him, but Grayson's words stop me. "Riley." I turn to face him, my heart aching at the sight of his glassy eyes. It reminds me of the day he found out about Aurora. He had that same sheen. Grayson may act cold and unfeeling, but if I were to hazard a guess, I'd say he feels more than the rest of us. Perhaps too much, even. "Will you come in with me?"

His plea is raw, a crack in the armor he's built around himself. I see the fear and vulnerability he's usually so good at hiding, and it breaks me. How can I deny him this? How can I not be there when he's pleading with such silent desperation?

"Only if you want to."

I nod, swallowing the lump in my throat and threading my fingers through his. Pain and fear are still prevalent in his stare, but his shoulders drop, some of the tension in them easing. His grip is firm, almost pleading, and I squeeze back, hoping to offer some semblance of comfort.

We step into the room together, the door closing softly behind us. The curtains have been pulled, the only light coming from a small bedside lamp that casts a warm glow over the room. Gran lies comfortably in her bed, frail and pale, her breaths shallow and labored. Beside her sits a nurse, who rises, moving over to greet us. Her face is etched with sympathy as she talks to Grayson in a hushed tone.

"I'm so sorry," she says softly. "She's been in and out of consciousness. She's comfortable and not in any pain." Reaching out, she squeezes Grayson's arm. "This is the end, Grayson. Sit with her. Talk to her. We'll give you peace to say goodbye."

Grayson's Adam's apple bobs, his eyes never straying from his Gran's frail form as he nods his acknowledgment before the nurse silently slips from the room.

Only when we're alone does he take a shuddering breath. That brave face he's been donning starts to crumble, and I direct him to the chair the nurse had been sitting in. The raw pain in his eyes is unbearable as he sinks into it, focusing intently on his Gran. His grip remains firm on my hand the entire time, like without it, he'd drift out to sea and never find his way to shore.

"Gran," he whispers, his voice breaking.

I stand beside him as he lifts the wafer-thin skin of her hand and presses his lips to it. His face crumples as he drops his forehead to rest beside her arm on the sheet, whispering words I can't hear but feel in the depths of my soul.

I don't know how to comfort him, how to ease the pain etched so deeply into his features. My heart aches for Gran, for Grayson, for the love and loss swirling around us. I want to say something, anything, but the words stick in my throat, unable to break free.

Instead, I focus on being present and letting him know he's not alone. I run my thumb over the back of his hand, a small gesture, but it's all I can offer. Tears blur my vision as I watch the man I've come to care for more deeply than I realized grapple with a pain that's tearing him apart.

Grayson's shoulders shake with silent sobs, and I feel my own tears spill over. The love in this room is palpable, even amidst the heartbreak. I squeeze his hand again, hoping he can feel my support, my unwavering presence.

Eventually, he sits up. He tugs on my hand, his other arm banding around my waist as he drags me into his lap so my back rests against his chest. He buries his nose in the crook of my neck, inhaling deeply before releasing a shuddering exhale.

"I don't know what to do without her," he confesses in a voice so low that if he wasn't breathing the words directly into my ear, I wouldn't have heard them. "She's been my rock. The one constant in all the chaos. I might not need her the way I did at eighteen, but I still *need* her." His eyes shimmer with unshed tears, and he takes a deep breath, trying to steady himself.

Still unable to find the right words, I lean back into his chest, letting him know I'm here. We're silent for a drawn-out moment, Grayson lost in his thoughts.

Eventually, he starts to speak. "Gran used to make the best apple pie," he says, a small, wistful smile tugging at the corners of his mouth. "Every Sunday, without fail, we'd have pie after dinner. I remember helping her in the kitchen whenever I stayed at hers when I was little. She'd let me roll out the dough, even though I always made a mess. But she never minded. She'd just laugh and tell me I was her little chef."

I can see the memories playing out in his mind, each one a bittersweet reminder of what he's losing. "She taught me how to drive," he confesses. "Dad was... busy, so Gran took me to an empty parking lot and let me practice until I finally got the hang of it. I remember how patient she was, never once losing her temper, even when I nearly ran into a lamppost."

Grayson's eyes drift back to Gran, and he brushes his thumb over the backs of her fingers. "She's the reason I am who I am today. Why I didn't end up completely lost in the dark. She believed in me when no one else did." He pauses, his voice trembling. "I just don't know how to do this without her. She's been my guide, my confidante. I feel like I'm losing a part of myself."

I swallow hard, shuffling sideways on his lap so he can see my face. His expression is one of devastation as I lift a hand, pressing my palm to his cheek. I wish there was more I could do. Wish I could take away this pain for him. "You'll always have those memories, Grayson. She's given you so much, and you've made her proud every step of the way. She'll always be with you in everything you do. Everything you achieve."

He nods, a tear escaping and sliding down his cheek. "I just... I wish I had more time," he says, his voice breaking.

I wrap my arms around his waist as he drops his forehead to my shoulder, and I soothe him as he falls apart in my arms. The minutes roll by, time losing all meaning until Grayson lifts his tear-stained eyes to mine. Beneath the thick layer of grief burns a fire, one aimed in my direction. "I'm done letting you hold yourself back from me."

"Grayson..."

He shakes his head. "We both know I fucked up, and we both know I'm not the type of guy to apologize for that. Not when it brought you back into my life." His eyes search mine, his hand moving to rest on the side of my throat. "I can't promise I won't piss you off. Hell, we both know I will. But I want to know that even when we're angry at each other, we still love one another. I don't want to waste any more time. I want to put the past behind us and move forward."

He continues, his grip tightening as if afraid to let go. "I want to start a new life with you, with Royce and Logan, and with Aurora. I don't have all the answers to how that looks, and I can promise you it won't always be smooth sailing, but I know I want it with you. The good times. The bad. The hard and the ugly."

His vulnerability, his earnestness, they pierce through my defenses. I reach up, cupping his face in my hands. "I want that too, Grayson. A life with all of us." My lips quirk in a teasing smile. "Although, for the record, I won't say no to you chasing me through fields or abandoned churches."

He smirks, a spark igniting in his eyes. "Good, because I had no intention of stopping." Then his lips are on mine. Coaxing. Demanding. Somehow both passionate yet chaste.

All too soon, he pulls away, the somberness of the situation settling between us once more as we turn to face Gran. I tense as I find her watching us, her eyes cracked open and a weak smile on her face.

"Grayson, my dear." Her voice is a whisper as her bony fingers squeeze Grayson's.

Shuffling me on his knee, Grayson leans closer, his face inches from hers. "I'm here, Gran."

She manages a small smile, her eyes filled with a lifetime of memories and unspoken words. "You've always been my strong boy," she croaks, her grip on his hand tightening slightly as a shadow casts over her face. "Don't let your father turn you into him. You're better than that, my dear."

Gran's hand trembles as she reaches out, touching his cheek with frail fingers. "I see you, Grayson. I see how hard you fight the world, how you keep everyone at arm's length. But you don't have to carry that burden alone. You deserve love, my boy.

Happiness. Strength isn't just about holding everything together."

Tears threaten in Grayson's eyes as he clings to every word, his emotions raw and exposed.

"You've built walls around your heart, my dear," she continues, her voice growing fainter. "But those walls... they keep out the love you deserve. Don't be afraid to let them down."

Grayson places her hand gently against his cheek, tears running freely down his face as she draws a shaky breath. "Let yourself love, Grayson."

"Gran," he chokes out, his voice thick with emotion. "I..."

She smiles faintly, a glimmer of pride in her cloudy eyes. Gran's next breath is her final one before she slips away. Grayson's face crumples with grief as he leans over, pressing a tender kiss to her forehead and whispering his goodbye.

Even after she's gone, we sit there for a while longer. The silence is peaceful, healing. The room steeped in a solemn hush. Gran's presence lingers in the air, a bittersweet memory mixed with the heavy weight of grief.

Minutes. Hours. Days.

However long Grayson needs, we'll sit here. *I'll* support *him*.

For now, everything else can wait.

My eyelids are heavy, and my muscles weary as I trudge into the house alongside Grayson; however, many hours later, Royce and Logan brought Aurora home and put her to bed hours ago. Thankfully, she's been out like a light all night.

Once we're home, Grayson heads straight for the stairs. I watch him go, sighing before I go to check on Aurora. I pop my head into her room, reassuring myself that she's safe and sound, before ducking across the hall to Logan's room.

"You okay?" he murmurs from where he was lounging on his bed. Getting up, he comes over and pulls me in against him.

"I'm fine."

"Grayson?"

I shake my head.

"He will be," Logan assures. "He's got us, whether or not he realizes that yet."

With a sad smile, I press onto my toes and plant a quick kiss on him. A thank you.

"I'm going to say night to Royce, then I think I'll stay with Grayson."

Logan nods as though he expected nothing else. He tucks my hair behind my ear, tracing my jawline with his finger. "You should. He needs you tonight. I've got Aurora."

"Thank you." With another press of our lips, I slip from his room and go to Royce's. He doesn't hear me enter, bent over his desk with headphones in as he draws. I tap his shoulder gently so as not to startle him, and lifting his head, he pulls the headphones off. "Ry." He glances past me toward the door. "You're both home?"

I nod.

The openness he always sports when he's drawing slowly shutters until his face is set in its typical hard mask. "I need to go... Lydia." I'd momentarily forgotten we left her tied up in the basement of Dax's club. I hadn't been joking when I said that she was dead to me. Still, we can't just leave her there indefinitely.

"Should you be going alone?" I question, worrying my bottom lip.

He gives me a sly smirk. "I'll be fine, James. You just take care of Grayson for us."

I give him a soft, weary smile. "I will."

His lips quirk in the semblance of a smile before he ducks in, kissing my temple. "Help yourself to something to sleep in," he offers, gesturing toward his dresser as he grabs his jacket before disappearing out the door.

I take him up on his offer, grabbing a t-shirt of his before making a pit stop at the bathroom to freshen up. Once I've stalled for as long as possible, I approach the stairs leading to Grayson's room. Dressed in Royce's top, my legs and feet bare, I pause with my foot on the first step, worrying my bottom lip. I've never been in Grayson's room, and suddenly, I'm second-guessing myself. Would he want me in there when he's grieving? Maybe he'd rather be alone?

Except, isn't that Grayson's problem? He shuts down and pushes everyone away. Knowing the stubborn asshole as I do, he's probably shoving every bit of emotion he's feeling into a box and snapping it shut.

Frowning, I march up the stairs, refusing to talk myself out of what I'm doing as I push open his bedroom door and step into the dimly lit room.

Grayson's bedroom is perfectly him—dark and moody. The walls are a deep charcoal, and the slanted ceiling adds unexpected coziness. A massive bed dominates the space with its dark, luxurious linens. The rich, deep tones of the bedding and furniture give the room a masculine elegance. Two doors are on the far side of the room, one presumably for the closet and the other for the adjoining bathroom.

The only light in the room is the bedside lamp. It creates a warm pool around the bed, the rest of the room fading into shadowy corners. A sharp, warm scent lingers in the air from Grayson's cologne, and feeling the plush carpet beneath my bare feet, I pad on silent feet into the room, quietly closing the door behind me.

Grayson lies flat on his back in the middle of the bed as he stares at the ceiling. Not once has he looked my way since I walked in. However, I know he knows I'm here.

"Go away, Riley."

Aaaand we're back to being an asshole.

Oh, how Grayson loves to give me whiplash.

"Yeah, no, I don't think so."

Done with letting him push me away, I move to perch on the opposite end of his bed.

He sighs but doesn't make any further attempts to get me to leave.

Because despite the walls he's putting up, he doesn't *want* me to leave. Stupid, stubborn male. The muscles in his face twitch before smoothing out one by one.

Stretching my bare leg across the bed, I poke him in the ribs. "Don't do that."

His head falls to the side, flat eyes staring unblinkingly at me. "Do what?"

"Shut down."

He sighs, returning his focus to the ceiling. "It's the only way I know how to deal."

"No, it's the only way you've *allowed* yourself to deal," I correct. "You're used to shutting everyone out, turning off your emotions to tackle the practical problem instead, but you can't keep doing that, Grayson."

"Says who? You?" He frowns.

"Yes. Me." Shifting my legs beneath me, I lean on my knees. "You say you don't want to waste time, yet here you are, *wasting time.*"

Snarling, he hauls himself upright to glare at me. "The only family I have just died! I'm allowed to take some time."

Before he can launch me across the room, or I can chicken out, I crawl into his lap, planting my knees on either side of his narrow hips as I grab his face between my palms.

"Your Gran was not the only family you have. You have us. You have me. You have *Aurora*." Holding his gaze, I lightly trail my fingers over the high rise of his cheekbones. "For once in your life, Grayson, let yourself feel all the hard emotions. Don't bottle it up. Don't push us away. You'll regret it."

He swallows, his Adam's apple bobbing. "I'm scared."

"I know, but you don't need to be. You're not alone. Isn't that what the three of you keep telling me? That I'm not alone? Well, it goes both ways, Grayson. If I'm not alone, then you're not alone either."

One minute Grayson is staring at me like he's never seen me before, his hands fisting the bed covers, and the next, his lips are on mine, his hands in my hair, dragging me closer as he swallows me whole.

"Grayson." My hands move to his chest, fisting his top. I intend to push him away. Instead, I pull him closer, eliminating the last of the space between us. "You're supposed to be feeling," I get out between frantic, desperate kisses.

"I am." His voice is a deep rasp, rougher than usual. "Believe me, Riley, I'm feeling *everything*."

I gasp as he lifts us, flipping me onto my back in the middle of his massive bed. With his hand planted on the mattress beside my head, he hovers over me, his weight a sensual comfort as he stares down at me with that stoic, unreadable expression.

Except his eyes say everything.

Despite being darkened by his pain and grief, they are also warmer than I've ever seen. His gaze holds mine, and in that moment, I see past the facade he presents to the world. The walls he's meticulously built around himself are still there, but there are cracks now, letting the light in. It's as if the loss of his Gran has stripped away some of his defenses, revealing a man who feels deeply, even if he rarely shows it. Seeing him like this, so raw and unguarded, stirs something deep within me.

"You're the eye of my storm," he murmurs in a voice scraped raw with vulnerability. "When I'm with you, there's this calm... this quiet I've never had before. Everything stops, and in that moment, I can just be."

Bringing my hand to his face, I run my fingers through the coarse hairs of his stubble. Lifting my head, my lips hover inches from his. "Get lost in the storm with me, Grayson."

It's all he needs to hear before his lips capture mine in an intoxicating, dominant kiss, and he settles his weight fully between my legs.

I moan, arching my back and fisting his hair, pulling on the ends as I attack his mouth with equal fervor. Grayson and I might have crossed some invisible impasse tonight, although that doesn't mean we aren't still a storm waiting to happen. That we don't still crave that harsh and demanding outlet from the other.

It's different, but it's also the same.

Just like when he chased me through the graveyard. It was the same as when he chased me through the field behind their house, but it was also different because I trusted him with my body that night—trusted him to keep me safe. To make me come. To make me forget.

Now... Now, I'm trusting him not only with my body but with my heart.

With rough tugs, he yanks my top over my head. He twists the fabric, my arms getting caught inside the material as he pins them to the mattress above my head.

Pulling away, he growls, his eyes raking over my face and chest. "I love it when you're pinned and helpless beneath me."

I moan, arching deeper as I grind my core along the hard length pressing against his jeans. With his free hand, he pulls down the cups of my bra, ducking his head to suck a pert nipple into his mouth.

He's not gentle about it. Nothing about Grayson is gentle despite the caged, refined appearance he puts on for the world.

And I wouldn't want him any other way.

Only when the skin is raw and sensitive does he move on to my other breast, lavishing it with the same attention before crawling down my body until his face hovers above the soft pink panties I'm wearing.

Working his way up my inner thighs with his mouth, there's a damp patch darkening the cotton by the time he presses his nose to the fabric and inhales, humming. He bites and sucks on my clit through my panties until they stick to me, and I'm desperate for more.

"These have to go," he finally declares, making quick work of peeling them down my legs and stuffing them in his jeans pocket before burying his face in my pussy like he's been dying to do exactly that for *days*.

"Oh god," I groan, lifting my hips to meet his talented mouth.

It amazes me how Grayson can infuriate me yet have me coming apart on his tongue in mere seconds. Perhaps that's part of it. The passion between us. The explosive chemistry. It can't only flow in one direction.

"Fucking delicious." Grayson's words are muffled, barely audible as he eats my pussy like it's his job—and we all know how seriously Grayson takes his job.

His fingers join the assault, and I'm primed to explode.

"Come, Tempest. Now."

Goddamn, I both hate and love how he just has to command it, and my body instantly obeys like it was born to follow Grayson's orders.

Like the crash of waves against the shore, I implode.

My limbs are still heavy, my breathing ragged as I push myself upright. Fisting the back of Grayson's top, I pull him up my body, ripping off the Henley so I can run my hands over the hard, lean planes of his torso.

Grayson smirks, the expression flooded with pure masculine smugness. "Eager, are we, Tempest?" he teases as I tear open the button of his jeans before shoving them over his ass.

"Are you saying you aren't?" I challenge with an arched eyebrow.

"Fuck no," he snarls, surging forward to claim my lips. The momentum has me falling back to the bed, Grayson settling on top of me as he kicks off his jeans and boxers. "Having you is all I've been able to think about since seeing you stand up to Lydia like that. That fucking slap, Tempest, had my fucking balls aching. I've never been so proud."

He nips my lip, and I yelp, before he slides the head of his cock teasingly along my slit, never actually entering me and giving me what I need. What we *both* need.

"Need you," I pant, rolling my hips and digging my heels into his ass in a bid to get him moving.

"Fuck, I love you like this. Wet and needy for me." Fucking finally, he pushes between my folds. Sighing, I stretch around him. His head falls to my shoulder as he seats himself inside me. "God," he groans. "You have no idea how much I needed this. Needed you. I don't know how you calm the chaos, but it's so fucking quiet."

Rapturous pleasure has smoothed the lines on his face as he lifts his head to look at me. Chemistry buzzes along my skin, yet what simmers in the air between us is so much more than simple attraction.

"We're in the eye of the storm," I murmur, feeling that same peace and contentment he does. Like the world has stopped turning. For a blissful moment, everything is frozen in time.

Then he begins to move, and that tranquility melts into a molten desire that sizzles along my nerves and fries every thought in my head until all that exists is the slide of skin against skin, the heat of Grayson's warm body, and the insane pleasure every grind of our hips elicits.

My nails dig into his skin, clawing marks down his back as he thrusts into me with bruising force while leaving marks all along the column of my neck with his teeth and lips. Despite his sweet words, this is not lovemaking. It's a battle of wills. A clash of titans. The way I imagine it will always be with Grayson.

Sliding a hand into my hair, he fists the auburn strands. Pain dances along my scalp as he wrenches my face to his. "Mine."

"Yours," I agree, because there truly is no denying the inevitable. I think I've always known it was the truth, but opening myself up to Grayson is terrifying. Scarier than falling in love with Royce or Logan. Not because of what he did when I first came to Halston, but because he's my teenage crush. The one man I put on a pedestal. Who seemed so far out of reach that he was nothing but a fantasy that I'd immerse myself in in my darkest moments. He was the spark in the night that kept me going when my demons were pressing in on all sides. He's the reason I didn't give up sooner. The reason I clung to hope for so long.

Without him, I'd have died before I was far enough along for that pregnancy stick to turn positive. Before I found out about Aurora. Before I found a reason to *live*.

"I've always been yours." I curl my hand around the back of his neck, squeezing. "I might be your eye in the storm, but you've always been my candle in the dark."

"Good. I'll be your guiding light, and you can be my shelter from the storm. Together, we'll make it through the night. Now, show me how those pretty eyes spark when you're coming on my cock."

Reaching between us, Grayson rubs his finger against my clit until stars blanket the clear sky, and there's no fear of either of us getting lost.

We spend the rest of the night in each other's arms. Every time one of us would stir, our hands and lips would wander until Grayson had me seeing stars all over again.

By the time the gray light of dawn battles the night for dominance, muscles I didn't even know I had hurt, and a sleepy smile graces my lips as I slide out from between the sheets. Not wanting to wake a sleeping Grayson, I tip-toe to the adjoining bathroom and quickly relieve myself.

The room is lit by only the weak daylight straining through the window when I step back into it. I don't immediately go back to the bed. Instead, I wander the room to the soothing backdrop of his soft breathing. I'm struck by how minimalistic it is, yet each item here carries weight and meaning.

On his nightstand is a framed photo of his Gran, her smile warm and loving. I pick it up gently, feeling a pang of emotion at the sight of her kind eyes. Nearby, I notice a small stack of ticket stubs tied together with a thin piece of string. I untie the string and carefully sift through them, recognizing one from Logan's championship game last year. The edges are worn from handling, and I imagine Grayson's excitement and pride as he watched his brother achieve such a milestone.

On a shelf above his desk, there's a sleek frame housing an article clipping. It's about a huge deal his company landed, demonstrating Grayson's pride in the company he has reconstructed in the wake of his father's actions. The headline is bold, praising his strategic mind and leadership. I trace the edge of the frame, feeling a surge of admiration for his accomplishments.

I trail my fingers over the rigid spines of business books and classic novels as I pass a modest bookshelf, before approaching his dresser. A small, intricately carved wooden box is perched on top that draws my eye. My fingers hover over the top of it before I open the lid. Inside, sit a pair of antique-looking cuff-links and...

... a bright pink scrunchie.

It can't be.

Gingerly, I lift it out, the fabric silky smooth against my fingers.

"I stole it from your bedroom when we were teenagers."

I whirl toward his husky voice. "Why?"

He's sitting upright in the bed, his lean torso on display, the sheet pooled around his waist as he stares at me. His hair is sticking up on end, and he has never looked sexier. Something about seeing Grayson undone gets to me—knowing that he'd never let just *anyone* see him like this.

"You had a part of me," he says, gesturing toward the bracelet I'm still wearing. "I wanted a part of you."

I arch an eyebrow. "You could have just asked. Instead of *snooping* through my room."

His lips twitch in a semblance of a smile. "Says the girl currently *snooping*." He gives a casual shrug. "Thought that might be weird. What with you being my sister and all."

"Stepsister."

"Same thing."

"I don't think it is," I argue with a genuine laugh.

"Besides," he continues. "I like the idea of you not knowing."

"You realize I spent weeks searching for this. I assumed one of the girls from school nicked it from my locker during gym."

"I'd apologize…"

"But it would be a lie." I roll my eyes, unable to control the muscles along my lips as they quirk upward.

Unrepentant, he merely shrugs before we're interrupted by the pinging of my phone. Scrunchie still in my hand, I move over to my bedside table. I find my phone on the charger and subtly cast a glance at Grayson's way, knowing he must be the one who retrieved it from where it fell on the floor after our first sexcapade and put it on the charger while I was sleeping.

Plucking it from the table, I settle against the head of the bed and check my notifications. The top one is a text from Royce. Surprised, I open it, wondering what he would have to message me about. Anything urgent, and he'd have come upstairs, and anything else could probably have waited until breakfast.

Reading the text, my mouth goes dry.

"What's wrong?" Grayson asks. His body heat practically burns as he leans closer.

The phone slips from between my fingers as I lift my head to stare into those depthless eyes. "Lydia escaped."

We're no longer in the eye of the storm.

LYDIA

CHAPTER TWENTY-NINE

The driver gives me a final wary glance in the rearview mirror as I tap my phone against his card reader and hustle out of his germ-infested cab. It's no fucking wonder he was giving me weird looks, with my hair a mess, makeup smeared, and my hands fucking bound.

Huffing, I awkwardly yank my dress down, stumbling in my heels as I march toward the front door.

I'd been *terrified* when those men had appeared out of nowhere on my way home after a night out with the girls, thrown a rancid sack over my head, and tossed me unceremoniously into the back of a van. I thought I was going to *die!*

A high-pitched laugh bubbles up my throat, and lifting one hand, I tenderly touch my face. My cheek smarts from where that little bitch slapped me, and steam billows from my ears.

How dare she.

How fucking *dare* she!

That Ruthless character... How long has my daughter been using her wiles to wrap him around her finger?

And Grayson! Just wait until his father hears who he's in bed with.

That little harlot!

She isn't content to simply steal my husband; she has to sleep with the entire student body at Halston U.

And she has the nerve to tell me *I'm* dead to *her*?! Well, we'll just see about that. I have no idea what she and her little friends had planned before they rushed out of there but thank god they did. They left in such haste that they didn't ensure the door was closed behind them. All I had to do was wait. The fools that they are, they underestimated me. Did they think I'd sit quietly in that chair and let them talk to me that way? Treat me with such disrespect? Once the thump of music was loud enough to cover any noise I might make, I snatched my purse from the corner it had been tossed into and hauled ass out of there, careful to keep to the shadows until I was out front of the club and able to blend into the crowd until I hailed a cab.

Now? Now I'm fuming. Vibrating with rage at the audacity of that little bitch. I'm so sick of her innocent act. So sick of her destroying my carefully laid plans. I'm going to make her *wish* that stupid idiot had hit her with his car.

"Bertram!" I bellow as I stomp into the house. My heels clack against the floor as I go straight for his office. Finding it empty, I storm into the kitchen to take a knife to these stupid restraints.

Rubbing my raw wrists, I huff as I march up the stairs to his bedroom. Also empty.

Where the hell is he?

Stomping back to the foyer, I'm breathing fire as I plant my hands on my hips and glare at the door, demanding he walk through it.

When that doesn't work, because Bertram loves nothing more than to defy me, I snatch my clutch from where I dropped it on the table and pull out my phone.

Dialing his number, the *ringing* of his phone echoes as I tap my foot and wait. I *hate* waiting. At this time of night, he should be at home. He should have been wondering where I've been all this time! Worrying for my safety!

So where the hell is he?

Aaaggghhh!

Releasing my frustration, I shove the vase off the table. It shatters with a satisfying *crash,* water spilling onto the pristine floor and the flowers scattering.

I've had e-fucking-nough!

I'm so sick of being treated like dirt. Bertram has no appreciation for me.

My daughter sure as fuck doesn't. Ungrateful bitch. I gave her *everything.* I worked my ass off to land a man of Bertram's wealth and prestige, and instead of saying thank you, she fucks him behind my back and has the *audacity* to lie to me about it.

What does she think is going to happen now? Does she think Bertram will actually want her and her sniveling daughter? That the three of them will be one big happy family?

I scoff just at the notion. There is absolutely no way in hell that I will allow that ungrateful child to steal my life. My husband. My money.

Done with this bullshit, I flick to the *find my phone* app that I had the good sense to connect to Bertram's phone one night after I'd distracted him with sex and he'd stalked to the bathroom to clean up, leaving his cell unattended.

Bertram thinks he can play me, but I can play him too.

The blue dot shows his location as Halston. What would he be doing in *Halston* at this hour? It's the same spot on the map where he's been on those nights when he doesn't come home until I'm already in bed.

I'd assumed it was some insignificant whore, but Riley's protestations, along with the ridiculous obsession my husband has with her, have me wondering...

Is this their love nest?

There must be somewhere they go to hook up since Bertram's plan to have her under our roof failed. Naive, gullible Riley probably thinks she'll have more time with him if they're somewhere *alone*. That he'll leave me if she pulls him far enough away.

Honey, he won't ever leave me for you.

And tonight, I'm going to prove it.

Grabbing the keys to my Bentley GT convertible, I pull up directions to my husband's location and climb into the car. The engine roars as I slam my foot on the accelerator, kicking up gravel before flying down the driveway toward Halston.

I fume the entire journey, and as I pull up outside a quaint apartment building, that fury boils over. Glaring up at the darkened windows, my lip curls in a snarl as I imagine the two of them in there somewhere, wrapped up in each other. Probably laughing at me. Do they think I'm that stupid?

Throwing open the door, I stand on the sidewalk and stare at the building. The lights are off in all but one window. Given that it's the middle of the night, it's not surprising. I don't care what time it is. I'll readily go door to door until I find those sneaking, lying snakes.

I march toward the entrance of the building and pull open the double glass-fronted door. The lobby inside is *okay*— nothing fancy. If it were me Bertram was bringing here, I'd demand something better, but clearly, my daughter can be bought for cheaper—foolish girl.

Going straight to the wall of mailboxes, I scan the various names in search of a familiar one. A frown pulls at my lips when I notice one I recognize, only it's not the name I'd been expecting.

Of course, I should have figured. Bertram isn't stupid enough to tie his own name to a secret fuck pad. Furtive tasks like this are precisely what he pays David so handsomely for. Memorizing the apartment number beside David's name on the mailbox, I stomp toward the stairs.

My anger has morphed into something glacial as I navigate stairs and hallways to apartment number eight. Finding the right one, I don't bother with such formalities as knocking. They didn't do me the courtesy of not fucking behind my back, so why should I offer them the courtesy of knocking? Instead, I twist the door handle and step into the apartment.

The lights are on inside, showing a vacant open-plan living-dining area. Giving it a cursory inspection, my focus moves to the hall leading to the bedrooms. My heels are silent on the thick carpet as I bypass the open doorways and approach the one at the end of the hall, which is closed. Pausing, I press my ear to the wood before quietly turning the handle. I slowly open the door, giving my eyes time to adjust to the dark interior as I peer into the room.

I make out the outline of a bed, except it's not the right size. I'd been so confident I would walk in on Bertram and Riley cuddled up together that it takes me a moment to understand what I'm actually seeing.

A single bed is pushed against the wall, and a small, plastic kiddie table and chairs are set up on a rug beside it. A cold chill seeps down my spine, and I clap a hand over my mouth. Riley wasn't lying. She has Aurora back, and they are living here—on *my husband's* dime.

This is so much worse than I imagined!

Whirling, I march for the door, moving directly to the next room down the hall.

Flinging open the door, I balk.

Again, comprehending the sight before me takes far longer than it should. Except this time, my world tilts. It topples. It crashes down around me.

"Oh my god! David!"

I rush to David's side, where he's lying on the floor, convulsing. Tears fall unbidden from my eyes as I fall to my knees beside him. My hands hover over his chest, but there's so much blood. It's everywhere, spilling relentlessly from a deep gash across his throat. *How? Why?* "David, my love," I cry. *What happened to you?* Despite the sickly pallor to his face, it's clear that he's been beaten to hell.

The sound of gurgling is loud, and when it stops, along with the convulsing, the room is suddenly eerily quiet. "David?" Leaning over him, I find a spot on his shoulders not soaked in blood and shake him. However, his glazed-over eyes never shift from the ceiling. He doesn't blink. Nothing.

Sobbing, I curl up in a ball beside him. *Nothing makes any sense. Why is he here, in Bertram and Riley's apartment?*

My poor David.

He was the only one who cared about me.

After my idiotic husband got sent to prison and my daughter saddled me with her kid, he was the only one who ever asked me how I was. Who wanted to spend time with me. Who *listened.*

In those early days after Bertram was arrested, he'd bring me flowers and a bottle of wine, and we'd talk for hours. If I had a problem, he'd step in and sort it. He was good like that. Useful. He knew the job of a man. Ensured I was taken care of while Bertram was indisposed.

As the years passed, he was the only one I could confide in. Bertram and I had an agreement that we'd stay together. He needed me to keep up appearances once he was released and to dispel the rumors my daughter started after whatever spat they got into. I wanted his money and to keep the lifestyle I'd become accustomed to.

However, it was David who gave me everything else. The

comfort I needed. The support. He provided me with everything my husband had failed at over the years. He'd seen how Bertram treated me behind closed doors—his indifference toward me—and said it wasn't right. That I deserved better. He gave me that better. He gave me something my husband never had: love. I *loved* him.

I sob. How can he be gone? This isn't how it was all supposed to unfold. We were supposed to go to Europe. David had wanted it just to be the two of us. We have plenty of money now, but I couldn't let Riley win. I refused to hand my husband over to her. Not after all the lies and backstabbing. He wasn't *hers*. He never was, and I'd never allow him to be. I *needed* David, but I *wanted* Bertram—at least until he no longer lusted after Riley.

The three of us would go to Europe after Bertram was released. I'd continue the charade with him for as long as it took for him to move on from his obsession or for Riley to marry, and David and I would have our stolen moments until then. David understood. He knew I couldn't just walk away, not after the two of them made me out to be a fool.

I had to make him suffer. Make *them* suffer.

After his incarceration, David had become more to Bertram than a mere employee. Bertram *relied* on David too much, so it wouldn't seem strange if he joined us in Europe, continuing his role alongside Bertram until such a time as we could offload him. At that point, Bertram could do whatever he wanted so long as it wasn't returning to my daughter's bed, and David and I would have each other. It would have been perfect. It *should* have been perfect.

A shadow falls over me, a chill running down my spine. Startled, I push myself upright, eyes going wide as a gasp falls from my lips.

"Lydia," he purrs, the corner of his lips curling upward. "How convenient."

My composure crumples, my gaze dropping back to David's pale face. "D-David." My lower lip trembles. "He's dead."

"Yes," Bertram drawls. "I am aware, since I'm the one who killed him."

My face whips toward his, and for the first time, I take in my husband as he looms over me, a dark figure of menace and dread. His eyes, blazing with an unholy fire, pierce through my very soul. Dark hair falls in wild, untamed strands around his face, framing a look of pure, unadulterated evil. He looks like a demon conjured from the depths of my nightmares, every inch of him exuding a terrifying, almost supernatural power.

"W-what?" Certainly, I heard him wrong. Why would he kill David? David did everything for him. Unless Bertram found out about me and David? Did he kill my lover in a fit of jealous rage?

Interest piqued, I look up at my husband through a new lens.

Bertram scoffs. "Get that starstruck look off your face. My reason for killing him had nothing to do with you."

His words may as well be a slap to the face. Sparks of the anger that drove me here break through the surface of my grief, and rising, I meet my husband's eyes, unblinking as I lift my chin.

"You won't get away with this! I saw who you're keeping in that bedroom! What is this place?" I sneer. "Your love nest? Are the three of you playing happy families here?" I spit the words at him. "How did you even find her?"

He chuckles, the sound like ice pellets hitting my skin. "Why, darling wife, you delivered her straight into my awaiting arms."

What? No...

He smirks, cold, dark eyes gleaming with triumph as he

leans in as though to share a secret. I remain carefully still, his face taking up all of my vision as he whispers, "*You* sold her to me."

No...

"Although, sold is probably the wrong word since that money has conveniently found its way back into my accounts."

"No."

He grins. "Yes."

Reaching out, he twists a strand of my hair around his finger. "My stupid, simple wife." His soothing tone is at odds with his demeaning words. "David has been working for me this entire time. He played you. Had you wrapped around his finger so you'd confide all your secrets to him." He tugs on my hair, making me gasp. "I've known about her since the beginning." If it's possible, his already menacing expression turns deadly. "When David informed me of your plan to get rid of her before my release, I made some plans of my own.

"David was the one who arranged for the cell phone to be delivered to your house after he gave you that ridiculous Craigslist message to post. He's the one you were communicating with." He chuckles humorlessly. "You didn't even question how someone obtained your address from that, did you? All you saw were dollar signs and a chance to screw me over."

"No." My voice cracks, the sound muffled by the shattering of my heart. "No," I repeat, shaking my head. "He loved me."

Lips pushed out, my husband tilts his head, giving me a look of faux sympathy. "No, wife. He was obeying my orders the entire time. Since the very beginning. Every late-night chat, every bouquet of flowers, every *fuck* was done on my say so."

The room spins. "Then why kill him?"

Tutting like I should have figured out the answer by now, he gives me an assessing look. "He had outlived his usefulness to me." He shakes his head, muttering to himself, "Can't even be trusted to look after a *child*." Shaking himself out of his thoughts, he focuses back on me with a dark, piercing stare that chills me to the bones. "I'm beyond ready to begin my new life."

"N-new life?"

"Not that ridiculous Europe plan you foolishly believed in." He cackles scathingly. One side of his lips lifts. "No. I'm finally about to get everything I ever wanted. I've waited *years* for this." He sneers. "Put up with being married to you. Rotted in a prison cell. I'm *owed* this. I *deserve* it."

Riley.

He's talking about *her*.

That stupid fucking bitch! Why is she always ruining my life?! Of course, this is all about her!

My limbs shake with restrained fury. "You won't get away with this!" A shrill laugh pierces the air. "I won't let you!"

"Oh, I know," he purrs, far too at ease. "You've made that perfectly clear." The hairs along my arms stand on end as he steps closer, eliminating the space between us. Menace pours from him, and I stumble backward. My foot catches on David, and I trip, hitting the ground with an *oomph*.

"Bertram." With one arm outstretched in front of me, I shuffle backward on my ass. Like an ominous shadow, Bertram follows, his steps silent on the carpet as he stalks me until my back hits the wall.

I'm shaking so badly I can't get to my feet as he stands over me. My heart is lodged in my throat, terror paralyzing me as he slowly lowers to a crouch. There's nothing in his eyes as he stares at me. It's like looking into oblivion—nothing but desolation and death.

"Y-you can't do this! P-people will question my absence."

"Will they? You made sure to tell enough of your girlfriends that we would be going to Europe. Unfortunately, work commitments have kept me here, but my darling wife needed a break after all the stress of the last few years, and the loving husband that I am, I told you to go alone and enjoy yourself." He waves a dismissive hand. "Eventually, I can tell people you loved it so much that you decided to move there permanently. The distance put a strain on our marriage, and ultimately, we decided to go our separate ways. Although, by then, I doubt anyone will really care. We will all have moved on, after all."

Reaching out, he touches the tip of his finger to my cheek. It's only then that I realize I'm crying. Coating his finger in my tears, he rubs it into his skin like he wants to preserve it. Remind himself of this moment. "I'll have my new family. The one I've wanted for years. Since the first time I saw her hiding out at the back table of the bar you were waitressing in."

My gasp gets stuck in the back of my throat, and I begin to choke. "Why?"

Tilting his head, he continues staring at me in that uncanny, utterly terrifying way. Like I'm an ant he's debating whether to crush.

"You've served your purpose. Now you're just a problem standing in my way, and I'm done with obstacles."

Strong fingers wrap around my neck, squeezing. I gasp, but there's no air. Bucking, I claw at his arm, his hand, as I stare pleadingly into those dead, uncaring eyes.

Black dots appear in my vision as I wonder what I did to deserve an end like this. My limbs grow heavy, and my energy drains out as my eyesight narrows to a tunnel before everything goes black—forever.

RILEY

CHAPTER THIRTY

Nerves make my eyes wider than normal, and my pale skin paler despite the makeup I'm wearing as I flatten a hand over the front of my black dress. It's been a long and melancholy week since Gran's passing. Grayson has been subdued and quiet. Other than planning the funeral and clearing out his Gran's room at the nursing home, he's spent a lot of time with Aurora, the two of them cuddled on the sofa watching daytime TV or on the rug in the living room while she showed him one of the numerous toys or games Logan bought for her.

It's sweet—watching them together. Seeing Grayson bond with my little girl. Watching her get to know her big brother—even if she doesn't know that's who he is to her. It pulls at my heartstrings. I just wish it was under better circumstances. That there wasn't this gray cloud perched over Grayson's head.

However, every time he smiles at my little girl, I know that too will pass. That he will learn to shoulder his grief. That this won't be a step back for him in bottling up his emotions. He truly seems to have turned a corner, even though it's obvious he's struggling. I'm proud of him. However, today will be the most challenging day yet. Today, he buries his Gran. Today, he says his goodbyes.

Grayson is a wreck, though I think he realizes now that he has all of us to lean on. We just have to make it through today.

Movement in the doorway catches my attention, and I meet Royce's hardened stare. His lips are pursed, face set in fierce determination, much like it has been for the past week. Lydia escaped the night Gran died. Royce offered to go after her, but I told him no. That's what she wants—to take up more of our lives. I truly am done with her.

Besides, Blue found flights for both her and David to Switzerland. I'm guessing they both decided to flee the country? Whatever. If I was a more vengeful person, perhaps I'd go after them, but all I want is to move on. To spend time with my daughter and my guys. To cement this family we're building.

"Ready?" Despite squaring his shoulders as though he's prepared to go into battle, Royce's voice is soft and gentle.

"No," I honestly admit. Lydia and David may no longer be a concern, but Bertram most definitely is. We haven't heard anything from him since we found Aurora, and with Gran's death, Grayson hasn't been in the office. However, we all agree he won't miss the funeral today, even if it's just for appearance's sake.

I wouldn't be so terrified if it were just me facing him, but none of us were happy to leave Aurora with someone we didn't implicitly trust, so we're bringing her with us today. *She's* who I'm most afraid for. What will facing him again do to her? Royce and Logan will do whatever it takes to keep her away from him. To keep his eyes from even touching her, but I have no doubt the second he sees her with us, he won't be able to stay away.

Pushing off the doorframe, Royce stalks toward me. My gaze drops over him. I so rarely get to see Royce in anything other than jeans or sweats, but today, a perfectly tailored black suit is stretched over his broad frame, hugging his muscles. The suit jacket makes his shoulders appear wider than usual, and the pants emphasize his narrow waist before wrapping around his tree-trunk thighs.

I bet if he turned around, his ass would look incredible. It's more than him just looking good in a suit, though. It's the fact that despite how smart and polished he appears, his wild recklessness can't be contained. It shines through in the scruff of his beard and the way he carries himself with predatory grace. No man with Royce's bulk should be able to carry themselves with such ease—like a panther.

Perhaps it's the situation we're walking into and the shit we've all been dragged through in recent weeks, but there's an intensity about him—more so than usual—a dangerous aura that seeps through the seams and crackles in the air around him.

Royce might *look* refined, but everything about him screams *stay the fuck out of my way.*

He groans, hand fisting my hair. "Babydoll, don't look at me like that."

My lips curl up in a coy smile. "Like what?"

"Like you're two seconds away from falling to your knees when we both know we don't have time to satisfy one another right now."

"Are you sure? I can be quick." I'm teasing. His eyes narrow to a glare, and I chuckle.

"Are you seriously going to make me walk into a funeral with a hard-on?" he growls.

I shrug a shoulder, untangling myself from his hold as I step away. "You have the car journey there to picture whatever you need to to get that thing to go down." I gesture toward his crotch.

Royce groans, a half-pained, half-frustrated sound. "Baby-doll, it won't go anywhere with you staring and pointing at it."

I merely smirk as he adjusts himself in his pants.

Eyes narrowed on me, he growls, "You're going to pay for that when we get home."

I smirk. "Promises, promises."

He dives for me, and I dance out of his way, darting toward the door. Before I can escape, though, his arms wrap around me from behind. I melt into his embrace, my head resting on his chest. Despite not wearing his usual clothing, he still smells of leather and something earthy, and I wonder if it's his cologne or shower gel. Whatever it is, it's perfectly him and exactly what I need right now.

The flirty moment passes, and the weight of everything against us hovers heavily overhead as I sigh. Royce drops his head, inhaling like he needs to breathe me in as badly as I need to fill my lungs with him. "Let's just get through today, sweetheart."

The car ride to the cemetery is quiet. The kind of quiet that feels heavy, like a blanket that's too warm and thick, pressing down on us. Logan's hands grip the steering wheel tighter than usual, his knuckles white against the black leather. Royce stares out the window, his jaw clenched, lost in his own thoughts. Grayson is in the back with me, his gaze fixed on Aurora, who's nestled between us, playing with the straps on her car seat.

Aurora, with her bright eyes and innocent curiosity, is the only one who doesn't quite understand the gravity of today. She looks up at me with that wide-eyed expression that makes my heart melt and ache simultaneously.

"Mommy?" she asks, her voice small and uncertain, "You

said we're going to say goodbye to Gran, but... where did she go?"

Grayson shifts beside her, his hand coming up to rest on her small shoulder. I see the pain in his eyes as he struggles to find the words. How do you explain death to a three-year-old? She might not have known Gran—never met her—but that doesn't make it any easier to explain to her the permanence of death.

I clear my throat, trying to keep my voice steady. "Gran... Gran is in a special place now, sweetie," I begin, choosing my words carefully. "She's up in the sky, like a star. Watching over us."

Aurora's brow furrows, and I can tell she's trying to process this. "Like the stars we see at night?" she asks, her voice full of wonder.

"Yes, exactly like that." I force a small smile. "She's up there, watching us, making sure we're okay."

Aurora nods, her little mind accepting this explanation for now. She turns her attention back to the straps on her seat, her fingers fiddling with them absentmindedly. Grayson's hand tightens just a bit on her shoulder, and I can see the struggle in his eyes. This isn't just about explaining something complicated to a child—it's about dealing with his own grief, his own loss.

Logan releases a long breath, glancing at me through the rearview mirror. We share a look, one that says so much without saying anything at all. We're all feeling it, the sadness, the loss. The car feels like it's filled with it, suffocating in a way that's hard to escape.

The trees blur past as we drive, the world outside moving while everything inside feels like it's standing still. We're heading to the cemetery to say goodbye to someone who meant so much to Grayson, someone who was there for him. The *only* person who was ever truly there for him.

While Grayson needs today to say goodbye, I'm attending the funeral to thank this incredible woman who gave Grayson a perspective he would never have had. A woman without whose influence I shudder to think what Grayson would have become. Just like his father, I imagine.

As we pull up to the cemetery, the car slows down, and I see the people gathered, dressed in black, standing in small groups. They're waiting, murmuring amongst themselves, the somber mood evident in their mannerisms.

The cemetery is a mix of old and new, with weathered tombstones standing alongside freshly dug graves. The sight of it all sends a shiver down my spine, a reminder of the finality of today. Grayson shifts beside me, his gaze fixed on the gathering crowd, his face unreadable, but I can feel the tension rolling off him in waves.

Logan turns off the engine, and the sudden silence inside the car is somehow even more deafening. Royce finally tears his gaze away from the window, glancing back at us with a look that mirrors how we're all feeling—heavy, tired, not quite ready, but knowing we have to be.

Aurora's small hand reaches for mine, her fingers curling around my own. "Mommy?" she asks softly, almost whispering, "Will Gran be okay up there?"

I squeeze her hand gently, leaning in to kiss her forehead. "Yes, baby," I whisper back, my voice catching in my throat. "Gran will be okay."

As we step out of the car, the weight of what's ahead of us settles in fully—the reality of it all. We join the others, making our way toward the small gathering. Each step is heavier than the last, and as we approach the crowd, I feel Grayson's hand brush against mine, a silent reassurance that we're in this together, that we'll get through it, no matter how hard it feels right now.

GRAYSON

CHAPTER THIRTY-ONE

The day we bury Gran is a beautiful spring day. It's early March, so there's still a bite to the air, but the transition from winter to spring is palpable. The sun hangs low in the sky, casting a warm, golden light over the otherwise quiet cemetery. The snow has mostly melted, and patches of green grass are coming back to life, although there's still the odd clump of white stacked against a headstone or lying beneath the shade of a tree.

Spring was Gran's favorite time of year. She loved watching the bare trees return to life, tiny buds blooming beneath the sun's rays. Bird song fills the air with a strangely cheerful symphony despite the mournful day. The priest rambles on as I watch a pair of robins flit from tree to tree, their vibrant red breasts a stark contrast against the pale sky.

Gran will be happy resting here amongst the plants and birds she used to enjoy watching from the large bay window in the nursing home. With Riley's warm hand tucked in mine, her presence a strength at my side, the world feels strangely peaceful, wrapped in a quiet serenity that's hard to describe.

The chirping of birds mixed with the crisp breeze that has

chilled my nose and fingertips reminds me that no matter how harsh the winter, spring always follows, bringing a sense of hope and possibility. I cling to that hope as they lower Gran into the ground, and I say a final goodbye to the last happy link to my childhood.

As dirt is thrown on top of her coffin, my gaze slides to the headstone beside her. My mother's. There's not that same grief as I linger on her grave, but that aching emptiness of loss resonates.

Riley squeezes my hand, her voice low as she leans in. "How are you holding up?"

"I'm hanging in there." For a moment, I fall into those hazel eyes. Today, the green in them is sharper. Perhaps it's the spring weather bringing her back to life, too. Now that we have Aurora back, it feels like all of us are trudging out of the frozen tundra. It doesn't need to be said that we were all starting to lose hope despite our efforts. Fear had crept into our systems, slowly paralyzing us. None of us wanted to be the one to admit it. To put that out in the universe, but we were all thinking it.

However, having Aurora back does not mean that she is entirely safe. Even now, I can feel the probing of my father's gaze on us. Specifically on *them*—Riley and Aurora.

When Aurora started to become restless, and Logan bundled her into his arms, murmuring quietly to her, I noticed from the corner of my eye how my father's jaw ticked. Admittedly, the way he has possessively watched them since we arrived has dampened some of the smugness I felt when we walked in—the five of us striding down the aisle as one. As a family.

I *know* my father. He won't be an easy nemesis to best, although we do have the upper hand now. Not to mention the fact that I *know* him—better than he would probably like to admit.

"Grayson." My name is nothing more than a whisper on the light breeze: a wariness, a warning. Blinking, I realize I've been staring into Riley's eyes for an inappropriately long time. Wrenching my gaze away, I focus instead on the pile of dirt now marking Gran's grave. My chest pinches painfully. I still can't believe she's not here. How many times in the past week have I grabbed my keys to go to the nursing home only to remember that she's not there?

Riley's hand squeezes mine, and I tear my gaze away from the grave, noticing that guests have begun to file out of the rows. I keep one eye on my father, who lingers nearby, while I accept condolences and thank people for coming. Quite a few of the older employees from the office attended, along with a few residents and staff from the nursing home.

As the last of the guests walk away, my father finally steps up. "Son." He claps a hand on my shoulder, his face the picture of polite grief. Except that's where it stops. That grief, that pain... it doesn't bleed into his eyes the way I know it has spilled into mine. Since discovering the truth, I've noticed the cold calculation in my father's eyes, the falseness of his actions, especially at that fucking dinner. Still, for the first time, I see how *fake* it all is. How fake *he* is. Does he even know what genuine emotion is? Is he capable of feeling *anything*? He's perfected the facial expressions, the right things to say, the correct way to behave in any given situation, but I highly suspect that's where it ends.

By the time I respond with a forced, "Dad," his focus has already slithered away, lingering on Riley for longer than is appropriate before skipping over Logan and Royce to land on Aurora. Wide-eyed, Aurora burrows herself deeper into Logan's chest. The action makes Riley stiffen, and I rub my thumb over the back of her hand in an attempt to soothe her.

Logan's arms tighten around Aurora and he shifts so she

can't see Bertram, ducking his head to murmur into her ear before my father interrupts. "What was your name again? Larson?"

Logan's responding stare is as icy as Royce's. "Logan." Not sparing my father another minute of his attention, he turns to Riley. "I'm going to take her back to the car."

Riley manages a small *thank you* smile. "Okay."

With a repulsed sweep over my father, he drawls, "I think today calls for milkshakes once you're all done here." With that, Logan stalks off toward the car, Aurora safely in his arms.

I'm not the only one who releases a breath of relief, knowing Aurora is no longer subjected to his presence. Now, I just need to get Riley away, too. We're all playing at being civil because this is not the time or place, but I'm so fucking done with pretending when it comes to my father.

In fact... Lifting an arm, I drape it around Riley's shoulders, bringing her flush against me as I kiss the top of her head, all while keeping my eyes on my father. I smirk internally at seeing the burning decimation of his rage blazing in his eyes.

"No Lydia today?" I ask casually, more out of curiosity than anything.

"No." Not looking at any of us, my father slides a hand down his wrinkle-free suit jacket. "She's had enough of all this cold weather. Decided to soak up some sunshine in Europe for a while."

"How nice for her," I drawl, all the while wondering if we scared her enough to send her running or if it's yet another lie. Another deception. Although, if it is, I doubt my father is covering for Lydia. I'm pretty sure the only reason he stayed married to her and decided to give things a go after his release was because he thought she could be of use to him. Or perhaps it was a case of keeping your enemies close. I can't imagine he was too happy to discover she had neglected to inform him of

Aurora's existence and then tried to get rid of her before his release. "Well, we should get going."

Arm firmly wrapped around Riley, with Royce at her other side, I move to step past my father. That's when he reaches up and grabs my arm. "Really?" he hisses, voice too low for anyone else to hear. "You think you can just walk off with what doesn't belong to you?"

Lifting my face to his, I keep my voice equally low. Only Riley can make out our whispered conversation, although she pretends not to as she stares at the car where her daughter is safely ensconced. "Which one of them are you referring to? Because as far as I'm concerned, they're *both* mine."

My father shakes his head at me, the corner of his lip lifting in this smug little smirk like he genuinely believes he will ultimately win. Doesn't he realize he's already lost? That this was never a fucking game—just him unable to accept not getting what *he* wants for once in his life.

"You'll regret crossing me, *son*." Standing tall, he straightens his tie and says loud enough for Royce to hear, "I'll see you Monday at the office."

We stand in a line and watch him stalk back to his car and drive away before Royce exhales loudly. Tilting his head, he gestures toward the car. "I'll be with Logan. Take your time. We can leave when you're ready; no rush."

When we're alone, Riley glances up at me. "I can go, too, if you want to be alone."

"Stay," I urge with a squeeze of her hand.

She rewards me with a rare, accepting smile. One that isn't often directed my way.

Turning back to face the grave, she rests her head against my chest, and we simply stand there, lost in our thoughts. At some point, my focus shifts to my mother's gravestone. Noticing, Riley's gaze follows.

"I barely remember her," I confess. "Anything I do remember, I'm pretty sure it's from photos and stories Gran shared with me as opposed to actual memories."

"How old were you when she died?" Riley's voice is tentative as she slides her gaze to mine, holding my stare.

"Three, I think. I don't remember it. I vaguely recall her being sick, but that's about it."

"What was wrong with her?"

I wrack my brain, trying to remember. "I'm not sure. I remember her sleeping a lot. Some days, she was so weak that she couldn't even get out of bed."

Riley seems to chew on the inside of her cheek before she spits out, "You said your dad abused her?"

Shoving my hands in my pants pocket, I nod. "I found photos Gran must have taken. Evidence." My voice is thick. "I don't think either of them ever did anything with them. There was also a journal. It was all pretty damning."

A steady touch on my arm snaps me out of that dark place, and I stare down at where Riley is touching me. "I'm sorry," she murmurs. Her gaze is tender with empathy. "Your Gran told you your dad killed her?"

"I mean, you can't trust everything she said—the Alzheimer's—but she was right about everything else."

Nodding her head, she seems to think.

"What?" I eventually ask.

"I just... with everything your mom went through, I'm wondering if she was depressed."

"You think she killed herself?" My tone is defensive, and Riley immediately straightens.

"No! No, that's not what I'm saying. I just think if I was in her position... Trapped. Traumatized. Helpless. I'd be so *tired*." She shrugs a shoulder. "Your body can only keep up the fight for so long." She squeezes my arm, emphasizing her next point.

"I'm not saying she wanted to die. I only wonder if her spirit, battered and bruised, finally surrendered to the peace she'd been searching for."

As we leave the cemetery behind, I cast one final glance over my shoulder to the graves sitting side by side: mother and daughter. The grandmother who shaped me into who I am today and the mother I barely remember. All I can hope for is that, in death, they have finally found peace.

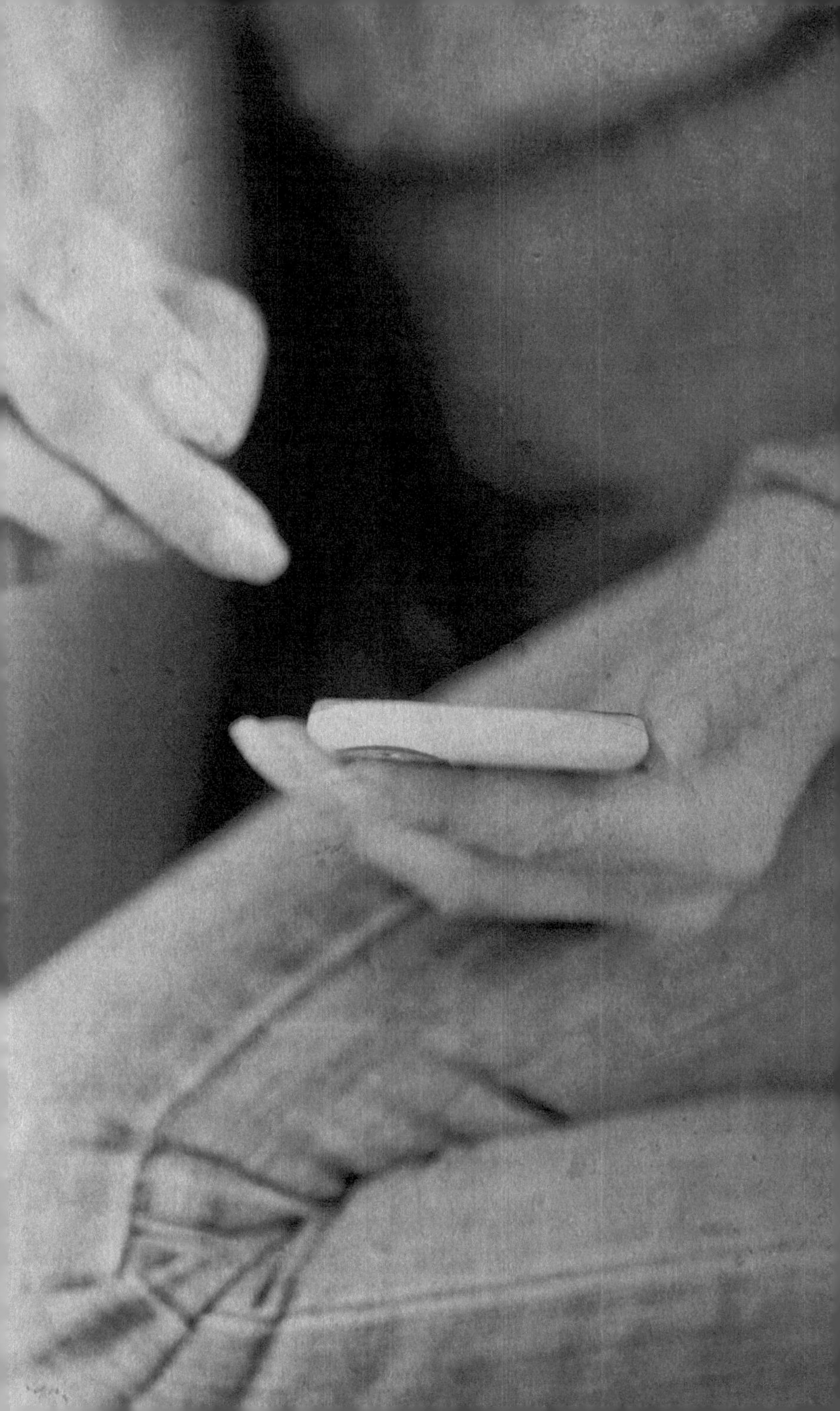

RILEY

CHAPTER THIRTY-TWO

That afternoon, we're chilling out in the living room with the remnants of our milkshakes. Royce and Logan egged Grayson into a video game battle while Aurora draws quietly on the floor, and I'm curled up on the sofa —content to be surrounded by my family. The guys' soft laughter and playful banter fill the air, along with the rapid clicking of the controllers and the occasional triumphant shout or groan of defeat.

"Come on, Grayson, is that all you've got?" Logan teases, his voice filled with mock incredulity. "You're getting your ass— *butt…* You are getting your *butt* handed to you!"

Aurora's eyes go comically wide at Logan's slip-up, and I smother a laugh behind my hand as he mouths an apology. Grayson chuckles, a rare sound that always makes my heart skip a beat. "Just you wait, Logan. I've got a few tricks up my sleeve."

Royce chimes in, his tone dripping with sarcasm. "Yeah, right. Like when you tried to beat me at that racing game and lost all five races?"

"My car was messed with!" Grayson protests, earning a snort from Logan.

"Dude, cars don't get *messed with* in video games."

I can't help but smile at their banter. Despite everything that's happened, despite the fear and pain, this moment feels almost normal. Their camaraderie and the easy way they rib each other... I imagine that's what having siblings is like growing up.

I let the soothing balm of their voices wash over me. Royce's laughter is deep and rich, Logan's is bright and infectious, and Grayson's is a rare but cherished sound somewhere in between. It's like a symphony of safety, each note playing perfectly in tune with the others.

"Right, girls," Logan announces. "Place your bets. Who do you think is gonna win?"

"Ro!" Aurora declares without a moment's hesitation. She can't say Royce or Grayson, so she calls them Ro and Gayson. Of course, Logan, feeling left out, insisted he needed a nickname too, and he's been trying to convince her to call him Lo—which just sounds ridiculous, if you ask me. However, when I said as much, he pouted and gave me those puppy dog eyes he's disturbingly good at.

In a flare of dramatics, Logan clutches at his chest as though mortally wounded. "Pumpkin, how could you do that to me?"

Smirking like the cat who got the cream, Royce flicks his gaze my way. "What about you, Mama?"—Another stupid nickname that has stuck—"Who are you betting on?"

"My money's on Grayson." Grayson's eyes widen in surprise as Logan makes a noise as though he's dying at my betrayal. The whole thing brings a smile to my lips, one Grayson mirrors. The two of us share a fragile moment that goes beyond simple video games and jesting among friends.

"Traitor," Royce mutters, reaching over to grab my foot and

tickling it until I squeal and plead for mercy. Aurora cackles at the entire thing, doing nothing to come to my rescue. *Traitor.*

The guys dive back into their game with renewed focus until Logan throws his arms in the air. "I win! Take that su— losers!" Standing, he spins in a victorious circle, pointing at Aurora and me. "Ladies, remember this moment. Don't bet on losing horses."

"You're ridiculous," I chide while Aurora throws her head back and cackles like a hyena.

After another few rounds of their game, the guys pause it and begin reminiscing about their earlier college days. Aurora has given up on drawing and climbed up beside me on the sofa. Her eyes are heavy, and I can tell she's moments away from falling asleep.

"Remember when we snuck into the dean's office and replaced his family portrait with a picture of that stray cat we found?" Logan chuckles, his eyes sparkling with mischief.

Grayson laughs, shaking his head. "Yeah, and he didn't notice for a whole week. Then he called a campus-wide assembly, and the look on his face as he berated us all was priceless."

Royce smirks, leaning back on his hands on the mattress. "That cat was the ugliest thing I've ever seen. How did we even come up with that?"

"It was Logan's idea," Grayson chortles. "He was always the mastermind behind our stupid pranks."

"Hey, I prefer the term *creative genius,*" Logan replies, puffing his chest in mock pride. "Besides, what is college without a few crazy memories?"

I smile, enjoying their stories. Despite their differences, they clearly share a deep bond forged through shared experiences and a lot of humor. Curiosity gets the better of me, and I can't help but ask the question that's been on my mind since I first started getting to know each of them.

"How did you all become friends? You're so different. It's hard to imagine how it all started."

The room falls silent for a moment as the guys exchange glances. It's Logan who speaks first, his expression softening.

"It was our freshman year," he begins. "We all had our reasons for keeping to ourselves…" He gives a one-shoulder shrug, not needing to fill in the gaps. Royce had just left the false rape allegation behind, and Grayson was dealing with his grandmother and the company off the back of his father's arrest. Logan… tilting my head, I give him a questioning look. "It was after I got kicked from that Michigan game," he explains. That's what I suspected.

Despite that dark time in his freshman year, he smiles at a memory. "I remember seeing Royce at one of the freshman football games. He was amazing on the field, but he always appeared guarded when stomping around campus."

"I did not *stomp* around campus," Royce gripes.

I chuckle. "You kinda do. You *stomped* right into me on my first day."

Challenge flashes across his brilliant blue eyes. "Babydoll, you're the one who ran into me. So desperate to get your hands on me."

Grabbing the straw from my milkshake, I flick it at his head while grinning.

Logan and Grayson burst into laughter as Royce easily catches it. "I figured he needed a friend, even if he didn't know it yet," Logan continues when we settle down again.

Royce rolls his eyes, but there's a hint of a smile on his lips. "Logan wouldn't leave me alone. He kept bugging me until I agreed to hang out with him." I don't even bother to smother my smile. That sounds exactly like Logan, and I bet it's precisely what Royce needed. After what he'd gone through, there was no way he would put himself out there to make friends. He needed someone like Logan to poke and prod and force him into a friendship.

"And then there was Grayson," Logan continues, turning to him. "We had a couple of classes together, and I noticed how he was always so focused. It was like the rest of us didn't exist. After seeing him so intent on his school work for several weeks, I decided he needed a break."

Grayson chuckles softly. "Logan practically dragged me out of the library one night. I was buried in work, struggling to balance school and the company, and I still visited Gran regularly. He insisted I needed to have some fun and dragged me to some frat party."

"But it wasn't until Royce got himself kicked out of a campus bar after Gray and I peeled him off some guy too dumb to realize who he'd picked a fight with, and spent the night bonding over stale coffee and pancakes that we truly became friends," Logan says, smiling fondly at the memory. "We realized we made a good team. Royce, with his determination and loyalty. Grayson, with his intelligence and strategic mind. And me, with my... well, charm and persistence."

Royce and Grayson laugh, and I find myself joining in. It's clear that Logan was the glue that brought them together, his easygoing nature and relentless friendliness breaking down their walls.

"You were the anchor." My voice is filled with awe, and I have so much love and respect for this husky of mine. The entire campus had turned on him, and instead of curling in on himself and putting up walls, he went looking for friends in the unlikeliest of places. "You brought all of you together."

He shrugs like what he did wasn't an incredible feat, but we all know, given Royce's prickly attitude and Grayson's obstinance, what Logan achieved is practically a miracle. "I guess you could say that, but it wasn't just me. We all needed each other, even if we didn't realize it initially. We became each other's support system, and that's what kept us going."

Throat tight, I nod, feeling a deep admiration for these three incredible men. Their friendship is a testament to the power of connection and the strength of having people who genuinely care about you.

The moment grows heavy, and in true Logan fashion, he breaks it with a more lighthearted memory. "Remember that wild party at the Delta Chi house?"

Grayson's eyes light up. "You mean the one where you got kicked out for trying to ride the mechanical bull in the backyard?"

Royce laughs, shaking his head. "And then you convinced us to sneak back in through the kitchen window."

Logan holds up his hands in mock surrender. "In my defense, I was trying to impress that girl from my international business class. But, yeah, that was a good night."

Grayson shakes his head, although a smile lifts the corner of his lips. "You ended up getting us all thrown out again when you tried to start a conga line in the living room."

"And then the sprinklers went off," Royce finishes, grinning. "We were soaked to the bone."

Later that night, Grayson and Royce are watching a movie with Aurora while Logan cooks dinner when my phone buzzes on the coffee table. I smile, seeing several new messages from Tara. I hadn't been very good at replying to her while everything was going on, but I've been making more of an effort to respond and actively participate in our friendship this past week.

TARA

Got a new shipment of feather boas. This one's neon pink! *photo attached*

Oh, and Xander ate the last slice of pizza. AGAIN. That little troll.

I'm thinking about switching the pink out for electric blue. What do you think?

But I like the girliness of the pink. It throws people off.

OMG, you'll never believe what happened at the club last night. This guy tried to pay for his drinks with a magic trick. Like, dude, coins don't magically multiply. *rolled eyes emoji*

My car made a weird noise this morning. Should I be worried? Or just blast the radio louder?

ME

You're insane. And you should tell Xander about your car!

Her response comes back immediately.

TARA

Xander?! I can't tell Xander! Do you have any idea how long he will lord it over my head? Telling me Betsy is a death trap is his favorite thing to do.

Snorting, I hesitate for only a moment before typing out:

ME

Any chance you'd have a spare spot for me if I came back to Lux next week?

Tomorrow night is Logan's last game of the regular season before regionals, and now that things seem to be settling down and we've developed a routine that works for everyone with Aurora, I'm keen to get back to work, even if it's just one shift a week. Even with Bertram still out there, I need this return to normalcy. Having a job gives me independence, especially now that I'm living with the guys and so reliant on their help with Aurora.

Bubbles form and disappear on repeat before a response finally comes through.

TARA

Biiiiitch, you better not be messing with me!
Hell yes, I've got a spot for you! Come to rehearsals on Tuesday!

I'm smiling as I respond and set my phone down. I know we still have Bertram's existence hanging over our heads, but it feels good to return to normal. Not that I can really call any of this normal since I've never had any of it before—unlimited time with Aurora, other people here to help and support me, three incredibly hot men to call my own.

No, this isn't normal.
It's so much fucking better!

RILEY

CHAPTER THIRTY-THREE

The crowd at Halston's ice rink is electric, buzzing with anticipation for the Huskies' final regular season game. The energy is contagious, and even though Grayson is absent—saying he wanted to catch up on work he'd missed out on this past week—I can't help but get swept up in the excitement around me. Aurora bounces up and down in her seat, her little hands gripping the edge of her tiny jersey—Logan's number emblazoned on the back, the fabric hanging loose on her small frame. She's never been to a hockey game before, and her wide eyes take in everything—the noise, the lights, the way the players glide across the ice.

I think back to sitting in my crappy apartment with Ava and Isabella, watching a previous game of Logan's, and wishing I could share the experience with my daughter. Now I can't believe that it's really happening.

Royce squeezes my hand as if he knows where my head has gone, and I give him a genuine smile.

"Mommy! Ro!" she squeals, pointing excitedly as the team skates out for warm-ups. "It's Lo!"

My heart swells at the sight of Logan, focused and determined as he circles the rink. When he spots us, his face softens into a smile, and he waves his hand. Aurora practically leaps out of her seat, waving back with all her might. "Lo! Lo!" she calls out, her voice somehow cutting through the crowd's roar.

Logan's grin widens, and he taps his chest where his heart is, then points at Aurora. It's a gesture that melts my heart, and Aurora's resounding squeal brings tears to my eyes.

As the game begins, Aurora's excitement only grows. She doesn't fully understand what's happening on the ice, but she knows it's important. Every time Logan skates by, she jumps up, cheering in that high-pitched voice that only a three-year-old can manage.

"Go, Lo, go!" she yells, her tiny fists pumping the air.

As the game progresses, a break in the action shifts everyone's attention to the jumbotron, which suddenly lights up with the familiar "Kiss Cam" graphic. The camera pans over the crowd, catching couples who lean in for quick kisses, sparking cheers and laughter from the stands.

I'm not paying too much attention until I notice the screen has stopped moving, and there, in bright, colorful clarity, is Aurora and me.

"Oh, look!" I laugh, pointing up at the screen. "We're on the Kiss Cam, baby!"

Aurora's eyes widen with excitement, and she immediately leans in, planting a big, wet kiss on my cheek. The crowd erupts into cheers, and I can't help but laugh, kissing her back.

But Aurora isn't done. She wriggles out of her seat and crawls into Royce's lap, her little hands cupping his face as she gives him an equally enthusiastic kiss. Caught off guard, Royce stares at her for a surprised moment, his cheeks tinted with color. He barks out a shocked laugh, his deep chuckle rumbling through him as he hugs her close.

I expect the camera to have moved on, so when I look up,

I'm surprised to find it still lingering on us as catcalls and cheers grow louder. "Kiss him!" a tipsy freshman yells behind us, stamping her feet as others nearby egg us on.

Royce meets my eyes, his grin widening.

"Looks like they want more," he teases, nodding toward the screen.

I laugh, feeling a rush of warmth despite the coolness of the rink. "Guess we can't disappoint them, can we?"

Still grinning, I lean in, and Royce meets me halfway. The kiss is sweet and brief, but the crowd goes wild, the noise almost deafening. Aurora claps her hands, squealing with laughter between us, clearly delighted by the attention.

As we pull apart, Royce ruffles Aurora's hair, and she beams up at us, her happiness infectious. I can't help but smile as the camera finally moves on, but the moment lingers, a bright spot of joy amid everything else weighing on my mind.

"Mommy," Aurora tugs on my sleeve as the team skates back onto the ice. "Is Lo winning?"

I glance at the scoreboard. The two teams are currently tied. "He's doing his best, sweetie. But even if he doesn't win, he's still our hero, right?"

Aurora nods vigorously, her eyes shining. "Right! And heroes get milkshakes!"

"Is that right?" I chuckle. "Just heroes?"

Her eyes widen as if she just realized her mistake before she shakes her head vigorously. "Little girls do, too."

The game continues, and I try to set my concerns for Grayson aside, for Aurora's sake and Logan's. Whenever Logan gets close to the boards near us, he glances up, searching for Aurora's face. And every time he does, she squeals with delight, her hands waving frantically to get his attention.

Royce nudges me again, a knowing look in his eyes. "He's playing for her tonight," he says quietly. "You can see it."

He's right. The score may be tied, but Logan is a force to be reckoned with on the ice. He'd told me before how having me in the crowd motivated him, and I guess the same can be said for Aurora.

But despite the sweetness of the scene, the fact Grayson isn't here with us sits wrong with me. I try to focus on the game, Logan, and Aurora's joy, but my thoughts keep drifting back to him. He's been quiet since the funeral yesterday. Distant. I just hope he truly did go into the office to catch up on work and not to drown his grief in the bottom of a bottle.

So when Royce's phone lights up with a call from him, I encourage him to take it.

He shakes his head. "I'm not leaving you here."

Rolling my eyes, I gesture toward the scoreboard. "There's less than fifteen minutes left. Just call him back and check he's okay."

"Exactly, there's *only* fifteen minutes left. Whatever he's calling for can wait."

"He buried his Gran yesterday and has been holed up in his office all day, alone—probably to drink. I know you're as worried about him as I am, so will you *please* just go talk to him?" I plead. "We'll be right here."

"Ry." He exhales, shaking his head before he grimaces. "Why do you make it so hard to say no to you?"

I smirk. "I don't know what you're talking about."

He snorts. "Sure you don't." The moment of levity gives way to a frown. "Stay here. I'll probably have to go outside to hear him, but I'll text Logan in case I'm not back before the end of the game."

"Stay here—Got it."

He rolls his eyes, a smirk quirking the corners of his lips before he presses a quick kiss to my cheek and stands, shuffling down the row of people and disappearing up the stairs.

"Mommy," Aurora says a moment later, and I can tell by her tone that it's urgent. "I need to pee." *Yup, of course.*

"Baby, the game is nearly over. Can you hold it?"

She shakes her head, staring at me like she's two seconds away from peeing her pants.

Sighing, I gather her things. "Okay, let's go." I glance across the rink, but Logan is deep in the game, so he doesn't see us leave. Holding her much smaller hand firmly in mine, we climb the stairs out of the stadium and along the hallway until I spot a sign for the women's bathroom.

"In here, sweetheart." The bathroom is otherwise empty, and we squeeze into a stall, Aurora doing her business before I dump our belongings at the sink and help her wash her hands.

"Go dry your hands." I point to the hand dryer as I grab our coats and bag from the floor. I'm bent over, my back to the door, as the sound of the hand dryer drowns out all other noise. That's why I don't realize someone else has entered the bathroom. Not until I stand up with our belongings in hand and turn to find Bertram holding my little girl hostage.

My heart pounds in my chest, each beat loud and desperate, as I take in the terrifying scene in front of me. Bertram's hand is still firmly clamped over Aurora's mouth, his fingers digging into her soft cheeks. Her wide, terrified eyes are fixed on me, and I can see the tears welling up, the panic seeping into her tiny body. The sight of it shatters something deep inside me.

"Please," I plead, my voice trembling as I hold out my hand, willing him to see reason, to stop this madness. "Please, Bertram, she's just a child. You don't want to hurt her."

"That's entirely up to you, Riley," he snaps, his voice sharp and fraying at the edges, lacking its usual cool confidence. There's something different in his eyes, something wild and unhinged, as if the careful control he's always prided himself on is slipping away.

I swallow hard, trying to keep my voice steady, my mind racing to find a way out. "I'll do whatever you want," I say quickly, "Just... let her go, and I'll come with you. I won't fight you, I won't try to escape. Just don't hurt her."

Bertram narrows his eyes, studying me as if trying to gauge the truth of my words. He's quiet for a long moment, and I can feel the tension in the air, thick and suffocating, as I wait for his decision.

"Promise me you'll be a good girl," he finally says, his voice tight. "That you won't try anything, otherwise she'll be the one to pay for it." He shifts his grip on Aurora, his fingers digging into her small shoulder as he slowly removes his hand from her mouth. Her chest heaves as she gasps for breath, and I can see her lower lip trembling, but she doesn't cry out. She's too scared, too stunned to do anything but stare at me, silently begging for help.

"I promise," I say, nodding fervently as I drop our belongings and step closer. "I won't try anything. I swear."

Bertram's eyes flicker over me, searching for any sign of deception, but I force myself to remain calm.

"Where's your phone? Leave it on the sink." With shaking hands, I do as he says. He gives me another sweep before nodding, satisfied, and jerks his head toward the bathroom door.

"Let's go," he orders, dragging Aurora along as he moves toward the exit. My heart seizes in my chest, but I force myself to follow, my mind screaming at me to do something, anything, to get Aurora away from him. But I know I can't risk it, not now, not when he's so dangerously close to losing control. I need to bide my time, to wait for the right moment.

As we step out into the corridor, the noise from the game hits me like a wall, the cheers and shouts of the crowd filling the space around us. I glance around, searching desperately for

Royce, for anyone who might help, but there's no sign of him—of anyone. With only a few minutes left of the game, everyone is inside, counting down the minutes. As for Royce, I don't know if he's still outside talking to Grayson or whether he's returned to our seats to find them empty. I never got a chance to message into the group chat to tell them where we were.

Bertram keeps a tight hold on Aurora, his other hand gripping my arm in a painful vise as we make our way through the stadium. The odd person we pass doesn't look twice at us, and I don't dare call out for help—not with Bertram's fingers digging into Aurora's little legs as he carries her, or the painfully tight hold he's got around my waist.

The cold air hits me like a slap when we step outside, and I shiver, but it's not just from the temperature. It's from the fear, the sheer terror of not knowing what Bertram plans to do next.

A black car idles at the curb, the engine running, and Bertram heads straight for it, his grip on us unrelenting. My mind races, trying to come up with a plan, a way to stall him. I scan our surroundings, praying desperately for Royce to be out here. To see us.

"Mommy." Aurora's trembling voice has my gaze snapping to hers. She looks at me with wide, terrified eyes, and all I can think about is keeping her safe and ensuring she makes it out of this alive.

"Everything's okay, baby," I try to soothe, noticing how my voice wavers unconvincingly.

We reach the car, and Bertram opens the back door, shoving Aurora inside before turning to me. His eyes are wild now, his breath coming in harsh, ragged gasps as he grabs my arm again, pulling me toward the car.

"Get in," he orders, his voice tight with barely restrained rage.

I glance around one last time, praying for some miracle,

some sign that this nightmare is almost over. But all I see is the empty street, the car waiting, and the man who once held all the power in the world over me, now on the edge of losing everything.

And then, I get into the car.

Bertram closes the door behind me, and I hold Aurora close while she cries into my chest, and I cling desperately to the thin thread of hope that the guys will find us before it's too late.

I'll do whatever it takes to keep Aurora alive until they do.

When I think this night couldn't possibly get any worse, the car slows to a stop outside my worst nightmare. I squeeze Aurora tighter against me, but the words of reassurance I'd been muttering the entire journey shrivel up and die as I stare unblinking at the mansion now looming before us, its grandeur undiminished by time.

The sprawling, elegant estate stands tall, its pristine white facade gleaming in the spotlights set to illuminate its resplendence. Tall, manicured hedges line the driveway, leading to an ornate front door flanked by massive stone columns. Everything about it screams wealth and power.

Everything about it is a torment.

Memories flood back, each one more painful than the last. This is where it all began. Where my nightmares took shape. I can almost hear Bertram's tender voice whispering in my ear, feel the suffocating grip of fear that choked me every day. My heart pounds in my chest, a relentless drumbeat of terror.

How did I end up back here? Of all places, why *here*? The sight of the mansion sends a shiver down my spine, my skin prickling with goosebumps. My knuckles have turned white from fisting my hands so tightly. It feels like a cruel twist of fate, dragging me back to the one place I swore I would never return to. My hands tremble, and I force myself to breathe, each inhale shaky and uneven. The fear is palpable, a heavy weight on my chest.

The car door is a welcome barrier between me and the past. One that is wrenched open all too soon.

"Out," Bertram grunts, already reaching out to drag me out of the car. My arms tighten protectively around Aurora, even as I stumble, my knees weak at the thought of being back here.

"W-why are we here?"

"What are you talking about? We live here."

Fuck me. He's gone insane.

I look up at the house. It's still as imposing as ever, a monument to the man who tried to break me. But I refuse to let it. I refuse to let *him*.

"I made sure to purchase the house when my son so daringly sold it upon my incarceration."

With Aurora perched on my hip, he begins dragging me up the steps to the front door, which opens for him. Walking into the house is like stepping into a time capsule. Everything is exactly as I remember it. The grand chandelier hangs from the ceiling, its crystal droplets sparkling in the dim light. The marble floors are polished to a mirror-like shine, and the sweeping staircase with its ornate wrought-iron railing curves gracefully up to the second floor. The portraits on the walls, the antique furniture, the grand piano in the corner of the room — it's all exactly as it was. The air smells faintly of lilies, just as it always did, masking the underlying scent of fear that once permeated these walls.

I stall in the doorway, the weight of the past pressing down on me. Memories assault me from all sides, dragging me back to moments I thought I had buried deep.

The first time I saw Grayson flashes before my eyes. He was

standing at the top of those stairs, looking down at us with a mixture of curiosity and reservation. I had felt so out of place, a stranger in this world of luxury and power. But there had been something in his eyes, a spark of something I couldn't quite identify, that had given me hope.

Then, the darker memories creep in. I remember the constant fear that gripped me every time I walked through this door, never knowing if tonight would be a night Bertram would come or if I'd be lucky enough to be left alone. I remember how my heart would race, my palms sweating as I braced to step inside and close the door, effectively locking me into my fate.

And then that final day... Grayson, standing in the middle of this very foyer, his face a mask of fury and pain. "Get out of my house! I don't want to see you again!" he had shouted at my mom and me after his father was arrested. The betrayal and hurt in his eyes had cut deeper than any wound Bertram had ever inflicted.

I bite down on my tongue until the taste of copper floods my mouth. I need the pain to ground myself. To stop the memories from sweeping me away. The weight of them is crushing, but I force myself to breathe. In and out. In and out. I'm not that scared girl anymore. I'm stronger now. I have to be, for Aurora. For the guys. For myself. For us—all of us. Our family.

Focusing on my breathing, I take a tentative step deeper into the house. My heart pounds in my chest. Everything is so painfully familiar, yet it feels like a lifetime ago. The house's opulence is suffocating, a gilded cage that once held me prisoner.

The sound of the front door snicking shut has me whirling. Bertram stands there, watching us with an unhinged sort of reverence that chills me to the core more than anything else in this mausoleum of a house. He's smiling at us like we're his whole world, and he's the indisputable king.

"How nice is this?" he says, sounding nothing like the menacing man who stepped into the bathroom and grabbed my daughter. He holds his hands out to his sides, indicating the house. "Everything can finally be how it should."

He moves closer, and I'm frozen in place, terrified of moving and setting him off. Standing over us, he cups my cheek. His touch burns like a brand. "My precious family."

The possession that drips from his every word...

His gaze slides to Aurora, who clings to me like a spider monkey as she stares at him with terror. He either doesn't notice or care as he smiles down at her, the expression more haunting than anything. "Why don't you go put the little one to bed? You remember which room it is." I shiver, and he seems to mistake my revulsion for something else as he smiles lovingly, like we're sharing sweet memories. Stroking a finger down my cheek, he adds, "Then you can join me in mine."

Nope. No. Abso-fucking-lutely not.

"It's her first night in a strange house—strange bed," I hedge, doing my best to keep my voice soft as I parse out the words in the way that's most likely to get him to leave us the fuck alone. "She won't settle by herself." A flash of that anger darts across his irises, and I'm quick to add with an apologetic grimace, "She'll just end up in with us."

He definitely doesn't want that. His lips purse, not pleased, but not enraged either.

"Fine," he eventually relents before flashing me another one of those terrifying smiles. "Stay with her tonight. Tomorrow, you can explore the house and get her settled, and we'll celebrate all of us finally being together with a special meal."

I have to engage muscles I don't typically use to force my lips upward into his desired response. "Sound's perfect." I nearly vomit.

With that same smile in place, he leans in, clearly intending to kiss me on the lips. I move my head at the last minute, and he catches my cheek. Thankfully, he lets it go. Not wanting to spend another moment in his presence, I hold Aurora close as I cross the foyer toward the stairs. "Oh, and Riley," he calls after me. Like before, there's an edge to his voice, which was all an act, and this is the real him. I pause but don't dare to look back at him over my shoulder. Instead, I wait. "Don't even think of trying to escape. I've got all the doors and windows sealed shut, and only I have a key for the front door. You cannot run this time."

Trembling like a leaf, my heart is lodged in my throat, and I'm seconds away from vomiting as I haul ass up the stairs. Despite the distance I'm putting between us, every step is like trudging through sludge. An invisible tug pulls me forward, my body seeming to know where I need to go even as my mind revolts at the idea of stepping foot back in *there*.

The hallway stretches before me, with its familiar cream carpet and white walls lined with portraits. About halfway down, my eyes lock on the white door, which appears so ordinary and so deceptively harmless.

But I know better.

The house is eerily quiet. Even my footsteps are muted on the thick carpet as I gingerly draw closer. The door seems to grow larger with every step I take, its plain surface mocking me with its normalcy. There are no visible signs of the horrors it conceals, no clue to the terror embedded in the wood. Regardless, I can *feel* it. The fear and desperation of my younger self seeps into my bones, a cold, suffocating presence that clings to me.

I remember every detail of what happened behind that door. The late nights when the house was dark and silent, save for the creaks and whispers that filled my head with dread. I remember how Bertram's voice would cut through the silence, soft and terrifying. How I'd freeze, my body going cold with fear. The way he'd smile, a predator's smile, as he slipped into my room. My bed. Every moment in his presence is designed to break me a little more.

My breathing grows shallow, the walls closing in around me as the memories press down like a physical weight. Needing a moment, I stop, hand flat to the wall to keep myself upright as I close my eyes and force deep, shuddering breaths into my lungs.

Still, that tug on my chest drags me closer.

I reach out with a trembling hand, fingers brushing against the door's cool, smooth surface. It's like touching a live wire, and a jolt of fear shoots through me.

I can see it all so clearly in my mind: the times I cowered in the corner of that room, trying to make myself as small as possible, the nights I wept into my pillow, the hours I spent hiding from reality in the back of my closet, Grayson's bracelet my only source of comfort.

The countless moments of hopelessness, wondering if I would ever escape. If I would ever be free.

And here I am, right back where it all started. Was I ever free of him? Was I ever truly safe, or has it all been some cosmic joke?

Unbidden, my fingers move to the handle, pressing it down. The door swings inward, silent on its hinges as I step into the room.

Same pink walls.

Same white carpet.

Same pink bedsheets.

I close my eyes, pressing my back against the door as I force myself to breathe.

"Mommy?"

I slowly open them, glancing down at my daughter, who

needs me more now than ever. I force my lips into what I hope is a reassuring smile before I walk over and set her down on the bed.

"Everything's going to be okay, baby. Mommy's going to get us out of here." Somehow.

LOGAN

CHAPTER THIRTY-FOUR

The final buzzer blares, the loud noise echoing through the stadium as the Huskies clinch their victory. A wave of euphoria surges through me as I chest bump Gavin, both of us grinning behind our helmets. Before I know it, we're surrounded by the rest of the team, everyone piling on top of one another in a chaotic, joyous dog pile. Feeling the weight and warmth of their bodies pressing against mine, I suck in a breath and howl. The others follow suit, the entire rink coming alive with the sound. It's our final game of the regular season— or it would be if we weren't top of our conference. Frozen Four, here we come, baby!

Finally extricating myself from the tangle of limbs, I get to my feet. My eyes seek out the familiar spot where Riley, Aurora, and Royce had been sitting. The arena is quickly emptying as fans stream toward the exit, and it takes me a moment to spot their empty seats.

My lips tug down in a frown. I'd wanted to see Shortcake's smile at our win and the excitement on Aurora's face, even though she doesn't really understand what's happening. That's the only prize I care about. Shaking off my disappointment, I skate toward the edge of the rink, eager to celebrate with them.

Stomping off the ice, I make my way to the locker room, each step filled with triumph and anticipation. Once upon a time, that excitement was to hang out with the team and celebrate our win. Now, the only celebrating I want to do is milkshakes at my favorite dinner with the most amazing kid in the world, or the naked kind in my bed with a certain redhead. A smirk tilts my lips as I recall our filthy foursome. I'd definitely be down for a repeat performance. Or perhaps I can convince Royce to babysit Aurora while me and Riley get hot and heavy in the treatment room again.

Reaching my locker, I snatch up my phone. My fingers fumble slightly from the lingering adrenaline before I manage to unlock it. There is a message from Royce, likely informing me they're waiting in the foyer.

ROYCE

Ducking out to talk to Grayson. Left the girls alone. Told Riley to stay in her seat until I was back. If you finish first, stay with her till I get there.

Brows furrowing, a niggling worry tickles the hairs on the back of my arms.

Both of their seats were empty when I left the ice.

The sweat clinging to my skin chills, and without a second thought, I shuck off my jersey, pads, and skates, forgoing a shower as I dial Riley's phone while hastily pulling on my clothes. It rings out, and I redial as I race for the door, ignoring my teammates calling my name.

When she doesn't answer for a second time, I call Royce while I jog down the tunnel back into the now-empty arena. The line doesn't even fully ring before he picks up, and the cheering crowd in the background practically deafens me.

"I'm coming!"

A cold spike of panic shoots through me, and ignoring the buzzing of the Zamboni, my focus is drilled on Riley's empty chair as I make a beeline for it.

"Royce." I have to yell to ensure he hears me. "Do you have Riley?" My voice is edged with fear as I march down her row.

"No. I was on the phone with Gray. She should be in her seat."

"She's not here!" I shout, panic rising in my throat like bile. "Their seats are empty."

There is a brief silence. I hear Royce curse at the end of the line. "Stay there. I'm on my way."

I'm only half listening as I reach their vacant seats, turning on the spot but not finding anything out of the ordinary. They're just... gone.

Staring down at my phone, I navigate to the app that enables me to track her phone. We all have it. Grayson insisted on it as a precaution, although I've never had to use it until now.

It says her location is still in the stadium, and I frown, zooming in on the blue dot. The relief nearly takes me to my knees when I realize she's in the bathroom.

"It's fine," I tell Royce. "They're in the bathroom. Aurora probably had to go."

"Which one?" he barks, not sounding the least bit reassured.

"The one right outside the entrance to where you were sitting." I climb the steps, intending to meet him there.

Standing in front of the bathroom, I knock on the door,

calling Riley's name through it. When I don't get a response, I poke my head in, frowning when I find it empty. That relief I was feeling becomes acid in my stomach when I notice Riley's phone sitting by the sink and her and Aurora's belongings piled on the floor beneath it.

Fuck. *Fuck.*

Why is her phone here? Where is *she?*

Grabbing it, I fist the device, surprised that the plastic doesn't crack beneath my grip. The door slams open behind me, and I whirl as Royce storms into the bathroom.

He takes one look at the scene, and his expression turns lethal.

"She's gone, Royce," I whisper, my voice breaking. "She's gone."

"I don't get why we're still fucking here," I snap.

Royce barely spares me a glance as he paces the length of the women's bathroom, continuing his phone conversation with Dax.

"We know who has her."

Royce's glare is withering, only I don't fucking care. We shouldn't just be standing here twiddling our thumbs. We should be out there looking for her—heading back to that apartment to see if they're there.

Grayson finally makes his grand entrance, striding into the bathroom with enough force that the door ricochets off the wall.

"What the fuck happened?" His fury is a match to the flame in an already gasoline-riddled room of frustration. Not bothering to wait for an explanation, he barrels into Royce, the momentum sending them both tumbling into the wall. Royce's phone goes skittering across the floor into one of the stalls. "You were supposed to be keeping an eye on her!" Gray snarls, glowering at Royce like he could actually take him on *and win.*

"I was!" Royce shoves Grayson backward before standing straight. "*You* were the one who called *me.* I stepped out to take your call because Riley was worried you were giving yourself alcohol poisoning all alone in your office."

Teeth gritted, I see the flash of remorse in Gray's eyes. "I wasn't drinking. I went because something about the way Dad said he'd see me Monday made me think he was up to something. So I went to snoop around."

"He *was* up to something," I chime in as Royce ducks to retrieve his phone. "Just nothing to do with work."

"Are we sure it's my dad?" Grayson asks, swiping a hand through his hair and looking entirely ruffled in his suit from this morning.

"Who else would it be?" I question while Royce goes back to his conversation with Dax.

Grayson shrugs. "Lydia? How do we know she actually got on a plane and left?"

I had opened my mouth to argue, except then I snapped it shut, realizing he was right.

"Fuck," I snarl instead, whirling to face the mirror. Leaning over the sink, I see my eyes are bloodshot, bags pronounced beneath my eyes. I'm fucking wrecked after giving that game my all to ensure we won. All because I wanted to win Aurora's first game. Hanging my head, I close my eyes and remember their happy smiles every time I skated past. Aurora's enthusiastic waves and her screaming my name.

We will find them.

We have to.

The alternative isn't an option.

"Here," Royce calls, and my spine snaps straight as he stalks over to me and Gray. He holds his phone out so we can all see, and presses play on a video clip. I swiftly realize it's video footage of the stadium. Then, a moment later, when Riley and Aurora come into view, content and oblivious as they enter this very bathroom, I realize it's of the hallway right outside.

There's nothing for several minutes, and then fucking *Bertram* sneaks along the hallway, looking shifty as shit, before he steps into the bathroom. My teeth grind to dust and the next few minutes, waiting for them to exit and not knowing what the hell he's doing to them in there are some of the worst of my life.

Eventually, they reappear. "That bastard," I snarl when I see he's holding Aurora hostage against him. "He's using Aurora to force Riley to leave with him."

Blue must have compiled the video clips as the camera moves with them through the stadium and outside until they climb into a sleek black car and pull away from the drive. But not before I catch Riley's pale face and terrified eyes as she scans her surroundings, pleading for someone to help... pleading for one of *us*.

And we fucking let her down.

"Where does the car go?" I seethe when the screen goes black.

Royce shakes his head. "Blue is working on that now."

"We're not just going to stand around here and wait for him to track them back to wherever the fuck they go."

"So what do you suggest we do?" Grayson drawls, though I can tell from the firm set of his jaw that he's just as furious as I am.

"Go back to that apartment. Maybe they're there, or there's a clue as to where he'd take her. Hell, we can ask the other resi-dents if they know anything."

Royce scrubs at the thick scruff on his chin. "It's not a bad idea while we wait for Blue. We might be able to find some clue that he hasn't."

I'm already stalking toward the bathroom door with the girls' coats and bag in my hand. "Let's go, then," I bark over my shoulder.

We're pulling up outside the apartment building in record time. Grayson views the speed limit as a guide rather than a *limit* as he drives like a maniac through the quiet town streets.

We don't dawdle outside this time, marching straight into the building and up to apartment eight. The door is closed, but I turn the handle and arch a brow at Royce and Gray when it opens.

Royce slides a gun from the waistband of his jeans, and I momentarily wonder whether he had that on him all night, before he's stepping in front of me, weapon raised as he moves into the apartment.

I'm on high alert as we enter the apartment, scanning it for any sign of our girls. It looks much like it did last time except... "What is that smell?" I pull the neckline of my t-shirt up to cover my nose against the heavy, cloying stench that smells like the garbage hasn't been taken out like *ever*. That smell definitely wasn't here last time.

As a unit, we move toward the back hallway leading to the bedrooms. With every step, the smell grows more potent. Even through the fabric of my top, the scent is suffocating. I can feel my throat closing over, the urge to gag overwhelming.

Gray and Royce don't seem to be fairing much better. They've also covered their mouths, the three of us sharing an ominous glance as we reach the door behind which the smell is strongest.

We all hesitate, none of us wanting to be the one to reach out and turn the door handle. Whatever the fuck is on the other side of that door, it's bad.

Really fucking bad.

Mumbling something indecipherable, Royce reaches out and turns the handle before pushing open the door. None of us make a move to step into the room. Thank fuck, because the second the door swings open, it's like hitting a brick wall of unbearable stench. I can fucking taste it. It's like rot and body fluid odor all rolled into one. My eyes water immediately, and I hunch over, gagging.

"Jesus." Gray turns his back on the scene, and I can tell he's as close as I am to losing the contents of his stomach.

Royce is the only one who doesn't appear physically affected. I guess he's used to being around the smell of blood and body odor, but holy shit, this is on an incomprehensible level.

"Who is it?" I manage to choke out. The good news is it can't be Riley or Aurora. Bad news is that it's not Bertram.

"Pretty sure I have an idea," Royce mutters before hedging into the room for a closer inspection. Yeah, I think I'll just stay here. I absolutely *will* vomit if I get any closer.

Keeping a safe distance from the bodies, he edges around the perimeter of the room. One of the bodies is lying flat on the floor in what I think is a pool of his own blood, while the other is slumped against the wall. That one is the worst because I can essentially *see* the extent of decay. I can only look at the body for a second or two at a time before I have to look away. However, from those brief glances, I'm pretty sure it's Lydia. I recognize the skimpy dress she was wearing when she escaped from Dax's club.

But who is the other one?

"Pretty sure that's David," Royce clues me in when he's

finished inspecting the room. He closes the door, and we quickly return to the hallway outside the apartment, only pausing briefly to check out the other bedroom and ensure it's empty.

I swear I can still smell the lingering stench of decay once we've closed the apartment door, and I'm wondering how we didn't notice it before or if it's now permanently embedded in my skin. God, I need at least five scalding showers before I dare to breathe through my nose again.

"Guess that answers our question about whether or not they got on that plane," I say when I can finally talk without gagging.

Gray shakes his head, staring wide-eyed at the door. "He just left them there," he states almost absently. "He's completely fucking lost it. Who just leaves dead bodies there for anyone to find? I'm surprised the neighbors haven't called the cops yet. It's only a matter of time."

I don't give two shits about that. Good fucking riddance, if you ask me. We'd planned to do the same with Lydia and David, so I couldn't care less. David deserved the ending he got after his role in Bertram's fucked up plan. "Well, Bertram definitely didn't bring the girls here," I say instead, focusing on what's important. "Which means he's got somewhere else he'd take them."

"Maybe he took them to his house?" Royce suggests.

Grayson sighs. "Maybe. I dunno where else he'd take her."

"So we go there next?" I ask, frustrated and feeling like we're running around in circles chasing our tails at this point.

"Let me check in with Dax," Royce says. He sounds just as defeated as I do.

He steps away to make the call, and I hesitate before striding to the apartment next door and rapping on the door.

"What are you doing?" Gray demands.

I shrug a shoulder because I don't fucking know. I just need to do *something*.

"It's unlikely the neighbors will know anything relevant," he continues.

Yeah, probably, but it's worth a chance, right? It's better than doing fucking nothing.

No one answers, and I knock again. After another moment of being left unanswered, I figure they're maybe out or away on holiday or some shit. It would explain why they haven't smelled the horrific stench next door.

Moving further down the hallway, I try to remember which windows had lights on inside when we pulled up. This one has light seeping from beneath the door, so I'm guessing someone is in.

I knock my knuckles against the door. Despite clearly not agreeing with my plan, Gray follows. "Hello," I call through the door. "I know you're in there. I just want to ask you a few questions about your neighbor down the hall."

Still, no one comes to the door. I knock again, sharper this time. My patience is long fucking gone. "I need to talk to you."

It's more of a demand this time, but I'm done with being fucking ignored.

In a moment of pure frustration, I fist the door handle. My eyebrows hitch when it turns, the door cracking open an inch. Who leaves their front door unlocked? I lift my gaze to Gray's, finding him frowning down at the handle in confusion. It was one thing for Bertram's apartment to be unlocked if he left in a rush, but a second unlocked door?

"Hello?" I call, pushing the door open another inch to peer inside. Just like Bertram's apartment, what little I can see is sparsely furnished. Straining my ears, I'm met with a silence that doesn't match the overhead light, which is turned on.

"Hello? My name is Logan," I explain in a loud, clear voice. "I was hoping to speak to someone about your neighbor."

Nothing.

I share another *what the fuck* look with Gray. "You shouldn't leave your front door unlocked," I try again. "You never know what type of crazy might just waltz inside and make himself at home."

Me. I'm that sort of crazy.

Officially done pandering, I shove the door open and enter the apartment. "Be careful," Gray whispers as he follows me inside.

I do a quick scan of the open-plan layout. No dishes are sitting beside the sink. No coffee cups on the end table. There isn't even a television in the living room. What sort of neanderthal doesn't own a TV? Stalking to the kitchen, I rip open the cupboards. Empty. Empty. Empty. No food. No cutlery. No plates.

What the fuck?!

"Gray," I bark. "Try the apartment next door."

He hesitates before leaving, and I move deeper into the apartment. The hairs rise on the back of my neck. Something isn't right here. It's possible this is just an empty unit and the realtor forgot to turn the light off earlier, but it feels like something more is happening here.

Every room I peer into is empty, and once I've checked the entire apartment, I move back to the door. Gray meets me there, his eyes wide. "Every apartment door is open, and they all look like empty units."

Except, there were names beside every mailbox downstairs.

"No one lives in this building," I deduce.

What. The. Actual. Fuck.

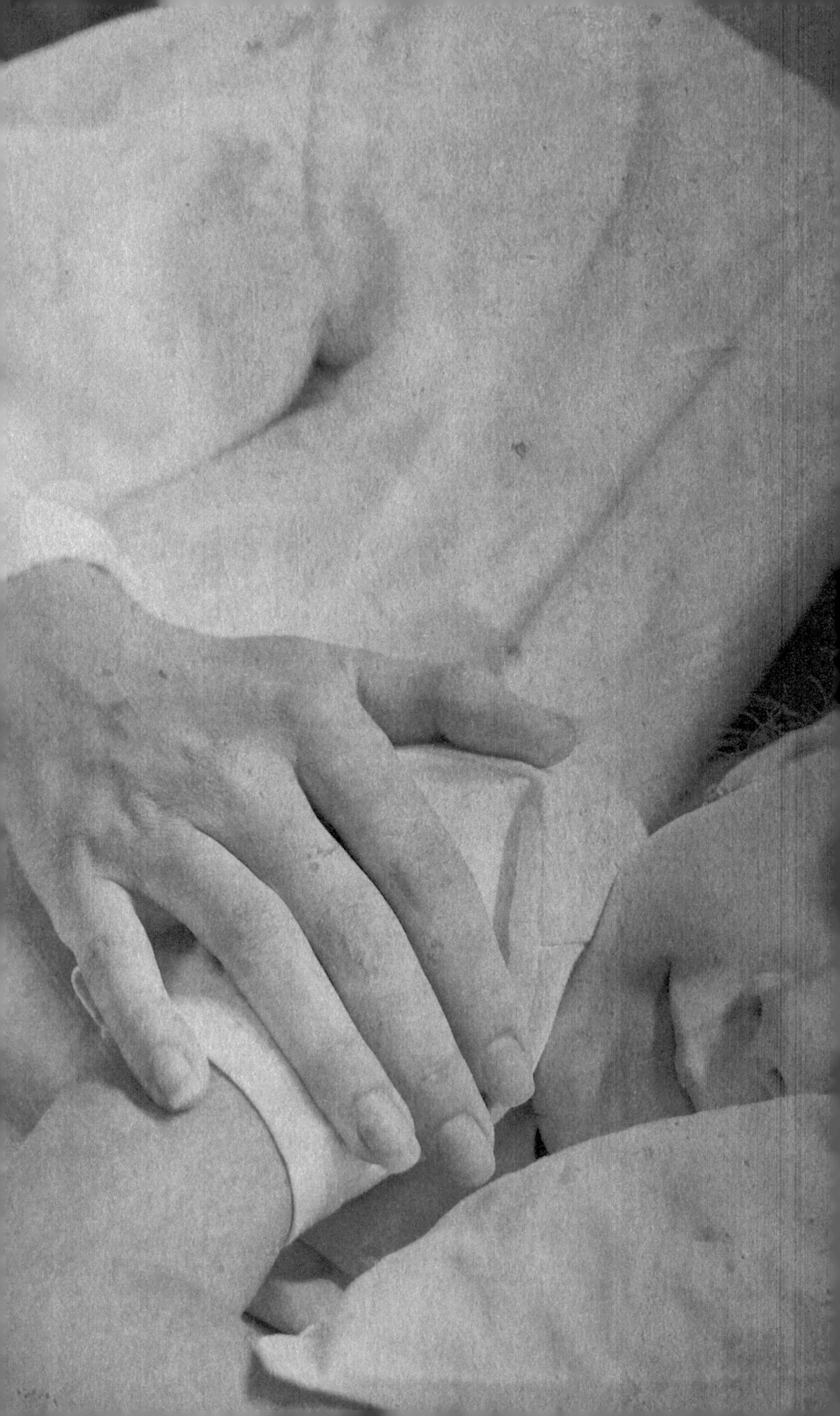

RILEY

CHAPTER THIRTY-FIVE

"There's my girls," Bertram greets with that creepy as fuck smile in place when we walk into the dining room that night, dressed in the outfits he picked out and left outside the bedroom door for us. I've never felt more uncomfortable, like we're dolls he's dressed up for his amusement.

He stayed true to his word and left us alone last night. At first, I was able to ignore our situation as I focused on reassuring Aurora and coaxing her to sleep. But once she was out, I was on alert. I lay awake, lying between her and the door the entire night, listening...

To every creak.

Every squeak of a floorboard.

The whistle of wind at the window.

The *tap* of the tree branch against the glass pane.

All of it served to startle me awake every time my heavy lids dared to close.

Except, not once did he come.

And all day today, he was absent—even when I crept from the room down to the kitchen to grab food for Aurora. I'd checked the front and back doors and various windows, finding them all locked and the keys conspicuously absent—just like he'd said—before trying the old house line, which was still where I remembered. Of course, the line had been disconnected, leaving us trapped in this house without a means of contacting the outside world.

It was only when I was starting to think we might actually be alone in the house that the clothing showed up, along with a note asking us to be in the dining room at 7 p.m. sharp.

Honestly, I'm not sure what's worse. The frantic stress of not knowing where he is and when he will just appear like an apparition, or having to endure his presence. To feel the brush of his gaze scraping like claws of possession over my skin.

It's all one big psychological game.

A mind fuck of epic proportions.

I'm just waiting for the actual games to begin because everything thus far has been about the waiting, the anticipation, and building up the tension.

Only it's not like the build-up when Grayson tells me to *run*. There's nothing fun about this. It's not excitement that has my heart thumping against my chest. The anticipation isn't what has me twitchy.

It's fear.

Blinding terror.

It seizes my muscles and clenches my stomach. It has taken control of my every action and plagues my every thought. Prevents me from acting rationally. Thinking logically.

Makes it so *how the hell do I get us out of here?* is the only question circling on repeat in my head.

And the answer: I have no fucking idea.

Aurora's hand is clutched tightly in mine. I gave her firm instructions to behave tonight. Not to say anything to him and to respond when he talks to her, even if it's just a smile. All I want is to make it through this dinner unscathed. I'm clinging to the hope that Bertram won't try anything too daring with her here, and after dinner... well, I'll worry about that later.

"Sit." He gestures toward the table where three place settings are laid out, food already waiting for us. "Dinner is served."

My stomach flips, and it's not due to hunger.

"This all looks lovely," I say politely, forcing a smile as I settle Aurora into her chair before sliding into the one next to her. Unfortunately, that places me within touching distance of Bertram, but better me than her.

He immediately clasps his hand over mine. Anyone peering in the windows would think it was a sweet family dinner. They wouldn't notice how I wince as his tight grip crushes my bones. They wouldn't see the tension fizzling in the air. Smell the fear that permeates the room.

With a fork in hand, I push my food around my plate. I can't bring myself to attempt a single bite. I have zero appetite. Unsurprisingly. How can I, when I'm sitting at a table opposite the last man on earth I want to be sharing a meal with, in the house that haunts my nightmares, with my daughter's safety on the line?

"Do you like your new room, Aurora?" Bertram asks. I immediately tense, my fingers tightening around the fork in my hand.

"Y-yes, Sir." Aurora's voice is small, and I *hate* this. The entire fucked up situation.

"Call me Daddy," Bertram says sternly, unaware of the crushing wave of revulsion that crashes over me. He pierces Aurora with a look that renders her incapable of saying anything. She merely nods, and I encourage her to go back to eating, hoping Bertram will turn his attention elsewhere.

He does. He begins rambling about how good life will be

now, just the three of us. He talks as though my mother never existed, and if I cared, perhaps I'd ask him about her, but I don't. I tune him out, simply nodding at the appropriate times. I keep one ear on the conversation and an eye on Aurora while I devise a way for us to get out of here.

I spent the day hoping the guys would show up and break down the door. I trust that they're doing everything they can to find us, but whatever Bertram has done to hide the fact he owns this house from prying eyes, it's clearly working. I don't know how long it will take Dax's IT guy to find this place and for the guys to get here, and I'm acutely aware that the clock is counting down. It's only a matter of time until Bertram wants more. Until his facade cracks, and I'm unable to put him off.

My gaze catches on a large, wrought-iron candlestick to one side of the fireplace, and I imagine snatching it up and wielding it like a bat as I smash it into Bertram's skull...

"Mommy." Aurora tugs on the maroon dress I'm wearing. Leaning in, she keeps her eyes on me and whispers, "Is he really my daddy?"

Unfortunately, her whisper is an average person's voice, and Bertram hears every word. "Of course I'm your father," he barks. "Who else would I be?" His gaze snaps to mine, hardening. "Have you not been telling her about me?"

Ha.

Holding Aurora against me, I keep my attention on Bertram. "She's just confused. It's a lot of change in such a short time. It'll take her a while to understand and adjust."

Rage simmers in the dark depths of his eyes, and I realize the falsely sweet front is gone. "Aurora, go to your room." Bertram's demanding tone cracks like a whip through the otherwise quiet room. Aurora stiffens at my side. Unsurprisingly, she doesn't leave the table, instead staring up at me with wide, fear-filled eyes.

"Now!" Bertram smacks his hand against the tabletop, making the cutlery clatter and glasses wobble precariously. "Don't make me tell you twice."

"Go on, sweetie," I say softly, pasting on my best attempt at a reassuring smile. "I'll be up for bath time and to tuck you in." *I hope.*

Aurora still hesitates, and I ask, "Do you remember where you're going?"

She gives a shaky nod, and I help her down from her chair, pushing her toward the exit before Bertram completely loses his shit. I don't breathe until she's out of the room and her footsteps have disappeared upstairs.

The scrape of chair legs squealing against the floor reminds me that I'm not so unfortunate as to have escaped this hell. Bertram pushes his seat away from the table before patting his thigh. "Come here."

Those two words are said with the same commanding tone he used on Aurora.

I don't want to.

Everything in me revolts against the idea, my body seizing up in its attempt to disobey. I'd remain obstinately in my chair if it weren't for some primal part of my brain, functioning based on survival, that takes control of my extremities and forces me to my feet.

The games have officially begun.

Aurora. Aurora. Aurora.

Her name repeats with every *clack* of my heels against the floor as, with laden steps, I close the distance between us.

Only when I'm standing at his side do my steps falter. He arches a knowing eyebrow in challenge. It's a dare. A command. A threat all rolled into one. With stiff movements, I step between his parted legs and lower myself to perch on the edge of his thigh.

Fuck, I hate this.

My breaths are shallow, my skin cold and clammy as I force myself to stay in the present. To resist the memories slamming like wrecking balls against my rapidly crumbling defenses.

With a concentrated effort, I force my mind back into that corner I would retreat to on those cold, hopeless nights when he'd sneak into my room. I shut down all thoughts, all emotions, until, when I look down and see his hand sliding up my thigh, it feels as though it's happening to someone else.

Except, as I feel his breath dance along skin that isn't mine, I realize I'm not alone in the corner anymore.

A tingle of sensation races over my palm—Logan's comforting hand.

A warmth envelops my back—Royce's protective presence.

Dark, fierce eyes raze my skin and lift the hairs along my arms—Grayson's silent strength.

This time, I'm not alone.

They might not be with me, but they are *with* me. Offering me what they can.

I've barely allowed myself to give them more than a passing thought since I left the hockey arena. In my bones, I know they're out there looking for me. Hunting for answers. However, I can't simply sit back and wait for them to find us.

Which means I'll have to play Bertram's twisted game until I can figure out how to get me and Aurora safely out of here.

Seconds.

Minutes.

Hours.

Time is an irrelevant thing as I sit numbly on his lap, cocooned in my own world, until my head is wrenched to the side with enough force to have tendons snapping along my neck.

My lips part on a gasp as a sharp pain skitters along my

nerves, my wide eyes clashing with dark ones that are so familiar and yet so distinguished from the ones I've gotten used to seeing every day.

"Isn't that right?"

An edge to his tone makes it clear he's been trying to get my attention for a while.

"Sorry," I apologize around a choked throat. "What were you saying?"

His eyes narrow, his hand on the top of my thigh tightening to the point of pain.

"That you're going to be a good girl and do as I say." Loosening his grip on the back of my head, he strokes a finger eerily gently down the side of my face. "That you've got this defiance out of your system." His nail drags across my lower lip, and I shiver at the sheer act of possession. At how he so brazenly touches me. Claims what has never been his. I don't know if he mistakes my disgust for pleasure or if he gets off on how I react to him, but his eyes flash with a gleam, stare raking over my face. "I'm done with the teasing and the games. I've cleared the path for us to be together, and I'm just about out of patience, so I would advise you *not* to push me any further."

Questions stick in the back of my throat, rendering me speechless as I slowly blink back at him. I swallow, his gaze dropping at my audible gulp before flashing back to my face. He tilts his head to the side, and it's the creepiest thing I've ever seen—being analyzed by someone so incapable of empathy but who is well-versed in reading my every emotion.

"Or am I going to have to call dear little Aurora down here again?"

"N-no."

His responding grin is the least bit comforting. It's like staring into the maw of a rabid wolf standing over you, getting high on your fear before it goes in for the kill.

"Good." His gaze flicks behind me. "Go make sure she's tucked up in her bed for the night then join me in my room."

At the offered escape, I slide from his lap. However, I barely make it to my feet before he captures my face. His fingers dig into my cheeks, and his expression is terrifyingly unreadable—kind of like Grayson's used to be back when he first hauled me into his house. Only now, I realize Grayson hasn't looked at me like that in a long time. Unlike his father, I can interpret the emotions behind his facade even when he doesn't want me to.

"Where are your manners?"

"S-sorry." He arches a brow, and another involuntary shiver wracks me. "*Daddy.*" I go to pull away again, but those punishing fingers threaten to slice through my skin.

He doesn't say anything. Simply waits for me to put the pieces together. To figure out what he wants. My thoughts scramble.

His free hand slides up the back of my thighs, over the curve of my ass, before it flattens against my lower back, forcing me closer.

No.

My eyes widen with understanding, satisfaction flashing across his face when he realizes I've connected the dots.

Using his harsh grip on my face and hand on my back, he forces me closer. I resist at first, internally screaming my protestations.

"This is not my good little girl," he rasps against my lips. I can feel the sting from where his fingers have broken the skin on my cheeks. "Maybe the time apart has changed you." Again, those dark, menacing eyes flick toward the door where Aurora disappeared. "Perhaps I need to start again with Aurora. She's a bit young for my tastes, but oh, how I could mold her." His lips quirk. "I could make her perfect for me."

"N-no," I stammer. "No. There's no need for that."

With his gaze thankfully riveted on me once more, he no longer drags me toward him. Instead, he waits, the picture of endless patience.

Forcing back the urge to gag, I drop my gaze to his chest. I place my hand over his sternum before slowly sliding it over his shoulder and along his neck. Dragging my attention back to his face, I force the words he wants to hear past my lips. "You don't need her. I'll be your good girl." I lick my lips, his gaze tracking the movement with a predatory focus. "I *am* your good girl."

Dark eyes meet mine, his voice husky as he says, "Prove it."

Wrapping my hand around the side of his neck, I inch closer. His hand is a brand on my lower spine, a crushing weight carrying me forward until my lips press to his.

Eyes squeezed shut, I count the seconds.

One.

Two.

His lips remain unmoving against mine.

Blood rushes in my ears. My heart thrashes in my chest.

I force my mouth to move over his. Force my tongue to sweep along his lower lip. Force myself to relax into him.

His lips part slightly, a silent order which I resentfully obey.

The second the tip of my tongue toys with his, his self-control snaps.

A wild snarl rips from his throat. The hand holding my face moves to the back of my head to keep me in place while the hand on the base of my spine forces me into his lap as he takes control.

I force myself to stay still. To take it. To give it back until we're both breathless and heaving.

"*Fuck*," he rasps, grip still bruising. His pupils are blown, his eyes black and wild with want. He nips at my lips, and I cringe at the sting. He chuckles. "I love it when you're good, but I think I love it more when Daddy's little girl is naughty."

Something must cross his mind as his gaze hardens, and in the next second, I'm choking, spluttering, fingers scraping at the hand wrapped tightly around my throat.

"Where did you learn to do that?" he practically yells in my face. "Was it that *hockey player*? Were you a slut for him? How about *my son?* You thought you could replace me with *him?*" he spits. "And that boy you were sitting beside at the arena—have you been spreading your legs for him, too?"

My only response is a suffocating gurgle as I fight uselessly against his superior strength. Bertram has morphed into something truly demonic, his eyes blazing with a raging fire and his body vibrating with fury as he squeezes tighter.

Tighter.

Tighter.

My muscles grow heavy, my body getting weaker.

Black spots steadily enlarge across my vision.

Royce's blue eyes. Logan's winter scent. Grayson's heavy weight.

Aurora's child-like laugh.

Those are the last thoughts bef—

Choking and spluttering, I ignore the jagged pain vibrating up my tailbone as I roll onto all fours and splutter over the tiled floor. Saliva trails from my lower lip, dangling as I drag in a raspy breath, hungrily filling my starved lungs as the room comes back into focus.

Black loafers appear in my line of sight, but I don't have the energy to peer up at their owner. "You have thirty minutes." His voice comes in and out as though he's yelling down a long tunnel before he stalks off, leaving me alone on the dining room floor, bruised and traumatized.

And the torture has only begun.

RILEY

CHAPTER THIRTY-SIX

With careful movements, I slide out from beneath a passed-out Aurora. A moan escapes as she rolls onto her stomach, and I reach down to brush her hair out of her face before sweeping a loving hand down her spine. Reluctantly, I make myself pull my hand away, tucking the covers around her tiny frame before I grab my heels, slip silently from the bedroom, and close the door behind me.

In the hallway, heels dangling from my fingers, I lean my forehead against the door and breathe deeply. Or, I try. I haven't taken a full breath since Bertram walked into that bathroom at the arena. Eyes closed, I try again. And again, until I at least feel like I'm not coming out of my skin.

I can wish and pray on falling stars that this isn't happening, but the truth is that *it is*. This. Is. Actually. Happening. And with every minute I waste standing out here, I'm risking my daughter's safety.

Squaring my shoulders, I push away from the door, bending to place my heels on the floor. I slide my feet into the shoes as I smooth out my wrinkled dress. I'd ducked into the bathroom to fix myself up after picking myself off the dining room floor before I put Aurora to bed. Only, neither it nor the time spent reading her a story did anything to abate the frenetic energy buzzing beneath my skin.

Since I didn't manage to eat or drink during dinner, I stop by the kitchen and fill a glass of water before downing the entire thing. Setting it by the sink, I stare longingly at the block of butcher knives taunting me.

Too obvious.

Not that I would have anywhere to hide one where he wouldn't find it.

Especially given *why* I'm going to his room.

Shuddering, I force myself to turn my back on the knives and leave the kitchen.

Each step I take echoes through the dark, empty hallways of the mansion, the sound bouncing off the walls and amplifying the dread curling in my stomach. The air feels thick and suffocating, as if the house itself is aware of the terror brewing inside me. At this point, I'm pretty sure my fear is embedded in the walls.

The hallway is dark when I reach the top of the stairs and turn toward where the primary suite is located. The double doors loom ahead. I've never been inside the suite before. Never had a reason, never mind a *want* to peek into that room. One of the doors is slightly ajar, forming a slither of light that runs down the wall and across the floor.

The sight is deceptively inviting. So at odds with what waits beyond. My footsteps falter just outside the door. A blade is lodged in my chest, the pain sharp and foreboding, making it impossible to suck in a full breath.

The longer I stand there, the louder the silence becomes.

"Don't keep me waiting, Riley."

His voice cuts like a knife. I can feel it flaying me open.

With a last, futile inhale, I tuck whatever fragmented pieces of my sanity still exist back into the safe corner of my mind, along with thoughts of my guys and Aurora, and I reach for the door, as ready as I'll ever be to face the horrors that await on the other side.

The smell of expensive cologne and something more sinister hits me first, flooding my mouth until I want to gag as I do a quick sweep of the room. It's dimly lit, the bedside lamps casting a warm glow over a large, perfectly made bed.

At first, I think the room is empty. That perhaps he is in the bathroom, but a flicker of movement from the corner of my eye has me whirling in my heels. Cast in shadows, he sits like a king on his throne. Beady eyes trained on me, his arm resting on the arm of his straight-backed chair, a glass lined with an amber-colored liquid dangling from his fingers. He's still dressed in the suit he was wearing at dinner. Not even his tie is loosened or top button undone.

For a long moment, we remain there. Him sitting. Me standing as we stare at each other from across the room. There's something different about this time. Perhaps it's the fact there's a light on, no matter how dim, as opposed to the shadows he would sneak around in when he'd slip into my room in the middle of the night.

It could be that I'm in *his* room instead of him being in mine.

Or that it's four years later, and regardless of my life choices —or perhaps because of them—I seem to have come full circle in some cruel twist of fate.

Have I been naively foolish all these years to believe I had a say in my future? For all I know, it would never have mattered what decisions I made in the last four years; I'd still have ended up right here. In this moment. In this room—*with him.*

Knocking back the last of his drink, he discards the glass on an end table before getting to his feet and stalking toward me.

He doesn't stop until the tips of his shoes touch the toes of my heels.

Reaching up, he toys with a strand of my hair, twisting it around his finger. "There's my good girl. I knew you were still in there. Waiting for me, just like I've been waiting for you."

His hands glide over my shoulders and down the backs of my arms as he eliminates the scant distance between us. My breasts brush against the front of his shirt, his cologne damn near suffocating me in its overwhelming stench. "Your hockey player doesn't make you feel this." There's a snarl behind his words. "Or that tattooed thug."

He's vibrating with his rage... or maybe it's me who's shaking as he wrenches my face up to his.

"Now there's *only* me and you."

"What about my mom?" As I said earlier, I don't give two shits about that bitch, but I'm all about buying time, and if I have to talk about her to do it, then I will.

"We don't need to worry about her anymore," is Bertram's vague response.

"Because she's in Europe?" My gaze darts between his. There's something benign about the way he dismissed my concern. Something more... permanent than Lydia simply being out of the country. "Right?"

Bringing his hands to my cheeks, he strokes his thumbs across them.

"There are no more obstacles standing in our way." Another stroke of his thumbs. "I should never have married her, but I had to keep you close, you understand? Once I saw you, I couldn't let you slip through my fingers. There was no other way..."

The lump in my throat solidifies.

"W-where is Lydia?"

I don't know how I manage to choke out the words.

Ducking his head, he nuzzles at my neck while I stand stock-still, rooted in place with bile burning the back of my throat as he plants open-mouthed kisses along my jaw.

"Gone." His voice is deeper, raspier. His hands glide up my hips and over my waist before sliding to my back. It's the caress of a lover, but the reverence of his touch doesn't mean it's wanted.

The mental mindfuck of being touched against your will in such a tender, reverential way is something you never come to terms with. Something that never gets easier. I think that's why I enjoy the way the guys manhandle me—their rough touches.

Although, even when they're gentle with me... it's different. It's there in the way their eyes soften. How they catalog my reaction to their touch and adjust accordingly, always taking their cues from me.

Unlike Bertram, who doesn't notice or care that I'm stiff as a board and silently screaming for him to get off me.

Gentle doesn't necessarily mean kind.

Just like rough doesn't mean uncaring.

How you touch someone doesn't demonstrate whether you care. It's the *intent* behind the action.

"For good."

His words don't get the chance to fully penetrate before his mouth covers mine, knocking the air from my lungs. His tongue forces its way past my teeth, and he groans into my mouth. The bile thickens, becoming suffocating. My eyes are squeezed shut, my fingernails leaving crescent moon indentations in my palm as I squeeze them at my sides, battling the urge to push him away, to piss him off, to anger him.

I force steady breaths through my nose. I need to control myself; I need to remain calm, to keep as much of my sanity tucked away as I can so that I don't lose the last fragments of who I am before I can get my daughter and me out of this alive and unharmed.

His tongue feels like a wet fish in my mouth. Intrusive. Nothing like the passionate kisses I share with the guys. Their possessive caresses. Their toe-curling kisses that make stars dance across the backs of my eyes.

That's what I focus on, what I use to get myself through this.

"This is why I never kissed you before." His voice is gravel, scraping against my skin and leaving dots of blood to bloom in its wake. "I knew once I did, I'd never get enough." A final brush of his lips over mine. "Get on the bed. It's been far too long since I've been inside you."

Whether it's the order or his words, my stomach cramps, and vomit floods my mouth, acrid and searing as I grit my teeth and swallow it back down.

"You *are* my good little girl, right, Riley?" he asks with an arched brow when I don't immediately move toward the bed.

With a shaky jerk of my head, I move toward the bed as though walking through a dream. I absently try to calculate how many minutes have passed since I stepped into his room. It feels like it's been hours, but it can't have been more than maybe ten minutes.

You can do this, I remind myself. *Just keep going.*

Climbing onto the bed, I settle on my back, my head resting against the pillows. It could be the comfiest bed in the world, and I'd be incapable of feeling it. My body is too stiff. My heart too numb. My mind too distanced.

The world around me no longer feels real. Color has drained out of it, leaving only a sepia tone. There's the hiss of a zipper as Bertram shucks out of his clothes before the mattress compresses and a weight settles on top of me. I feel like I'm wearing one of those VR headsets. I can see the scene playing out, even though I can't feel it. It's like it's happening to someone else, and I'm nothing but a casual onlooker.

My dress is pushed up to my hips, and there's a faint sensation as his hand covers my breast. His lips are moving, but the words don't penetrate.

My legs are shoved apart.

Fingers snaking a path up my thigh.

An explosion rocks the entire house.

My surroundings blink back into high-definition as the walls shake and windows rattle from the force of the blast.

Bertram topples off me, collapsing onto the floor as I plant my hands on the mattress and push myself upright. My eyes are wide as the floor trembles violently, the explosion reverberating through the structure of the house followed by a hot, oppressive wave of heat. The acrid smell of smoke begins to fill the air. I'm wracked by a coughing fit, which startles me out of my stupor.

Oh my god, it worked!

"What the—" Pushing to his feet, Bertram cautiously approaches the door but makes no move to open it.

A second later, the blaring of the fire alarm threatens to deafen me. Jumping into motion, I snatch the lamp from the bedside table. It's a solid, metal design. Perfect for what I need. The alarm covers any noise I make as I quietly creep up on him from behind. Taking advantage of his distraction, I lift the lamp above my head and bring it down on his.

He goes tumbling to the floor in a shriek of pain, but I don't stop. With a war cry, I bring the lamp down again.

And again.

And again.

Until blood covers one side of his face and his eyes are half closed, glazed over, and distant. Heaving and arms shaking, blood drips from the lamp as I stare down at his still form.

There are bright red splatters across the back of my hand and even bigger blots on the cream-colored carpet, growing larger until they form a pool around his head.

Ignoring it, I fall to my knees, dropping the lamp as I feel around in his pockets. He said he was the only one with a key for the front door, and I *need* it. I check both pockets in his pants, coming up empty, before frantically stuffing my hands into the pockets of his suit jacket.

I groan aloud when I don't find what I'm looking for. Turning, I quickly scan the room but don't see any signs of a key. I can't waste any more time looking. Aurora will have heard the explosion, and I can't risk her leaving the room. This house is massive and it would be difficult to find her. She could get hurt if she goes wandering off alone.

Without the key, I race from the room. In the hall, I kick off my heels. My bare feet smack against the carpet, which is oddly warm against my soles as I pump my legs harder.

Reaching Aurora's room, I skid to a stop, throwing open the door and hurrying inside. I know I don't have a lot of time, especially without that damn key. I need to act quickly.

"Mommy!" Her eyes are wide with fear as she clutches the duvet to her.

"Everything's okay, baby," I assure her as I hurriedly wrap a blanket around her tiny body and haul her into my arms. "Everything's going to be okay."

Arms wrapped protectively around my daughter, I rush from her room. Smoke is already gathering in the hallway upstairs, far quicker than I'd anticipated. It makes my eyes stream as I cough and splutter, squeezing my daughter closer to my chest.

Her face is buried in my neck, and I raise the blanket. "Hold this over your nose and mouth," I order her.

"Mommy," she cries, but does as I say. I tuck her face back

into my neck, the smoke growing thicker until I can barely see through it to where the stairs should be. I crouch low, moving as quickly as I safely can until I spot the hazy outline of the banisters through the thick cloud of smoke.

One hand braced on the back of Aurora's head, I keep the other on the wall as I descend the stairs. As we reach the ground floor, I regret not lifting something to cover my own mouth. I'm already feeling light-headed, and the lack of visibility is disorientating.

"We just have to get out of here," I murmur, spinning in a circle. As I do, I catch sight of a wall of red. No, not a wall. An *inferno*. Where the kitchen once was is now overcome by flames licking at the walls and ceiling. Hungry for more, the flames are already moving down the hallway, engulfing the entire back corner of the house.

Spinning away, I lose my balance as a wave of dizziness takes over. I stumble, grunting as I fall to one knee. Aurora sobs, her tiny body shaking with the force of it. It's fear for her that forces me back to my feet. I move to the opposite corner of the house, putting as much distance between me and the destructive fire and suffocating smoke.

Hurrying into a den with a large eighty-inch TV on the wall and sofas crowding the small space, I slam the door closed. The smoke is mild here, and breathing heavily, I take a second to get my raging heart under control.

Settling Aurora into the corner of a sofa farthest from the door, I move to the only window in this room.

"God damn!" I snarl, thumping my fist against the glass when the damn thing doesn't open. I can feel myself beginning to break. The tears are right there, my shoulders shaking with the restraint it takes to hold them back.

Not yet. Just a little longer.

Putting my back to the window, I scan the room for

anything I can use to smash the glass. It's a simply furnished TV room. There's nothing here I can use.

A sob slips free.

"I'm scared, Mommy."

At Aurora's small, terrified voice, I rush over to her, crouching to her height. I brush a hand over her hair. "I know, baby. You're being so brave for me. I'm so proud of you. I just need you to be brave a little longer. Can you do that?"

She seems to think about it, looking at me with tear-stained cheeks before she gives a slight nod. Giving her what I hope is a reassuring smile, I lean in and kiss her forehead. "My big brave girl."

Standing, I do another sweep of the room as I swipe a hand through my tangled mess of hair. I'm desperately searching for something I missed before, but a second scan confirms there is nothing here.

I remember the heavy-looking candlestick I saw in the dining room earlier. That would be strong enough to break the glass. Staring at the door, I chew on my lower lip as a plan forms.

Yes, okay. It's the only shot we have.

Turning back toward the sofa, I snatch up a throw pillow, hurriedly ripping out the inside stuffing until I'm left with just the cover. Clutching it in my hand, I crouch in front of my daughter. My stomach is in knots, but I know I must do this.

"Baby," I hedge, forcing my voice into a calm I don't feel. "I need you to stay here for Mommy."

"No, Mommy!" Aurora cries earnestly.

"Yes, baby." My voice is firm. "You're my brave girl, right? I need to go get something, but I'll be back as soon as possible."

She's still shaking her head and sobbing hysterically.

"Do you remember the adventure Perry the Caterpillar goes on?"

Sniffling, my daughter frowns but gives me a confused nod. It's her favorite book. We've read it so many times she knows the entire thing word for word. It takes less than ten minutes to read from start to finish.

"Recite Perry's Adventure, and I'll be back before you finish, okay?"

Hiccupping, she clutches her blanket, but again, she nods. I brush my hand over the side of her face, drinking it in before pushing myself to my feet and forcing myself to leave her behind. It's my only option if either of us is going to make it out of this house alive.

The smoke is already thicker in the hallway, and I hold the pillow cover over my nose and mouth as I keep low and hurry to the dining room, squinting to see through the smoke. My eyes burn, and my lungs feel like they're on fire. The dizziness in my head grows more substantial.

I make it to the dining room on pure adrenaline, finding the candlestick. The metal is deceptively cool in my hand amidst the sweat licking my spine and dotting my brow.

With one hand holding the pillow cover to my face, I haul it back to the den, coughing and spluttering. I have to stop and lean against the wall more than once when the spinning becomes too much. My mouth tastes like ash, and no matter how big a breath I suck in, it never feels like enough.

I'm acutely aware that I'm running out of time.

Reaching the den, I hear Aurora's hacking cough through the door. I wince at the smoke, which has grown deceptively thicker in the room since I left.

"I'm back, baby. We're going to get out of here, okay?"

My voice is weak, hoarse. I don't sound like myself.

Marching for the window, the room sways. Black spots have taken up permanent residence in my vision, however I push past them as I plant my feet in front of the window. Mustering the last of my strength, I tighten my hand on the candlestick before swinging it at the window.

Glass shatters, and I bring a hand up to my face as I turn away. Shards embed in my skin, scraping against my arms and leaving little nicks in their wake. However, I don't feel any of that as fresh air sweeps into the room, bringing sweet relief with it.

I use the candlestick to knock out the remaining shards of glass before dropping it with a clatter. Glass slices into the soles of my feet as I hurry back to Aurora, bundling her in my arms before moving back to the window.

"Ugh." I blink furiously as I fall against the wall with her in my arms. The room is spinning so fast that everything is a blur. *Nearly there*, I tell myself as I squint. Focusing on the dark shape of the window, I stumble toward it.

"I'm going to lift you out the window, sweetheart. Then I'll follow right behind, okay?"

I'm not even sure if she answers me. My throat is so dry. My eyes are filled with sand. *God, all I want to do is sleep.*

"On you go," I somehow manage, ensuring the blanket is wrapped securely around her to protect her from any stray bits of glass or wooden splinters before setting Aurora on the windowsill and ushering her through.

She slides across the sill before dropping down on the other side. She's so tiny that all I can see is the top of her head as I lift a leg to follow her through.

That's when everything goes sideways. The world tilts upside down, spinning around in a whirl of color until everything goes black.

I'm not sure if it's in my mind or not, but the last thing I hear is my daughter's terrified scream.

ROYCE

CHAPTER THIRTY-SEVEN

The car roars down the dark roads, its headlights piercing through the inky blackness. My hands grip the steering wheel so tight my knuckles are white, urgency throbbing in every beat of my heart. Grayson sits beside me, his eyes locked forward, with a tension in his jaw that mirrors mine. Logan is in the back, his leg bouncing faster with every passing mile.

"I can't believe I never considered our family home," Grayson chastises himself with a shake of his head.

After tracking Bertram's car, which shows it's been sitting outside his house all evening—and hacking into his security system to check he definitely didn't have our girls there—Blue turned his focus to the apartment building in Halston and was able to identify the corporation that owns it. Once he discovered that, he tracked down other assets the company owned.

The second Grayson saw the list, he recognized the address of his childhood home. Within minutes of that discovery, the three of us were in the car racing away from The Depot, where we'd spent the past twenty-four hours helping Blue scour video footage and scan documents in search of a clue as to where to find our girls.

She's there. *They* are there. It's the only thing that makes sense. This entire fucked up situation has come full circle, and you can bet your ass it's going to end tonight. Bertram's a dead man walking. We're going to get our girls, and that sick fuck isn't going to live to see the sunrise.

"You couldn't have known." The words come out harsher than I intend, but I genuinely mean the sentiment. "How could you have known the house you sold four years ago had worked its way back into your father's hands?"

The how of it all is unknown, but we know enough to connect the dots.

Grayson makes a noise of disagreement but doesn't voice his objections. Glancing his way, I suspect he's unable to unclench his jaw long enough to get a word out. Instead of forcing him to talk, I push my foot down further on the accelerator. The engine roars in response, the car speeding up. We're so far past the speed limit that the landscape is a blur out the side window.

As we round the bend, Logan's sharp intake of breath makes me glance to the left. Smoke. Thick, black plumes billowing up into the night sky. My heart skips a beat, a cold dread settling in my stomach.

"No," I breathe. Despite our dangerous speed, the car feels like it is moving in slow motion as my gaze takes in the landscape.

"Do you think that's..." Logan's voice trailed off, the fear in it palpable.

"Hurry," is all Grayson says, his voice tight.

My foot is flat to the floor, my body urging us to go quicker, to move faster. The winding road feels endless as I fly into another bend. All the while, my focus keeps flicking back to the smoke, growing thicker and darker as we approach.

Finally, a set of open gates loom ahead. The back of the car fishtails, Grayson and Logan grappling for the *oh-shit* handle as I turn onto the driveway, gravel kicking up beneath us as we fly down it.

We crest a hill, and the sight before us makes my blood run cold. Flames lick up the side of the house, bright and fierce against the night. Once a picture of wealth and power, the elegant mansion is now a blazing inferno.

"Fucking hell," Logan rasps, jaw slack as he leans between the two front seats. The flames are almost blinding against the dark backdrop, growing in size as we careen to a stop at the front of the house.

I slam the car to a stop, and we are out instantly. Panic floods my veins, an icy terror that scatters my thoughts as I scan the house's exterior. Where are Riley and Aurora? Are they inside, or have they already gotten out?

Whirling, I scan our surroundings, but there's no sign of anyone other than us.

"Riley!" I shout, my voice lost in the roar of the flames as I rush up the front steps. The heat is oppressive, the air thick with smoke.

"Riley! Aurora!" Logan's voice joins mine, desperate and frantic, as the three of us race for the door.

Grayson is a step ahead of me. He grabs the door handle only to recoil in pain. "Fuck, it's scorching hot!" he yells, clutching his hand.

"Shit!" I run a hand through my hair before stepping back and bringing my leg up. My foot connects with the door, but it doesn't budge. Frantic, I kick out again and again with the same useless response.

"This isn't working," Logan snarls, before yanking on my arm and taking off along the side of the house.

I'm peeking through windows, growing increasingly concerned for Riley and Aurora's welfare, when I hear it—a scream, piercing and filled with fear. My heart lurches. "Did you hear that?"

The others nod, and we sprint faster, desperation fueling our steps.

"There!" Grayson shouts as we round the side of the house. Aurora stands at a window, dressed in soot-stained pajamas and wrapped in a blanket. Tears stream down her face as she cries and calls for her mom.

"Aurora!" When she hears Logan calling her, she turns to face us. She sobs, her entire little body heaving with the effort. She's dusted with soot, a tattered blanket wrapped around her.

"Lo!" She cries, pointing through a broken window with a trembling hand. "Mommy needs help!"

Logan doesn't hesitate to bundle her into his arms, holding her tight like he's afraid to let her go as he mutters assurances. My focus is on the window as I peer inside. Smoke is thick in the room beyond, billowing out the broken window and making it impossible to discern anything. Grayson and I exchange a glance, fear and determination mirrored in our eyes.

Glass breaks beneath my boots as I approach the window and brace my hands on the sill before Grayson stops me. "You're too big, dude. You'll get stuck. I'll go in, find Riley, and lift her out to you."

He's shoving me aside and climbing in before I can argue, and a moment later, all I can make out is his silhouette.

"Shit," he curses from inside the room.

"What is it?" I bark.

"She's unconscious." He has to shout to be heard over the

creaking of the house and roaring of flames. Fuck, the entire structure is going to come down.

"Move it, Van Doren, before the fucking roof caves in!"

The silhouette moves before Grayson's lean frame appears in the window. His sweater is pulled up to cover his nose and mouth, and in his arms is a bruised and bleeding Riley. My heart shatters at the sight.

"We're going to get you out of here, Tempest. Just hold on," he murmurs, voice tight with tension. I reach for her, my hands shaking as Grayson passes her to me. Feeling her in my arms, relief floods me. Even in this state, holding her is a balm to my terror.

"I've got you, sweetheart." Holding her close, I murmur reassurances in her ear. She feels so fragile in my arms, so vulnerable, but her chest rises and falls, her eyelids fluttering. She's alive.

I carry her safely away from the blazing house and gently set her down on a patch of grass. The blades are cool beneath her heated skin as I brush her hair, darkened with soot, away from her face before kissing her forehead. "Come on, baby, open those gorgeous eyes for me," I plead.

Sirens blare in the distance, and I'm aware of Grayson kneeling at my side. His hand is wrapped around hers as he kisses her knuckles, murmuring similar pleas.

Her chest rises and falls, breaths shallow but steady. Still, she doesn't stir. Tears sting my eyes, and I turn away as I force myself to keep them at bay. My gaze connects with Logan's. He's standing off to one side, keeping Aurora's attention away from her mom, but Logan's face is etched in pain, and he does nothing to stem the tears streaking down his cheeks as he looks at Riley as though he's watching his heart shatter into pieces.

Seeing him break, my own tears wriggle free until the three of us are crying and pleading with Riley to wake up.

To come back to us.

To survive.

To live.

My fingers curl around Riley's limp ones, my focus intent on the air that fogs up her oxygen mask every time she exhales. She regained consciousness momentarily before the fire trucks and ambulances arrived, and several more times while she lay on a stretcher on the way to the hospital. Every time, she'd been groggy and confused, and the EMT had advised her not to talk.

I'd given the paramedic a menacing glare as he'd tried to close the doors and climbed into the back of the ambulance before they'd peeled away from the still-burning house.

Aurora was sitting in the back of another ambulance, Logan keeping her entertained while she was checked over. She doesn't appear to have suffered the same extent of smoke inhalation as Riley. Likely thanks to the blanket that was wrapped around her. Grayson had been deep in conversation with the fire chief and police, giving a statement when the ambulance left. He's still absent, but Logan joined me in Riley's room, carrying a passed-out Aurora a little while ago.

Neither of us says a word. Exhaustion and worry rim his eyes, likely mirroring my own as he stares transfixed at Riley's sleeping form. The doctors have assessed her and assured us she's fine, minus some minor smoke inhalation—hence the oxygen mask.

She's merely sleeping. Exhausted from the night's activities... and whatever the fuck has gone down in the last twenty-seven hours since I stupidly left her alone at the stadium.

All in all, she's lucky.

We're lucky.

Bowing my head, I press a kiss to each of her knuckles. Tonight could have ended so differently. The fire could have got her. Bertram could have destroyed her before the fire even started. We could have been too late. We nearly were.

"Any word from Grayson?" Although he keeps his voice low, his words are a thick rasp as though Logan was the one caught inside that burning house.

I shake my head. I'd messaged him and Logan earlier with an update on Riley's condition. Although he's read the message, he hasn't responded.

"He's probably still dealing with the fire chief."

"Do you think Bertram was still in the house?" he asks after a moment.

I merely shake my head, not knowing. I fucking hope so, though. I hope he met a slow and agonizing end in those flames.

"I hope he was," Logan continues, voicing my thoughts aloud. "I'm done with this. I want him gone. I want a normal life for the five of us—one where we aren't afraid to let Aurora out of our sight or where Riley is constantly looking over her shoulder."

What I wouldn't give for that, too.

A twitch against my fingers has my gaze snapping to Riley's face. Her eyelids flutter before opening, and I let out the first real breath since I got Logan's call as I take in those stunning hazel eyes.

She stares at the ceiling briefly before her head falls to the side, her gaze catching on mine. "You're okay," I assure her, giving her fingers a squeeze. Her eyes are clouded with confusion, and she lifts a hand, touching her oxygen mask. I can see the events of the night play out across her mind before her head whips toward Aurora.

"She's okay, too." Relief floods her features as she stares at her daughter, sleeping soundly on Logan's lap.

"I haven't let her out of my sight, Shortcake," Logan says softly, a relieved smile tugging at the corner of his lips. "Docs checked her out, and she's perfectly healthy. Not a hair harmed on her head."

Riley seems to melt into the bed at that confirmation, her throat bobbing as she swallows. Her eyes close, and for a moment, I think she's fallen back to sleep before she pushes the oxygen mask off her face.

"How—" She stops, licking her lips, and I hurriedly pour her a glass of water and bring it to her lips. She drinks the cool water down greedily before trying again. "How long have I been out?"

"Not long." Unable to help myself, I smooth my hand over her hair. "A few hours. You passed out from smoke inhalation." My own voice is thick. "You were unconscious when we found you."

She gives a small, tired nod, her brows furrowing as she tries to piece together her fragmented memories. "The last thing I remember is breaking the window to escape."

I take a deep breath, my heart aching at the thought of what she had endured. "When we got there, we saw smoke and flames. The door was locked and burning hot. We heard Aurora scream. Grayson climbed in and got you out."

At the mention of his name, her eyes scan the room, searching for him.

"He's still at the house," Logan says by way of explanation.

She grimaces at the mention of that house, her gaze falling back on Aurora like she can't bring herself to look away for more than a few seconds at a time.

The questions I've been stewing over for the past day that have only become more insistent in the past hours stack on the tip of my tongue. Unable to hold them back any longer, they slip free. "What happened?" I croak. "Did he hurt you?" Fuck, he better not have. "Did he..." I can't even bring myself to voice that last one aloud.

She gives my fingers another squeeze, those tired eyes fixed on mine. "No."

A weight I didn't realize I had been carrying finally lifts from my shoulders, my muscles relaxing for the first time since we found her things in that bathroom.

"He was at the game," she explains, voice thick and raspy.

"We know," I interject so she doesn't have to hurt her throat by talking. "We saw the video footage. You did what you had to to protect Aurora."

She nods, but her eyes are shiny with tears. "H-he left us alone that first night and all day." More lines form along her forehead as she frowns. "I think he wanted us to be comfort-able. Or perhaps he was trying to get in my head, I don't know."

She goes quiet, and I know there's more. He did *something*.

Leaning forward, I rest my elbows on my knees and brush my thumb across the back of her hand. "You're safe," I assure her, holding her bloodshot eyes until her shoulders inch down from her ears.

"Maybe we should wait for Gray," Logan suggests.

Riley gives a firm shake of her head. "No. He doesn't need to hear the details..."

I catch Logan's gaze, his posture deflating as he agrees, and we patiently wait while Riley gathers herself.

"A-after dinner... he... he made me sit in his lap." Her face scrunches in disgust. "He touched me." Her voice breaks over the word, and it takes all my self-control to remain seated. To not storm out of here and hunt down the sick, twisted bastard. "He made me kiss him." Her fingers lift to her cheek, trailing the little red nicks as she gets lost in the memory, shuddering. I'd assumed they were from when she broke the window, though now I'm guessing they aren't, and yup... Bertram is a fucking dead man. Assuming he isn't dead already.

My gaze slides to Logan, and despite his comforting hold on Aurora, his eyes spark with the same murderous intent. Jaw clenched, he lifts his gaze to mine, and we're in agreement.

If Bertram made it out of that fire alive, he will meet his end at our hands for daring to touch Riley. For traumatizing her. For terrorizing her by kidnapping Aurora.

"H-he told me to meet him in his bedroom after I put Aurora to bed," Riley continues, utterly oblivious to how fucking strong she is at this moment. Sure, her voice is hoarse, her skin pale and coated in soot, but without her having to say anything, I *know* she fought like hell to get Aurora and herself out of there.

A tear gathers on her lower lid before spilling over, and I reach up to swipe it away. "I-I couldn't," she stammers, wide eyes holding mine. "I knew if I did that, he'd break me, and I don't think I would have recovered this time."

Squeezing her hand, I state earnestly, "You would have, Ry. You would have because, this time, you wouldn't have been healing alone. But whatever the hell you did to make sure that didn't happen, I'm so fucking glad for it."

"I-I lit the burners on the stove." She sniffles, wiping at her nose. "B-before I went to his room, I turned on the gas and draped a towel over the stovetop.

"I didn't know how long it would take. I just kept telling myself to keep him occupied until it ignited. I..." Her eyes go wide with fear. "I didn't expect the fire to get so big so quickly. I thought I'd have more time to get us out of there."

Brushing my hand over the back of her head and down the length of her hair, I assure her, "You did. You were so brave."

Logan clears his throat, and Riley looks his way. "What, uh, what happened to Bertram?"

Exhaling, Riley gives a slight shake of her head. "I hit him over the head with a lamp. I-I don't know if he is... I just ran. I-I don't know."

"It's okay. Grayson will be here soon, and he can update us."

"I hope he's dead."

They're the first words Riley has spoken tonight that haven't been coated in hysteria or panic. The steel in her tone, the sheer strength. Well, fuck, now might not be the time or place, but it gets me fucking hard.

"If he's not, he's going to wish he was, real fucking soon."

Logan's tone drips with menace, eyes flashing with delight at whatever torture he's imagining. He might be a golden retriever. He might come across as the laid-back, easy-going one of us, but if anyone hurts someone he cares about, he can be just as ruthless as me.

It's what makes the three of us such good friends.

Grayson is like a phantom—silent and deadly.

Logan is the fist to the face you never see coming.

And I'm the brick wall you slam into when you try to flee.

Together? We're fucking deadly.

Especially when you come after either of our girls.

Riley's eyes begin to droop, exhaustion weighing her down. "Go to sleep, sweetheart," I encourage, bringing my lips to her knuckles. She gives me a small, sleepy smile as she sinks deeper into the pillows. "We'll look after Aurora and be here when you wake up."

With that reassurance, her lids drop closed, and knowing she'll be alright, I finally allow myself to relax as my head drops to the mattress beside our joined hands, and I close my eyes.

GRAYSON

CHAPTER THIRTY-EIGHT

I watch as the ambulance speeds away, its sirens blaring and flashing lights cutting through the night like a blade. My lips are flattened into a grim line at the thought of Riley inside, unconscious. She better be okay! Royce is with her, and he said he'd keep me updated—which is the only reason I'm still standing here.

Another ambulance follows, taking Aurora and Logan. I can't help the knot of worry tightening in my chest. It's been squeezing tighter since I first spotted those flames in the distance. Arriving to find the house engulfed in flames was like waking up in a living nightmare. Then, seeing Aurora and Riley like that—Aurora scared out of her mind and Riley so fragile... It broke something inside me.

Turning my back on the ambulances, I stare up at the blacked-out carcass of what was my childhood home. The flames have mostly been subdued, and the firefighters are methodically working to put out the last stubborn pockets of fire. The smell of smoke hangs heavy in the air, acrid and suffocating. I stare at the wreckage of what was once a house, now reduced to charred remains.

The only reason I'm still here is to hear if there is any word on my father. Not because I care, but because I want to make sure the bastard is truly dead. I need to see it with my own eyes.

After what feels like hours of waiting, the fire chief finally approaches me. His face is grim, eyes shadowed with the weight of what he has to say. "The cause was a gas stove left on," he explains. "The fire spread quickly, probably started in the kitchen. If there's any consolation, it was an accident."

An accident? I nearly snort aloud. This was no accident.

There's no stopping the curl of my lips as it dawns on me, and I turn away, pretending I've got a bit of ash in my eye. Riley. My smart, fierce Tempest. I bet it was her. She must have turned it on when my father was distracted, creating an opportunity for them to escape—even if it meant risking everything. I mentally praise her for being strong and clever, even in the face of danger.

When I turn toward the fire chief again, my face is impassive as I listen to him explain how the fire spread, what his men are doing to combat it, and the likely outcome. I have no interest in saving anything, so I don't give two shits if the entire building is razed.

"Any signs of anyone else in the house?" I ask him.

"Nothing yet," he says grimly. "But we'll keep clearing rooms."

Time drags on as I continue to wait, watching the firefighters move through the wreckage, their shouts and orders filling the air. Then, suddenly, there's a commotion. Voices rise, and the controlled chaos escalates as a group gathers near the front door.

My heart pounds in my chest, a mix of dread and anticipation swelling inside me. I take a few steps closer, trying to see through the haze of smoke and steam rising from the scorched earth.

Then I see it—a body being lifted out. He's burnt, his skin charred and blistered, but there's movement. He's alive. Barely. EMTs rush over from a standby ambulance, scurrying around him, working quickly to stabilize him. Their efficiency is clinical and detached, and I watch as they check his vitals, administer oxygen, and prepare him for transport. He's unconscious, a mere husk of the man I despise, but he's still breathing.

Before they can lift him onto the stretcher, I step forward, catching their attention. "Where are you taking him?" My voice is sharper than I intend, the words laced with the remnants of my anger.

One of the EMTs glances up at me, her expression professional but unyielding. "Springview Medical."

A cold knot of dread settles in my stomach. The same hospital where Riley and Aurora were taken. The idea of them being under the same roof again—of my father being anywhere near her—fills me with a deep, simmering hatred. "Take him somewhere else," I demand, my tone edged with desperation. "Anywhere else."

The EMT shakes her head, already turning back to Bertram. "We can't. Protocol dictates that we take patients to the nearest hospital."

I stand there, fists clenched, as they lift him onto the stretcher and load him into the ambulance. The doors slam shut with a finality that echoes through the night, and I'm left standing in the middle of the charred remains of the house, helpless as they drive away.

I stalk over to Logan's car while I dial Royce to fill him in on Bertram's determination to not fucking die. I no longer need to be here. If my father is under the same roof as Riley and Aurora, then you can bet your ass I'm going to be right there with them the entire time!

RILEY

CHAPTER THIRTY-NINE

Despite the heaviness in my muscles and the slight scratch at the back of my throat, I feel much more rested when I wake up. Opening my eyes, I immediately latch onto the dark orbs staring unblinkingly at me as though I might disappear if they dare close for even a fraction of a second.

His hair is a mess, sticking up every which way, and he's pale-looking. His eyes are slightly bloodshot, possibly from the smoke since Royce said he went in to get me or from lack of sleep. Probably a mixture of both.

Despite his appearance, a weight lifts off my chest at seeing him, knowing all three of them are okay and that they all came.

We stare at each other for a moment, a whole host of emotions transpiring in that simple exchange. With only our eyes, we acknowledge everything that's happened in the past twenty-four hours. I silently admit how fucking terrified I was, and he confesses to nearly losing his freaking mind when he discovered I was gone.

He apologizes for letting me down even though he doesn't have to.

I apologize for leaving the arena without one of them that night, even though we both know I had no other choice. That I'd make the same decision time and again if it meant rescuing my daughter.

He says that he wishes they'd gotten to me sooner.

I tell him it doesn't matter because they arrived in time.

The only thing neither of us brings up is his dad. Is he alive? Did they find him inside the house? The questions cycle on repeat in my mind, but I'm not yet ready to hear the answer. To know if I killed him or, at the very least, was responsible for his death. Or if he somehow managed to escape.

My gaze drops to his hands, noticing the thick white bandage wrapped around one.

"You're hand," I croak. Thankfully, I no longer sound like a twenty-pack-a-day smoker, although my voice is still not my own. Presumably, that will heal in a day or two.

He glances down as if only now realizing it's bandaged.

"It's nothing." His own voice is thick. "Minor burn. Nothing that won't heal."

I frown down at his wrapped hand, before I slide my gaze away, feeling guilty. "Where's Aurora?" I ask, realizing the seat Logan had been sitting in earlier is now vacant.

"Logan took her home so she could sleep in an actual bed," Grayson explains. "Royce went with them. Doctors said you could be discharged once you woke up."

Silence falls heavily between us as I stare at him before he exhales heavily. The top half of his body curves forward and his stoic expression fractures into one of heartache.

"Fuck, Tempest." His voice is deep and thick, coated with anguish. "When I saw that godforsaken house on fire, I thought I was going to lose you. That we were too late. I'd never have fucking forgiven myself if you or Aurora had..."

"Hey," I soothe, opening my arms, and he practically falls

into them, his long, hard body resting against mine as he buries his face in my neck. "We're both okay. We made it out."

His shoulders shake, and I simply stroke my hand up and down his back, breathing in the comfort of being this close to him.

"Can't say I'm sorry to see that fucking house *burn*," he eventually says, steel in his voice.

"You and me both. I just wish I could have witnessed it from the *outside*."

Lifting his head, he pins me with a glare. "Not funny."

I can't help it, I grin. The last twenty-four hours or so might have been harrowing. An emotional rollercoaster. But *fuck me,* I am so happy knowing Aurora is safe and that the guys came for us.

The levity of the moment passes, Grayson's brows furrowing. "My dad," he begins. I stiffen. I can't help it. It's an involuntary reaction. He notices, grimacing before he continues. "He's here. In a room down the hall. It's another reason why Logan took Aurora home."

I swallow, feeling for the first time since I woke up like my throat is clogged with soot. "He's alive, then."

"Burned, but yeah, he's alive."

Guess it was foolish of me to hope I'd hit him hard enough to kill him or that the fire had taken care of what I couldn't.

"I'm sorry, Tempest."

I shake my head, not trusting my voice to speak.

"Did you talk to the police?" I finally ask. "Maybe if we tell them he's been stalking me, they'll arrest him again. Send him back to prison?"

Although Grayson nods, his tight expression says he disagrees.

"Or he could say that you've been keeping him from his daughter," he counters. "Either way, I don't want him going back to prison. Not when he can still stalk you from there or get released in several months or years and start this shit all over again. You deserve to move on. Aurora deserves a normal childhood," he states with unflinching finality. "He needs to go."

Glancing around the room, I ask, "Do I need to stay here, or can I go?" Now that I know Bertram is in a room just down the hall, I want to get out of here.

He's on his feet in an instant. Pointing at a duffle bag at the end of my bed, he says, "There's a change of clothes in there. If you're up for it, go shower and get dressed. "I'll hunt down a doctor and have you out of here in no time."

A shower sounds amazing. I *reek* of smoke. However... "Grayson," I call out, stopping him in his tracks. My gaze slides to the door. "What about *him*?"

"I'm down as his emergency contact, and since he's unconscious, the nurses are communicating with me daily about his progress, so we will know as soon as there is any change in his condition."

I nod, and he disappears out the door before I can tell him not to bully whatever doctor he finds first.

With the advice to take it easy for the next few days and to stay hydrated, I'm discharged. Half an hour later, Grayson brings the car to a stop outside the guys' townhouse.

Streaks of gray brighten the horizon, dawn breaking on a new day as I walk through the front door, a smile tugging on my lips. Who would have thought mere months ago I'd be so relieved to be walking into this house? The me from back then would have laughed in your face and said you must be crazy. But hey, if this is what crazy feels like, then I guess you can call me in-fucking-sane because I wouldn't trade this feeling of belonging for anything in the world.

Despite the early hour, the smell of eggs and bacon is thick in the air, and my stomach grumbles in appreciation. "Mommy!" Aurora squeals as she bounces over, then launches into my arms.

"Whoa there kiddo," Royce chastises, chasing after her. "Remember what we said about being careful with Mommy for the next couple of days."

"Oh." Her lips tug down as she loosens her hold. "I'm sorry, Mommy."

"You're okay, baby. It's so good to see you."

She nods, wriggling to be put down before she grabs my hand and pulls me toward the living room. "Look!" She points toward where a mattress has been laid on the floor, covered with a duvet and piled high with pillows. "We're having a snuggle day."

"A snuggle day, huh?" I smirk at Royce who winks at me. "That sounds pretty perfect to me."

"Why don't we let Mommy get some food while we pick out a movie for us all to watch?" he suggests, distracting Aurora while Grayson tugs me out of the room and down the hall to the kitchen.

Pausing in the doorway, I smile at the sight of Logan in front of the stove, shirtless, wearing low-slung sweats and a bright red apron. Seeing him takes my breath away, and I allow myself to simply admire him for a moment.

Leaning against the door frame, I run my eyes over his exposed back, the muscles flexing and rippling as he flips bacon and shuffles pans around. The power beneath his skin is mesmerizing, a testament to the hours he spends training and pushing his body to its limits. Each muscle is perfectly defined, his body a temple of perfection. The curve of his shoulders, the hard lines of his biceps and triceps, and the way his lats taper down to his narrow waist is breathtaking.

His movements are fluid and controlled, each one high-lighting the power and grace he possesses. He turns slightly, and although his apron blocks what I know is a spectacular view, I don't need to see it to picture the deep V of his hip flexors and the hard plane of his abdomen.

His skin glows in the soft morning light, every contour of his physique illuminated. There's a raw, masculine beauty to him that I can't tear my eyes away from. I haven't had much time recently to stop and appreciate him, and I take this moment to do precisely that—to appreciate Logan in all of his glory. His dedication, strength, and unwavering support shine through in this simple, domestic scene.

He catches sight of me out of the corner of his eye. "Short-cake!" Logan's greeting is as enthusiastic as Aurora's as he hauls me into his chest. "Fuck, you're a sight for sore eyes. How are you feeling? Do you need anything? I'm making breakfast. I Googled earlier, and the internet said you should drink lots and eat soft foods, so I have eggs, pancakes, yogurt, and fruit. Royce got you your favorite coffee." He frowns. "But maybe you shouldn't drink hot liquids. Hold on, let me Google that real quick." He's already typing away on his phone. "We have water, and I made you a smoothie—"

I place a hand on his arm to stop him, and his gaze snaps to mine. "Everything smells amazing, Logan. You didn't have to go to all this effort, but thank you."

Pressing onto my toes, my hand snakes around his neck as I pull him down to me. Our lips brush, and he groans. The spatula hits the floor with a light *thud* as his hands clamp down on my hips, fingers squeezing against my flesh as if ensuring I'm real.

"Fuck, baby. I missed you. Don't scare us like that again. I don't think my heart could take it."

Pulling back, I stare up into his concerned face. "I'm sorry," I say the words loud enough for the others to hear, including them in my apology. "Believe me, I have no intention of doing that again. If I'd thought there was any other way…"

"We know, baby," Logan assures. "Now, go sit down so I can bring you breakfast."

"What about me?" Grayson grouses. "Are you going to bring me my breakfast?"

Logan looks him up and down. "You have working arms and legs, don't you?"

Sneering playfully at Logan, he walks me over to the table and pulls out a chair for me, even though I'm perfectly capable of seating myself, before he stalks over to fill a plate with food.

Logan brings me one with double the amount of pancakes and eggs Grayson loaded onto his plate, and I give him a look as he sets it down in front of me. Aurora and Royce join us, and the five of us sit around the table while Grayson and I eat.

Once we're done, Aurora grabs both of us by the hands and drags us into the living room, where we all squish onto the makeshift bed. *Toy Story* is queued up on the TV, and someone hits play. With Aurora curled up on one side and the guys surrounding us, it's the perfect day.

I must have fallen asleep, as when I open my eyes next, it's only Logan and me in the bed. He's sitting upright with his back pressed against the bottom of the sofa, typing away on his phone.

"Good afternoon, sleepy head," he teases when I stretch. "Did you have a good nap?"

I nod. "How long was I out for?"

"A couple of hours."

I glance around the room, listening for sounds deeper in the house. "Where are the others?"

"They took Aurora to the park and out for ice cream."

"You know she's going to become a sugar addict with the amount of treats you guys give her."

He only grins like that's exactly what he wants, and I roll my eyes.

"While we're alone, I wanted to talk to you. Aurora is meant to start daycare this week, but with everything with Bertram, if you want to hold off, I can call to push it back."

I purse my lips as I think about it. "What do you think I should do?"

"I think you should do whatever you think is best," he starts, making me smile. "However, I also think we need to stop letting Bertram dictate our actions. He's in the hospital and in no condition to come after either of you right now."

I nod. "I agree. I think we should stick to the plan of enrolling her this week. I'm also going back to Lux this week. I had already messaged Tara before—" I wave my hand in the air, not actually saying the words—"but I don't see the need to change my plans."

Logan grins down at me. "I think it's a perfect plan."

Feeling warm from the glow of his praise, I take advantage of the time alone, just us, as I crawl up his body until I'm straddling his lap.

Dropping his phone onto the mattress, he lifts a hand to brush my hair away from my face. "How are you, really?" he asks, searching my eyes.

"I'm better than I probably should be," I tell him truthfully. "Physically, I feel fine; I'm just sore and tired. I-I don't want to think about what he made me do or the fact he's still alive." I slide a hand up his chest, loving that he never put on a shirt so I can feel the warmth of his body seep into my palm. "I'm here with you guys and Aurora, and that's all that matters. That and how distractingly hot you are without a top on."

He chuckles, his hands sliding down my arms and running up my thighs. I'm wearing an oversized top that belongs to one of them—I don't even know who—and a pair of leggings that have seen better days, but with his heated gaze on mine, I feel like I'm wearing the sexiest lingerie.

Once I'm done exploring his chest, I drag my fingers down the center of his abdomen until they meet the fine hairs of his happy trail. Reaching the waistband of his sweats, my gaze catches on the date he has tattooed over his hip. I brush my fingers over it and bite my lower lip as I look up at his face through my eyelashes. "I want you, Logan."

He groans, a pained sound that's half growl. "Just me, huh?"

I give him a coy smirk. "Well, all of you, truthfully, but since the other two aren't here, I guess that will have to come later."

"Sucks to be them," he agrees huskily, fingers kneading my skin as he rocks me over his growing erection. "Fuck, Shortcake." He glances toward the door. "We'll have to be quick, though. I dunno how long we have until they get back."

"I think we can manage that," I tease.

He groans again before shuffling down the mattress and flipping us so I'm on my back, and he hovers over me. With tender, careful movements, he pulls my top over my head before dragging my leggings and panties down my thighs.

Wedging his broad shoulders between my legs, his breath fans the sensitive skin of my pussy before he leans in and swipes his tongue along my slit. I sigh, my head falling back against the cushions as I lift my hips. "God, Logan," I breathe as he sucks and licks at me. His touch is soft and gentle, slowly coaxing me to life. "That feels so good."

His fingers caress my skin, swiping over my lower abdomen, my hips, my thighs. Each touch sends a jolt of want to my needy core until I'm grinding against his face, chasing my fast-approaching release.

Back arched, head thrown back, I come with a scream.

Breathing heavily, I watch through half-lidded eyes as Logan shoves down his sweats and climbs up my body until he hovers above me. His broad, muscular frame is a protective canopy that shields me from the world, and his chestnut eyes, ordinarily light and playful, have darkened with a potent mix of want and desire. As he looks down at me, I can see the shift in those eyes, how they soften and deepen, holding a promise that makes my heart race.

His gaze roams over my face, drinking me in as if he's memorizing every feature, every freckle. There's a tenderness there, a carefulness in the way he touches me, his fingertips ghosting over my skin with reverence. He's always been gentle, but now there's an intensity that takes my breath away. How he looks at me makes me feel like I'm the only person in the world, the center of his universe.

I watch as his eyes trace the lines of my jaw and the curve of my lips. There's a heat in his gaze, a fire that burns just beneath the surface, barely restrained. He wants me, and it's written in every line of his body, in the way his muscles tense and release as he holds himself above me.

"You're beautiful." His breath fans across my face, warm and sweet, and I can feel the controlled strength in his arms as he supports his weight.

"Need you." My hands flatten against his back, urging him closer.

His responding smirk is cocky, full of masculine pride, yet his touch is soft and gentle as he notches himself at my entrance. His lips part slightly as if he's about to speak but can't find the words, before he shakes his head and presses his hips forward.

I gasp as my walls stretch to accommodate his girth. He lowers his head, and his lips brush against mine in the whisper of a kiss so gentle it sends shivers down my spine. His eyes never leave mine, even when his hips meet mine, and we share a moment of profound connection before he begins to move.

Ducking his head, his lips trail a path of fire wherever he touches as he drives us toward oblivion. There's a reverence in his actions, a worshipfulness that makes my heart swell with love and something deeper, something primal.

Logan's desire is tangible—a living, breathing entity that wraps around us, drawing us closer. It's in how he looks at me, his eyes dark and smoldering, filled with a promise of what's to come. And in that moment, as I clench around him and he fills me, I know that I am his, just as he is mine.

RILEY

CHAPTER FORTY

Despite spending the past two days resting and recovering, I'm exhausted as I climb the stairs to bed. Grayson had offered to put Aurora to bed while Royce and I snuggled on the sofa—okay, I was totally sleeping and drooling on his shoulder—and Logan is out with the team. I practically had to kick him out the door, but if the team is going to make it to the championships, then they need their captain to be present. Now that we have Aurora back safely, there's no excuse for him not to give hockey and the team his all.

Yawning, I mumble goodnight to Royce outside his bedroom, only pausing briefly to glance up to Grayson's floor before crossing the hall. He never reappeared after tucking Aurora in, so I assume he went to his own room afterward. Easing open my bedroom door, I slip inside. The only light is the soft pink hue of the mushroom nightlight Logan purchased.

On silent feet, I pad toward the lump on the bed, expecting to find my daughter starfished on her stomach and sound asleep. Except I pause at the bedside as I take in the sight before me. Yes, my daughter is passed out, sprawled out across the entire bed. However, a sleeping Grayson is beside her, perched on the very edge, with one leg hanging off the bed and his foot planted on the floor to stop him from face-planting the carpet. A book is propped open on his chest as though he fell asleep while reading, and one hand is outstretched toward Aurora as if, even in his sleep, he needed to assure himself that she was still here.

For several moments, I simply drink in the scene before me. It's still all so surreal, seeing the two of them getting along. There were nights when I'd watch Aurora sleep and wonder what it would be like if Grayson knew of her existence. Knew he had a sister out there in the world. But even in my wildest imagination, I could never picture this.

On the balls of my feet, I tip-toe across the room and lift the book from Grayson's chest before setting it on the bedside table. He's lying on top of the duvet, so I grab a blanket from the bottom of the bed and drape it over him, pressing a chaste kiss to his cheek. He stirs but doesn't wake, and when he rolls further onto his side toward Aurora, I bite back a smile before creeping out of the room and silently closing the door behind me before slipping into Royce's room.

"Do you mind if I sleep with you tonight? Grayson passed out in my bed."

"You know you never have to ask," Royce says with a soft smile, pulling back his bedsheet. My eyes rake over the sight of him, bare-chested and with tattoos on display, as he sits up in bed, back resting against the headboard and a drawing pad on his lap.

"What are you drawing?" I ask as I strip out of my clothes and pull a discarded t-shirt of his over my head before climbing in beside him. He tilts the sketchpad my way, and I suck in a gasp. "Was this yesterday?" I ask, and he nods. He's drawn all of us at the breakfast table, Aurora in Logan's lap as the two munch on a humongous stack of pancakes. My more modest stack has been forgotten as I watch them with a smile on my face. However, it's the slight smile on Grayson's lips that captures my attention... it looks so similar to mine—filled with warmth and awe.

That tiny little smile transforms his entire face.

It reminds me of the teenage Grayson for whom I fell head over heels.

"Royce, is this... real?"

He huffs a small breath beside me, moving closer so I can feel his answer against my skin. "I wanted to draw it when I saw your expression, but when I noticed Grayson's, I *knew* I had to capture the moment. I wanted you to see how he looks at that little girl." He nudges me with his nose. "He's in love with her. Who knew all it would take was a three-year-old to demolish the last remnants of those walls."

Yeah, who knew?

Grayson was the one I'd been most anxious about getting along with Aurora. I knew Logan wouldn't be an issue. He's basically a giant child himself. While quiet and stony-faced, Royce has a heart of gold that I knew would melt once he spent some time with her. But Grayson? He's a hard nut to crack— believe me, it's taken a long time for me to break through that tough exterior. However, all I had to do was see how he looks at Aurora, interacts with her, and any hesitation, any fear I once harbored, went up in smoke.

"It's a superpower," I mumble absently, unable to look away from Royce's sketch. "Can I have this when you're done?" When he doesn't answer, I look up at him. "It deserves to be framed— put on the wall. I'm thinking in the kitchen?"

I'm not sure if I'm crossing a line or pushing him too far, but when he gives me a soft smile, it fills me with hope. He presses his lips to mine in a soft kiss. "Hang it wherever you want, Ry. This house is as much yours as it is ours. Make it your home."

I smile into his kiss. "Can I ask you a question?"

"You can ask me anything, James."

"Why do you not show others your sketches? They're so good, Royce. Your talent deserves to be appreciated by the world."

His smile is soft and endearing, his gaze flooded with love as he lifts a shoulder in a casual shrug. "I draw for me. Not for the world or money or any of that."

"So you'd never consider selling any of your drawings? There's this cafe in Halston that Logan took me to once. It has artwork from local artists on the wall that customers can buy."

"Never say never, but I'm happy just drawing for me for now." He nudges my shoulder. "And for you."

I grin up at him. "You best accept now that I'm going to want to cover every square inch of wall space with your drawings."

He chuckles, shaking his head at my teasing.

Wriggling my toes under his calf, my head falls to rest against his headboard, and I watch on silently while he draws and shades. Watching him is like watching magic happen. How he's able to bring the drawing to life... it's incredible.

"Please tell me you plan on doing something that involves drawing once you graduate. It would be a travesty not to."

His eyebrows hitch. "A travesty, huh?"

"Yup. A literal *travesty.*"

"I mean, my degree is in architecture. There's drawing in that."

"Wow, sound less enthusiastic. Please. You're blowing my mind with your excitement. AHH!" I squeal as he dives in, his fingers tickling me.

"Someone's feeling bratty tonight."

"Royce!" I squeal, his name coming out breathless as I writhe and wriggle in a bid to escape him.

I've slipped down the bed by the time he relents, and I swat at him while pushing my hair out of my face. He smirks down at me, but his stare shows a hesitant vulnerability.

"I have been working on something…"

My eyes widen as I scour his face. "Will you show me?"

He pauses before nodding and climbing off the bed. Wearing only his boxers that cling to his tight ass and thick thighs, he saunters over to his desk and lifts a larger sketchpad before coming back to me.

Perching on the edge of the bed, he hands it over to me, and I meet his gaze before dropping it to the pad of paper. With careful movements, I open it, a gasp falling from my lips as I take in the various frames filled with colorful characters.

A slow grin splits my face. "Is this… a children's book?" I question, awed as I flip to the next page, then the next. "Royce." His name is said with raw reverence. I can't tear my attention from the sketchpad as I take it all in. "This is… incredible."

"Yeah? You think so?"

"Are you joking?" I exclaim, whipping my head to gape at him. "I *know* so. You should submit to whoever you submit children's books to. No, you *need* to. I mean it, Royce. If you don't do it, I will do it for you because this is *insane*."

He's chuckling now, his initial hesitation having melted into relief. "That's actually what I was thinking of doing. It's not finished yet, but once it is."

I nod, gaze falling back to the page as I go back to the beginning before patting the empty spot in the bed beside me. "Sit with me. I want you to read this to me. Tell me what the story's about."

Huffing a laugh, he does as I ordered, and we snuggle up on his bed together as he begins, "Well, it's about a little girl who gets lost and is trying to find her way home…" and I fall even more in love with this passionate, creative man.

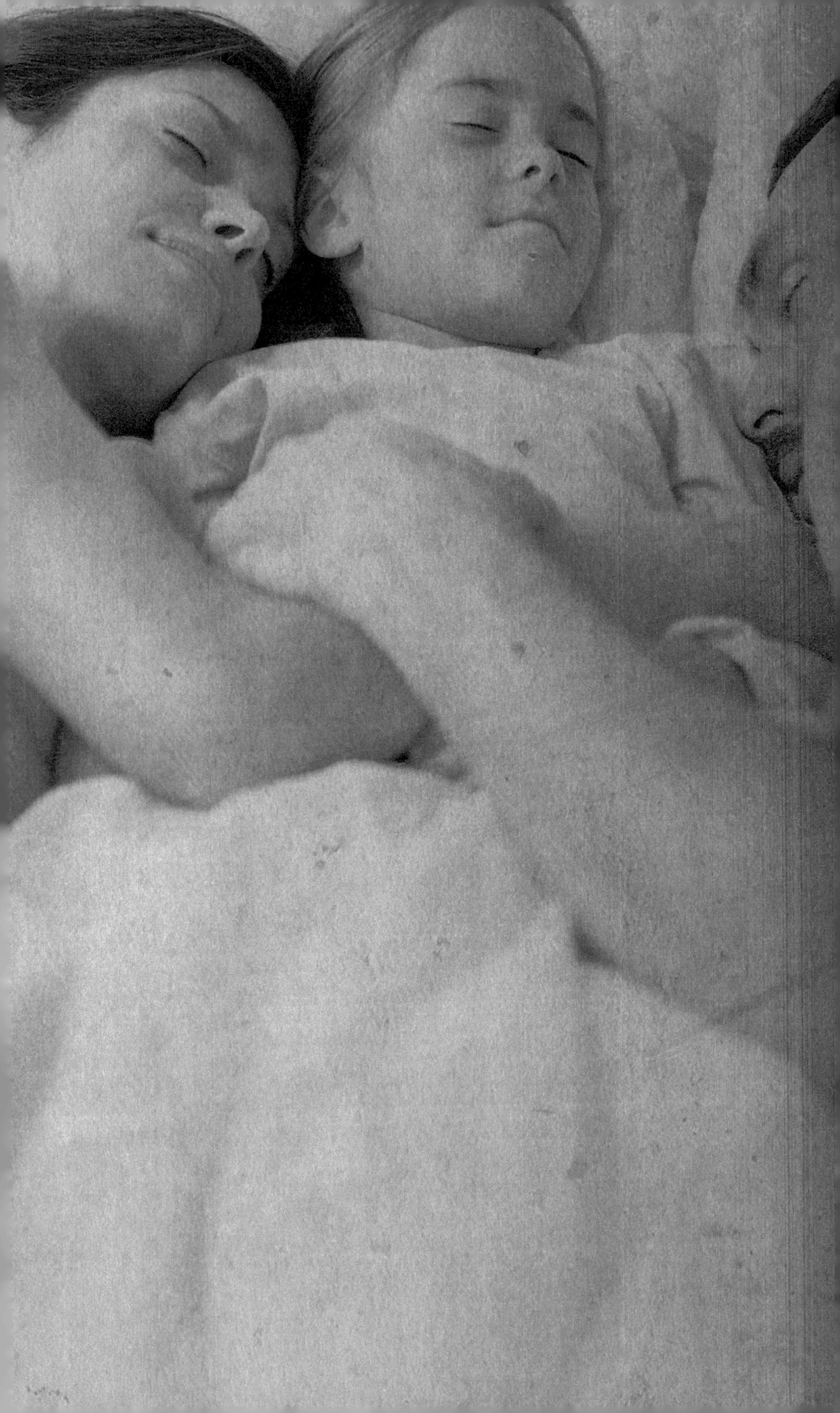

GRAYSON

CHAPTER FORTY-ONE

"Grayson."

"Mmmph." I roll away from the voice. It's too early to get up yet. Whatever the hell Logan wants can wait another couple of hours.

"Grayson," the voice repeats, a small hand coming to rest on my shoulder and giving it a quick squeeze. A little more awake now, I realize the voice isn't Logan's. It's too feminine. Too sweet.

My eyes snap open, and I blink up into Riley's face.

"Sorry," she whispers. "I thought you might want to catch a few hours' sleep in your own bed."

Her words struggle to compute through the fog in my head until I turn, noting the sleeping girl spread out over ninety percent of the bed, leaving me with a narrow strip to sleep on. Damn, I'm lucky I didn't fall on the floor.

"What time is it?" I ask, voice rough and scratchy as I swipe a hand through my hair, likely mussing it up.

"Early, still."

"Sorry. She didn't want to sleep alone last night."

"You don't need to explain," she murmurs. "Thank you for staying with her."

Like I would have left her. I'd told Aurora I'd go get her mom, but she refused to let me leave the bed. I'd planned to only stay until she fell asleep, but honestly, I'm not sure which of us passed out first—her or me. The events of the past few days wiped me out.

"Mommy," Aurora's sleepy voice interrupts, her eyes still closed.

"Shh, baby, go back to sleep," Riley soothes, reaching over me to stroke the back of Aurora's head. I love watching these private moments between them. The way Riley cares for her daughter. The way Aurora looks at her mom. It's clear that Riley is that girl's entire world. She looks up to her in a way I never remember worshiping my dad. He was always this imposing figure. I felt like I had to impress him, and he always fell a little short.

That's not how it is with Riley and Aurora. Riley praises every single one of her achievements, even if it's as simple as drawing a stick figure or eating her peas. Even when Aurora gets a word wrong or mispronounces it, she isn't chastised or ridiculed. Riley simply offers her a soft smile for her effort before correcting her.

Watching them together... puts everything into perspective. It makes me realize I never had my father's love. I see now that he never truly loved me. I was a possession, an extension of *him*. I was never my own person, never just Grayson, never his *son*.

Not the way that Aurora is Riley's daughter or how she's effortlessly becoming *ours*.

Becoming *mine*, and I'm not talking in a *half-sister* kinda way. I mean fucking *mine*. Mine to care for. Mine to protect. Mine to love.

Looking at her, I don't see a sister nearly twenty years

younger than me. I see a little girl who I fell in love with the second I learned of her existence. A bright, bubbly child who lights up when I walk through the door after a long day at work and classes. A kid who can make me crack a smile at the stupidest of things and has suckered me into watching a plethora of Disney movies.

I see a little girl who I want to watch grow up. Who I want to comfort when she has her heart broken for the first time. I want to help her with her homework when she's stuck and scare off every adolescent male because none of them are fucking good enough for her. I want to worry about her when she breaks curfew, and sit up waiting until she gets home after prom.

I feel myself coming undone with every minute spent in Aurora's presence.

She's... everything.

"Sleep with me, Mommy."

Aurora's sweet voice brings me back to the here and now, and I move to get up so Riley can climb in beside her daughter. Except, as soon as I shift, Aurora's hand snaps out to fist my top. "No," she complains sleepily. "Bed cuddles."

Smothering a silent laugh, Riley attempts to explain, "Baby, Grayson needs to go sleep in his own bed."

Eyes still closed, Aurora shakes her head, lips pulled down in a frown as she rubs her face against the pillow. Her hand tightens on my top. It's clear I'm not going anywhere. Remaining where I am, I arch an eyebrow at Riley. *Well, what are you going to do now?*

Rolling her eyes at me, she moves to the other side of the bed and slips beneath the cover. This bed is not made to fit the three of us, meaning we're all squished onto it, and Riley and I end up looking at each other over Aurora's head. Our faces are so close that I can see the light dusting of freckles along the bridge of her nose, Aurora's restful breaths the only sound as we stare at one another.

Long seconds pass, but for once, when Riley and I are in the same room, it's not strung tight with tension. It's calm. Peaceful. Like how it is when I'm inside her and everything wrong in my life slots into place. For that blissful moment, all is right in the world.

This moment is the calm after the storm.

It's a tranquility I can see myself enjoying for the rest of my life.

"She's perfect," I tell Riley, gaze dropping to the little girl snuggled between us. I've thought that plenty of times over the past couple of weeks that we've had Aurora, yet I don't think I've ever said the words aloud. Not to Riley.

Riley's smile is soft and endearing as she glances down at her daughter. "Yeah, she is."

"I don't think her time spent with my dad has harmed her in any way."

Riley's lips flatten, but relief shines in her eyes. "You think so? I mean, she seems to be doing okay. Logan said they talked, and it sounded like Bertram mostly ignored her." She sighs, staring down at her daughter with concern. "I hope that's the case but I haven't wanted to ask her outright in case it upsets her or triggers something."

"Nah, I think there would be signs if he had traumatized her in some way. Other than being a little shy around one of us initially, which is understandable, she has adapted to being here really well."

Sinking deeper into her pillow, Riley smiles down at her daughter.

"What about you?" she asks somewhat hesitantly.

"I want her here, Riley." I infuse my words with sincerity, hoping she hears what I'm saying—believes it. "She's family.

Blood. But even if she wasn't, she's your daughter, which means I want to know everything about her."

She chews on her bottom lip, those fathomless green-brown eyes holding me captive and slowly reeling me in. Not that I'm putting up a fight. Not anymore. Not when it comes to her.

"I don't know how to explain to her..." She trails off, but she doesn't need to finish that sentence. I understand.

She doesn't know how to explain to her daughter that I'm her brother. But I'm also so much more than that.

Her arm stretches across the distance between us, fingers tangling with mine on top of the bedsheets. "I want her to know. Want you both to have that relationship, regardless of whatever you may be to me. Whatever else you may be to her."

Wriggling closer, I eliminate any spare space until Aurora is a warm body pressed against us, and I can lift my hand to rest it on the side of Riley's throat. I give it a light squeeze. "*Whatever you may be to me* is everything. *Whatever else I may be to her* is whatever she needs. We're done dancing around this, Riley. You, me, Royce, Logan, and this little girl... we aren't an eventuality because we're already happening. We *are*. We *always will be*."

Her cheeks are tinged pink, her lips pressed flat to smother the smile I know she's struggling not to let loose. "When things are going good, it's hard for me to believe it will last."

"Well, this is forever, so get used to it."

"So possessive," she mumbles—a deflection.

"Damn right." My chest vibrates with the confirmation. "You're ours." I practically snarl the words. "*She's* ours."

"You realize that means you're all mine?"

My eyes flare, and I hiss, "Say that again."

I swear, the green in her eyes shimmers. "You're mine," she repeats.

In the next moment, I'm stretching over Aurora, careful to keep my weight off her as my lips hover inches above Riley's. "Say it again."

"You're mine." Her declaration tastes so fucking sweet as I bring my lips to hers.

I can't claim her the way my blood is urging me to do, and instead of deepening the kiss, I'm forced to pull back.

"You can bet your fucking ass I'm yours."

We must doze off at some point. When I next open my eyes, curious dark ones eerily similar to mine stare back at me. A tiny finger comes up to poke my cheek before moving to outline my eyebrow.

"You look like the mean man."

My eyes widen, my body stiffening as my brows likely disappear into my hairline. My focus slides to Riley, pleading for help, but she's still asleep. *Well, shit.*

"Erm." I clear my throat, buying myself an extra few seconds. "That's because he's my dad."

I've gone and opened the lid on this conversation. Maybe that wasn't the right thing to say? I should have distracted her. Bedtime stories and movie cuddles I can do, but the hard-hitting questions? I haven't a clue how to handle that.

Except, didn't I just tell Riley I was all in? Co-parents? That means I need to be here for the complicated stuff, too.

Yeah, but I was thinking about deciding on punishments if she misbehaves or discussing whether or not she needs braces when she's a teenager, not whether or not to tell her I'm her brother.

That decision should firmly be Riley's.

Aurora's lips twist into a frown, and despite her young age, I can see her mind working. "He said he was my daddy, too." Before I can figure out what to say, she asks, "Did he play with you?"

My throat bobs as I swallow. "No, he didn't."

She pouts. "He wouldn't play with me, either." She bites down on her bottom lip in a way that mimics Riley's, and it almost makes me laugh. "He was scary."

"It's okay," I reassure her, covering her tiny hand with mine. "He scared me, too." Leaning in, my forehead rests against hers. "Do you want to know a secret, though?"

Her eyes round, excitement lighting up her face as she nods eagerly.

"You don't need to be afraid of him. He'll never scare you again. I'm going to make sure of that."

Feeling a weighted stare, my gaze flicks to Riley, finding her watching our interaction. Concern creases her forehead, even as a softness enters her eyes.

Shuffling closer, her voice is raspy with sleep as she cuddles Aurora and says, "That man, he isn't really your dad, but he did help make you. Just like he helped make Grayson." She pauses, waiting. "Do you know what that means, baby?"

I go still. Swear, I don't even breathe. Don't dare to blink as I watch on.

Aurora gives a slight shake of her head.

"It means the two of you are siblings." She waits, the two of us watching Aurora closely. "Grayson is your brother."

My nerves buzz like a live wire beneath my skin as I wait for her reaction. This little girl is all the blood family I have left, and the weight of that truth presses heavily on me. I want her to accept me, to see me as someone who can be part of her world despite everything. I don't want to make the same mistakes I have with her mother. Don't want to give her any reason to distrust me.

Aurora's brow furrows, and she remains silent while she processes Riley's words. The seconds stretch on, each one feeling like an eternity. Panic spikes. I glance at Riley, who gives me a reassuring smile, but it does little to calm my racing thoughts.

Then, something shifts. Aurora's eyes light up with a spark of realization. She looks up at me, her expression a mix of awe and excitement. "You're my brother?" she asks, her voice filled with wonder.

I nod, my throat tight with emotion. "Yeah, I am."

A huge grin spreads across her face, and she squeals with delight, bouncing in place on the bed. "You'll play dress-up with me? And have tea parties? And—and we can be princesses together?"

"Rora, baby, Grayson might not—"

"Yes," I interject, cutting across whatever out Riley was giving me as relief washes over me, so intense that I almost feel dizzy. "We can do all those things. Anything you want."

She throws her arms around my neck, hugging me tightly. "I've always wanted a big brother!" she exclaims, her joy infectious. "This is the best day ever!"

Chuckling, I return her embrace as my teary-eyed gaze connects with Riley's. She's watching us, her own eyes shimmering with unshed tears and a soft smile playing on her lips.

Aurora's acceptance, her pure and unconditional excitement, wraps around my heart, soothing wounds I've carried for so long. This tiny, fierce little girl is giving me a chance to rebuild a family from the wreckage of our past. And for the first time in a long time, I feel like maybe, just maybe, I deserve it.

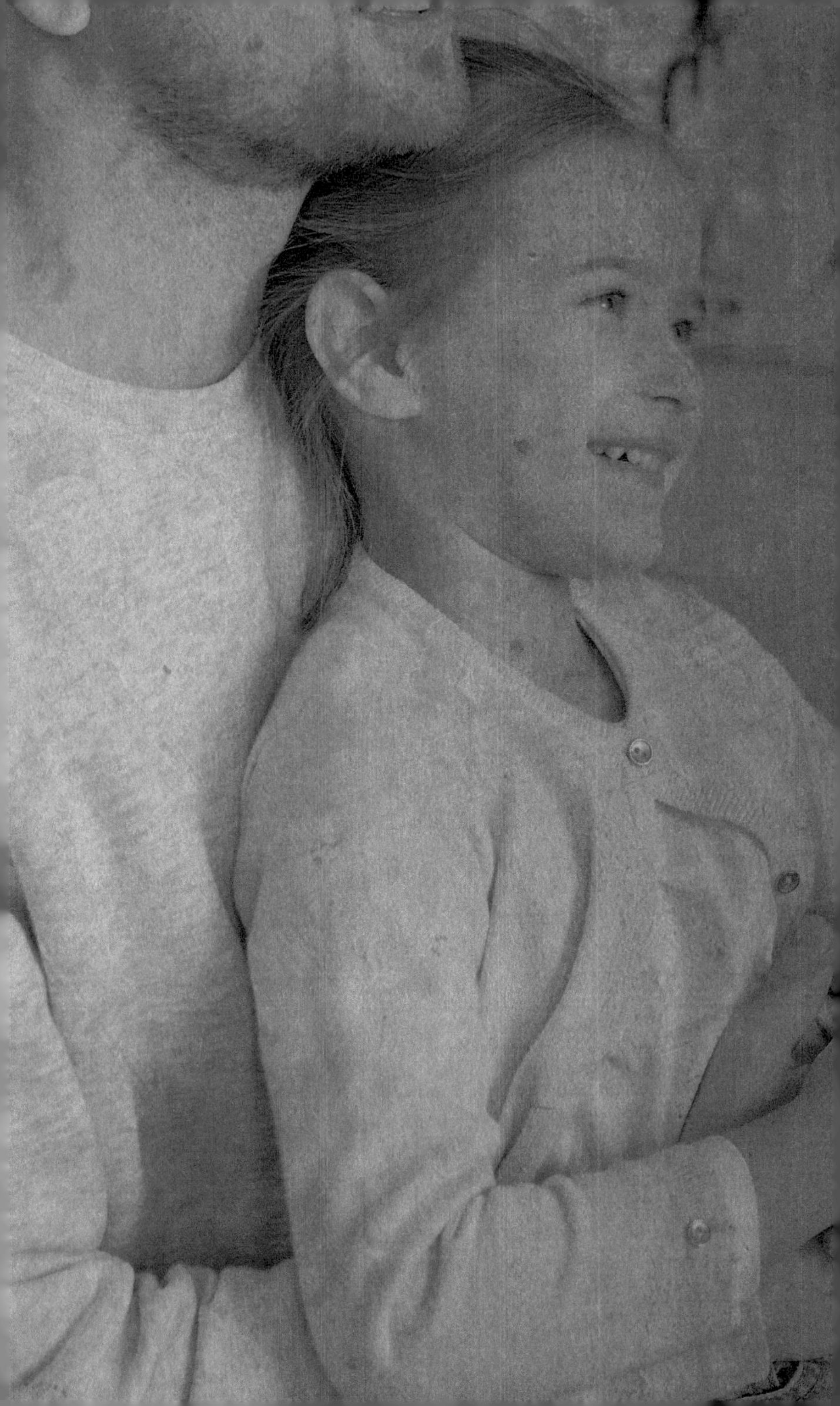

RILEY

CHAPTER FORTY-TWO

"Guess what!" Aurora announces as she bounces into the kitchen a short while later. Logan and Royce are already there, and Logan immediately scoops her up, throwing her into the air and making her squeal in delight.

"What?" he enquires. He tries to settle her on his hip but she squirms to get down, grinning like it's Christmas morning as she bounces over to Grayson. She's barely left his side since I told her he's her brother.

I'd been half asleep, refusing to admit it was time to get up when I heard their whispered conversation.

It broke my heart, listening to them bond over their shithead of a father—albeit on two very different levels. If scaring her and not playing with my daughter is the worst Bertram did to her, then I can live with that.

May she never know the horrors I've faced at that man's hands.

Still, it made it clear to me just how much they *needed* one another, even if Aurora didn't know it yet.

The excitement when I told her...

The sheen in Grayson's eyes...

It's a moment I'll never forget.

"Gayson's my brother!"

Except, she can't say brother so it comes out more like *brov-er*, and the entire sentence is just adorable! Including the way Grayson's chest swells with pride.

"He is?!" Logan exclaims, his grin broad and genuine. "Well, this is cause for a celebration. How about pancakes?"

"And milkshake?" Aurora enquires because, yes, Logan has gotten my daughter addicted to strawberry milk.

"Obviously. No celebration is complete without milkshakes with extra cream and chocolate sprinkles."

"Yes!" Aurora throws her tiny fist in the air, abandoning Grayson's side in favor of the promise of sugar.

While Logan gets her to help him with breakfast, Royce strides over to clap Grayson on the shoulder. Nothing is said, but the two of them share a loaded glance.

"Can I eat in front of the TV, Mommy?" Aurora asks, precariously carrying her plastic plate of maple syrup-covered pancakes.

"Sure, baby." Bringing over her milkshake, I settle her in front of the TV with a cartoon program before returning to the kitchen. "However, remember, we have to get dressed soon. Today's your first day of daycare, and we can't be late."

I'm fairly certain she's not paying attention, too engrossed in her cartoons as I leave her to it.

"You ready to go back to class?" Logan asks when I sit down at the kitchen table with them. "You can take another day or two if you need it?"

I give him a soft smile. "I'm fine, Logan. I'm ready to get back to a normal routine." My gaze slides to Grayson. "Your dad is still in hospital?"

He nods, sipping on his coffee. "Yup. They've had him in a

medically induced coma while he's intubated. He's not going anywhere, Tempest."

I ask for an update on Bertram every day, and every day, the relief at hearing he's still there is lifting.

Between mouthfuls of food, I tell the guys, "I think he did something to Lydia." I don't honestly care, but I'm curious to get their perspectives. Is she dead like Bertram implied, in which case I never have to worry about her bothering us again, or is she really on some island in Europe, where she can just pop on a plane and return at any time?

All three of them stop mid-chew to look at me.

"Uh, baby," Logan hedges.

"She and David are dead," Royce states, laying it all out there.

"We found their bodies," Grayson adds. Logan makes a gagging emotion before dropping his fork to his plate and pushing it away.

"Thanks for that reminder, man. Just what I needed—skipping breakfast before a practice session. Real cool."

"What do you mean?" I ask, ignoring Logan's antics.

"After Bertram... took you both," Royce hedges, "We went to the apartment we found Aurora in case he took you both there. Obviously, you weren't there, but Lydia and David were."

My eyes go wide. "So they really are dead."

"Deader than dead," Logan deadpans. "You ain't ever getting their stench out of the apartment."

I have no idea what he's talking about, but it feels good to know Lydia is gone.

"Good," I say, picking up my fork and continuing with my breakfast.

The guys all share a glance, but that's the end of the conversation. None of us care to spend any more time discussing the heinous bitch that was Lydia.

A wall of muscle is at my back as I bend down to give my daughter a hug and a final pep talk. "You're going to have the best time and make so many friends."

"But no boys," Grayson interjects.

Sighing, I pray for patience. Dropping Aurora off for her first day of daycare *should* be straightforward, but with all three of them in tow, it has turned into a full-blown operation—one that has drawn the eye of every other parent here.

"You can be friends with whoever you like," I tell Aurora, ignoring Grayson altogether. Emotion churns in my chest as I pull her in for a tight hug. "You remember the most important thing?"

"To have fun." Her words are muffled against my chest, and I smile as I pull her back, holding onto her arms as I give her a big, reassuring smile. "Go on," I urge. "Go play."

Loud sniffling behind me has me looking over my shoulder as my daughter skips away, not a second's hesitation as she makes a beeline for the play mat where a bunch of toys have been set out. His eyes glisten with unshed tears. "She's just so... brave," he says, his voice trembling.

"Logan, it's daycare, not boot camp." It's a struggle to keep the humor from my tone. He's as dramatic as Aurora—worse, maybe. The two of them definitely rub off on one another. I can only imagine the hysterics when Aurora hits her teenage years.

"Who's that kid? He looks like trouble," Grayson grumbles. Following the line of his suspicious glare, I find Aurora talking to a little boy. He holds out a red firetruck for her to play with, and when she accepts it, he sits beside her.

"He just sat down beside her!" He sounds so ridiculously outraged. I can't decide if his brooding protector shtick is entertaining or migraine-inducing.

"He's a *kid*," I remind him, because he seems to have forgotten that.

"Yeah, he's a kid now, but one day he's going to be all grown up with a chip on his shoulder and a cocky swagger."

"Oh, sorry. I didn't realize he was *your* kid."

That glare of his swings my way. "Har har."

I merely smile sweetly up at him.

"That's my big brother!" Aurora's sweet voice carries over to us, and while still maintaining his glare, Grayson stretches to his full height, chest puffing outward. The little boy Aurora was chatting with takes one look at him before whipping his gaze away so fast I'm surprised he doesn't snap his neck.

Annnnd now we're terrifying the children.

"Grayson," I hiss, smacking him in the chest with the back of my hand.

"Finally," Royce grouses. The next second, he's striding away, and I whirl in time to watch him stride up to the teacher. *Oh my god, I'm never bringing any of them ever again.* It'll be a miracle if Aurora isn't kicked out before drop-off is even over.

"Ms. Evelyn," I hear him saying. His superior height makes him tower over the poor five-foot-three woman, and his tattoos are on full display, intimidating every other parent in the room. I don't even want to know what the teacher thinks of our crazy family. I'm on the verge of disowning three-fifths of us anyway.

"I want to know that a close eye will always be kept on Aurora. No leaving the room without an adult." Okay, well, at least he's just doing his due diligence. Understandable, given everything.

I miss the teacher's response, and I groan when I next tune in to what Royce is saying. "Now, she doesn't like the crusts of her bread. They need to be cut off. And she prefers squares to triangles. For nap time, it—"

I clamp a hand on Royce's arm, giving him a tight smile as I scream at him with my eyes to *shut up*. "We have taken up enough of the woman's time," I hiss before turning to Ms. Evelyn. I really hope my smile is less crazed looking as I say, "Ms. Evelyn, thank you. I'm sure Aurora will be just fine in your care."

With a glance between us, Ms. Evelyn smiles before walking off, and I cast a quick look in Aurora's direction. Unfazed by the commotion we're causing, she has moved on to exploring the room. Spotting a table with colorful blocks, she sits down and begins playing with them.

My heart swells with pride and a touch of sadness. My little girl is growing up. Still holding her little backpack, I move to the wall of coats and bags. Her name is already written on a peg, and I set her backpack on the bench beneath it.

"Time to go," I hiss at the others when I'm done.

Grayson frowns. "I dunno…"

"Grayson." I pinch the bridge of my nose. "This is a daycare. The entire point is that we leave her here while we go to work and class."

"The teacher assured me she'd call at lunch," Royce reassures him, glaring fiercely around the room.

"Oh my god, please tell me you didn't." I throw my hands in the air before whirling to find Logan. He's still watching Aurora. In fact, I'm certain he's inched closer, and looking at his face, I can tell he's two seconds from pulling out a chair and joining her at the table.

"Logan," I bark, keeping my voice low and a smile plastered on my face for the sake of the children and other parents present. "We're leaving."

His head whips toward mine. "Already?"

How are they not grasping this concept?!

"Yes. I thought you had class at nine?"

He waves a dismissive hand. "I can grab the notes from someone."

"Or you could just go to the class." I stalk toward him. "I assure you, you cannot hang out here all day."

He gapes at me in outrage as though how dare I suggest he can't do that. "Says who?"

"The teacher, for one, if we don't leave soon. Probably the other parents when they find some weirdo is playing with their kids all day. Your teachers and Coach when you inevitably don't show up for class or practice." Affronted, he grunts at me.

Rolling my eyes, I give him a playful nudge. "She'll be okay. She needs to make her own friends." He makes a noise of disagreement. And in some miraculous feat, I manage to wrangle them all out the door.

"Hey!" At the sound of Aurora's voice, we all whirl.

"What is it, Pumpkin?" Logan's voice is filled with concern as he crouches, and she immediately runs into his arms.

"You didn't say bye!"

"I'm sorry, boo."

Burying her face in his shoulder, she wraps her tiny arms around his neck, squeezing tightly. After a moment, she stretches out an arm, making grabby hands. "Gayson. Ro."

Despite the nonsense that has been this entire ordeal, it is an incredibly sweet moment, the three of them blocking the entire hallway as they crowd in for a hug. Aurora mastered the art of wrapping them around her finger in less than a week. The girl deserves an award. They are absolute suckers for her.

Eventually, she wiggles to get down, before skipping away. "Bye, Gayson. Bye, Lo. Bye, Ro." Reaching the door to her classroom, she waves, and just before she disappears, she tacks on, "Bye, Mommy."

Well, better an afterthought than completely forgotten, right?

"Can we please go now?" I grouse.

"Awww." Logan fake pouts at me as he drapes his arm over my shoulder, and we walk out of the daycare. "Someone's just salty because they were nearly forgotten."

"I am not."

He gives me a knowing look, and I *accidentally* jam my elbow in his ribs.

Outside, I take a deep breath, feeling the weight lift from my shoulders. "She's going to be just fine," I say, more to myself than anyone else.

Grayson moves to my other side, Royce at my back. "She's got this," he assures. "Besides, if anyone gives her any hassle, we'll soon sort them out."

That's not the ringing endorsement he thinks it is.

RILEY

CHAPTER FORTY-THREE

"*Oh my god!*" I clap a hand over my mouth to hide the hysterical laugh threatening to burst free as I close the front door behind me after spending the afternoon studying in the library. "What did you let her do to you?"

"We're playing dress up, Mommy." My daughter stares at me with the sweetest smile, wearing a princess dress Logan undoubtedly bought for her. She looks cute, but that's not what has me frozen in the doorway to the living room.

It's the six-foot-three dark-haired behemoth with cherry red lips, matching rosy cheeks, and bright blue glittery eyeshadow that sweeps from his lashes all the way to his eyebrows. On the plus side, at least the color matches his eyes. However, he also looks completely and utterly ridiculous.

Perhaps it's the tattoos.

The best part is the scowl on his lips and his crossed arms. Sitting in a child-sized chair for my daughter, Royce was voluntarily allowing her to brutalize his face even though he clearly hated every second of it.

"Blame Logan! He's been telling her all week she can have a princess tea party."

"And you were the idiot who caved and threw one for her?" I'm teasing and laughing, but I can't get over how incredibly sweet it is of him.

This past week has been heaven—going to class, collecting Aurora from daycare, cooking dinner with Logan, and cuddling on the sofa before crawling into bed with the guys. Without the threat of Lydia or Bertram hanging over my head, I've gotten so much studying done. I still have a ways to go, but if the rest of the semester is like this, I should be able to pull my grades back up.

"Well, you've never looked better." It takes every ounce of my self-control to maintain a straight face, but the second Royce's gaze cuts to mine, those astute blue eyes narrowing, I howl with laughter. "Please let me take a picture." I'm already pulling the phone from my pocket.

I mean, if this isn't a prime example of what a sucker Royce is for my little girl, I don't know what is. I swear, all she has to do is give him those puppy dog eyes of hers and pout, and he does whatever she wants. Aurora isn't the slightest bit intimidated by his large size or tats.

"Don't even think about it, James," Royce growls, a thread of promise behind his words that sends shivers skating along my spine.

"Just one." As soon as the sound of the photo being taken penetrates, he shoots out of his chair and lunges for me.

I squeal, dropping the phone as he grabs me around the waist. We crash to the couch, him twisting at the last minute so he's beneath me.

"No!" I squeal, writhing as his fingers tickle my ribs.

"Tickle party!" Aurora yells before diving on top of me, adding her fingers to the mix.

"That's it, Aurora. Tickle Mommy."

"No! No! Please." Tears stream down my face, and I can

barely get the words out between heaving breaths and bursts of laughter.

"Aurora," I attempt to chastise between gasping breaths. "There will be no dessert after dinner if you don't stop."

"Don't worry, sweetheart." Royce winks conspiratorially at my daughter. "I'll make sure you get dessert."

"Royce!" I squeal, twisting against him. The two of them attack me until I wheeze out, "Stop. Please. I surrender. I surrender!"

Royce falls still, Aurora following. "I dunno, Aurora, what do you think? Do we accept Mommy's surrender?"

"You can go get a bar of chocolate from the sweetie tin if you do."

"Bribing your daughter?" Royce tuts in my ear, causing me to shiver for an entirely different reason.

"Okay. We accept your surrender, Mommy," Aurora says brightly. "Can I have my chocolate now?"

I huff out a laugh, shaking my head. "Yeah, okay. You know where it is; go get it."

She's racing from the room before I've even finished speaking.

"That was mean." I smack Royce on the arm, but he just laughs.

"And you taking photos of me in pain, wasn't?"

I twist so we're chest to chest. "You look like you fought with a clown, and he won."

Royce groans, his head falling back against the armrest. "That bad?"

"Have you looked in a mirror?"

"God, no. I planned to jump straight into the shower as soon as she finished. I didn't realize what time it was."

"Thank you for playing dress up with her."

Lifting his head, there's a softness in his gaze now. "You

need to stop thanking us for spending time with her. We all love her; we love spending time with her. She's exactly what each of us needed." His fingers trail down my temple, brushing a strand of hair from my face as he stares at me with so much openness that it's hard to believe this is the same closed-off, sharp-edged man I accidentally crashed into on campus that first day. "This house had gotten so quiet and bogged down with all our issues. Logan's been the light that keeps Gray and I from drowning ourselves in misery, but I know carrying that task sometimes weighs on him. It's an unfair burden for us to place on his shoulders. But Aurora emits that light so effortlessly. Having her here puts everything into perspective." He squeezes my waist. "Having you both here feels *right*."

Leaning in, I press my lips to his, his sweet words making it easy to ignore the fact his face practically shimmers from so much blusher. One of his large, calloused palms slides to the back of my head, holding me firm as his tongue slides along the seam of my lips before dipping inside.

"Eww!" A voice interrupts, and Royce and I jolt apart, heads turning to where Aurora is standing in the doorway, nose adorably scrunched as she stares at us. *Damn, I'd completely forgotten she was here. That's what happens when I get sucked into one of these guys' orbit. The entire world ceases to exist.* "That's gross."

I huff out a breath of laughter as I move to sit upright, Royce following. "You won't think so one day."

"No, Mommy," my three-year-old daughter says with all the seriousness in the world. "I'm always going to think that."

Royce points a stern finger at her, which does not have the impact he thinks it does, considering he looks like a drag queen. "Even if you change your mind, you're not allowed to kiss any boys until you're forty."

With more attitude than such a small body should be able

to contain, Aurora crosses her arms over her chest and cocks her hips. Where the hell did she even learn that move? "I'm *never* changing my mind. Boys are icky."

Swallowing my laughter, I climb to my feet. "You ready to watch Logan on the TV tonight? Then Mommy's gotta go to work, but Grayson will tuck you into bed later."

Yup, I'm going back to Lux tonight. I was there earlier in the week for rehearsals, but tonight is my first official shift back—much to Grayson's disapproval. I need this, though. As much as I appreciate everything the guys have done, I still need to maintain my independence. More than that, I *enjoy* working at Lux. Especially now that my bestie is in charge and sleazy Ben hasn't been heard from since Royce ran him out of town.

Aurora nods enthusiastically, bouncing on the balls of her feet as she claps her hands. "Yes! But why can't we go see him play?" She pouts, and it's so freaking adorable. Royce must think so, too, as his hand comes up to cover his mouth as he coughs to disguise his smirk.

A smirk that quickly turns into a scowl of disgust when he notices his fingers are stained red from all the gunk on his face.

Lifting Aurora and placing her on my hip, I explain, "Because he's not playing his game here, baby." Even though he's only playing at a stadium an hour away, none of us is ready to attend a live game just yet. While I wish we could be there to cheer him on in person, I believe he'll be able to better focus on the game if he knows we're at home and safe. If we were in the stands, he'd constantly worry that we've disappeared again. I hate that that fear has been instilled in him. "He'll be home by the time you wake up tomorrow, and when the team makes it to the Frozen Four, we'll go see him play."

While it might not be the championship game, tonight's game is still important. A conference tournament that Logan explained, if they win, guarantees them a spot at regionals and potentially competing for a national championship. Although, from what I gather, they are at the top of their group. So, even if they lose tonight, they will likely be selected to play at the regional level. It's all too complicated for me; I just want him to win.

My precocious daughter purses her lips as she chews over my words before definitively nodding in acquiescence. "Okay. But can we call him now?"

"We did promise him we'd call. Do you wanna put your jersey on so we can show him?"

Her eyes blaze with excitement as she squirms for me to put her down before racing from the room.

"No running up the stairs!" I call after her. The rapid thump of her feet barely slows, and Royce and I chuckle as we share a look.

"You're still sure about returning to work tonight?" he asks, watching me closely.

"I am. I'm excited to get back on the stage. I've missed dancing."

Crossing the room to me, his hand slides up my arm and across my shoulder before cupping my neck. "You know you can dance any time you want? One of us will take you to the dance studio." Despite Bertram still being unconscious in a hospital bed, they've all shown an inability to let me go anywhere alone, and poor Ms. Everly gets hounded by all of them, demanding updates every day.

"I know. Th—"

A growl cuts me off. "Do *not* thank me. In fact, I'm banning those words from this house." I chuckle. "Instead of a swear jar, perhaps we should make you put a dollar in a jar every time you say thank you for something you shouldn't be thanking us for."

"In that case, I definitely need to go back to work," I tease, patting one of his rigid pecs.

The thundering of what sounds like a herd of elephants trampling down the stairs precedes my daughter skidding back into the room. "Ready!" she declares. She has thrown the black and gold Huskies jersey over the princess dress she was wearing before. I press my lips together to smother my laugh. My daughter has a very interesting fashion sense; however, I can't deny that she makes the whole ensemble work for her.

"Alright, let's go into the kitchen to call him." Using my hands, I usher her from the room. "Meanwhile, Princess Royce can grab a shower."

"I heard that!"

I glance back at him over my shoulder, smirking. "You were supposed to, *Princess*."

Eyes flaring, his words chase me out of the room. "You're going to pay for that one later, Babydoll."

God, I fucking hope so.

⸻

"I don't want you going back to that club," Grayson grumbles in his irritating, frustrated tone.

"Oh, you don't? Huh, why didn't you say something earlier?" My voice is thick with sarcasm, which he doesn't appreciate as he glowers at me. He's only made his opinion clear *every day* since I announced I was going back.

Rolling my eyes at his infuriating alphaness, I drawl, "Ben hasn't been seen since Royce ran him off, and I'm excited to work with Tara and see the other girls. I've missed them." I pin him with a look. "I *want* to go back."

That doesn't appease him, so I merely move on. It's a point

of contention that neither of us will yield on. Whatever. He'll get over it—he has no other choice because I am not quitting my job. Not when I'm finally rid of Ben, and I can actually enjoy it without stressing.

Instead, I direct the focus back to Aurora, who Grayson is looking after tonight. "She'll probably pass out as soon as we leave," I tell him. "She's already in her jammies and brushed her teeth, so you just need to put her in bed. She'll demand that you read her at least three bedtime stories, but just read her the one. It's already past her bedtime." I worry my bottom lip. I don't know why I'm feeling so anxious. "She fell asleep during the game, but don't let her fool you into thinking that means she can stay up. It's already *way* past her bedtime."

"You're talking like I haven't put her to bed before or like I wasn't sitting beside you on the couch all evening. It was *my* lap she fell asleep in," Grayson grumbles. He's looking at me like I've grown a third eye on my forehead. Hell, maybe I have.

"Right." I chew on my bottom lip, trying to think if I've forgotten anything, until a gentle squeeze of my shoulder snaps me back into the room.

"We'll be fine," he rumbles, seemingly irritated at my over-bearingness. However, his shoulders marginally relax when his eyes meet mine, and a gentleness softens his gaze. "I promise she's safe with me."

I blow out a breath, holding his piercing stare. "I know. I'm just nervous. It was last Friday..."

"I know," he says, giving me another squeeze. "My dad is still in hospital. Everything is fine. Go shake that ass." His nose scrunches. "On second thought..."

He begins to drag me in against him, the jesting breaking the tension as I wriggle free.

"We're going to be late," Royce informs us as he helps me

into my coat before ushering me out the door. "She'll probably sleep the entire time we're gone," Royce says reassuringly as we make the short trip to Lux. "She's safe with Grayson."

"I know. I know she is." I blow out a breath. "I'm sure it will get easier with time." Somehow, it never feels so challenging to drop her off at daycare or to leave her with one of the guys during the day. It was dark out when my mother abandoned her in a parking lot, selling her just to get back at me and her husband. It was dark when Bertram frog-marched us out of the hockey stadium. It was dark when I pushed her through a broken window to avoid the flames licking up the walls.

Bad things happen in the dark.

I don't even realize I'm biting my nails until Royce reaches across and encapsulates my hand in his, holding it hostage for the remainder of the journey.

"You're back!" Tara squeals when I walk into Lux. I don't have a chance to respond before she's strangling me to death in a fierce hug. "It's so good to see you, mama." My arms come up, returning her hug. It's damn good to see her too. What with being the manager and all now, she wasn't at rehearsals on Tuesday, and with everything going on with Aurora these last few weeks, we haven't done more than exchange a few texts. We did, however, catch up for a quick coffee earlier in the week when I filled her in on everything that happened last weekend and confirmed I was still good to start back tonight.

"How's the little one?"

"She's great. Absolutely *loves* all the attention from these guys." I thumb Royce, making Tara smirk.

Wagging her eyebrows, she teases, "She's got good taste." I snort while Royce shakes his head. Turning so she can link her arm through mine, Tara points toward an unoccupied table. "I have a table reserved for your Rottweiler with a perfect view of the stage because I'm nice like that. Does he need a treat or anything before we leave him?"

"Har har." Royce narrows his eyes on her in fake warning before he stalks off to take his seat.

"Remember not to pee on the furniture," she calls after him before dissolving into a fit of giggles.

"Having fun there?" I tease, but I'm grinning at her antics. *Damn, I've missed her.*

"Soooo much fun, you have no idea."

We walk arm in arm across the club floor and into the back hallway. "How have things been here? Not regretting accepting the manager position yet?"

She shakes her head. "It's been great so far. I still haven't met the new owner, but he seems happy enough for me to do whatever I think is best."

"Well, that's handy." I glance her way out of the corner of my eye before daring to broach the subject. "What about Dax? Have you seen him recently?"

I hadn't bothered to leave out his role in getting Aurora back when we'd talked earlier in the week. I'm not sure how exactly she feels toward him, but I thought she should know that despite his reputation and whatever he'd done to her in the past, he had been instrumental in rescuing Aurora.

Royce mentioned that he'd left town shortly after the night of the fire, and I have no idea how long he'll be gone or if he'll be coming back. I know he's got his club in Springview, but other than the occasional drop-in to The Depot, I don't know if he'll be back in Halston any time soon.

Growing somber, she shakes her head. "Nope. He left town as quickly as he arrived, unsurprisingly without saying a word to me."

"I'm sorry," I say, nudging her shoulder in support.

She shrugs. "Whatever. I'm used to it by now. It just sucks

when he stops by. It's like, I manage to convince myself I've moved on, and I'm over him, and then *bam*, he shows up. It all becomes a harsh reminder that I'm nowhere close to being over him." Her sigh is heavy. "I don't know if I ever will be."

I wrap her in a brief hug. "Good thing there's plenty of eye candy to drool over at The Depot in the meantime."

Smiling now, she agrees, "True dat."

RILEY

CHAPTER FORTY-FOUR

Congratulations! Another step closer to the Frozen Four! You out celebrating with the team?

Thanks, Shortcake. Yup, just grabbing a beer with some of the guys.

He follows his text with a photo of him winking at the camera, with some of his teammates in the background.

Wish I was at home with you, though. I missed tucking Aurora into bed tonight. Grayson, the fucker, sent me photos to make me jealous. You should withhold sex from him as punishment.

ME

I'll think about it

"Wha—"

I nearly drop my phone as warm lips swallow my scream. Instantly recognizing that possessive, demanding touch as Royce's, I groan into his mouth. His hands are all over me as he presses me into the brick wall as the fire exit door I'd just walked through clatters shut. We are out in the open, but I was one of the last girls to leave the club, and if anyone else walked out now, the open door would obscure us until they were out of sight.

"Fuck, James. I'd forgotten how fucking *intoxicating* you are on that stage." Hips pressed against mine, I can feel the hard length of him against my stomach. "I've had to endure this damn thing for the last four hours."

Despite myself, I laugh into his mouth, making him growl. "You think this is funny?" His large hand slides into my hair, pulling on the strands until I expose my neck for him to trail tantalizing kisses along. "I want to know what you're going to do about it?"

I moan because, *holy fuck*, I love when he talks to me like this. Love how much he needs me.

Wriggling my hand between us, I place my palm over his crotch. Wetness floods my panties as I feel him pulse beneath my touch. "This." My voice is thick and raspy as I rub my hand over his erection before sliding deeper to cup his balls. His breath hitches, and it turns me on to see how affected he is.

"That's a start," he grinds.

Popping the button of his jeans, I slide my hand beneath the waistband of his boxers. His cock is warm and hard in my hand as I fist him with slow, teasing strokes.

"What about this?"

"Better." His breathing is labored as I work him over, his hips thrusting in time to my steady tugs. "Fuck, Riley. It's crazy what you do to me."

His breath is an aphrodisiac as it dances across my heated skin. Goosebumps pebble in its wake, a shiver running down my spine when he sucks on the sensitive spot beneath my ear.

"So sexy. So fucking hot."

His hips rock, his hands setting me ablaze as they roam my body. God, why are we wearing clothes? I'm heating up. Melting. I'm a frickin' fire hazard.

I no longer give a shit about who sees us as I spin us around. Royce smirks at me as his back hits the wall, but it quickly morphs into an agonized groan when I sink to my knees.

"*Fuck.* Such a dirty little whore on your knees for me in the back of an alley." The blazing in his half-lidded eyes makes every word out of his mouth irresistible. I have to clench my thighs together as I fumble to pull down his jeans and boxers. His thick, silky cock springs free, the piercing at the tip taunting me.

Wrapping my hand around the base, I lick along the throbbing purple vein before wrapping my lips around the tip. My tongue swipes over the bead of precum, and I smirk to myself when Royce hisses.

"Yes, Babydoll. Swallow my cock."

I don't immediately do as he says, choosing to toy with him some more as I fist the base while slowly running my lips and tongue over every warm, hard inch of him.

One of his hands comes to the back of my head, tenderly stroking at my hair. However, his touches become rougher and more demanding as he loses himself to the chase.

"Jesus Christ, Riley. I need to fuck your face."

I can't make out his expression in the dim light of the alley. He probably can't see mine either, so I pop my mouth off him, and in a voice that sounds nothing like mine, I taunt, "So fuck my face."

He makes a pained sound before his hand applies enough pressure to the back of my head to hold me down on his dick as he thrusts his hips, fucking in and out of my mouth. All I can do is dig my fingers into his ass and hold on for the ride. Saliva dribbles out of the corner of my mouth, mixing with the tears streaming down my face, and I'm so unbelievably turned on by the dirtiness of what we're doing that I shove my hand in my panties and begin rubbing at my clit until bright lights dance across the backs of my eyes.

"Shit. Fuck. I'm going to come," he warns a split second before warm seed fills my mouth and spills down my chin. Before I have the chance to swallow, I'm hauled to my feet in a daze, and Royce slams his lips over mine. His tongue pushes its way into my mouth, and he groans as he swirls his ejaculate around our mouths.

His hand shoves into my panties, and I moan as he sinks two thick fingers into my wet heat.

"Swallow," he orders as he licks across my chin, soaking up what spilled as he roughly finger fucks me. My ragged breaths intertwine with his, and it takes mere seconds for him to bring me to the edge. "Come for me, Ry. I want to lick you off my fingers so I can taste both of us on my tongue."

Well, Jesus, when he says it like that.

I'm a goner, my release flooding his fingers as he rubs at my clit and leaves me unable to stand on my own two feet. He carefully maneuvers us so I can sag against the wall, keeping one arm around me for support as he brings the one he had in my panties to his mouth.

Eyes closed, his features are smoothed in sheer bliss as he sucks his fingers between his lips and hums. Even when he opens them to look at me, his eyes are darkened with lust, pupils blown.

"Fuck, yeah. Never listen to a word Grayson says. Dude's an idiot. You should *absolutely* keep working here so we can do this after every shift."

And now I'm standing outside of my place of work, cheeks red from an orgasm and laughing my head off.

Royce watches me with a quirk of his lips and an endearing look in his gaze before he leans in and presses a quick kiss to my lips. "You're beautiful when you laugh." My hand fists in the front of his shirt, keeping him close as I deepen the kiss.

I keep it short, and as I pull away, I murmur, "I love you."

Wrapping me in a bear hug, he brings his face to my ear. "Love you too, sweetheart. Ready to go home?"

He links his fingers through mine when I nod, and hand in hand, we head for his car.

RILEY

CHAPTER FORTY-FIVE

"You're doing so good, sweetie!" I wave when Aurora glances my way.

Ava and I sit on the cold metal bleachers, bundled up in our coats and scarves, as we watch our kids on the ice. We introduced Aurora and Isabella a couple of weeks ago, and they've been inseparable ever since. They both play on the Hot Shot Huskies together, and they've also begun dance lessons. The girls also demand play dates if they go more than a day without seeing one another. They're besties, and it's so adorable to watch.

It means I see a lot more of Ava, and I've really enjoyed having that girl time and, more importantly, having *mom* time. I've never been friends with someone else who has a kid, and it is unbelievably therapeutic to have someone who gets it—the juggling, the challenges, the highs and the lows. I may no longer be doing this alone, but that doesn't mean raising a kid is easy.

"Mommy!" Aurora calls.

"I see you, baby. Well done!" I give her the thumbs up before she turns away, focusing on whatever new move Logan just taught her. She wobbles in her tiny skates and oversized helmet but manages to keep her balance. Isabella, who's a bit older and more confident, skates circles around her.

Just thinking his name has my gaze sliding his way. Logan looks every bit the hockey coach in his jeans and skates, guiding them both with patience and enthusiasm. He's got a knack for this, for teaching and making it fun.

"Look at Aurora go," I say, my voice filled with pride as she manages to skate a few feet without falling. "She's loving this."

Ava chuckles. "Isabella's been talking about it non-stop. I think we have a couple of future hockey stars on our hands."

We laugh, but my eyes never stray far from Aurora. Now that we've all settled into a comfortable routine, we've brought Aurora to the rink as often as we could these past few weeks. She's taken to it like a duck to water, always eager to lace up her skates and glide across the ice. At home, she cheers for Logan during the Huskies' games, her little voice echoing through the living room. Unfortunately, since the team has reached regionals, all their games have been away, but if they win the semifinals next week, we've promised her we'll go to the championship.

Not only would Aurora love that, but so would Logan. Having us all standing rinkside cheering him on. My heart swells with pride and anticipation as I imagine us all there. Logan killing it on the ice. The Huskies taking home the trophy. My gaze slides to Logan, who's now showing the older kids how to execute a perfect slapshot. He looks effortlessly handsome, his jeans hugging his frame just right, and his movements on the ice are fluid and powerful. There's something about how he commands the rink, a natural authority that's simultaneously attractive and reassuring.

My eyes follow him as he skates back to Aurora, kneeling to her level and demonstrating a simple skating drill. She watches him intently, her little face scrunched in concentration. He places his hands gently on her shoulders, guiding her movements, and she beams up at him, trusting and eager to learn.

"He's so good with her," Ava comments, nudging me with her elbow. "It's like he was made for this."

A warm feeling spreads through me as I watch them. "He really is. They all are. The way they all pay attention to her, make her feel special... it's incredible."

Aurora tries the drill again; this time, she gets it right. She squeals with delight, and I find myself cheering alongside her. Logan's face lights up with a proud smile, and he gives her a high five. My heart melts a little more each time I see them together. The way he interacts with her so effortlessly makes it seem like he's always known how to be this wonderful with kids.

Ava chats about the dance studio, and I tell her about my class load, but even as we discuss mundane things, my eyes keep drifting back to Logan and Aurora. Logan looks up and catches my eye, giving me a wink that sends a flutter through my stomach. I smile back, feeling the warmth of his gaze even from across the rink.

Life has been pretty perfect these past few weeks. Bertram is still in the hospital, although Grayson got a call today to say they were taking him off the intubation. I'm not sure what exactly it will mean for us if he starts to heal. I'd honestly been hoping he'd just die or have a cardiac arrest when they tried to remove the tube from his throat. Unfortunately, it seems I'm not that lucky. However, we have time to figure it out.

Otherwise, I've been happy. Blissfully so.

Yeah, there are still kinks to work out. Aurora has taken over my room, meaning I bedhop most nights after she falls asleep. The four of us struggle to fit in one bed comfortably, except for the odd night when we all pass out. Then, I usually sleep with two of the guys and switch over the next night. But for the most part, we've settled into a comfortable routine that suits us.

Royce refuses to let anyone but him escort me to Lux for my shifts, and Logan and Grayson tend to take turns staying home with Aurora while the other attends Royce's fights with me. Grayson is managing to balance work and class, and is back to enjoying his CEO role at Van Doren Holdings now that his father is not constantly undermining him. As for me? My grades have been steadily improving, and I'm once again loving being in a learning environment.

"Mommy, did you see me!" Aurora shouts as she clomps off the ice.

She tries to run toward me, but Logan loops an arm around her waist, nearly lifting her off the floor. "Hold on there, Pumpkin. Let's get those skates off you before you take someone's eye out."

She giggles but drops to the bench and begins talking animatedly to Isabella as if they haven't spent the last hour on the ice together. Logan crouches to help her out of her skates, and Ava moves to do the same with Isabella.

"Ready to go home?" Logan asks a short while later, once he's said goodbye to the other kids and parents, and we're the only ones left in the rink.

Aurora yawns, tuckered out after her busy day. She's already bundled in Logan's arms, her head resting against his chest as she nods.

Throwing his bag containing his and Aurora's brand new skates over his shoulder, he takes my hand, and together we walk out to his car.

It's perfect. Him. Them. This life we have.

Everything.

"There we go," I say later that night as I tuck the covers around Aurora. "Snug as a bug in a rug." I give her my best attempt at a smile, but damn, I'm tired.

Bath and bedtime were not the smoothest tonight. After crashing when we got home from the ice rink, Aurora found a second wind and threw a tantrum when I mentioned it was bathtime. Even Logan couldn't sweet-talk her into the tub. It took me, him, and Royce promising her everything under the sun before she finally relented. Lucky for Grayson, he is working late in the office tonight, so he missed out on all the mayhem.

"Mommy!" Aurora suddenly cries, sitting upright. "Hank!"

"Where is he?" I ask, exasperated, as I gather her scattered clothes off the floor. She's talking about the stuffed husky toy Logan gave to her. She's carried it with her everywhere ever since.

"I don't know."

I pinch the bridge of my nose.

"Well, when do you last remember seeing him?"

Pouting, she gives me a helpless shrug.

"You had him when you got home from daycare," I tell her, remembering him being strangled in the crook of her arm when she walked in with Grayson earlier. "Did you take him skating?"

"Oh!" I take that as a yes.

"You probably left him in the car. I'll go get him, you stay here. I mean it, Aurora. Do not move from that bed."

With a stern look, I leave her in bed, pulling the door over most of the way before hurrying down the stairs and snatching Logan's keys from the hall table. On my way past, I heard the water running in the bathroom, so he's probably showering. Royce retreated to the solitude of his bedroom when Aurora dictated she wanted me to read her bedtime story tonight.

Light spills out from the hall when I open the front door, leaving it wide as I hurry down the steps toward the SUV parked at the curb. Pressing the clicker, the headlights flash, and the car makes that *click* noise that indicates it's unlocked.

I'm not paying attention to my surroundings as I yank open the back door and begin feeling around in the semi-darkness for the stuffed toy.

"Come on," I groan, not feeling it anywhere. "Where are you?"

I know she won't settle without him, and if she doesn't relax, then I won't sleep, and I really, *really* like sleep.

"Ha, gotcha!" I hold up the soft toy like it's my own personal Stanley cup. Clutching it firmly in one hand, I duck back out of the car. A chill runs down my spine, and I glance down the street. Lights are on in the neighboring houses, but otherwise, it's empty.

Shaking off whatever that was, I gently close the car door, not wanting to slam it at this late hour. As I turn toward the house, a shadowy figure appears before me. My heart leaps into my throat as I stumble back against the side of the car.

My hand comes up to minimize the glare of the lights from the house, which casts the man's form in shadow. I know, though. I know before I can disseminate his features that it's *him*.

Bertram.

Or what's left of him.

The fire has ravaged his once-imposing figure, leaving behind a grotesque version of the man he used to be. His skin is mottled and uneven, patches of raw, red flesh standing out against the blackened, charred skin that covers most of his face and hands. The burns have twisted his features, his lips pulled tight in a permanent sneer, his nose half-melted, and one eye almost swollen shut. The sight of him is nightmarish, and it takes everything in me not to recoil in horror.

But it's his voice that genuinely chills me. When he speaks, it's nothing like the cold, calculated tones I remember. The fire has stolen that from him, too, leaving behind a rasping, guttural sound that grates against my ears. It's as if each word is being dragged out of him, scraping against his raw throat, but the malice behind it is unmistakable. "Riley," he growls, the sound barely human, more of a hiss than a voice. "Did you truly think you could get away from me? That I'd let you go."

The words slither through the darkness, wrapping around me like a vice. The sheer venom in them paralyzes me. Despite his injuries, despite the burns that have left him a disfigured shadow of himself, Bertram is still terrifying. Still a force to be reckoned with. His eyes, one swollen and bloodshot, the other a dull, glazed-over orb, bore into mine with a malevolent intensity that makes my skin crawl.

"You think you can build a new life without me?"

He moves closer, and I can see how the burns have affected him. His movements are stiff, jerky, as if each step causes him pain, but the determination in his eyes is undiminished. His clothes hang off him in tattered, singed rags, clinging to his ravaged body, and the smell—God, the smell—hits me like a physical blow. The acrid stench of burnt flesh, mixed with the antiseptic tang of hospital air, turns my stomach.

I step backward, my spine hitting the side of the car, but he lunges forward. "If I can't have you, then no one can!" The light from a nearby streetlamp reflects off the sharp edge of a blade. I dodge instinctively, chucking the husky at him in a moment of panic.

The blade sails past my ear and connects with the glass behind me, the car window shattering. I duck under his arm, but his hand—raw, blistered, and trembling—catches my wrist. "You did this to me," he rasps, the sound more of a strangled wheeze now.

I move on autopilot, noticing where his thumb is and grabbing it with my other hand, twisting. He curses, but I'm already rotating my arm, exactly as Xander showed us. With a final pull, I'm free.

But I'm not yet out of danger.

I stumble back a step, whirling toward the front door. The second my back is turned, he's on me. I cry out as my head is wrenched backward, hair ripping from my scalp as he yanks on it. "You're not going anywhere," he snarls.

I realize I must have dropped the car keys at some point, and I'm utterly helpless as I'm dragged backward. The cool edge of the blade touches my throat, and blinding terror renders me immobile. I couldn't scream even if I wanted to.

"This is the end for you, Riley," he growls.

I can't wrench my gaze away from the taunting warmth of the hall light. I can see Aurora's coat hanging on the peg next to mine. Her shoes set neatly by the door and looking hilariously small beside Logan's sneakers.

Home.

I reach out a hand, wanting to feel its warm comfort one more time, but it's just beyond my grasp. Out of reach. Leaving me in the cold.

Bertram digs the knife into the soft flesh of my throat, and a tear rolls down my cheek, knowing this is it.

There's a sharp stab of pain...

... Before I'm knocked forward. Bertram's presence at my back disappears, replaced with the thud of fists and pained grunts.

I stumble on my feet before I find my balance, whirling in time to see Grayson drive his fist into his father's face.

"You twisted fuck!" he screams into Bertram's face. "You think you can take her from me! She's not yours." Another gut-wrenching punch. "She never was." Bertram's head whips to the side, blood trickling from his mouth. "She's mine." His nose shatters. "Ours."

Punch after punch after punch.

Grayson lets out every single one of his pent-up emotions.

Everything I imagine he's kept bottled up for years. For a lifetime.

All of it comes pouring out while I watch on, shocked, and some part of me understands that he needs this—this catharsis.

"What the hell—" Logan comes barreling out of the house in sweats and a t-shirt, his feet bare. He strides toward Grayson, but I reach out and stop him.

"Don't."

"He can't do this here." His voice is strained as he vacillates between interfering and letting Grayson go to town on his shithead father. He must decide to give him another moment as he pulls out his phone instead, bringing it to his ear. A moment later, he says, "Yeah, you might wanna come out here."

Royce's broad frame darkens the doorway a moment later.

"Jesus Christ, he's going to kill him." He stalks over to Grayson, and this time, I don't interfere as he grabs him by the back of his shirt and drags him off his unconscious father. "That's enough," he hisses, voice low as he scans the street.

Grayson grunts and shakes him off but makes no move to attack his father. Instead, he spins toward me, stalking across the short distance between us until his hands cup my face, his gaze raking over every inch of it before dropping to my neck.

His gaze turns molten as his nostrils flare, his thumb moving to scoop up the droplet of blood before sucking it into his mouth.

My hands slide up his chest, resting over his thundering heart. "I'm fine," I assure him.

"Aurora?"

"She's in the house, hopefully asleep."

With a curt nod, he whirls on the guys. "And where the hell were you two while *he*—" he stabs a finger in Bertram's direction—"was attacking our girl?"

"We had no idea." Logan grimaces, chagrinned. "He's supposed to be in the hospital!"

Grayson shakes his head. "That's what I was coming to tell you. I just got a call from the hospital to tell me he'd absconded." Snarling, he turns away and begins pacing the sidewalk.

"Well, I don't think we'll be returning him," Royce drawls, sneering down at what remains of Bertram. Between the burns and Grayson's beating, he's unrecognizable.

"What do we do with him?" Logan asks, jutting his chin out toward Bertram.

"I'll call Dax. I'm sure he's got somewhere we can take him."

Royce makes his call, and a short while later, they have an unconscious Bertram bundled up in the back of his truck.

"How are we doing this, then?" Logan asks as we huddle around the back of the car.

"I'm staying here," I tell them. "Someone needs to stay with Aurora, and honestly, I don't want to know." I meet Grayson's gaze. "I'm not letting him steal any more of my happiness. Knowing he's gone is all I need to know."

He holds my stare before nodding—an understanding passing between us.

"Royce can come with me. Logan, you stay with the girls."

"What?!" Logan protests. "No way. I want my pound of flesh, too."

"All of you can go," I tell them, waving toward the truck. "We'll be fine. Our only threat is currently zip-tied and soon to leave the land of the living."

The three of them share a look, a silent communication going on between them. None of them look terribly happy about it, but ultimately, they all agree, and I watch the taillights of Royce's truck disappear into the distance before heading back into the house.

I shower quickly before pulling on Logan's sweats, Grayson's t-shirt, and Royce's hoodie and crawling into bed beside Aurora. I snuggle into her, breathing in her scent that is uniquely hers.

Burying my face in her neck, I smile because, finally, I'm free.

LOGAN

CHAPTER FORTY-SIX

Arms crossed over my chest, I lean against the tiled wall as I watch Bertram dangle from a chain hooked to the ceiling. It feels fitting that we've come full circle. That we're back in the same room we interrogated Lydia in.

Except, this time, our victim won't be leaving alive.

"He's waking up." Royce takes a step back from where he'd been standing sentinel over Bertram, Grayson pushing off the wall on the far side of the small room to stalk closer.

"About fucking time," he growls, like he's not the reason we've been waiting *hours* for his shitstain of a father to regain consciousness. Not that I can blame him.

I'm still fucking furious with myself for not realizing Short-cake was in trouble only *feet* from the house, and I had no fucking clue. I shouldn't have left her alone.

I can tell Royce is carrying the same guilt; the tightness in his shoulders and the flexing of his biceps let me know he's itching to take out all that guilt on the man, who is slowly rousing.

Bertram groans, and when his eyes finally flutter open, the three of us are standing shoulder-to-shoulder in front of him.

He's truly never looked worse, half charred, half beaten with skin literally sloughing off. It's a disgusting sight.

"What is this?" His words are slightly slurred, his voice raspier than it used to be. His bloodshot eyes scour the room, taking it in. "W-where am I?" Before finally lifting to where he's dangling from the ceiling. "W-what... Get me down!"

"Yeah, that won't be happening," I tell him.

He finally seems to realize *who* is standing in front of him. His gaze narrows on me, then turns wary when it slides to Royce before finally landing on his son.

"Grayson."

Contempt lines his cracked voice. It raises my hackles. Despite his dire situation, he doesn't seem to realize *he's* not the one in charge here. He should be cowering in fear. Begging for his life. How the fuck is this asshole even still conscious?!

"Dad."

Bertram's lip lifts in contempt. "If I'd known you were interested in my sloppy seconds, I'd have let you have a go with Lydia before I killed her."

Grayson's hands fist at his sides, but instead of acting on the violent impulse I know is riding him hard, he smirks arrogantly at his father. "This isn't about you, old man. And for the record, Riley was never yours. You *took* from her. But what she vehemently refused to give you, she gave willingly to me. To *us*. Because she's ours."

Grayson's chest expands with pride, and I silently clap to him for finally getting on board with Team U*s*.

"But thanks for taking care of our Lydia problem," Grayson continues.

His father merely grunts. "So what is your plan now?" the asshole drawls, still not fully grasping the situation. "We both know you haven't got it in you to kill your own father."

Grayson scoffs. "You're no father to me." Stepping forward,

he glares intently at Bertram. "I *know* what you did to my mother. The abuse. The bruises." His voice rises with each statement he directs at his father until he's shouting, "You're the reason she's dead!"

Unaffected by his son's accusations or the palpable rage billowing off him, Bertram snarls, "Your mother was weak. Weak-willed. Weak spirited. *Weak.*"

He doesn't get the chance to say anything more. Grayson drives his fist into his already beaten and burned face.

Despite the ache that's likely settled into his muscles from the earlier beating, Grayson pummels Bertram anew.

Royce and I stand back, knowing he needs this. Needs the closure. To burn off everything he's bottled up regarding his father.

By the time he's done, Grayson's knuckles are split and caked with blood, and his father sways listlessly from his manacles. His toes barely touch the floor, his body bowed forward. The chains are the only reason he's still standing.

His face is a bloody pulp, so swollen and charred that he resembles Lydia and David's corpses more than a human being.

Ass pressed against the far wall, Grayson is bent at the waist, his hands on his knees as he catches his breath.

Meanwhile, I step forward. Bertram's eyes, swollen and bloodshot, unfocused when they meet mine.

"Remember me?" There's no mistaking the blade of menace in my tone.

Missing a few teeth, and with his mouth likely filled with blood, he merely makes an indistinguishable noise in the back of his throat.

I take my time, cracking my knuckles as I stare him down. "You've had this coming from the moment I found out what you did to my girl. Even if you'd left her alone after you got out of prison, you'd still be right here, swinging from a chain and counting down the minutes until your death."

Then I drive my fist into his stomach, throwing my entire weight behind it. He doubles over—well, as much as his chains will allow—an agonized sound ripping from his throat as red-tinged spittle hangs from his mouth, swaying precariously before dropping to the blood-splattered tiles.

I go to do the same again when a hand on my shoulder pulls me up short. "Here," Royce grunts, shoving a baseball bat into my hands instead. "Riley will have all of our nuts if you damage your hands while giving this fucker what he deserves."

He's not wrong, even if it does feel good to use my fists. I never use my fists. Never get in fights or do anything that could potentially jeopardize my hockey career, yet the second I saw this sack of shit on our doorstep, I had no concern for my future, only that penance was paid.

That Riley got her justice.

That Grayson got his closure.

That we all got our vindication.

Twisting my hands around the handle, I give it a few test swings before slamming it into the side of Bertram's knee. He cries out. A noise that sounds like the tearing of ligaments makes me smile as I line up for another shot. "Oh yeah, that felt good."

I hit the same leg again. This time, there's a pop, his kneecap dislocating. When his leg is completely fucked up, I move on to the other one, doing the same to it.

I'm breathing heavily, and sweat dots my brow by the time I'm done, and Bertram is officially dangling by his manacled wrists, his legs completely fucking useless.

If only it were his dick.

Actually...

He's half-conscious when I shift my stance, lining the bat up before driving it directly between his legs and into his balls.

His strangled scream is music to my ears.

"Your turn, man." I toss the bat to Royce as I turn my back on the shitstain. I feel ten times lighter than I have in months. Like a weight has been lifted off my chest, and I can finally breathe again.

It feels fucking great.

"Gee, thanks. You two fuckers have left me so much to work with." Royce gestures in Bertram's direction. "The asshole is half dead already."

I shrug, not the least bit apologetic.

"Whatever," Royce grumbles, shaking his head. "I'm not interested in beating on him, anyway."

"You sure, man? 'Cause it feels pretty fucking epic." Arms out to the side, I spin in a circle with a manic grin. "I feel like I'm on top of the world."

"That's the adrenaline," Royce drawls.

"Nah, man, this is the sweet, sweet high of vengeance."

Dismissing me with a roll of his eyes, he turns to Gray. "Gray, you done?"

Still leaning against the wall, Gray's expression is shut down as he stares at his dad. "Yeah."

Royce searches his face before he nods. "You can step out—"

"No. I'm staying."

Royce doesn't ask if he's sure. He simply pulls the gun Dax gave him several weeks ago from the waistband of his jeans.

Flipping off the safety, he stalks over to Bertram, who puts up absolutely zero fight. I don't even know that he's aware of what's happening right now. If he realizes he's about to die.

With the muzzle pressed to his forehead, Royce doesn't say any last words as he pulls the trigger.

The sound bounces off the walls and vibrates down my

bones as Bertram's head snaps to the side before falling forward.

In the deafening silence of the aftermath, the three of us stand there, staring at the empty carcass dangling in front of us.

Good fucking riddance.

Hands shoved in my pockets, I glance at the others. "Well, I dunno about you guys, but I'm ready to get home to our girls. I think this calls for a celebratory breakfast."

Freshly showered and wearing only a pair of gray low-slung sweats, I silently enter Aurora's room and scoop a sleeping Riley into my arms.

"What time is it?" she mumbles sleepily, burying into me as I carry her out of the room.

"Early, still."

"Is everything…"

"Everything's perfect, Shortcake."

"It's over."

At the foot of the stairs leading to Grayson's room, I look down at her, finding both eyes open and intently fixed on mine.

"It's over. He's dead. Your mom is dead. You and Aurora are both safe. No one will get to either of you again. Not without going through all three of us first."

"Aurora?" she enquires when I begin ascending the stairs.

"She's sleeping still. We have a couple of hours until she wakes us."

It felt like it took forever for us to get back home. Dax offered to take care of the body, and we agreed since, like, what the fuck were we going to do with a dead body?! Then we had to strip out of all our clothes and hose ourselves down with ice-cold water before donning some shitty garb Dax managed to find last minute.

Frozen to the bone, we all went to shower as soon as we got home. Royce, the fucker, called dibs first on using our shared one, so I had to wait for his slow ass to finish before I could get in, then *finally* go see my Shortcake.

There's no way any of us would agree to be parted from her tonight, and since Grayson has the biggest room and, hence, the biggest bed, it made sense for us all to congregate in his room.

Which is exactly where the other two are when I walk in carrying Riley.

Her face lights up when she sees them before her lips part on a gasp. She's scrambling out of my arms before I've even fully set her on the bed.

"Grayson," she gasps, crawling between his legs to the head of the bed, where he's sitting with his back against the headboard.

"It looks worse than it is, Tempest. I'm fine," he assures her. Not that she listens as she lifts his hand, inspecting the bruises already beginning to bloom, and nicks along his knuckles with a frown tugging on her lips.

She gives his other hand the same thorough going-over before she lifts her face to his. A silent moment passes between them—a conversation without words.

Royce and I can be angry at what both of them had to endure. We can want vengeance for them, but Riley and Grayson are the only two who fully understand what it was like to be at Bertram's mercy—albeit in different ways.

His hands come up to cup her face, his thumbs brushing reverently over the apple of her cheeks. "I swear," he murmurs, seemingly in answer to something she silently asked. "This is our new beginning. A new life. Together. All of us."

One of his hands slides down to gently caress her neck, the

other threading through her loose strands of hair. "Now kiss me, 'cause, after tonight, the only thing I want is to feel your body against mine while we show you how *sweet* this new life of ours will be."

He doesn't give her the chance to move of her own volition as he uses his hold on her to drag her lips to his in a possessive yet hot-as-hell kiss. She moans into his mouth as she crawls into his lap, straddling him.

I suddenly understood why watching us that day in the treatment room was so painful. Riley's still fully dressed in the ridiculous outfit that looks as though it's a piece of clothing belonging to each of us, and my dick is already tenting my sweats. Another minute and there will be a wet patch for everyone to see just how fucking gone I am for this girl.

Not that I give two fucks if these guys see that. Hell, I don't give a shit if the rest of the world does. I'll gladly scream from the fucking rooftop for the entire universe to hear that I am head-over-heels, maddeningly, deeply, irrevocably in love with Riley James.

Unable to withstand another moment of not touching her, I stalk over to the bed and climb onto it behind her.

Breaking her kiss with Grayson, she looks at me over her shoulder. Those delectable swollen lips stretch into a smile. Needing to taste her, I duck my face to nip at her lower lip before sucking it into my mouth.

Her arm wraps around my neck, pulling me closer as she arches her back. Her ass grinds against my throbbing cock, and I nearly lose it right there and then.

I can't get enough of this girl. She's fucking everything.

"Riley," I groan.

"Need you," she moans, one hand draped over Grayson's shoulder while he lavishes her neck and collarbone with open-mouthed kisses.

Her gaze flicks to the side, and I realize Royce has moved to kneel beside me on the bed. "All of you."

Jesus, just when I think she can't get any more perfect.

I'm not the only one who thinks so, as Grayson voices his agreement while burying his face in her hair.

His hands have slid beneath her clothing, inching her hoodie up and over her head. Her top comes with it, leaving her naked from the waist up, tits on display, and her nipples screaming to be sucked.

Ducking his head, Grayson sucks one into his mouth while Royce twists the other between his thumb and forefinger.

Throwing her head back, my hands move to her hips, steadying her as she rubs herself on my cock.

"Such a wanton little slut for us, aren't you, Babydoll?" Royce purrs in a voice that is filled with sinful promise.

"Yes," she pants, even as a blush dusts the tops of her cheeks and blooms across her chest.

"Bet you're already soaked," Royce taunts. "So desperate to take all of us at once."

"Find out for yourself."

Sliding one hand from her hip, I push it beneath the waistband of the sweats she's wearing. Her heat has me god damn nearly combusting before I sink two fingers inside her.

"Fucking drenched," I confirm.

I steadily move my fingers in and out while she grinds against my hand. Between the three of us, we tease her to the brink of release before Royce's filthy words send her careening over the edge.

"You're going to come for each of us. Then you're going to come *on* all of us. So drench Logan's hand, James."

Fucking her with my hand, ensuring my fingers brush that sweet spot inside of her, she detonates, crying out as she comes all over me.

Grayson doesn't give her a second to catch her breath before he shoves her sweats down. He flips them so she's splayed on her back in the middle of the bed.

Her auburn hair fans out around her, and she looks like my every fantasy with her glittering eyes, swollen lips, and flushed chest.

Shoving her legs apart, he dives between her thighs, making her practically jolt off the bed as he licks and sucks his way along her slit.

"Hold her down," he barks, coming up for breath before diving back in.

Royce and I are on either side of her, and while he claims her mouth, I set to work tasting every inch of her skin.

Her hand fists the back of my head when I suck her nipple into my mouth, and it isn't long until she's murmuring "Oh God," on repeat before screaming out for a second time.

"You're doing so good for us, Ry. One more," Royce encourages.

She shakes her head. "Can't."

"Yes, you can. One more, then we'll give you what you want."

Flipping her over so she's on her stomach, Royce hauls her up by the hips. She sways on her knees, but he steadies her with a hand on her hip while he lines his cock up at her entrance. His piercing glints in the dim light of the room before he pushes his way inside.

She moans, back arched and lips parted as he fills her. The sound of skin slapping against skin fills the room, along with her sweet moans.

I know when Royce goes to stretch her ass as she gasps at the feel of his thumb pushing against her tight ring of muscle.

"Shh, baby, relax," I soothe, stroking a hand down her spine.

Releasing a held breath, she relaxes, and Royce wiggles his thumb all the way in.

"Oh," she gasps, before thrusting back against him.

"That feel good, baby?" I ask, chuckling at her blissed-out expression.

"So good. But I need more."

Royce chuckles. "So greedy."

"It gets me so fucking hard seeing how much you want us," I tell her.

"Yours." Her breathless claiming goes straight to my cock, and unable to hold back any longer, I reach into my sweats and fist myself.

Her pupils dilate as she watches me pump my cock.

"Damn fucking straight, you're ours," Grayson growls, appearing just as mesmerized with her as I am while he watches Royce coax her toward another orgasm. "Ours, always," he barks, lifting her face with a finger beneath her chin as he lowers his to hers. "And we'll always be yours."

With that, he slams his lips down on hers. She comes instantly. Cum is still leaking from Royce's cock when Grayson rips her way. "All of us. Inside you. Now."

He practically shoves her into my arms. "I want your ass first." *Possessive fucking asshole.*

"Is that what you want, baby?" I ask her.

"I don't care which of you goes first, so long as you hurry up about it," she snaps. Even doped up on orgasms, she's still impatient to have us all.

Grinning, I give her lips a quick peck before falling back on the mattress and bringing her with me. "Ride me," I tell her, steadying her hips with my hands as she reaches between us to grab my engorged cock, bringing it to her entrance before sliding down.

My head falls to the mattress as I groan. Her wet heat feels like silk against my skin as I thrust up into her, forgetting about everything else in the room as I become fully engrossed in all things Riley.

It's only when I feel her tighten around me that I snap my eyes open, not remembering when I closed them, to find Grayson looming behind her.

"It's just my fingers," he assures her, his voice surprisingly gentle.

"Oh, God," she groans a moment later. "That feels so good."

"Here." Royce tosses him a small bottle of lubricant. "Brought that in case we needed it."

Grayson pulls away, and a moment later, he's back. His hand on her spine pushes her down toward my chest, and I murmur, "Kiss me, Shortcake."

She doesn't hesitate, her tongue infiltrating my mouth in a sloppy, wanton kiss.

I feel it the moment Grayson breaches her walls. She stiffens against me, and I whisper words of encouragement which become increasingly strangled as I feel his cock slide against mine inside her, separated only by a thin barrier.

If I thought Riley was tight before, it's got nothing on how it feels now. My dick is in a vice grip, and I'm pretty sure if one of us so much as wriggles, I'm going to explode.

Grayson is cursing under his breath while I'm struggling just to breathe, and Riley's fingernails leave crescent moon marks on my chest.

"Oh my god," she whimpers. "I feel so full."

"But a good full, right?" I ask, needing the clarification.

"Uh-huh." She gives a shaky nod of her head, her eyes closed and her entire body trembling with the onslaught of ecstasy. "But I really, *really* need one of you to move."

It takes a few moments for the three of us to find a rhythm that works, but holy shit, once we do, it's like fucking nirvana up in here.

Sex with Riley is fan-fucking-tastic. But sex with Riley when it's all of us is out of this world.

I'm absolutely going to come in record time.

"I'm so close already," Riley moans, echoing my thoughts. "Royce."

"I'm here, Ry." He appears at my head a moment later, and it's the hottest fucking thing I've ever seen, watching him thread his metal dick into Riley's mouth so she's taking all three of us at once.

"That's it, Babydoll," he praises. "Look at you taking all of us. You were fucking made for this. For us."

She makes a noise of agreement around his thick cock, still somehow managing to bounce on my dick in tandem with Grayson's thrusts.

The entire scene is erotic.

"Fuck, I'm going to come," Grayson grunts. His face is scrunched as if he's fighting to delay the inevitable. I can't fucking blame him; I've been attempting to recall old hockey stats just to keep myself from coming. I'm not ready for this to end yet.

"You going to come, Riley?" Royce asks. He's now fucking her face relentlessly. Tears streaming down her cheeks as he holds her hair out of the way.

She mumbles what I seriously hope is a yes, and wedging a hand between us, I rub at her clit.

She tights around me a moment later. Royce's thrusts stutter, and Grayson curses vividly while colors I've never seen before dance across my vision before my balls draw up, and I come.

Panting and breathless, we collapse in a sweaty heap on the bed.

When I finally catch my breath, I say aloud, "Please tell me we can fit one more round in before Aurora wakes up."

40
29

RILEY

CHAPTER FORTY-SEVEN

Aurora is practically bouncing on my lap, her tiny body buzzing with excitement as she watches the Huskies Championship game with wide, sparkling eyes. The arena is electric, filled with the deafening roar of fans, but all I can focus on is her joy and absolute awe at finally seeing Logan play live again. She's been talking nonstop since we left the house this morning, her excitement growing with each mile we drove closer to the arena.

"Look, it's Lo! That's him, right, Mommy?" she asks for what must be the hundredth time, pointing eagerly toward the ice. Her voice is shrill with anticipation, making me smile every time.

"That's him, sweetie," I say, my heart swelling as I watch Logan skate across the rink. He looks so focused, so determined, every muscle in his body taut with concentration. The game is tied, and there's less than a minute on the clock. It's been a grueling match, with each team fighting with everything they have, but the Huskies have held their ground. They always do.

Beside me, Grayson is leaning forward, his elbows resting on his knees, his eyes locked on the game. He's as tense as I've ever seen him, his fingers curled into tight fists. Royce, on the other hand, sits back in his seat, exuding a calm confidence, but I can see the flicker of nerves in his eyes, the way he clenches his jaw every time the puck changes hands.

Logan secured tickets for Ava, Isabella, and Tara to join us. I'm pretty sure Tara's just here for the hot hockey men—and quite possibly the violence—but Isabella has become as avid a hockey fan as Aurora.

"The Huskie's goalie," Ava muses, leaning over to talk in my ear. "Who is he?"

"I think his name is Nico." I glance her way. "Why?"

She shakes her head. "Just asking."

"He's hot."

She scoffs. "Don't go getting any ideas, I've sworn off all men. I was only asking because he's doing an incredible job of stopping the pucks."

"Uh-huh," is my only response. I'll let her hold tight to that belief for now.

"Go, Lo! Go!" Aurora yells, drowning out any further conversation. Her little fists pump the air, her voice shrill as she cheers Logan on. She's been waiting for this moment for weeks. All those nights spent watching him play on TV, her tiny voice cheering him on even when he couldn't hear it. And now she's here, in the thick of it, watching her newfound hero in action. My heart aches with love for her, for how much she adores him.

How much she adores all of them.

And how much they dote on her.

Logan lit up like a firework on the Fourth of July when he skated onto the ice. His gaze instantly found us and zeroed in on the matching jerseys Aurora and I are wearing, the number seven standing loud and proud on our backs. Even Gray and Royce are wearing Huskie beanies in support.

The seconds tick down, and the tension in the arena is

palpable. I can feel it in the way Grayson's fist clenches and Royce's foot taps restlessly against the concrete floor.

And then, like a dream unfolding in slow motion, Logan takes the puck, weaving through defenders with a grace and agility that leaves the crowd breathless. Aurora is on her feet now, standing on my thighs as she grips the railing in front of us, her eyes glued to him.

"Go, Lo! Go, Lo!" she chants, her voice nearly drowned out by the thunderous roar of the crowd.

Logan moves in, his stick a blur as he dekes past the last defender. The goalie lunges, but it's too late. The puck sails past him and into the net with a satisfying thwack. The arena explodes with noise, the cheers so loud they rattle the seats. Aurora screams with pure, unfiltered joy, her little body bouncing up and down as she throws her arms around my neck.

I'm not even sure she fully understands what's happening; she's just caught up in the excitement.

"Did he do it, Mommy? Did he do it?"

"He did it, baby." I laugh, pulling her close, my heart so full that it might burst. "He did it."

Grayson and Royce are on their feet, their faces split with grins. Grayson lifts Aurora out of my arms, spinning her around as she squeals with delight. Royce pulls me into a hug, his laughter rich and deep in my ear.

The Huskies swarm Logan, their victory chants echoing through the arena as they pile on top of him in celebration. And there he is, at the center of it all, his eyes searching the crowd until they find us. He grins that familiar, crooked smile that melts my heart every time and raises his stick in a silent salute.

In this moment, everything feels perfect. All the struggles, all the heartache—it all led us here, to this—to a family, to love, to a happiness that I never dared to dream was possible.

Eventually, Logan breaks away from his team and skates

over to us. His hair is slick with sweat, and his helmet has been forgotten somewhere. Happiness oozes from his every pore, shining in his eyes beneath the bright stadium lights and evident in the brightest grin I've seen yet on him.

He stops in front of us, clapping a gloved hand against the plexiglass right in front of where Aurora and I are sitting. She hurries to stand on my knees, practically falling as she leans forward to press her hand to his.

"Careful there, sweetheart," Grayson chastises as he catches her, settling her on his hip so she can safely reach Logan's hand.

She giggles, staring up at Logan with something akin to hero worship. Her hand is so much smaller against his large, gloved one, and I take a mental snapshot, wanting to remember this moment for years to come.

His gaze is soft as it rests on hers before flicking to me.

"Congratulations," I mouth, knowing he won't be able to hear me over the chaos of celebration.

His lips hitch higher, and he glances pointedly down at his hand when Aurora removes her much smaller one. "Come on, Shortcake," he mouths. "Give me what I want."

Rolling my eyes, I cannot suppress my grin even if I tried as I press my hand to the glass. Logan smirks, winking at me before he skates to center ice when the announcer calls for the captain of the Huskies to come forward.

An award ceremony has been set up in the center of the rink, and the NCAA Championship trophy gleams under the bright lights as it's handed to him, and for a moment, everything seems to stand still.

Logan accepts the trophy, hoisting it high above his head, a look of fierce pride and accomplishment etched on his face. And then, just as if it were the most natural thing in the world, his eyes find mine. The connection between us feels electric, pulsing with the shared emotion of the moment. His gaze then shifts to Aurora, who is waving frantically at him, her joy infectious, and he smiles—a smile that's meant for us, for this family we've fought so hard to build.

As he passes the trophy to his teammates, the celebration intensifies. They pass it from player to player, each taking a moment to bask in the glory of the win. The arena buzzes with excitement as the photographers gather the team for the official championship photo. The team clusters together at center ice, the trophy front and center, as they pose for what will become a lasting memory of this victory.

Suddenly, I feel Grayson's hand on the small of my back, guiding me down the stairs toward the ice. Aurora, still bubbling with excitement, nearly drags Royce along as she runs ahead of us. The security at the gate steps aside, allowing us onto the ice, and the cold bites at my cheeks as we step onto the surface.

We step carefully toward the team, Aurora's giggles echoing as she slips and slides, clinging to Royce's hand. When we reach Logan, he doesn't hesitate—he scoops Aurora up in his arms, spinning her around as she squeals with delight. The rest of the team greets us warmly, patting Grayson and Royce on the back, pulling me into hugs as if we've all been part of this victory together.

Logan pulls me close, his arm wrapping around my waist as we stand in the midst of it all. Aurora is in his arms, her small hands reaching out to touch the trophy that glimmers in the light. It's a moment I'll never forget, this feeling of unity, of love, of everything falling perfectly into place.

The crowd begins to thin, players skating off the ice until only the five of us remain. Aurora is snuggled against Logan's chest, half asleep. Grayson drapes an arm around my shoulder, Royce's large hand wrapped around mine as we huddle close in the middle of the ice, soaking up this moment of triumph.

Not just for Logan's win.

But for everything we've faced and overcome.

For everything we've endured to get to this moment.

To find one another.

To create this perfect family.

And I know, without a doubt, that this is our happily ever after.

ROYCE

EPILOGUE

I glance in the rearview mirror for the fifth time since I picked Aurora up from daycare. She's been reticent and looked almost... sullen when I arrived. Now, I take in her lips, tugged down, and the sadness in her eyes, and I want to murder whatever little asshole has upset her.

"Do you want to stop for ice cream on the way home?" I ask her.

She merely shrugs, not lifting her head, and now I *know* something is wrong. In the months Aurora has been living with us, she has *never* turned down ice cream.

"Sweetheart, won't you tell me what's wrong?" I try again. I asked her this already when I picked her up, but she just shook her head. Which is the same response I get this time.

My hands tighten around the steering wheel, and I have half a mind to drive straight back to the daycare and demand answers from Ms. Everly. I knew she couldn't be trusted to take care of our little girl. We shouldn't have left her alone there with those snot-nosed little shits.

What if someone is bullying her? Did one of those little twerps make fun of her?

You can't beat up little children, I fruitlessly remind myself as I miraculously keep the car heading homeward and don't do a U-turn in the middle of the street.

"It's supposed to be a secret, but we have a surprise for you and your Mom later," I tell her, knowing Grayson is going to blow a gasket that I've said anything. I'll endure his wrath if it means I can get a smile from her. Except, not even a secret surprise can get her to perk up. *Damn, it really must be bad.*

Instead of pushing her to talk, we drive the remainder of the way home in silence. She's unbuckling her car seat as soon as I've parked, and the second I open her door, she's jumping down, her little backpack in her hand as she races into the house.

The TV is already on, the vibrant colors of cartoons assaulting my vision when I walk into the house. I stop long enough to find her sitting on the floor in front of the television. She's too close, but I don't bother to reprimand her as I stalk past the living room and into the kitchen, where Grayson is sitting at the table, his laptop open in front of him.

We have just finished our final exams, and none of us have any more assignments due. This means Logan, Gray, and I are officially done with college, so whatever work Gray is doing must be for his company.

Logan is heading off to development camp for the Timber-wolves in a few weeks before starting training camp in the fall. Thankfully, the camp is in Springview, so he can travel and still be here every night.

I turned down Dax's offer to join the underground fighting circuit. I still enjoy the occasional fight at The Depot, but I don't *need* the outlet like I once did, and I'm not inter-ested in doing it professionally. Especially since it would mean a lot of time away from Riley and Aurora. From my family.

I'm still working on the children's book I've been toying with. I've even elicited Aurora's help with the story, running adventure ideas past her and showing her some of my sketches. I'm not sure if anything will come of it. If I'll even submit it to a publisher or publish it myself once I'm done. For now, I'm simply enjoying a project that's just for me and Aurora.

Riley has her last exam today and should be home in a couple of hours. I'm so proud of her. She's worked her ass off to improve the grades that had slipped at the beginning of the year, and she's once again at the top of her class. I have no doubt that she will pass these exams with flying colors and move on to her Sophomore year in the fall.

And we have a celebratory surprise for her tonight.

However, that won't happen if we can't determine why Aurora is in a bad mood.

"I need you to remind me we can't hurt children," I grouse to Gray.

"Why do we hate children?" he asks, looking up from his laptop.

"Because some little shit has upset Aurora, and she won't tell me what they've done."

In the blink of an eye, Gray is on his feet, the legs of his chair scraping against the floor. "What the fuck did they do?"

Yeah, he's going to be absolutely no help in talking me down.

"I just told you, she won't tell me."

He looks downright murderous as he glowers at me from across the kitchen.

Before he can stalk into the living room and demand answers from her, we hear a key in the front door, and Logan walks in. We hear his low murmur as he talks to Aurora before the heavy tread of his feet before he appears in the kitchen.

"What the fuck is wrong with Aurora?" he demands.

"We don't know. She was like that when I picked her up," I tell him.

"And she won't tell you what's wrong?"

I shake my head, and he huffs, rubbing his hand along his chin as he thinks.

"Maybe we should cancel tonight?" I suggest.

"No," they both argue. "We've been planning this for months," Logan grouses. "Today's Ry's last exam. We're officially done with college. We have two weeks before camp begins and life gets hectic. I'm not waiting another day."

Fired up, he stalks toward the fridge and begins lifting shit out before reaching up to a cupboard for glasses.

"What are you doing?" I ask him.

"I'm going to find out who hurt our little girl and why, then I'm going to deal with them and make it all better so she's her bright, bubbly self by the time Shortcake gets home, and we can show them the surprise we've been planning for *months*."

Gray and I share a look before he shrugs. We both know if anyone can get answers from Aurora and cheer her up, it's Logan.

Five minutes later, he's calling Aurora into the kitchen.

"What?" she demands, standing in the doorway with her arms crossed. I swear, she's like a mini Grayson at that moment with her mother's fiery attitude and his stubbornness.

"I made you a milkshake." He gestures toward the tall pink drink, layered with whipped cream and sprinkles and complete with a red and white straw, sitting in front of a bar stool on the kitchen island.

Her eyes narrow in suspicion. "Why?"

Crouching down, he gets to her height. "Because you had a bad day at school, didn't you?"

She stares at him for a moment before her shoulders drop an inch, and she nods.

Goddammit, I fucking knew it. I knew I should have gone back to that damn school and demanded to know what happened.

"Well, there is no problem a milkshake can't fix," Logan tells her, scooping her into his arms and depositing her on the bar stool. However, before she can clasp the glass in her hands, he pulls it out of her reach. "I have one condition, though... You have to tell us what happened today while you drink it. Can you do that?"

Lips pursed, she seems to think it over while staring longingly at the pink drink, before eventually nodding.

"That's a brave girl," Logan praises, pushing the drink in front of her.

We wait impatiently while she takes a long sip of the drink, smacking her lips together. A small smile brightens her face for the first time since I picked her up, and it loosens some of the anxiety rattling around in my chest.

"Tell us what happened, Pumpkin," Logan encourages, his arms resting against the top of the island opposite her. "Did somebody say or do something to upset you?"

Her eyes drop to the tabletop, and that sadness is back. I fucking hate seeing it. She nods, her bottom lip trembling before she says in a small voice, "Sally and her friends were making fun of me because I don't have a daddy." *Sally and her friends are dead.* I don't care if they're practically babies. Tears well in her eyes. "They said it's because I'm not love-ble." *God fucking dammit.* I really am going to have to scare a three-year-old into line, aren't I?

I arch a brow at Grayson, hoping he knows how the fuck to fix this since Bertram is—was—his dad, too.

Lips pursed, he appears resigned as he moves to sit on the stool beside Aurora.

"I think you mean loveable, sweetheart," he begins slowly, "And you're plenty loveable. In fact, you're *so loveable* that you have *three daddies*." Logan holds up three fingers to emphasize my point.

"I remember Sally," I say.

"She's the one with that weird nasally voice," Logan unhelpfully interjects, making Aurora laugh as he imitates her.

"The way I see it," I continue, ignoring him. "Sally is jealous. Only very special people get to call three people daddy." The three of us move to surround the stool where she's sitting. "We all love you so much, sweetheart," I tell her. I don't need to look at the others for confirmation because I already know they feel the same way when I say, "You're our baby girl. Our kid. We're always going to be here for you. Support you. Love you. No matter what."

"What are we doing here?" Riley asks when we step out of the car in front of a sprawling single-story ranch-style home with a craftsman twist to fit the northeastern landscape. It has a wide, welcoming front porch that runs the entire length of the house, with sturdy stone pillars and wooden beams.

I can't take my eyes off her as she takes in the mix of natural stone and sage green siding that blends seamlessly with the surrounding landscape. Oversized windows allow plenty of light and offer unobstructed views of the surrounding land-scape. Since the house is located in the country between Springview and Halston, we are surrounded by forested wood-land that I imagine will make a picture-perfect landscape when the snow begins to fall.

"Let's just go inside," Grayson says vaguely, already striding toward the front door and letting himself in. Frowning, Riley hesitates before following, not exactly being left with much of a choice when her daughter bounds in behind Grayson, seeming keen to explore.

The inside has an open floor plan with high, beamed ceilings and plenty of space. The living area is central, with a large stone fireplace as a focal point. It is perfect for cozy evenings spent huddled in front of the fire with a movie.

At the back of the house is a modern kitchen with rustic accents, granite countertops, and high-end appliances. There's a large island for all of us to gather around and a dining area that opens up to the backyard through sliding glass doors.

"What do you think?" I hedge, watching as Riley spins in a slow circle, taking it all in.

"It's beautiful, but I don't understand. What are we doing here?" Tearing her gaze away, she looks at each of us, puzzled. "Are you thinking of buying this place?"

"Mommy!" Aurora's loud screech jolts her into action as she moves through the house in search of her daughter, the three of us on her heels.

"Mommy! Look!" Aurora is standing in the doorway of one of the bedrooms, and Riley gasps when she steps up behind her. She peers into the perfect princess bedroom we have spent weeks setting up.

In fact, we've spent the better part of the last two months getting the house ready—upgrading it, painting, and making it a home fit for the five of us... and hopefully more one day.

"Look, Mommy, there's a princess bed!"

The princess bed is a large, pink four-poster bed with gauzy drapes hanging above it. On the wall opposite, a castle resembling something from a Disney movie has been painted, along with unicorns and other girly things I recall from Aurora's room at Lydia's.

Mouth agape, Riley whirls toward us as Aurora moves to explore the room. "How?"

Crowding around the doorway, the three of us surround her.

"The townhouse is too tiny," Grayson tells her. "Aurora needs her own proper room, and we need a bed big enough for the four of us."

"Five for the mornings Aurora wakes early and climbs in with us," Logan adds teasingly.

Tucking my finger beneath her chin, I direct her focus my way. "What do you think about making this place home, Ry?"

"Live out the rest of our days here," Logan murmurs, ducking his head to run his nose up the column of her neck. "Watch Aurora grow up."

"Give her a couple of siblings," Grayson adds, stepping up behind her and wrapping his arms around her waist.

"So what do you say?" I encourage, when it seems all she's capable of is gaping at us. "Wanna spend forever here with us?"

"I—" Gaze filled with love and shining with unshed emotion, she looks at each of us before her eyes fall on Aurora, who is playing peacefully with her new toys in her new room. "Yes."

THE END

FOLLOW ME

Join my reader group—Rachel's Rebel Rehab—to stay up to date on all new releases and for access to bonus material.

ACKNOWLEDGMENTS

Every now and again, a character pops into your head, and you just resonate with them. This book was that for me. I connected with not just Riley but Logan, Royce, and Grayson. Their pain and heartache. Their hope and how they strived for a better future for themselves. These characters sucked me in and wouldn't let me go until their story was out in the world for you all to read. I hope these characters have ingrained themselves in your DNA as deeply as they are in mine.

Certainly, this book would be nowhere near as good as it is without the help of my amazing team. Nikki who is always ready to listen to my rants and suggest ideas when I get stuck (which is a lot). Thank you so much for being on this crazy journey with me.

Another thanks to my alpha and beta readers for trudging through the mess that was my first draft and still loving it.

A massive thank you to my editor and friend, Angie for handling the dumpster fire I gave her initially and helping me build this book into what it ultimately turned out to be.

A special mention to Caitlin too for everything she did to make this book and these characters story perfect!

I also have to thank my tiktok and street teams, and those who signed up for the blog tour with Peachy Keen to help promote and spread the word about this series. I appreciate all your hard work promoting every week.

I need to thank my husband who is always my rock and support.

Lastly, thank you to all of you, the readers, for picking up this book and reading it. Without you none of this would be possible!! If you loved this book, please help me spread the word by leaving a quick review.

ALSO BY R.A. SMYTH

<u>Crescentwood Series</u>

A dark, high school bully reverse harem with a stalker and gang element.

<u>Pacific Prep Series</u>

A dark, academy bully reverse harem with a taboo relationship.

<u>Black Creek Series</u>

A rival gang-mafia reverse harem with a vigilante FMC. Contains MM.

<u>The Ruthless Boys of Ridgeway</u>

A college, friends-enemies-lovers, second chance reverse harem with a stalker and secret society elements.

<u>Halston U</u>

A college, hockey, stepbrother, enemies-to-lovers reverse harem with a revenge plot.

ABOUT THE AUTHOR

R.A. Smyth is best known for writing contemporary dark romance filled with unexpected twists, mystery, and plenty of steam. Rachel lives in the UK with her husband and two golden retrievers, and when she's not busy thinking up crazy cliffhangers to drive her readers insane, she enjoys inflicting the same torture on herself by reading incomplete series.

She has always been an avid reader, starting from the Harry Potter books as a kid. It's an interest that has grown into an obsession over the years and becoming an author has been a secret lifelong dream of hers.